We hope you enjoy this book. Please return or renew it by the due date.

You can renew it at www.norfolk.gov.uk/libraries or by using our free library app.

Otherwise you can phone 0344 800 8020 - please have your library card and PIN ready.

You can sign up for email reminders too.

EXPOSED

Paul Ilett

PublishingPush

FIRST EDITION

ISBN 978-1-80227-655-8 (hardback)
ISBN 978-1-80227-613-8 (paperback)
ISBN 978-1-80227-614-5 (ebook)

Typeset using Atomik ePublisher from Easypress Technologies

www.paulilett.co.uk

For Suzanne and Donna.
Thank you for not killing me
x x

PROLOGUE

THREE DAYS AGO

Shaking with fear, he could only watch helplessly as the screen on his mobile phone dimmed and all the signal bars vanished once more. He had already checked the stable door and found, somehow, it was now jammed, as though locked from the outside. And inside, the creeping darkness no longer felt exciting or intoxicating. Instead, it closed in around him, trapping him alone and with no way to reach his car or contact anyone for help.

His evening had been one of giddy anticipation, the promise of a sexual liaison with a much younger woman he had met on a dating app. But he now realised the liaison had been a trick. There was no sexually adventurous 20-something on her way to meet him, and no one was going to realise he was missing.

The stable was in the middle of nowhere, a dead zone with no signal for his mobile phone and too remote for anyone to hear a cry for help. His wife had little interest in his comings and goings. Most likely she would be sat at home binging on her Netflix dramas, assuming she had not already passed out in her armchair after too many gins. It would very likely be days before she even noticed he was gone.

He knew he did not have the luxury of sitting it out until morning, of waiting for the staff to arrive and begin mucking out. That final message, that *impossible* message; a few moments when his mobile phone had somehow connected to a signal just long enough for him to receive a call. And the message had been clear; the howling, distorted voice and the terrifying words. Someone was coming for him and the clock was ticking.

He had looked about the stable when he had first arrived, to locate a stall that was empty and clean enough for his planned sexual encounter. There were six stalls, four with horses. The stink of hay and manure had been acceptable to him earlier in the evening when he had been excited and sexually charged. But now the stench and the darkness frightened him, and his pounding heart was forcing him to draw deeper breaths, leaving him light-headed and feeling sick.

He heard a noise from the back of the stable, from within the darkness, a door creaking quietly, and it occurred to him there might be another entrance into the stable, one he had not noticed before. But the quietness of the sound frightened him, as though someone was attempting to enter the stable secretly. And he began to feel a strange sensation that he was no longer alone.

Up until that point the horses had been mostly quiet but now seemed restless, as though reacting to the suddenly changed atmosphere. He could hear them stomping, snorting and blowing as though preparing for a fight.

"Hello?" he called, attempting to sound casual and unafraid. And for a moment he hoped the response would be that of a woman's voice; his co-conspirator, hiding in one of the stalls, playing a silly prank to heighten the excitement. But there was no reply.

His eyes had adjusted to the absence of light, and he peered through the darkness to try and find the second door. But before he could step forward, he heard the snap of a metal bolt and the gate to one of the stalls suddenly swung open before him.

There was a noise, a loud cracking noise, the sound of a whip perhaps, and a man shouting. And suddenly a horse was in front of him, squealing and rearing up over him, its eyes wide and its nostrils flared. He fell to the floor, stunned by a glancing blow from the horse's hoof, and cried out in shock and pain. He felt his head open up and blood spray out.

"No, no!!" he screeched, and tried to put up a hand to protect himself. But the horse ploughed down onto him, pounding heavily with its hoofs, squealing as it did so. By the third blow, he was unconscious. By the fifth, he was dead.

CHAPTER 1

Javier García sat quietly in the rambling, sumptuous lobby of the Royal Hotel in Mayfair, gently fingering a small piece of paper in his hand. It contained a list of names: people he blamed for ruining his life and his career. And if the evening ahead played out as Javier hoped, he would soon be in a powerful position to take his revenge against them all.

He had been invited to the hotel to meet someone who had promised to change his life forever. The arrangements had been made covertly, through a number of nameless intermediaries using different email addresses and phone numbers. Every communication reiterated the offer of a meeting with a mysterious benefactor who had promised to reignite his career. There had been promises of money and resources too, more than enough for Javier to deliver retribution on everyone he blamed for his downfall; promises appealing enough to coax him out of hiding and persuade him to take the meeting, even though he still did not know for sure who it was with.

For years Javier had been one of the world's most feared and influential journalists; the *Daily Ear*'s most celebrated undercover operative who posed in numerous guises to trick celebrities and politicians into startling and often career-ending confessions.

One week he would be a European media mogul offering high-profile actors the chance to pitch a new movie idea. The following week he would be a wealthy international businessman willing to pay cash for the services of any avaricious MP. But Javier was most renowned for his Fake Spanish Prince, a guise he had used only a few times but with great and terrible success. He had lured numerous well-meaning celebrities to a suite at one of London's swankiest hotels under the pretence he was offering an opportunity for them to make a pitch for their chosen charity.

He would charm them, make them trust him, pour glass after glass of champagne and then jovially coax them into shameful personal admissions or outrageous jokes or statements. His subterfuge had successfully destroyed many careers and marriages whilst elevating him to a position of almost unparalleled power and resource within the newspaper industry. His readers both loved and hated what he did, relishing every detail of his appalling exposés whilst taking to social media to deplore him and his deceitful tactics.

Within the newspaper industry, opinions had been equally split. Some looked upon the 'Fake Spanish Prince' with a begrudging awe for the uncompromising ruthlessness with which he pursued his prey. Others ridiculed the way he attempted to legitimise his work as serious journalism and, in particular, his claims that his personal safety was as much at risk as a war correspondent on the front line in Iraq.

But one thing no one could challenge was the financial rewards each of his exposés brought the *Daily Ear*. Sales of the paper would skyrocket on the day his latest exclusive was plastered across its front page, and the subsequent editions would maintain the bounce in sales as he filed his follow-up stories. The paper's website would also see an enormous wave of additional traffic, and social media would be ablaze with angry discussions about his story.

But then, two years earlier, everything he had worked for came crashing to a very public and humiliating end. He had realised the *Daily Ear*'s senior team were increasingly unhappy with one particular celebrity who had become something of a national sweetheart: Sophia Ferrari was a clever and talented singer and reality TV judge who used her fame as a platform to fight for LGBTQ equality. Javier's bosses felt she had become too influential, and her positive views on gay rights had created a shift in public opinion in support of gay marriage. And that went against the *Daily Ear*'s very clear editorial line that marriage was a Christian institution between one man and one woman.

Javier knew if he could entrap Sophia into some devastating revelation, it would strengthen his position within the *Daily Ear* and also be the highlight of his career. And so, with high hopes, he arranged a sting. But it soon went wrong.

He lured his prey to a hotel suite in London to discuss her work with Stonewall, dangling the offer of a sizeable cash donation to sweeten the pot.

And, once he had her settled in his room, he followed the usual routine of charm and alcohol to coax her into trusting him.

They discussed her work with the LGBTQ community, and after a while, he suggested to Sophia he might be gay himself. Gently, and with great care, she had coaxed him into discussing the issue further. And then he had elaborated wildly, describing the pressures of hiding his sexual orientation from the King and Queen of Spain, and how it might affect his accession to the throne. He talked about loneliness, and the lack of physical intimacy he had suffered.

And Sophia had been incredibly sweet and gentle, and reassured him she would tell no one. But then he asked if she knew anyone who could arrange for a young man to visit his suite. A *very* young man. And he was happy to pay, handsomely, if the legal age of consent could be overlooked. And for a while she discussed his request because, at first, it was clear she had misunderstood and believed he was simply asking her to set him up on a date with one of her many gay friends.

But he needed her to understand. He needed her to state clearly, for his secret recording equipment, that she understood what was being asked of her and was willing to agree to it; to procure an underage gay teenager. But as he pressed the point, she quickly become angry, and accused him of the sexual exploitation of children.

Sophia stood, threw her champagne over him and then slapped him around the face before walking out. Javier had been furious that she had so selfishly ruined months of planning and so, undeterred, he altered his recordings and ran the story anyway. He then worked with two pliable, dim-witted officers at the Met to ensure a criminal prosecution was brought against her.

And he wanted her to go to prison. In fact, by that stage, he *needed* her to go to prison. Javier had always wanted his work to be considered legitimate and important and had grown increasingly aware that his journalism was often ridiculed by his peers. But a criminal prosecution would change that. If he could get Sophia Ferrari prosecuted for child sexual exploitation, it would give him legitimacy. And what better way than sending the nation's sweetheart to jail.

But when the high-profile case against her collapsed the Crown Prosecution Service brought charges against Javier and it was he, instead, who ended up in prison. He served 18 months for perverting the course of justice and spent every single day of his internment planning revenge.

"Are you Mr García?"

Javier looked up and found one of the hotel's uniformed staff standing in front of him, with an electronic door card in his hand. Lost in thought, Javier hadn't realised how busy the hotel lobby had grown over the previous half-hour. An angry thunderstorm was raging outside and some of the city's more affluent pedestrians appeared to have ducked inside to use the bar and facilities until the rain had passed.

Javier didn't like hanging around in busy hotel lobbies. During his time as the Spanish Prince, he had always been concerned his secret identity would be blown. Now, he simply didn't want anyone to recognise him and start posting comments about his location on social media.

"Yes, yes I am," he replied.

The concierge, a slight elderly man with an impeccably clear voice, spoke again. "Your suite is ready, sir. May I take you to your suite?"

"My suite?" Javier asked.

The concierge nodded and smiled. "The Margaret Thatcher Suite on the 13th floor, just as you requested."

This was something Javier had not anticipated. He had expected the meeting to take place in the restaurant, or a simple hotel room. Instead, an entire suite had been booked for him, a clear sign that a new and exciting opportunity was on the cards. This was, indeed, going to be the day Javier was put back on the path to greatness. "Yes please. That would be good."

"Do you have any luggage?" the concierge asked.

Javier stood and gestured to the empty floor around him. "Nope. Nothing. I don't have anything," he said. "Just me."

"Very good, sir. Please follow me."

Javier followed the man into the lift and up to the 13th floor. The Royal Hotel, and hotels just like it across London, had been his stomping ground for years. What for many would seem lavish and aspirational had become routine for Javier, a day at the office. And as he was shown into his suite, a pleasing expanse of quiet opulence and comfort, Javier began to feel at home.

The hotel had recently undergone a huge refurbishment to embrace the building's roots in the 1920s. Every remaining aspect of its Art Deco heritage had been lovingly restored and, where it had been removed, masterfully reimagined. Javier's room, gently lit by lamps, was a luxurious mix of geometric shapes, bold colours, dramatic mirrors and metal finishes. The furniture had been arranged around the entrance to the balcony to make the most of the view.

"Is this adequate?" the concierge asked. "May I pour you a glass, sir?"

On the circular glass coffee table, a bottle of champagne was nestled into an oval shaped silver cooler filled with ice and engraved with the hotel's crest.

"Yes please," Javier responded. It would be his first glass of champagne in far too long.

The concierge expertly opened the bottle with little fuss, poured a glass and handed it to him. "If there is nothing else, sir, you can access the concierge service at any time by dialling zero on the phone. May I wish you a pleasant stay." And with that the man left.

Javier walked across the sitting room and looked through the glass doors which led to the balcony. It had been a long time since he had been able to enjoy a view of London from anything other than ground level. But now here he was, gazing across the city from the 13th floor of one of London's premier hotels. And even though the night sky had been consumed by a thunderous rainstorm, he could find only beauty and inspiration in the view.

A flash of lightning darted across the skyline in front of him, but the thickened glass muffled most of the noise from the rain and thunder. The wind and the storm were for the plebs, he thought, those dull and ordinary people who were rushing through the streets on their way home from work. The warm extravagance of the Margaret Thatcher Suite was for him.

"Thatcher?" he whispered to himself, and for a moment he pondered the name. He had used this hotel several times over the years for some of his most successful stings. But he had never heard of the Margaret Thatcher Suite before and he felt it was something he would have noticed, being a true-blue Tory. He would have noticed if one of the suites was named after his greatest political hero.

And as he looked around, he began to feel as though he had been there before. Not just that hotel, but that very room. The decoration was different but the layout, and the view from the balcony, and the walk from the lift suddenly all felt very familiar. It occurred to him that he had used this very suite years earlier for one of his stings. Not Sophia Ferrari, because that had been at an entirely different hotel. But someone, most definitely, had fallen victim to him in this very room.

"But who?" he asked himself. "Who was it?"

CHAPTER 2

Valerie Pierce sat quietly in the back seat of her Uber, carefully studying the app on her mobile phone to check the car did not divert unexpectedly from the planned route in any way. Her handbag was tightly pressed to her lap for easy access, within which she had an array of personal safety devices her daughter had recently sourced for her. This included an attack alarm, a spray repellent and a hand-held, high-voltage personal stun gun called "The Paralyzer". She suspected at least two of the items in her handbag were illegal, but she did not care.

She was happy enough with her driver, Ionuţ, who had a four-point-six rating on the app and had been perfectly polite and jovial from the moment he had collected her from Fenchurch Street Station. But the thunderstorm had unnerved her and she no longer had the ability to pretend she was not scared. She peered through the car window, rainwater clinging to the glass, and tried to make sense of the collage of lights, colours and shadows as she was driven through the dark streets of the city towards the venue where she was meeting her contact.

She could not shake a terrible feeling of dread, a feeling that out there, somewhere, in the streets of London, someone was watching her. And planning to kill her.

"I haven't seen it this bad before," her driver said. "Not in London. The police have closed several streets due to flooding. It's coming down very quickly and very hard."

Valerie had already decided it was safe to trust Ionuţ and was desperately pleased he had offered the opportunity to participate in a normal conversation, if only for a moment. She had noticed he kept looking at her through the rear-view mirror, as though he recognised her but could not place her. And Valerie was familiar with that situation.

Through a long career in journalism, she had achieved a certain level of public recognition, helped mostly by the fact that she had maintained almost the same appearance throughout her entire adult life. Her dark brown hair was typically cut into a shoulder length bob, and she had proudly maintained the exact same dress size since she was a teenager. Her choice of clothes was always influenced by her signature colour, purple. Now at the age of 57, she was occasionally recognised when out in public, and it was always flattering, at least at first. But, as with Ionuţ, that initial flicker of recognition always seemed to fade so quickly and leave Valerie in the awkward position of having to explain who she was and why a complete stranger might think they knew her.

"I have to be at the restaurant by eight thirty," she said. "Do you think we will get there on time?"

"I think so, I think so," Ionuţ replied. "The traffic is not too bad. I think the rain is keeping more drivers off the roads. I will let you know."

Valerie had been told there was a discreet entrance in a little back street close to Kensington High Street, and she could see Ionuţ's sat-nav device was using live traffic information to predict their time of arrival which, despite the appalling weather, continued to show 8.26pm. She still had a few minutes to rehearse what she was going to say and evaluate the different possible outcomes of the evening.

It was going to be a difficult conversation because Valerie was not used to asking for help. She was not accustomed to being scared. For three decades she had enjoyed the spoils of writing one of the best-read and most influential weekly newspaper columns in the world. With just a few choice words she could destroy a celebrity's career or overturn a government debate.

She had not always been liked, nor her opinions always been popular, and over the years she had occasionally suffered abuse or received veiled threats. But she had existed within the powerful machineries of the world's most successful tabloid newspaper, the *Daily Ear*, and had always felt insulated from the nastier repercussions of her job. Over the years, there had been a few awkward occasions; a glass of wine thrown in her face by a reality TV star whose wedding Valerie had called 'trashy', and a confrontation at an awards ceremony by a TV presenter she had fat shamed. There had been many other similar incidents, but mostly she had always felt safe.

Four years earlier things had changed. During a particularly stormy period in the paper's history Valerie had quit her job and attempted to reinvent herself as a freelance writer, must-have television guest and social media commentator. It had all seemed very simple at the time, but Valerie soon found the reality of being a lone voice in the crowded, screaming void outside the newspaper industry harder to navigate than she had anticipated.

Now, she had transformed herself into a proudly pro-Remain Thatcherite freelance writer and commentator, who spoke in a far more measured way about a whole host of social issues. After a few false starts, she had successfully found her niche and had been able to monetise it quite effectively. Valerie Pierce had become the former *Daily Ear* columnist who proved you were never too old to change your ways. And her reformed public persona had been embraced and celebrated by a whole generation of new readers.

But although she had been able to maintain her professional profile to some degree, she no longer felt protected. She had built a following of more than two million on Twitter and was still able to create a tidal wave of debate and discussion with a single tweet. However, the darker aspects of social media had proven a shock for her, a minefield of misogynistic abuse and sexual threats. Eventually she had decided to employ her daughter, Alice, as her Social Media Manager and she knew Alice was now protecting her from much of the abuse aimed at her accounts.

Things had gone more smoothly since, apart from one mishap. She and Alice had decided to use an app to manage the content of her various feeds by lining up a hundred posts in advance (some of Valerie's funniest and most cutting comments). The app ensured these were posted regularly over the coming weeks, smartly targeted to build her followers. However, they had both lost the password for the app and now couldn't switch it off.

And so, no matter the news story of the day, Valerie Pierce could often be found posting about the inanest of topics. Today, Twitter's Valerie Pierce had been highly critical of any restaurant or café which claimed to offer a poached egg if it were cooked in a microwave rather than in water on the hob. Valerie hoped to God nothing important had happened.

The car drew to a halt and Ionuţ leaned across the passenger seat and pointed out of the window. "The doorway is just up there," he said, "but it's a one-way street. To drop you right outside the door I'd have to go the long way round, and we wouldn't get there by 8.30pm."

Valerie's eyes shot to the sat-nav which was now predicting they would not arrive until 8.51pm. And she could not be late. She was surprised her guest had agreed to meet her at all, and she knew if she were late, he would have the perfect excuse to simply leave. She peered through the rain and the darkness and could just make out the name of the restaurant, its unpretentious and modest façade concealing a favoured retreat for the rich and famous.

"No, it's fine. I'll walk," she replied and gathered her possessions. "Thank you Ionuṭ." She fastened the buttons on her purple raincoat and prepared her umbrella so she could open it quickly, and then stepped from the car into the rainstorm.

A gust of wind immediately caught her face-on and blew her umbrella inside out. As she struggled to bring it under control, she could hear her Uber drive away. And then she realised she was completely alone in the middle of a dark, rainswept London street. Tucking her bag tightly under her arm, she pulled her umbrella back into position and took a deep breath. She would not allow herself to arrive looking dishevelled or upset. She would not allow *him* the satisfaction of seeing her looking anything other than confident and powerful. It was bad enough she was asking him for help. *Him* of all people: the man who had tried to destroy her career and credibility, the man who had publicly revealed one of her greatest secrets and exposed her to ridicule and accusations of hypocrisy. But after the events of the previous few days, she had come to the crushing conclusion he was the only person who could help her, the only person who might believe someone was trying to kill her.

In spite of the rain and the wind, she managed to collapse her umbrella with little fuss and entered the venue with most of her dignity still intact. She was met at the door by a young man who took her coat and umbrella and checked her reservation. The lobby was partitioned by lights and curtains making it impossible to see the tables or the guests, although Valerie could clearly hear the noise of a busy venue – conversations, clinking cutlery and the gentle tones of a live piano.

"Your friend is already in your booth," the young man said. "Please follow me."

Valerie did not care for his use of the word 'friend' but on this occasion chose not to pick him up on it. As she followed him through the partition, she was surprised to find a much smaller venue than she had anticipated. The walls were lined with books and paintings, and a grand piano took centre stage in the middle of the space. There were only about 20 tables and booths, and all were full. She knew many faces, mostly from the arts or entertainment industry; a few composers and musicians, a couple of singers and one table populated by a number of artists she recognised and mostly despised. If she had more time, she would have stopped at their table to tell them none of them could paint.

She was led to a secluded booth, concealed by a screen for additional privacy.

"This is you," the young man said. "I believe your friend has already ordered the wine. Will you be eating with us this evening?"

"No," she replied. "Not tonight."

"That's fine. I'll be back later to check your drinks."

Valerie took a moment to gather her thoughts and then stepped behind the screen and took her seat. At first, she couldn't bring herself to look at him. She could see him out of the corner of her eye and noted he did not move as she arrived. But once she was settled and comfortable, she looked directly into his face without saying a word.

And there he was, sat directly opposite her in a private booth of one of London's most exclusive restaurants. A man who had once declared war on Valerie and the entire top team at the *Daily Ear*. A man who had successfully brought not only the newspaper to its knees but its parent company, and all but destroyed the family who owned it. She considered this man her personal nemesis. But also, now, he was the one and only person who might be able to save her life. The actor, Adam Jaymes.

She was immediately annoyed by how handsome he looked. His thick dark hair was brushed away from his face, his brown eyes sparkled in the light from the candles on the table. He was wearing a navy three-piece suit, but no tie. The top two buttons of his white shirt were undone in a way that, Valerie thought, made him look like something of a gigolo. And although she knew he was in his thirties, he still had the arrogant self-satisfied look of a man in his twenties. Adam sat calmly, with one arm resting on the back of his chair and a glass of red wine in his other hand. "I hope you don't mind, Valerie, but I ordered a nice Rioja. I think you will enjoy it," he said, and then poured her a glass.

"Thank you," Valerie replied. And without a second thought, she threw her drink in his face.

CHAPTER 3

With no sign of his mystery patron, Javier was beginning to feel deflated. With little to do but wait, he had finished the bottle of champagne and started to work his way through the rest of the bar. He knew the alcohol was a mistake. He could manage only small amounts before it would affect his mood, making him morose and then anxious and upset. He had hoped to off-set the effect of the alcohol with the food he had ordered for his room, but he had insisted on a number of off-menu dishes and these were clearly taking longer for the kitchen staff to prepare.

He had spent much of the previous hour sitting on the armchair closest to the balcony, staring out of the windows at the London skyline, the rain still pouring outside of the balcony doors. And he wondered what his family were doing, or if they knew he was out of prison. If they did, would any of them actually care? He had lost touch with them many years earlier, through a series of events so destructive they had not even made contact when he was sent to jail.

Javier had conflicted feelings about his childhood in Brentwood, a quiet and predominantly white town in Essex. The Garcías were known locally as 'that Spanish family' and his immigrant parents had a reputation for being hard-working and happy, but poor. They were never able to offer Javier the luxuries he always felt entitled to, and so he had decided at a young age he would have to make his own fortune. But Javier's path to success had not come without sacrifice, and the first thing he had forfeited was his relationship with his brother.

Daniel García had been the bane of his childhood; a beautiful younger sibling who succeeded at everything and was loved by all. Whilst Javier had been plump, awkward and selfish, Daniel was athletic, confident and kind. Worse still, he seemed to surpass Javier in every aspect of life.

When Javier had been runner-up in a school writing competition, Daniel had entered the following year and took first place. At college, Javier won a place as a reporter on the college newspaper, but Daniel joined a year later and was appointed editor. There was no spite in anything Daniel did; indeed, he had always shown great affection and loyalty to his older brother. But Daniel's constant success and Javier's spiteful jealousy prevented their relationship from ever fully evolving.

And when both sought a career in journalism, Javier found himself working his way through the exhausting route of regional press whilst Daniel was selected by the BBC for a graduate programme in broadcast journalism. Javier had feared his younger brother was headed for a successful career in television whilst he would be left behind, rotting away in the thankless world of local newspapers. And he hated him for it.

In a desperate attempt to break free from the grinding cycle of stories about annual A&E targets and district council planning rows, Javier managed secure a few weekend shifts at the *Daily Ear* newspaper in London. He had hoped it might lead to a permanent job, but he quickly learned the newsdesk thrived on temporary arrangements and if he wanted a permanent contract, he would have to deliver something big.

And that opportunity was handed to him on a plate by his unsuspecting younger brother. One night, 20 years earlier, *BBC Radio Essex* had been named Local Station of the Year at the Sony Awards and Daniel invited Javier along to celebratory drinks at a bar in Chelmsford. Daniel had spent the evening proudly introducing Javier to his colleagues: his *Big Brother* making waves in the national press. But Javier had not been so gracious. He kept his ear to the ground, hoping the celebratory atmosphere and the booze would lead to a startling revelation about the BBC he could sell to the BBC-hating *Daily Ear*. And, as an additional provision, he had a small tape recorder hidden within his jacket pocket so he could capture the revelations as evidence.

And that was the night Javier made his first baby-steps towards the creation of his Fake Spanish Prince. He coaxed Daniel's drunken colleagues into discussions about their expenses, their 'unpredictability allowances' and every other additional financial payment they could claim from TV licence payers. Their words, little more than honest and accurate responses to Javier's questions, proved to be perfect fodder for him, and he twisted each factual answer into a contemptable brag. The *Daily Ear* splashed the story on its front page two days later; 'Champagne boasts from smarmy BBC parasites'.

Shortly afterwards, Javier was offered a permanent contract with the *Daily Ear*, and on that same day his brother and six of his colleagues were dismissed by the BBC. Daniel and their parents never spoke to Javier again. Sometimes, he wondered what had happened to his family in the intervening years. Daniel had never appeared on television, and Javier had never heard his name or voice on the radio either. It was as if his younger brother had simply faded away.

His parents had often spoken of one day returning to the city of San Sebastián, their family home, for retirement. And he wondered if that is where they were living now. And perhaps Daniel had gone with them. Unlike Javier, Daniel was fluent in Spanish and it might have been an easier place for him to relaunch his broadcast career than in the UK.

And he wondered if they had ever suspected Javier was the brave undercover reporter delivering exclusive after exclusive to the world's biggest selling daily paper. The *Daily Ear* had always kept his identity a closely guarded secret. But, even so, they *must* have known it was him, Javier thought.

But no one had ever reached out to him, not his parents or his supposedly kind and forgiving younger brother. Year after year had passed without a single word from any of them. Even in his darkest hours, those terrifying and lonely days in the dock at the Old Bailey, not a single member of his family had been there for him, or even contacted him to see if he needed any help or support. Or even just a hug. They really had abandoned him completely.

"Fuck them," Javier said, and raised his empty crystal tumbler into the air as a flash of lightning lit the room. And then he crumpled back into himself and wished Daniel and his parents were there so he could tell them how sorry he was, and that he missed them. But they weren't there. No one was there.

It was 8.35pm, and there was still no sign of his host. Javier was beginning to worry the whole evening had been a waste of his time. He pushed himself out of his chair and gazed back into the room and tried to prise a memory free from the back of his mind.

He could visualise clearly how the suite had looked during his previous visit, all those years earlier, when he had used it for one of his set-ups. At that time, it had been presented far more plainly with unassuming furniture and a few paintings. And there had been daylight too, a warm sunny day. He seemed to remember a last-minute panic when his hidden tape recorder appeared to have stopped working.

He recalled a woman's voice, softly exchanging pleasantries with him about how warm the weather had been and how the sun always brought out the best in people in the city. He recalled her dark hair and delicate porcelain features. There had been a frailty to her he had not expected, so very different to the loud and ballsy character she had played on television. He had a sense she was not going to lead a long or happy life. And as his memory became clearer, he was able to put a name to her, the actress he had charmed with champagne and then tricked into revealing behind-the-scenes secrets from TV's most popular soap.

"It was Pearl Martin," he said. "This is the suite where I met Pearl Martin."

CHAPTER 4

By the time Adam Jaymes had finished wiping red wine off his face and shirt with his napkin, Valerie was calmly settled in her seat and smoking a well-earned cigarette. She was fascinated with the calm manner Adam had handled the situation. He hadn't even flinched as she had thrown her wine at him, almost as if he had been expecting it. And he had spent the past few minutes patting dry his face and shirt in a most remarkably silent and dignified way.

Finally, he spoke. "I knew I should have ordered the white," he said. "And you know you cannot smoke in here, Valerie. Please put that out."

"I will not," she replied.

"May I remind you I am here at your request," Adam said. "I understood you needed my help. But my presence is not an endorsement of you, Valerie, and should not be considered a victory either. And it does not give you carte blanche to behave however you please."

Valerie stubbed out her cigarette on the olive dish and folded her arms. "And why, may I ask, did you agree to meet with me? I am very grateful, of course, because as much as I hate to admit it, I do need your help. But you have never before, not once, agreed to meet with me or even just speak to me over the phone. Not so much as an email. All those years I spent writing articles about you. News stories, comment pieces, features… I always reached out to give you the chance to give your side of the story. I offered to interview you repeatedly, but I always had the same answer. Or lack of. You didn't even have the decency to decline. You just ignored me."

She could see Adam was almost smiling, as though pleased by the knowledge that by passive-aggressively snubbing Valerie for all that time he had clearly gotten under her skin.

"But not this time," she continued. "This time I contact your agent and tell him I need your help. The next thing I know you've booked a table at this restaurant and are pouring me wine. So why, Adam Jaymes, after all of these years did you finally agree to meet me?"

Adam did not respond immediately and for a moment Valerie was sure she saw a glimpse of doubt on his handsome face, as though he suddenly did not know what to say. But then he sighed, deeply, as though unhappy with the answer he was about to give. "Because believe it or not, Valerie, someone convinced me I owe you a favour. But to be clear, I am here listening. *That* is the favour. I do not owe you anything more than this. So please tell me what you need my help with, and I will let you know if it is something I am willing to do. But my help is not a given."

Valerie wished he had told her that before she had thrown her wine in his face. She opened her bag and delved through the array of personal safety devices to a white A5 plastic folder. She took it from her bag, put it on the table and slid it across the wooden surface to Adam.

"Six nights ago, a man named Chris Cox was killed at his home in Leeds," she said. "Does the name ring a bell?"

"Of course," Adam replied. "Cox on the Box. He used to write the TV review page for the *Daily Ear*. He always gave me very flattering reviews. Until I came out as gay. After which he repeatedly called me the worst actor on television. But I have no doubt you will deny those two points are in any way connected."

"Yes, well," Valerie said, "that is neither here nor there. The point is he was killed, Adam."

Adam nodded.

"Aren't you going to ask me how?" Valerie said, bewildered by the actor's apparent lack of interest in her news.

"I assumed you planned to tell me, Valerie," he replied, and then sipped his wine.

Valerie huffed. "Fine," she said, and realised the conversation was going to be far more hard work than she had anticipated. "He was at home, alone, watching television. At 9pm he received a call on his mobile phone and, moments later, his wall-mounted television somehow unhinged itself from the wall and crashed down onto him. It killed him instantly."

Adam placed his glass on the table. "I wasn't aware a wall mounted television would be heavy enough to kill a grown man," he said, with the air of someone barely paying attention.

"It was almost 160 inches, Adam. It filled an entire wall at his home. It was his retirement gift from the *Daily Ear*."

Adam nodded, as though the information now made sense. "Well," he said, "I am very sorry for his family. I am sure they loved him very much." His response was calm and measured but lacked any warmth or concern. And even though he had a reputation for being aloof, perhaps even a cold fish, Valerie had still expected a greater response from him. Granted, he had said the right things, but he had failed to emote any shock or sorrow at her news.

"*Three* nights ago, there was another incident. This time at a private stable in Berkshire," she continued. "At 9pm one of the horses, Pepper Gay, was freed from its stalls and appeared to become spooked. A man who was in the stable at the time was trampled to death."

Valerie gestured towards the folder and Adam opened it. Inside were several photographs from the scene of the two incidents and a few folded pages of what looked like confidential police reports. At the bottom was a photograph of one of the victims, a man in his early fifties with thin hair and a weak chin.

"You might remember Derek Toulson," Valerie said. "He was the *Daily Ear*'s PR chief for many years."

"Yes," Adam said. "Valerie, I have to be honest, I do not understand why this might involve me, or how I might assist you."

This was the part of the conversation Valerie had practiced the most. It was the part where she knew she could easily sound like little more than a paranoid lunatic. It was the part she needed to get just right. "No one knows why Derek was there," she said. "The stable was closed for the night. None of the staff knew Derek or had ever seen him before. No one knows how he got into the stable or how or why the horse was freed from its stall. His wife didn't even know he had gone out for the night."

"Well, I am certain the police will work it out, Valerie. Again, this is very sad, I am sure, but I still cannot see—"

"Chris received a call on his mobile phone at 9pm, just before he was killed," Valerie said, interrupting him. "The same for Derek. A phone call at

9pm. And their deaths were three days apart." And then she sat back, folded her arms and stared at Adam with an expression which suggested she had just proven a point.

Adam frowned, still puzzled by the conversation. "Accidents happen, Valerie. And as far as Derek is concerned… well… perhaps the noise of his mobile phone spooked the horse," he suggested.

"Adam Jaymes, don't you dare play dumb with me," Valerie retorted angrily. "A phone call at 9pm? Three days apart? Doesn't that ring a bell?"

And there it was. Finally. An expression on Adam's face that made sense to Valerie. A realisation of what she was talking about. "You are linking this to *Project Ear?*" he asked, a tone of genuine surprise to his voice.

Four years earlier Adam had launched 'Project Ear', a ruthless and high-profile campaign aimed at turning the tables on the *Daily Ear*. Drawing on the resources of his billionaire husband, Adam had hired a team of researchers, private investigators and former journalists. His objective, very simply, was to expose the private shames and secret scandals behind the top team of the *Daily Ear*, to give them a taste of their own medicine.

His team quickly amassed a shocking dossier of sexual indiscretions, perverse behaviour, lies, fraud and hypocrisy. But rather than release it all at once, Adam had taken his time to savour the revelations and spread his reveals over a period of weeks. He had wanted to ensure each individual exposé gained the maximum amount of exposure.

And so, every three days at exactly 9pm, he would upload an article to his website, some shameful disclosure about someone at the *Daily Ear*. But not without warning. He personally telephoned each victim at the same time, to let them know he was publishing a story about them. Valerie had received one of his calls, and Adam's shocking revelation had nearly cost Valerie her career.

"Chris Cox and Derek Toulson did not die in freak accidents," Valerie stated. "They were both murdered. And whoever killed them is copying your despicable campaign."

"Despicable?" Adam replied, raising his eyebrows. "All these years later and you still believe you can take the moral high ground? All I did, Valerie, was do to you and your colleagues what you had been doing to me and my friends for decades. I found out your darkest and most embarrassing personal secrets and then I published them for all to see. How is that any different to what you did for a living?"

"Because what we did was journalism," Valerie snapped, a spiteful tone becoming evident in her voice. "What you did was petty revenge. Revenge on me. On Colin. On poor Leonard."

Adam sat back in his seat and stared directly into Valerie's face. "Really?" he said. "You are still trying to argue that the garbage your paper slopped out onto the streets of the UK every day was journalism? And there was me believing you were the tabloid hack who had turned over a new leaf. How quickly the veil falls, Valerie. How quickly the lie is revealed."

Valerie was ready to tell this contemptable, spoiled and entitled 'star' exactly what she thought of him. What she had *always* thought of him. But for once she bit her tongue and instead quietly poured herself a replacement wine. She sat back and sipped from her glass, distracted momentarily by the Rioja's soft and supple flavour and its charming aroma of summer fruits. "You bastard, Adam Jaymes," she thought. "You even know how to pick a good wine."

"You have one minute, Valerie," Adam said. "*What* do you want?"

Valerie focussed her thoughts and remembered her script. "Every three days at 9pm on the dot," she said, "you published one of your nasty little exposés about someone working at the *Daily Ear*. But you always called beforehand. Your victim would get a personalised call from you. I remember mine like it was yesterday. '*Hello Valerie Pierce. This is Adam Jaymes. I just called to let you know it's your turn*'. I assume you remember that? Apart from tonight, it's the one and only time you and I have ever spoken."

Adam should his head. "Are you suggesting I murdered these two men?" he asked.

Valerie groaned. "Of course not," she replied. "You might be the most awful person I know, but I also know you're not capable of murder. There are many things I do not think you're capable of. Acting, for instance."

Adam sat quietly, patiently, and refused to rise to Valerie's insult.

"But someone out there is capable of murder," she continued. "Someone dropped a massive television on Chris and made it look like an accident. Three days later, someone lured Derek to a stable and killed him in a way that would also look like an accident."

Adam gestured to the papers and photographs on the table in front of him. "How did you even get these?" he asked, clearly unconvinced.

Valerie smiled proudly. "I may not work for a national newspaper any longer," she said, "but I still have my contacts. I heard about what happened to Chris through friends, and at first it didn't strike me as being anything other than a terrible accident. But a police contact told me what happened to Derek. And a few things began to sound familiar. Like a pattern."

"I assume you have spoken to the police about this?" Adam asked. "If you think Chris and Derek were both murdered, surely you should speak to them?"

"Yes. I did," Valerie replied and, trying not to look awkward, continued, "They didn't believe me. And I can't say I blame them. Adam, I know exactly how this sounds, how I am making myself look. But the truth is the only version of events that makes sense to me, that Chris Cox and Derek Toulson were both murdered. And if I am right, someone else from the *Daily Ear* is going to be murdered tonight."

She looked at her watch, and saw it was approaching 9pm. "And they'll get a call from the killer any minute now," she said.

There was a pause, as though the world was holding its breath, and Adam realised Valerie genuinely feared her mobile phone was about to ring, that she might be the next victim of a murderer she had convinced herself was targeting those soiled by their association with the *Daily Ear*.

And as much as he wished he did not care, he found himself reassuring her. "You are safe, Valerie," he said, gently. "You are here, with me, in a public place. A very public place. Nothing is going to happen."

But Valerie was immediately repulsed by how earnest and concerned Adam was being. "I came here to ask for your help, not your pity," she said. "Please do not pretend to be the sort of hero in real life that you play on television. It doesn't wash with me."

Adam sipped his wine then placed the glass back on the table. "I think we are done here," he said, with a tone of defeat in his voice. "This is our one and only conversation, Valerie. I hope you found it useful. Do not expect to get a response from me again."

He went to stand, but Valerie quickly interjected. "It is not easy asking for help," she said. "Asking *you* for help. Of all people, *you*. But this isn't a simple

PR problem, or a reputation management issue. I'm not being threatened with a lawsuit or being trolled by some misogynist idiot on Twitter. This is death, Adam. Murder and death. Out there somewhere, in the dark, is a killer. Someone targeting people connected with the *Daily Ear* newspaper. I am terrified I am going to be next and you are the only person who has the resources to help. Will you help me, Adam?"

Adam settled back into his seat and sighed. He looked back over the table at Valerie and then simply shrugged. "I don't believe that is the case," he replied. "I don't believe someone is trying to kill you and I don't believe you need my help. I am not accusing you of lying, Valerie. I simply believe you are mistaken."

"But Derek—"

"Whatever happened to Derek Toulson in the stable, I have no doubt he was up to no good," Adam stated, bluntly. "He was a deeply unpleasant human being. And whilst it is very sad for his family that he is dead, I imagine when the facts are known it will be proven he ultimately brought it on himself. I am sorry, Valerie, but I won't help you."

He stood and buttoned his jacket ready to leave. But Valerie had one last trick up her sleeve, something she had hoped she would not have to rely on. But it was her trump card, something that would leave Adam Jaymes with no option but to do her bidding.

"Adam if you don't help me," she said, "I will expose Pearl Martin's daughter. I know who she is. I know where she is. And I will expose her."

CHAPTER 5

Javier was sitting alone in his suite, glumly eating the meal that had finally been delivered. He had not complained about the delay. In fact, he had asked the concierge to pass on his gratitude, as the kitchen staff had provided several exquisite bespoke dishes that, for Javier, were a much-needed taste of home; tortilla de patatas, salted sliced tomatoes in olive oil and a paella with mussels and squid. These were the sort of meals he had grown up with. His parents had been keen to ensure their sons appreciated their Spanish heritage even though both boys were born and raised in Essex.

The meal had been delivered on a platter under a silver cloche, something Javier had quickly dispensed with. He had never been interested in the dressings of fine dining. He had always strongly believed that either a meal was good, or it wasn't. Serving it on an expensive plate under a silver dome would make no difference in the end. Instead, he had piled all the dishes onto a single plate and returned to his chair by the window, where he spooned it into his mouth and continued watching the storm.

The memory of his one meeting with Pearl Martin had darkened his mood. For many years she had been the face of the country's biggest soap opera, her loud and brassy TV character the complete opposite of her true self; quiet, private and frail.

For various reasons the *Daily Ear* had become obsessed with her and launched a campaign of character assassination the likes of which few reporters had ever seen. Javier knew he had played a small part in that, drawing Pearl to that very suite at the Royal Hotel with the pretence of being a European philanthropist looking for charities to donate to. Pearl had attended the meeting in good faith, hoping to make a case for a charity which offered free legal support to immigrants and those seeking asylum in the UK. He remembered the conversation had started quietly. Pearl spoke about her grandparents; immigrants who had sought a better life for themselves and their children after the war by moving to England. At first Javier had feigned interest in her story, but he quickly took advantage of Pearl's addiction issues and offered her glass after glass of champagne, until she had drunk enough to thoughtlessly reveal many back-stage secrets from her soap. His exclusive story was a significant stain on Pearl Martin's career, an unforgiveable mistake which soon led to her being sacked from her job. Not long after, Pearl's daughter was taken into care, and not long after that Pearl took her own life.

The destruction of her career and her life was something that sat comfortably within the range of Javier's conscience. But her death, her sad, lonely suicide at Beachy Head, did not. Throughout a life of callous disregard, Pearl Martin's death was the one event Javier had struggled to accept.

After a few moments of silence, the sound of a ringtone returned Javier from his inertia. He put down his plate and fumbled for his mobile phone, tightly jammed into his trouser pocket. After a moment of struggle, he managed to release it into his hand and looked at the screen which displayed the words "Withheld Number".

"Uh," he muttered. "Must be him." He pressed the answer button and held the phone to his ear. "Hello. This is Javier."

The voice that responded was not human. It was digital and distorted, a deep and howling scream of abnormality. "*Hello Javier García. This is your murderer. I just called to let you know it's your turn.*"

A sharp jolt of terror shot through his body and Javier bolted to his feet and threw his phone to the floor. His heart was pounding in his chest, and he found himself pinned against the balcony doors, staring back into the room. The phone call had shocked him, frightened him, and he tried to work through his searing panic to take stock of where he was, and how he could get out. How far away was that door, and could he reach it without any interference? But as his frightened mind rushed through a dozen different scenarios, suddenly the lights went out and the room was plunged into darkness.

Javier ran forward as quickly as his tired legs would carry him, out of the room and to the elevators. He pressed for the lifts repeatedly, but the button did not light. The phone call had terrified him; that horrible distorted voice and those cruel joy-filled words of murder. Someone wanted to kill him. Someone was going to enjoy killing him.

"Come on!" he yelled and stepped back to see if the display above either lift indicted one of the elevators was on its way to the 13th floor, but the displays were blank. He then tried the door to the stairs but found it locked. It was as if the 13th floor had suddenly ceased to exist. Someone was coming for Javier and he was trapped.

"Oh my God, oh my God," he said, over and again. "Maybe it was a prank, just a stupid prank. Whoever called me here, trying to teach me a lesson." And then he thought about his revenge list and wondered if someone on that list was responsible for the events of the evening. Had someone tricked him to come to the hotel with false promises, because they felt his time in jail had not been punishment enough?

But then he remembered that voice, that horrible screaming voice, and it did not feel like a prank. It felt like someone meant it; someone wanted to murder him. Without thinking again, he dashed back into the Margaret Thatcher Suite and slammed the door closed behind him. He *had* to find his mobile phone. It was the one and only thing that could help him, the one thing that still connected him with the world outside the 13th floor.

The room, now dark apart from the occasional flash of lightning, was no longer luxurious and welcoming. It was suffocating and menacing, a crushing enclosure of sharp metal and glass objects, any one of which could easily be turned into a deadly weapon.

He had no idea where to find a light switch, but as all of the lights in the room had gone off at the same, he had assumed the power had been cut. He slowly moved from the door and back towards the balcony, certain his phone was on the floor somewhere in that area. But he was reflected in the countless surfaces of the Art Deco furniture which, in the darkness, now created a gathering of movement and shadows that followed him as he crept through the room. With each step Javier caught sight of something out of the corner of his eye and would stop and spin round, only to find it was his own reflection or shadow. And then he would turn back and start to walk forward once more.

As he reached the balcony a sheet of lightning lit the room, just for a second, and in that moment, he clearly could see the chair he had been sitting in and the plate and cutlery he had placed on the floor next to it. He dropped to his knees and began to stroke his hands across the carpet, trying to locate his phone, or even just nudge it with his fingers, enough to make the screen light up. "Come on, come on," he whispered, angry and frustrated he had been so stupid to throw it to the floor in the first place.

And then he heard his own ringtone, and for a moment his heart leapt with joy and relief. Someone was calling him, and that meant his phone would light up like a beacon right there on the floor in front of him, a lighthouse drawing him back to shore. He was just seconds away from speaking to someone and calling for help.

With his eyes fixed downwards he glanced from one spot to another, hoping to see his phone glowing against the carpet. But then, out of the corner of his eye, he could see a dim light above him. His phone was not on the floor, it was in the air. There, just a few feet from him. His phone was in the air, being held by someone else. Javier was not alone anymore.

On his knees, he slowly shuffled away from the figure and raised himself back to his feet, gripping the handle to the balcony door for balance. The intruder was silent, stood still with Javier's phone held out towards him. The dim light from the screen offered little clue as to who was there, but Javier was sure he could just about make out the outline of a hood slightly obscuring the intruder's face.

"That's mine," Javier said unexpectedly, his words a surprise even to himself. The figure did not respond, and in that silent moment Javier could only hear his own ragged breaths, loudly parading his fear to the other person in the room. "That phone is mine," he said again, his terror now obvious with every syllable from his lips.

The intruder's head tipped to one side, like someone attempting to understand a foreign language, and then Javier's phone was casually tossed over one shoulder, its job clearly done. A prop that was no longer needed.

Instead, the intruder reached down into a pocket, and withdrew another object and held it up for Javier to see. A volley of lightning bolts lit the room and Javier screamed. The object was a carving knife, long and sharp, eager for Javier's blood. And beyond that, beneath the hood, a nightmare face, pale and almost featureless, stripped back to little more than a skull under a thin layer of white flesh.

Javier screamed again and pushed down hard against the metal handle. The door sprung open behind him and he stumbled backwards into the rain and freezing, howling wind. For a moment, a brief split-second, simply being out of the room made him feel safe. He turned and slammed the door behind him, and a last hope flashed through his mind, a hope that he could frighten off his assailant by raising the alarm, by screaming at the other balconies for help.

But with his first steps he tripped and lunged forward, sent flying by a wire stretched invisibly across the width of the balcony. Robbed of his balance, his feet slipping across the watery surface of the floor, he spun around and fell backwards, momentum lifting him partly over the balcony wall. With his legs flailing in the air, Javier grabbed downwards, hoping to grasp the ledge and pull himself back to safety.

But then he felt steadied, as two strong hands grabbed his ankles and gently pivoted him towards the floor. Javier glanced down; a shocking recognition of the 13-storey drop he had just avoided. "Oh God, oh God. Thank you. Thank you," he squealed, freezing rainwater falling onto his face.

But the intruder did not manoeuvre him back to safety. Instead, Javier was held in a state of balance, like a seesaw, the balcony wall wedged into the base of his spine, his legs one side and his torso hanging over the other. Javier tried to lean forward, to grab hold of something and pull himself to safety. But when he saw that horrible, twisted smile again he knew he had not been saved. His death had simply been delayed, savoured. Apart from the falling rain, there was silence and stillness. A moment of respite before his end.

The intruder stepped forward and lifted Javier's feet into the air, gently pushing his body to an increasingly sharp angle until there was nothing left but gravity and a 13-storey drop.

CHAPTER 6

There was no pretence in Adam's reaction, no suggestion he did not know who Valerie was talking about. There was no charade. Instead, after a moment of thought, he simply sat down again and looked Valerie directly in the eyes.

She had taken a photograph from her bag and placed it on the table directly in front of him. "Elizabeth Patricia Martin," she said. "Known to friends and family as Beth. But she has other names, of course. Many aliases. All part of the subterfuge to keep her true identity a secret. But I eventually worked it out. Did you honestly think I wouldn't?"

Adam stared down at the image of a young woman he had known since the day she was born; her bright, smiling face, caught in the street as she was casually chatting with a friend or perhaps a fellow student. She was completely unaware her privacy, protected throughout her life by a wall of family, friends and social workers, was lost. She was exposed. And after a moment of quiet reflection, he replied.

"I don't believe you," he said, calmly. "After everything you have done to that girl, everything you are responsible for, I do not believe you would take away the one thing she has left. Her privacy. No matter how desperate you are."

Valerie was uncomfortable with Adam's criticism. She was no longer Valerie Pierce of the *Daily Ear*, the shameless columnist who would happily parade her views on anything and anyone without a care in the world. Once outside the insular world of tabloid news, she had learned people had been hurt, genuinely hurt, by her actions.

Pearl Martin had been one of those people; an emotionally vulnerable TV actress who had caught the attention of Valerie early in her career and become the subject of countless highly critical columns, articles and comment pieces. Privately, Valerie had conceded her own part in Pearl's suicide. And she certainly did not feel comfortable threatening Pearl's daughter. But Valerie was desperate and, in that moment, would say anything to force Adam into helping her.

Adam moved forward, leaning towards Valerie with his hands together, almost as though he were praying. "The media was obsessed with Pearl," Adam replied. "You and your colleagues did that. You fuelled the public's curiosity of a TV actress and then watched it burn out of control, become a public obsession. You made Pearl the most famous woman in the country, and when she took her own life, she became the most famous woman in the world. You turned her into an icon. But in doing that you robbed me of my best friend, and you robbed an innocent child of her mother.

"I have done my best to stop anyone finding out what happened to Pearl's daughter. We all have. There are reporters who have spent years trying to track her down, to get her story, or even just a photograph. The moment someone finds her, she will never know another moment of peace in her life. And I do not believe you would do that to her, Valerie."

Valerie knew her ruse had failed, and she began to collect her things together. "Will you help me, Adam?" she asked, hoping against hope her desperate ploy had not backfired. "I know this all sounds surreal, and I am not asking you to believe me. Not here, not right now. But I am asking you to use all the resources at your disposal to investigate what happened to Chris and Derek, and to keep an ear out for any other questionable events. If the result of all of this is that you simply reassure me, beyond all reasonable doubt, that I am wrong then that will be enough. I just want to feel safe again."

Adam sat back and then, unexpectedly, he nodded. "Very well," he said. "Give me a few days. I will give you all the evidence and information my team can put together. If necessary, I will contact you directly to set up another meeting."

Valerie was so taken aback she was briefly rendered speechless. She had convinced herself the conversation had been a humiliating failure and she would leave the meeting empty-handed. But, instead, Adam had agreed to help her. Valerie quickly gathered her thoughts and handed Adam her business card.

"Thank you," she said. "All my contact details are on here." And with that, she stood up and left.

Alone once more, Adam retrieved his mobile phone from his pocket and dialled a number. "It's me," he said. "I need to see you. There's been a development."

At 9.45pm, Valerie Pierce was sat in an Uber travelling to Fenchurch Street Station to catch a train back to her home in Leigh-on-Sea. The stress and fear of the evening had lifted, not just because she had Adam's pledge of support but also because she had not received a phone call at 9pm. She hadn't realised how exhausting the previous days had been, and sat with her head resting against the window, only just paying attention to the world around her.

"We need to take a detour," the driver said, waving at a wall of ambulances and police cars which came into view in front of them.

Stirred from her inertia, Valerie leant forward in her seat and peered through the windscreen at the line of flashing lights and reflective jackets. "Goodness, what's happened?" she asked.

"Probably a flood or something," the driver replied. But then he suddenly jolted in his seat and reached backwards towards Valerie. "Don't look," he yelled. "Don't look."

Valerie slapped his hand away. "What do you think you're doing?" she asked. And as she looked through the windscreen, peering beyond the emergency vehicles, she saw it. A car parked outside the Royal Hotel, its roof crushed downwards, and a body lying on top, like a broken ragdoll thrown from the skies.

"Oh my God," she cried.

"Don't look, madam. Please. It is too upsetting."

The Uber came to a necessary stop as the police spoke to the driver to direct him elsewhere. But Valerie had to know who had died. She had to know if she was right. And so, she let herself out of the car and strode confidently through the circus of police, fire fighters and paramedics to the body. It was a skill she had developed over many years at party conferences and awards ceremonies, an ability to pretend she was supposed to be there.

And within moments she was right beside the car, staring into the open eyes of a dead man. She wondered if he had been alive right until the moment he had hit the roof. Had he had seen the car blazing towards him as the final seconds of his life flashed to an unequivocal end?

"Madam, no. No entry. Step back," an officer called to her.

Valerie ignored the command and continued to stare at the face of the man who had died.

"Madam, now!" the police officer yelled, and took Valerie firmly by the arm. "You cannot be here."

"But I knew him," she replied quietly. "I knew him."

CHAPTER 7

"…fell to his death from the 13th floor of the Royal Hotel in Mayfair at just after 9pm last night. Staff at the hotel are said to be deeply shocked by the incident. Police are investigating but say they are not looking for anyone else in connection with…"

"…counted members of the royal family, TV actors, popstars and politicians among the targets of his countless exposés…"

As expected, everyone is celebrating the #FakeSpanishPrince's (literal) fall from grace. So, none of you hypocritical bastards ever bought a copy of #TheDailyEar?

"…however, the eyewitnesses I have spoken to this morning say they clearly overheard him speaking to staff at the hotel and saying he hadn't brought anything with him. He had booked the hotel's Margaret Thatcher Suite, a room he had used several times in the past to lure celebrities and politicians to fake meetings with his infamous Spanish Prince and other characters he assumed over the years. One hotel contact has told me he ordered a number of traditional Spanish dishes as his final meal, which could well be reflective of those he enjoyed growing up with his family in Essex. Certainly, Javier García's final night was a lonely, low-key affair where he appeared to be revisiting many aspects of his life with some measure of regret."

My mother told me to only speak good of the dead. The #FakeSpanishPrince is dead. Good!

Paparazzi pervert Jason Spade should be out soon. Let's hope he doesn't take a dive from the 13th floor. He'd obliterate an entire block! #FakeSpanishPrince #JasonSpade

"…his brother Dan Martínez, a Pulitzer Prize winning reporter with the New York Times, released a statement on behalf of Javier's family stating: "We are very sad to hear of the passing of Javier García. We would ask for our privacy to be respected during this sad time." Dan, a former BBC journalist, moved with his parents to the United States two decades ago. There he quickly carved out a successful career as an investigative journalist, exposing numerous corrupt politicians and, most recently, documenting the resurgence of white supremacy in relation to the upcoming 2016 presidential election. He married supermodel Bridget Eastwood 10 years ago and the couple have three children…"

"…does raise issues about aftercare for those released from prison, and whether enough is being done to ensure ex-inmates feel supported and able to return to life as free and useful citizens…"

"…it was when the case against her collapsed that García's fate was sealed. Whilst not directly commenting on his death, Sophia Ferrari has, with typical compassion, posted a link to the Samaritans website on her social media accounts and urged those suffering from depression or suicidal thoughts not to suffer alone…"

"He was very amiable and funny. He played the part well. And he certainly knew how to keep the champagne flowing. I remember thinking 'this is all well and good but when do I get to talk about the funding for this art project?'. Instead, he kept asking me about prostitutes and whether I'd ever cheated on my wife or taken drugs. And that was never journalism. I never think of him as a journalist. In that respect he was an absolute fraud. What he did was cruel. Simply that. Cruel and self-serving."

@ValeriePierce53 *I had an electrician in to fix my traditional two-tone ("ding-dong") doorbell. Without asking me* *he replaced it with a modern electric "melody" doorbell. It took me 15 minutes of uninterrupted dialogue to explain to him what a terrible, terrible human being he was.*

CHAPTER 8

Lucy Strickland knew she was the most famous person in the room. Despite having, by far, the least journalistic experience of any of the *Daily Ear* staff in that morning's editorial meeting, that fame gave her a sense of power and importance that could not be abated. As she looked around the cramped office and the dozen reporters and editors embroiled in a punchy discussion about the day's news agenda, she wondered if any of them felt intimidated by her. Or even unworthy. She always enjoyed a sense that other people were unnerved by her presence.

She was dressed in a way that emphasised her most compelling attributes, to ensure she could never disappear into the background of any meeting. That day she wore a black trouser suit which accentuated her height, with a large diamond and gold scorpion brooch on her lapel. She had also pulled her long red hair into a tight ponytail which she knew was not the most flattering of looks as, in profile, it simply emphasised her large nose. But Lucy had long since given up any pretence of prettiness and, instead, embraced the attention that came with being 'striking'.

As usual she was only half listening to the discussion but wanted to appear fully engaged and so gurned her face through a range of different expressions; concern, deep thought and contemplation, indifference, a joke no one else had picked up on. And occasionally she would jot a pretend reminder into her notebook, something that appeared clever or important just in case one of the other journalists caught sight of it. That morning she had written down *'review and analyse document'* and *'schedule TV appearances to promote issue'*.

Lucy was doing what she did during every morning editorial meeting she attended. She was simply biding her time before triumphantly grandstanding on whatever issue she had decided to write about that week. Whilst a team of experienced journalists and editors were busily filling the following day's paper, Lucy was simply waiting for an opportunity to show off.

"We'll bury him at the bottom of page 23," Sydney Corrigan, the *Daily Ear*'s fourth interim editor in three years, stated. He had the air of someone who was permanently tired and stressed, an overweight, balding 60-year-old with enormous bags under his eyes. Sydney had hoped to quietly cruise to retirement on the features desk but was forced into his current role when his predecessor had been unceremoniously sacked.

"But he had a long and high-profile career with this paper," one of the news editors argued back. "It will be noticed if we don't acknowledge his suicide."

"Yes, yes but despite his long, high-profile career with this paper," Sydney responded, "he went to jail for corruption."

"Actually, it was for perverting the course of justice," one of the reporters chipped in.

Sydney sighed heavily. "Which is a form of corruption, for fuck's sake," he only partly muttered under his breath. "But the point is his prison sentence leaves us no room to manoeuvre. Our position is the same now as it was when he was sent down. We had no idea what he was doing. We don't support what he did. It was right he went to jail. And now he's dead. If we ignore it, then by tomorrow everyone will be talking about something else. If we run a load of features, we'll be pulled back into a whole fucking discussion about media ethics. So, as I said, the bottom of page 23."

"Well, I will be writing about Javier García in my column this week and I am going to say the opposite of everyone else," Lucy announced with great pride, standing up. She paused, as though waiting for a ripple of applause, but the room was silent.

Sydney stared at her with the look of a man who would rather have suffered a fatal heart attack that morning than be chairing the daily news meeting. "What's your angle?" he asked, despondently.

"I am going to tell the British people the truth," Lucy replied. "I am going to remind them that Javier García exposed corruption and lies on an unprecedented scale and they should all be on their knees mourning the loss of one of the UK's greatest undercover journalists. I am going to defend his legacy and challenge the British media and – yes – the *Daily Ear* itself to offer up someone, anyone, to take on the mantle of The Spanish Prince and continue his great work. I know I am the only person brave enough to tell the truth but, as usual: I. Will. Do. That."

Once again, Lucy waited for a round of applause, which she did not get, and so sat down.

"Did you ever meet Javier?" Sydney asked.

Lucy shrugged and shook her head. "Well, no," she replied.

"I knew him well," Sydney said. "Believe me, the man was an absolute bell end and I'm glad he's dead. Right, what's next?"

Despite her editor's disparaging words, Lucy left the meeting victorious. Nothing made her feel more intelligent than shouting an opinion that was at odds with everyone else in the room. The meeting had left her with an excited buzz and so she decided, rather than head straight home, she would take a brisk tour of the newsroom. It was a way to gain further attention from colleagues who were not senior enough to be in the morning meeting.

When she had first joined the *Daily Ear* she had been assigned Valerie Pierce's old office, its glass walls offering an electrifying view of the paper's vast newsroom, a blur of reporters and editors, dozens of top spec computers and, suspended from the ceiling above all of that, three enormous screens hung, channelling news feeds from around the world.

But equally it had offered a view from the newsroom into her office and so had provided an opportunity for Lucy to turn the busy hub of reporters into her own personal audience. Each day she would pace the floor, waving her arms in the air and speaking her thoughts aloud which, she imagined, for those on the other side of her glass wall would look as though she was in the middle of some grand, hands-free phone discussion, probably with someone very important. And Lucy adored it.

However, the *Daily Ear* had relocated its offices the previous year to Southwark as part of a major cost-cutting exercise that also saw several hundred staff made redundant. The new offices were simpler and more functional, with fewer open plan areas and absolutely no glass walls.

This had frustrated Lucy's theatrical attempts at attention-seeking and so now she only travelled across the city to attend the occasional editorial meeting and mostly worked from her office at home. But her husband was away on a stag holiday with his friends, and Lucy had found their large house surprising lonely without him. And so, she had decided to attend the office a little more frequently until he returned.

When she did work at the main office, she enjoyed doing the rounds to ensure as many people could see her as possible although she didn't want to speak to any of them. She just wanted to enjoy their gaze.

She entered the lift and said "ground" to the young man already there. "I'm going to the newsroom," she said.

"Oh, I thought you might be going to the memorial," he replied as the doors slid closed.

"Pardon?"

He nodded at her. "Your suit. I thought you were going to the memorial."

Lucy realised her companion in the lift was also wearing a black suit, but his ensemble included a black tie which gave the impression he was in mourning. As a rule, she did not like being spoken to at the office by people she didn't know just in case she was wasting her time on someone unimportant. And so, she leaned forward and stared at his security pass, a passive-aggressive display of her displeasure that he had chosen to speak to her.

"Communications Officer, Lewis Greene," she read out, and stood up straight once more. "So, Lewis, is this memorial for Javier García? Because I am dedicating my column to him this week. I am going to celebrate his work; endorse his undercover journalism for the courageous venture it truly was. You might want to send out a few press releases about it."

"Erm, no," Lewis replied. "It's for Derek Toulson. He used to be the PR director at the paper. He died a few days ago. A few of us are getting together for a brunch to remember him."

"Never heard of him," Lucy replied, abruptly. "I assume you liked him though. Good bloke?"

Lewis shrugged. "God, no," he said. "He was a complete tool."

Lucy took a dramatic step backwards and stared at him. "Then why are you commemorating him?" she asked.

"Oh, it's not being done respectfully," Lewis replied, with a bright smile on his young face. "God, no. Everyone hated him. It's more of a celebration to be honest. You're more than welcome to join us."

Lucy was tempted. She quite liked the idea of celebrating someone's death and had instantly changed her opinion of the young man in the lift who, up until that point, she had considered somewhat impudent for speaking to her.

But she had already committed emotionally to her tour of the newsroom and didn't feel the memorial would necessarily offer her the same level of attention. "I'll pass," she replied. "Why was he hated so much?"

"Oh, awful man," Lewis replied. "Bully. Sexual predator. Racist. Homophobe. He was fired a few years ago. Turned out he had been misusing company funds to bribe local councils into defunding charities he didn't like. Anything that was for single parents, gay people, the BAME community, the disabled…"

"Well," Lucy said, warming to the idea of Derek Toulson, "I can't say I entirely disagree with the man's motives. There is a ridiculous amount of public money wasted on politically correct nonsense. I'm surprised he was fired, to be honest. I know the paper was a little wet back then, but still."

She could see Lewis' eyes widen slightly, as though either surprised or disappointed by her comment. And then she remembered many of her colleagues did not hold the same extreme right-wing values as the paper and were only there for the monthly pay cheque.

"Derek was kind of famous," Lewis said. "You must have heard the story. There was an animal charity called Gay's Horse Sanctuary, named after the woman who set it up, Sally Gay. But Derek thought it was a charity for *gay* horses."

"Gay horses?" Lucy asked, gurning again. "He honestly thought someone was running an animal sanctuary for *gay* horses?"

Lewis laughed. "Yes, and he actually used *Daily Ear* funds to bribe the local council into closing it."

"Oh," Lucy said, disappointed that Derek had gone from hero to zero in her mind so quickly. "You're right. He does sound like a tool."

As they arrived on the ground floor Lucy realised, rather unexpectedly, that she had quite enjoyed her brief conversation with Lewis and was intrigued by his job title. She had mostly created her own publicity in her time with the paper and knew she had often misjudged how some of her comments would land, publicly. And she liked the idea of getting some additional support to promote her weekly column.

"I usually work from home," she said. "But could we catch up, soon? I would very much appreciate some extra PR, and it sounds like you could help."

Lewis nodded politely. "Yes of course," he said. "I'll have a look at your calendar and pop something in." He stepped from the lift and starting walking in the opposite direction. "Have a great day," he called cheerfully, as he left.

Lucy enjoyed a brief tour of the newsroom, and then retreated quietly to her office until the buzz had worn off. She was also excited about her meeting with Lewis, and the opportunity to give her profile and her column some additional publicity.

Her rise to public prominence over the previous few years had been as fast as it had been surprising. She had assumed her role at the *Daily Ear* on her 36th birthday, soon after a controversial stint on a reality TV show. During a brief tenure in the *Big Brother* house, she had proven herself to be slightly more articulate and knowledgeable than most reality TV stars. She had argued with the other housemates on topics such as race, poverty and immigration and her right-wing beliefs and rude, aggressive persona won her a cult following among some of the show's fans.

After *Big Brother* she continued to spew her angry opinions across social media, and her Twitter followers grew by hundreds of thousands. This quickly led to a succession of invitations to appear on television programmes to discuss some of the issues she raised. Her views on 'ugly babies on buses' won her a spot on the couch on This Morning, whilst her tirade against 'lazy nurses who are failing to keep our hospitals clean' saw her go head-to-head with her local hospital's Chief Executive live on BBC Breakfast.

But it was her unrelenting vitriolic diatribe against immigration that captured the mood of the Right and elevated her beyond the other attention seeking former reality stars on Twitter. More than that, her utter indifference at accusations of racism or hatemongering soon made her the poster girl for Brexiteers. The harder and faster the accusations came, the angrier and louder she promoted her views.

Lucy Strickland's star was in the ascension just as the *Daily Ear*'s new owner decided to recruit a female columnist to fill the void left by Valerie Pierce. He wanted the *Daily Ear* to move even further to the right in its tone and the opinions it projected and endorsed. And he considered Lucy to be the perfect voice to herald a new era for the paper.

And she had grabbed at the opportunity with glee, but perhaps also some naiveté. She had immediately found herself the subject of ridicule and, worse, undesirable comparisons with her predecessor. And this had puzzled Lucy because she knew Valerie had been neither universally loved nor respected. But within weeks of the launch of her *Daily Ear* column she was confronted by a retrospective admiration for her predecessor, one which left Lucy caricatured as the 'ASDA-price Valerie Pierce'.

Where Valerie was praised for having had "clarity and consistency on government policy and social issues", Lucy was accused of "stretching a little knowledge as far as it could reasonably be expected to go".

Valerie's mastery of the English language, "her flair and passion for words that gave her such power and influence over the opinions of her readers" was compared unfavourably to Lucy's writing style; "using the English language like a blunt instrument, with which to beat her readers into submission by simply repeating the same limited, well-worn opinions over and over again".

But rather than cave in, Lucy had doubled down. She set aside the criticisms and comparisons and decided to carve out her own path to success.

Whilst Valerie Pierce could skilfully influence and persuade, Lucy would make people angry. She would offer whichever facts suited her argument and then use her column to shout and yell at her readers until they were as angry as she was. And she picked her targets with consummate judgement, knowing which would push those 'angry buttons' with her readers; immigrants, non-white communities (generally, but particularly Muslims), fat people, poor people, Labour politicians and supporters, NHS employees, teachers and illegal immigrants, gay people and, in particular, transgender people.

Over the previous few years her impact had grown measurably, and it was now a generally accepted truth that many on the right would wait for Lucy to air her opinion on an issue before aligning their own arguments with hers.

But she also set the tone for the new *Daily Ear* itself. Gradually the paper had adopted her shouty, angry style across much of its news until Lucy's opinion was the benchmark for the *Daily Ear*'s coverage. At some point her column was renamed "Lucy Strickland. I'm Right!" and even her most adamant detractors had to acknowledge her success.

But she had a begrudging and resentful respect for Valerie's work, and on occasion, when bereft of ideas, she would revisit one of Valerie's old columns and plagiarise its content whilst ensuring it was re-written in her own unique and angry tone. One of her personal favourites had been a rewrite of a feature Valerie had produced many years earlier; a scathing attack on Pearl Martin. Valerie had cited the actress's apparent non-stop partying and drinking, from within a beautifully crafted article that left the reader believing Valerie had not attacked Pearl, but simply raised legitimate middle-class concerns about a lack of positive role models for girls.

Lucy, however, lacked Valerie's incredible journalist skill, and so had simply spewed a hate-filled article in which she attacked the memory of Pearl Martin and accused the actress, as if from the beyond the grave, of actively promoting drinking and drug-taking to girls and young women.

And as Lucy contemplated how to address the death of Javier García, she recalled Valerie had once written an article in defence of the Fake Spanish Prince, during the hey-day of his career. And that was all Lucy needed. Valerie Pierce's words would once again become her next column.

CHAPTER 9

"Mum. Mum, it's almost eleven. I'm going to put some pastries in. Will you come down?" Alice Pierce stood at her mother's bedroom door and waited for a response.

It had been an unpleasant night. Late in the evening, Valerie had called from London, clearly too distressed to board the train to Leigh-on-Sea, and so Alice had contacted her mother's ex-husband, Ray, to collect her and drive her home. Valerie had arrived in tears, too shocked and too frightened to explain what had happened. And then she had simply retired to her room and locked the door.

Alice had managed to glean some understanding of events from the few rambling comments Valerie had offered before she retired to bed, and she had been able to work out the rest from various news articles and Twitter posts that had appeared online, overnight. But what alarmed Alice the most was her mother's bizarre prophecy of a third death had come true. *Exactly* true. To the precise minute.

"Mum?" she called once more. And then, to her great relief, she heard Valerie's croaky voice in reply.

"Yes, darling. Give me 20 minutes. I want to have a quick shower."

"OK," Alice replied, and walked down the two flights of stairs to the kitchen on the ground floor. She made herself a latte using her mother's expensive coffee machine, switched on the oven and placed several shop-bought pastries onto a baking tray, ready to go in. And then she sat back at the breakfast bar, her tablet in her hand, and pondered the events of the previous week.

Alice had been somewhat bewildered by her mother's claim that two of former colleagues from the *Daily Ear* had been murdered. And after the police had rejected Valerie's version of events, Alice had been even more puzzled by her mother's insistence that only Adam Jaymes had the resources and the knowledge to investigate her claims, a man she knew her mother despised. It had all seemed too fantastical; the suggestion of murder and her mother's assessment that the only person who could help was a world-famous actor, married to an American billionaire.

But now, after a third death, exactly as her mother had predicted, she was beginning to feel frightened. And so, unable to sleep for most of the night, she had spent long periods on the ground floor, either caring for her mother's ailing dog, Jasper, or drinking herbal tea at the breakfast bar, searching the internet on her tablet for any suggestion Valerie had been spotted at the scene of Javier's death.

Alice's two daughters were visiting their father in Australia, and so she had temporarily moved in with Valerie rather than be alone in her flat while the girls were away. She missed them terribly. It was the first time they had been separated for anything more than a few days. But despite Alice's many misgivings about their trip, she had begun to feel relieved they were safely tucked away on the other side of the world.

Valerie had made it very clear she disagreed with Alice's decision to let them visit their father and his new wife. *"He knocked you up, flew home to Australia, and you don't hear from him for eighteen years,"* Valerie had said. *"But now he is settled and has a wife, he suddenly wants to play dad. Oh, I bet he does. Now you've done all the hard work. I bet he does."*

But Alice felt she had no right to prevent the girls from meeting their father or enjoying an all-expense paid trip to Melbourne. And she did not personally hold any grudges against their father. He had just been a kid, like Alice, when they met. Christopher Miller. A cute teenage boy sent to his English grandparents in Barnet while his mum and dad were going through a particularly difficult divorce.

Alice had met him in a coffee shop in the high street. She had been intrigued by his accent, and almost immediately fell in love with him when she heard the reason he was in the UK. They were kindred spirits, she had thought, both wounded by the actions of their parents. It was only after he had returned to Australia, she realised she was pregnant.

Alice wrote to him; told him the news. But she knew the letter was written in a way that had offered him every opportunity to opt out. She had not asked him for money or support. She had not placed any pressure on him to tell his own parents, or to be involved in any away. And after that, Christopher became little more than just a name, someone Alice's twin daughters, Hannah and Emily, knew existed. And that was all he was until a few months earlier when Alice received a letter from him, completely out of the blue. It was filled with stories, and information, and photographs. And suddenly, Christopher Miller became a real person once more. He asked if Alice would let him meet Hannah and Emily, to introduce them to the Australian side of their family. And Alice had agreed.

And although Valerie had contested that decision as strongly as she could, Alice believed her mother had also been quite happy to have Alice as a house guest while the girls were away. Their relationship remained uncomfortable, sometimes prickly, and Alice knew there were still many conversations they were yet to have.

Over the years there had been countless arguments, many of which had quickly and unnecessarily spiralled out of control, leading to long periods of estrangement. But over the previous few years, precariously at times, she and Valerie had found a new rhythm for their relationship which had mostly worked. And Alice had found a sort of peace, as she tried to let go of years of animosity and work towards a kinder connection with her mother.

That morning, Alice had thrown on her thick woollen jumper, blue skinny jeans and boots. It was a style she knew her mother particularly disliked, but she also knew Valerie would not say anything about it. Of late, her mother had begun to keep her opinions to herself. And her mother's silence had become an important part of their new and improved relationship.

"I'll put these in," Valerie said, unexpectedly appearing in the kitchen and breaking Alice's trail of thought. Valerie lifted the tray of pastries and placed them in the oven. Her dark hair was still wet, swept back from her face, but she had managed to get dressed; a pair of black trousers and a deep purple jumper. "How's Jasper this morning?" she asked?

"I fed him," Alice replied. "Or tried to. He's not eaten much. I think we need to get him back to the vet."

"Thank you, darling," she said. "I was hoping this new food would make a difference, but he seems even thinner. And I think his back legs are looking weaker. He stumbled quite a few times on the beach yesterday morning."

"Mum, he's 14 years old and he has kidney failure," Alice replied, softly. "At some point you know you're going to have to make a decision about him."

"I know," Valerie said. And then she stood and walked over to the French doors that led to the garden, and gently touched the glass. "Another miserable day," she said, reviewing the grey clouds that continued to darken the sky. "I can't remember the last time I saw any sunshine. It feels like it's been raining for weeks."

Alice chuckled. "You know when you do that, you look and sound just like an actress from a 1940s melodrama," she said. "Honestly, one hundred per cent Bette Davis. Dark Victory or Now Voyager."

"When I do what?" Valerie asked, turning to her daughter with a look of genuine innocence. "I was just talking about the weather."

Alice put down her tablet and walked over to the coffee machine. "Would you like one?" she asked. "I've finally taught myself how to use it. I'm getting quite good."

Valerie smiled. "Just an espresso. Nice and simple. Like me."

"And I can drive you to the police station again, if you like," Alice suggested. "It might help if you know what they're doing about it. It's three people now, not just two. They're bound to have linked them."

Valerie sighed and returned to her seat. "One would hope so," she replied. "We could give it a go. But not today. I just want to stay at home today. It's not as though I'm a witness. I was there afterwards. After it had happened."

"That's fine," Alice replied and then, daintily, enquired: "And your meeting with Adam Jaymes. I didn't get to ask. Did he turn up?"

Valerie nodded. "Oh yes."

"And?"

On the topic of Adam Jaymes, Alice's loyalties were severely compromised. On the one hand she knew, a few years earlier, he had used his fame and wealth to publicly humiliate her mother and had almost destroyed both her reputation and her career. But Alice had also been a fan since his time on the science-fiction show Doctor Who and, later, his guest starring role on the vampire drama True Blood. As much as she *knew* she should be appalled by the very thought of him, she could not help feeling somewhat starstruck and excited that her mother had actually met him.

"He agreed to help," Valerie replied, casually. "He wasn't convinced. Not at all. He told me as much. But I talked him into investigating. And I know this sounds awful, darling, but Javier's death is the proof I needed. Even Adam Jaymes cannot deny something is going on now."

Alice found herself unduly excited by the idea she was only two degrees of separation from having met Adam Jaymes herself. She placed her mother's coffee in front of her and sat down again. "How did you convince him to help?" she asked. "It's not as if there's any love lost between the two of you."

Valerie sat back and crossed her arms. She knew Alice would be appalled if she knew the truth, that her mother had threatened to publicly expose the identity of Pearl Martin's daughter to get what she wanted. And so, instead, she replied: "I told him everything I knew. And he agreed. It was simple."

Alice desperately wanted more information, to ask how Adam had looked, and whether he was genuinely as handsome in real life as he appeared on TV. But she did not want her mother to know she was a fan, and so changed the subject. "I'll go and check on Jasper," she said. "I'll dish up the pastries when I get back." And then, with an uncharacteristic show of affection, she casually kissed her mother on the cheek and left the room.

Valerie picked up the tablet and swiped across the screen, revealing the pages Alice had been reviewing beforehand. And within seconds Valerie was staring at a photograph of Javier, his mugshot from when he was arrested and charged with perverting the course of justice. It was one of the few pictures of the Fake Spanish Prince made publicly available.

And then, for a moment, a split second, Javier's cold, dead open eyes flashed before her. She was transported to the night before, the rain falling around her once again, the cold wind, the flashing lights from all the emergency vehicles. But at the centre of it all was a dead man, staring her in the face. A man she had known, somehow thrown to his death. She dropped the tablet back onto the counter and collapsed forward, holding her head in her hands, and tried not to cry.

CHAPTER 10

"Is this how far I have fallen?"

Steve Gallant was sat in a toilet cubicle at the National Baking School on the South Bank. He was there to interview the three finalists of the Great British Bake Off, and regular trips to the loo were a usual part of his routine. When it came to formal press events, he never liked to stand with a tape recorder or pad, writing things down. He had always felt it created a barrier and would often put people on their guard. And so, instead, he would simply chat, and then take himself to the toilet to email himself key points and quotes he could use later on.

"They're not even fucking celebrities," he muttered to himself. "They're just fucking competitors steaming puddings on a fucking TV show about baking."

He finished his emails and then slotted his phone back into his jacket pocket and sat with his head in his hands. He could feel every ounce of his 183lb body, his fitted shirt threatening to pop some buttons at any second. And he felt every second of his age. He was no longer the young, golden boy of entertainment journalism in the UK. He had transformed into a portly, orange-faced, middle-aged man with blond hair plugs and ill-fitting suits.

And this was how he had spent his 48th birthday, interviewing TV cooking show contestants and emailing himself story suggestions from a stall in a public toilet. As always, he put on his happy face as he made his way from the toilets and to the exit, exchanging pleasantries and praise with the contestants, producers and PR execs as he left.

Little did they suspect his smiles and overly courteous persona were masking a number of devastating exclusives at the expense of the finalists. He was already formulating an overarching theme of "The Curse of the Great British Bake Off" to tie all the stories together.

He had coaxed the first contestant into admitting she thought one the show's judges had nice eyes, something Steve would deftly link to online comments that she had flirted her way to the final. The second contestant had cracked a joke about drinking prosecco with breakfast to deal with her nerves, which as far as Steve was concerned was an open admission the pressure of being on the show had turned her into an alcoholic.

The third had made a passing comment about being upset by some of the negativity towards him on social media, and Steve was pondering if he could stretch that into a story about the contestant's mental health and potentially that he was now a suicide risk. He decided he would chat to the *Daily Ear*'s GP advice columnist when he was next in the office to see how they could spin that narrative.

Steve managed to hail a cab quickly and sat in the back seat checking through the calendar on his phone to double-check where he needed to go to next. "Hold on. I think it's the Saatchi Gallery," he said, vaguely remembering something about the launch of the Celebrity Painting Challenge.

The cab driver peered at Steve through the glass screen separating the front of the cab with the back. "You're the American one, aren't you?" he asked.

Although he had lived in the UK for twenty years, Steve had proudly clung to his native accent and never allowed it to diminish. He knew it was part of his brand, something which added a certain level of glamour to his role, a suggestion, albeit a false one, that he worked at an international level. "Yes," Steve replied. "California."

"I know you," the driver replied. "I've driven you loads of times. The guy from the *Daily Ear*?"

Steve looked up from his phone and stared into the smiling face of his driver, a man in his forties who had maintained both a healthy BMI and a full head of blond hair. It was like looking into a cruel mirror, that wanted to show Steve how he *could* have aged.

"Yeah, yeah of course," Steve replied, brightly. "How are you doing? Good to see you again."

The smile on the man's face lessened slightly. "Sorry to hear about your friend," he said, glumly. "I know he did a bad thing and went to prison for it, but he was still a human being and it's hard on the people he left behind."

Steve assumed one of his pretend showbiz pals had died but for a moment he could not remember which of them had spent a period in jail. His first thought was to wing it, to pretend he knew who the driver was talking about in the hope he would offer more information. But he found his patience lacking that day, and so simply asked who the driver was talking about.

"Oh. I'm so sorry. I thought you would know. That guy who pretended to be the Spanish prince."

It was news Steve had not been expecting, and his heart skipped a beat. "Javier García?" he asked, a coldness spreading through his veins.

"That's him."

"He died? What, in prison?"

The driver shook his head. "No, he was out of prison. He killed himself last night. Jumped from the 13th floor of a hotel. One of the posh ones too. The whole area was blocked off for hours."

It took a moment for the news to sink in. Steve realised the driver was still staring at him, and so he double-checked his calendar and confirmed the Saatchi Gallery as their destination. As the cab set off, Steve actively lost himself in the screen of his mobile phone, not wanting to speak any more about Javier. Instead, he swiped through different news pages and social media feeds, trying to absorb the news that a former colleague had taken his own life.

He and Steve had joined the *Daily Ear*'s editorial team at about the same time, both handpicked by the Ear's then-owner, Howard Harvey. Steve had been the rising star of showbiz news, a handsome charismatic American who had the same star qualities as the celebrities he wrote about. And Javier was the clever, determined undercover reporter whose use of disguises quickly made him the stuff of legends among his peers.

They had never directly competed against each other, and so had always rubbed along quite happily. Never friends, but close colleagues, happy to share in each other's successes and occasionally offer each advice when things were not going their way. And as he sat in the back of the taxi, en route from one abysmal press event to the next, he suddenly felt very old. There was something aging about Javier's death, like the loss of a first classmate from high school. And the finality of the loss was all-defining. Steve knew his life and his career were indisputably linked, and if he could not give his career a much-needed kiss of life, he might as well take a walk from the 13th floor himself.

CHAPTER 11

"You may not use the internet. You may not use or own a personal computer, tablet or mobile phone. You may not use or own a device of any kind capable of taking photographic images or videos. You may not present yourself as being a professional photographer or a member of the press. You may not attend any swimming pool or fitness centre that includes changing rooms or showers. You will take part in a sex offender programme and attend polygraph test sessions as and when required. You will stay at home between the hours of your curfew and you will report to a police station to give details of any car you use. Is there anything I have stated that you do not understand, Mr Spade?"

Jason Spade stood quietly as the house manager rattled off the list of rules as though reading from a shopping list. These were the rules that would define how Jason could live his life for the foreseeable future, delivered to him as though they were as mundane as the restrictions on the use of a library card.

"Yes, I understand," he replied, begrudgingly.

"My name is Mrs Warwick and I am the manager here. The house is staffed 24-7 and so there is always a member of staff here to assist if you need anything. And, to reassure you, we have had great success helping registered sex offenders, like yourself, reintegrate into society. Your Aunt Gail visited yesterday and delivered your belongings to your room. You have clothes, toiletries, towels, books and a few photo albums she wanted you to have. Do you want to go to your room now? I think you should clean yourself up."

His exit from prison had not been simple. A small crowd of protestors, about 20 or so, had lined the street opposite the main gate with banners and angry voices. One had tossed a milkshake at him with remarkable precision and it had exploded against his chest just as his Aunt Gail arrived in her little red Hyundai Getz to pick him up. He had mopped up much of it using several packets of tissues he found in her glove compartment, but his clothes were still wet and sticky, and the stench of strawberry shake had become quite nauseating.

"Yes, I will," he replied. Mrs Warwick led him up a flight of stairs to a large bedroom sparsely filled with a single bed, a cupboard, a desk and chair, a wastepaper bin and a chest of drawers, all of which looked as though they had been donated by a charity shop. A door led to a small, adjoining, windowless toilet and shower.

"We have seven residents, all males. We ask you keep to your own room and respect the privacy of the other tenants. Is there anything else I can help you with?"

Jason shook his head and Mrs Warwick left, closing the door behind her. Jason stripped off his clothes and threw them into the bin. They were the same clothes he had worn the day he had been sent to prison, returned to him that day as part of his release. But they were now far too big for him. His time in prison had enabled him, although not willingly, to lose more than 100lb in weight and so his Aunt Gail, the only member of the family still speaking to him, had bought him a whole wardrobe of new clothes for his new slimmed-down frame.

He also had a small bag of personal belongings that had been returned to him; a watch, his wallet and the keys to a house and a car he no longer owned. Jason's many victims had jointly sued him for damages and successfully relieved him of every one of his belongings. He had entered prison a man of considerable means but had left without a penny to his name.

Jason showered, quietly, and then wrapped a towel around his waist and lay down on his bed. He stared at the ceiling, sulking and overwhelmed by a grinding sense of injustice that so much had been taken from him. His house, his money, his career. All of it gone. And just because he had used specialist photographic equipment to capture images of women in various stages of undress, including some of the female athletes in private changing rooms at the 2012 London Olympics.

Jason had never understood the public outcry, the anger or the legal case against him. The hundreds of pictures found on his hard drive were no worse than those he had captured during his work as a press photographer for the

Daily Ear. For years he had hidden in bushes or neighbouring properties to photograph female celebrities sunbathing nude at holiday villas around the world. Or he had laid on the pavement to photograph up the skirts of female celebrities getting out of cars, so the *Daily Ear* readers could see for themselves whether or not that celebrity had any underwear on.

He had been told many times that his incredulous reaction to the guilty verdict was a key reason his sentence had never been commuted, and his sense of entitlement over women's privacy had gone well beyond any legitimate professional arguments; his activity was considered criminal, but to that day he simply did not believe he had done anything wrong and his refusal to accept any misconduct had nearly kept him in prison even longer.

During his incarceration, a group of women powered by a national sense of outrage and supported by a hatefully competent legal team (who had offered their services free) had taken everything from him; his house was gone and all his money. Every possession he owned, sold with the proceeds distributed amongst his victims. And as Jason lay on his uncomfortable bed, he decided the only victim was himself.

He rolled onto his side and stared at his room, and then noticed an envelope on his bedside table, propped up against the lamp, with '*Jason*' typed on the front. He supposed it was a good luck card from his Aunt Gail, so he sat up and opened it.

Instead, inside was a short, typewritten note: *"Jason. I am happy you are finally free. You have served your time and deserve the chance to recoup your losses and continue your career. the Daily Ear has changed a lot over the past few years – a new top team and a new focus. I want you back. I will send you a package in the next day. I appreciate you have conditions attached to your release, so keep this package private for now. But welcome. I look forward to meeting you. YM."*

Jason knew Yves Martineau well, a shameless and controversial British entrepreneur who had adopted a pretentious French name and made a fortune from soft porn and trashy satellite TV channels. He was also the new owner of the *Daily Ear*. And his letter proved that whilst Jason had lost all his material possessions, he had not lost his reputation as the world's top paparazzi photographer. the *Daily Ear* wanted him back, and soon he would retake everything that had been so unjustly stolen from him.

CHAPTER 12

Adam Jaymes had long since mastered the art of being inconspicuous, able to walk through the busiest of London's streets almost invisibly without being recognised. He had learned as a child star on TV's most popular soap that it was an essential talent if he ever wanted to reach a destination on time. And on the few occasions he was recognised and stopped, perhaps by some sharp-eyed Whovian or West End fan, he was always kind and gracious, happy to give autographs or pose for photographs. But mostly he was able to get from A to B without any interference.

Adam's incognito attire was simple and unassuming and would typically include a hat or cap and spectacles, sometimes with clear glass and sometimes tinted. His clothes were fashionable but not enough to draw anyone's attention, and he would walk swiftly to give others little time to acknowledge his face and realise they had just passed Adam Jaymes.

He arrived at a small office block in a quiet backstreet in Shoreditch and pressed the doorbell. He took off his glasses and cap, smiled into the small camera embedded into the entrance panel, and then pushed the door when he heard it buzz. It was the new location of a small, but successful charity, one that supported single parents, but particularly those suffering from mental health issues such as depression and anxiety. It had been set up shortly after the death of Adam's best friend, Pearl Martin, by her sister Patricia. Adam had recently become one if its patrons.

He jogged quickly up the stairs to the offices on the first floor, where he had expected to be met by the usual small team of enthusiastic staff and volunteers. But today he found it empty. All the computers were off; the telephones were silent.

"Hello?" he called into the air.

"My office, Adam," a familiar voice replied. "Come through."

He walked across the creaking wooden floor to a door that had a "Chief Executive" sign fixed to it. The door was slightly ajar and so he pushed it open and stepped inside. The room was sparsely furnished and plainly organised; a cheap MDF desk with a laptop and a telephone, two chairs, a couple of battered metal filing cabinets and a single, partly broken faux-wood venetian blind hanging across the window. The only decoration the room had received was the addition of two potted bird of paradise plants on the floor, although Adam was unsure if either was real.

The charity was relatively well funded, but little of that money was ever spent making the office environment more comfortable. 'Sparse' had been a financial choice and a reflection of the organisation's values. As much as was possible, every penny donated supported the services it delivered.

Patricia was stood by the window, arms folded, her expression and body language leaving Adam with no pretence of a warm welcome. They had always had a strained relationship, and he had often wondered, although never asked, if she considered him to be something of a usurper within the Martin family.

He knew the media often referenced the fact that he had played Pearl's little brother on television, and their relationship had been similarly close off-screen. Pearl's daughter, Beth, had always called him Uncle Adam, and treated him like a member of the family. And, perhaps as a final insult, Patricia's own son, Ben, had developed a familial relationship with him, too.

The only member of the Martin family who had never truly accepted him was Patricia, Pearl's sister. She always made Adam feel he was walking on eggshells, and her coldness had been particularly difficult for him because she looked so much like Pearl. The physical similarity was so strong many people wrongly believed Patricia and Pearl had been twins; they had the same soft features, pale complexion, big blue eyes and long black hair.

But the resemblance was purely physical. Their personalities were very different. Adam remembered Pearl clearly, her warmth and kindness, her quiet and clever sense of humour and her unassailable loyalty to a small circle of close friends. Patricia, by comparison, had always treated Adam with a cold abruptness that sometimes felt more like contempt.

And, on that day, the difference between the sisters was even more striking because Patricia had taken action to diminish her physical resemblance to Pearl, too. Her long black hair had been cut and dyed, replaced by a short lavender bob. She had also abandoned her contact lenses and was now wearing black, thick rimmed spectacles.

"This is quite a change," Adam said, trying hard not to sound or look disappointed.

"I was tired of being told how much I looked like my sister," Patricia replied, bluntly.

"Well, you do look like Pearl," Adam said. "There's nothing wrong with that. She was a very beautiful woman."

Patricia took her seat. "Perhaps I should say I was tired of being told how much I looked like my *dead* sister."

The flippant comment took Adam by surprise. He knew Patricia carried her sister's suicide with a heavy heart, as if she were in some way personally to blame. Pearl was the reason Patricia had set up the charity, and it was completely out of character for her to reference her sister's death in such a glib manner. Something was very wrong.

"You seem to be settling into your new offices," he said. "Do you miss Hackney?"

Patricia gestured for Adam to take the other seat and, as he sat down, she said: "I asked everyone to work from home for the rest of the day. I wanted a clear space for us to talk without interruption."

Adam nodded. "Yes, I can understand why. Valerie Pierce?"

Patricia narrowed her eyes. "You know damn well what I want to talk about," she replied. "Valerie fucking Pierce has a photograph of Beth? That is not OK. For God's sake Adam, this is all your bloody fault."

"Wait a moment," Adam retorted loudly, and sat down on the opposite side of the desk. "This is not my fault. I have worked as hard as anyone to protect Beth, to keep her identity secret."

"You have been reckless," Patricia replied, "baiting the press to come after you, to come after Pearl's legacy. To come after her daughter all over again. All of that bloody stupid 'Project Ear' nonsense. For God's sake, Adam." Patricia dropped her head into her hands, as though exasperated Adam would not take full responsibility for what was happening. She then looked up and, more quietly, said: "You got married and moved to America. Why couldn't you have just stayed there? Every time you come back to the UK, people start talking about Pearl all over again, about her death. And suddenly there are more articles in the papers about Beth. Whatever happened to Pearl Martin's daughter? Where is she? Who is she?"

Adam did not respond; an action Patricia took as an admission of guilt. "You are a constant reminder to the press," she continued, "to monsters like Valerie Pierce, that there is a part of Pearl's life they never got to. If you weren't here, don't you see how they would all just gradually forget? Move on with their scummy existences and leave my niece alone."

"Patricia, like it or not, this is still my home," Adam replied. Whenever they were faced with a challenging situation, he would usually allow Patricia room to vent or shout or make accusations. He knew it was one of her coping mechanisms. But on that day, he found he had little patience for her. "I split my time fifty-fifty," he continued. "My parents still live in England. I have friends here, too. And sometimes I'm here for work. I can't just boycott the UK."

"Fair enough," Patricia said, with an anger in her voice that made it clear she still considered Adam to be very much in the wrong. "But then explain to me, Adam, why you are suddenly wining and dining Valerie Pierce? Hmm? Perhaps you can explain it to me."

Adam did not respond, and in that moment Patricia's anger waned as she sensed he was keeping something to himself, that perhaps his silence was not an admission of guilt, but he was withholding something from her, a secret. "What?" she snapped. "What aren't you telling me?"

Adam sighed. "It's complicated," he said. "But I had a reason for meeting Valerie, and ultimately it is better we know Beth's identity has been compromised."

Patricia sat back in her chair and laced her fingers together. "And Valerie? I assume she is writing her story as we speak. Have you warned Beth's adopted parents? Or told Beth herself?"

Adam shook his head. "Actually no," he said. "There isn't going to be a story. To be honest, I don't believe she had any intention of exposing Beth. I think it was a deception. And she has given me her word she will keep our secret if I help her with something, and I have agreed. Believe it or not, under the circumstances, I trust her to keep her word on this."

Patricia appeared to flinch slightly, when Adam said he had offered to help Valerie 'with something' and scowled at him. "You are working with that woman?" she said, an accusation more than a question. "I assume it is something significant, if she's willing to keep the story of the decade to herself."

Adam sat back in his seat and realised he no longer had the luxury of choice. The situation had every possibility of spiralling out of control, and he and Patricia needed to put their differences aside for the sake of Beth. And so quietly and calmly, he told Patricia the truth. "Over the past week, two men have died," he said. "Men who used to work for the *Daily Ear*. Each of them was accidents, but Valerie convinced herself they were both murdered. She believed someone was targeting people connected to the paper."

"Has she gone to the police?" Patricia asked.

"Yes," Adam replied, "and they don't believe her. And, to be honest, I rather thought it was ridiculous, too. But in return for her silence about Beth I agreed to look into it. I have people looking into it right now."

"And you will find nothing," Patricia said, flatly. "All you will prove is that Valerie is a mad, attention-seeking old has-been."

Adam's shoulders dropped, as though unhappy with what he was about to say. "Well, therein lies the problem," he replied. "When I met with Valerie, she predicted a third death. She said someone else from the *Daily Ear* would be killed. She said it was going to happen last night, at 9pm exactly. And it did. It looks like a suicide. That's certainly how the police are treating it. But ..."

"But it is nonsense, Adam," Patricia said, finishing his sentence for him. "If the police say it was suicide than why pretend otherwise just to pander to some hysterical old bag?"

Adam sighed and shrugged. "Patricia, I know it sounds insane but... you know... maybe there's something to it." His words did not convey much conviction, and Patricia wondered if he was simply trying to justify the use of his time and resources.

"Come on Adam," she said. "Sometimes bad things just happen. And sometimes lots of bad things happen all at once. Don't let yourself get dragged into Valerie's nonsense."

Adam shook his head. "Perhaps. But I struggle with the idea of coincidence.

And it worried me when I heard the news. I've spent the past day looking into the details. And if you are not minded to immediately call it suicide, there is a lot there to be concerned about."

Patricia's demeanour changed notably. She suddenly seemed warmer, as though she had let off just enough steam to speak to Adam with a more civil tongue. "Adam, promise me you will just do the absolute minimum for Valerie," she said. "She is not a friend of our family and she does not deserve our help. And I am including you in that. Whatever it takes to keep her silent, do it. But nothing more, not a bit more. Promise me."

Patricia's conciliatory words took Adam by surprise. It was the first time she had ever referred to him as family, and he felt a little flutter in his chest. "Yes, yes of course," he replied. "But I want to tell you something else. I'm going to see Beth's parents."

"*Adopted* parents," Patricia snapped.

"Denise and Jay," Adam offered as a compromise. "Chris and I are going to pay for the three of them to go on holiday. For the next few weeks at least. Just to get them all out of the country. Chris has quite a few villas and summer houses with lots of security, so they'll be well cared for."

Patricia nodded. "OK. Well, that sounds a little over the top, to be honest. But if Valerie Pierce is flapping about London with a photograph of Beth in her handbag, I suppose it is a good idea."

Adam paused and then added: "I would like you and Ben to go, too. I thought you might enjoy the chance to spend some quality time with Beth, and you know how well Ben gets on with Beth, too."

Patricia stood and smiled at Adam in a way that made him feel she was unhappy with him again. "No, that won't be necessary," she replied. "I'm busy with my charity and I've finally got Ben to restart his studies again. He's been mucking about for the past few years and I've persuaded him to take up a masters. But I am sure it's a good idea for Beth and her adopted family to go, so I support you on that."

Adam recognised Patricia's tone and knew there was no point attempting to persuade her further. But the conversation had offered a half-win for Adam, so he decided that was enough for that day. "Very well," he said, and stood. He and Patricia had never embraced or shared a kiss on the cheek, either as a greeting or a farewell. Such moments always proved awkward.

And so, Adam simply held out his hand and Patricia shook it. "Thank you for coming," she said in a business-like manner.

Adam quietly made his way to the door but stopped when Patricia spoke again.

"And Adam .... I wasn't being completely honest about Project Ear," she said.

He turned and stared at her. "What do you mean?" he asked.

"I can't pretend I didn't get some enjoyment out of it. Watching you take them all down, one by one," she continued, with surprising candour. "You brought the *Daily Ear* to its knees. You ruined the family who owned it. If truth be told, I enjoyed every second of it, seeing them all get a taste of their own medicine."

Adam stared at her, not quite knowing what to say.

"And I do know how hard you work to protect Beth. How much you have risked to keep her safe," she said, softly. "I'm sorry I haven't said it before."

Adam smiled and nodded and then left, his heart singing from the praise he never expected to receive from Patricia.

CHAPTER 13

Valerie checked her watch again and wondered if her request to see the investigating officer had been forgotten. She had been trying to catch the eye of the uniformed receptionist in order to urge him to put out another announcement over the station's speaker system, but he was dealing with a steady stream of locals. Having listened to their conversations, Valerie assumed most were handing themselves in for crimes against the English language.

She had spent some time checking her social media where, it appeared, Alice had still been unable to switch off the app randomly posting to her Twitter feed. Two days after Javier's death, when so many high-profile journalists were reflecting on his work and his suicide, all Valerie's followers would have seen was a post which pondered the question: "*When you visit someone at home and find they have 'Live Life Love' painted on the wall of their sitting room, how many seconds need to pass before you can walk out, without it appearing rude?*"

Her attention was drawn away from the queue when a woman's voice said her name: "Ms Pierce?"

Valerie stood immediately. "*Mrs* Pierce," she retorted. "It is always *Mrs*."

"My apologies, Mrs Pierce," the woman replied, sternly. "I am Detective Inspector Sally Price. I understand you wish to speak to me regarding a suicide?" The officer was slim and surprisingly young with long, glossy black hair tumbling to her shoulders rather than tied back behind her head (as Valerie felt it should be). She wore a pair of fashion spectacles which Valerie suspected held plain glass, and a dark blouse and skirt rather than a uniform, which again disappointed Valerie. She always preferred to speak to uniformed officers. She felt there was more clarity about their role and their powers when they were in a uniform.

"Yes," Valerie replied. "But in private." She looked back to the queue of people. "It's not something I wish the world to hear."

Detective Inspector Price had an electronic fob hanging from her belt and used it to open the door into the non-public part of the station. "Of course. Please come with me."

Valerie had expected to be taken on an extended tour of the station, through a rabbit warren of corridors and open plan offices to a quiet meeting room some distance from the reception. But on this occasion, she was shown into a small, empty office just the other side of the door. There was a window overlooking the car park in front of which sat a small wooden table and two chairs. It was hardly the venue for the important conversation she planned to have with the Detective Inspector but, under the circumstances, it would have to do.

"My officers tell me you ignored the police cordon at the scene of Javier García's suicide, Mrs Pierce, and approached the body," DI Price said as they both took a seat on either side of the table.

Valerie was immediately defensive. "I did not interfere with the scene if that is what you are going to try and suggest," she snapped.

"No, Mrs Pierce, I -"

"And didn't touch any evidence, nor did I -"

"Mrs Pierce!" the Detective Inspector interjected, loudly, and Valerie was silenced. "I simply wanted to advise you we can give you information about support services if you saw anything last night which upset you. It is not pleasant seeing a dead body, particularly in those circumstances. As much as we are a police force, we also have a duty of care for our citizens."

Valerie sat back in her chair, feeling somewhat irritated. She had been prepared for a fight, a good old-fashioned verbal bust up, but this dreadful young woman was going full 'political correctness' on her and she was not happy about it. "I do not need support. Not that sort of support anyway."

"Then may I ask what you would wish to speak to me about?"

Valerie did not want a repeat of her conversation with Adam Jaymes from the night before. She did not want another pitiful stare or the sympathy and politeness which came hand in hand with being told her story was not credible. She wanted action.

"Javier García did not take his own life. He was murdered," she said, plainly. "He was pushed to his death by the same person who killed Derek Toulson three days earlier. And Chris Cox three days before that. All these men used to work for the *Daily Ear*. And all died at 9pm. And, if you check, you will see they all received a phone call from an unknown number just before they died. Someone is murdering people connected with the *Daily Ear* newspaper. And I am frightened I am next."

Detective Inspector Price pushed her hair back behind her shoulders and then took her spectacles off and placed them on the table between them. "May I call you Valerie?" she enquired, softly.

It was a tone Valerie did not like, suggesting she was little more than a confused old woman who needed to be handled rather than believed. "No," she replied. "I'm happy with Mrs Pierce."

"Of course, of course," the officer replied, a little surprised by the rejection.

"And you can put your glasses back on too," Valerie said. "I don't like the theatrical way some people use their spectacles."

"Now Mrs Pierce," Detective Inspector Price replied, her voice gaining volume, as she put her spectacles back on.

"And while I'm at it, you should tie your hair back, too. You are a police officer not a bloody French teacher."

"Mrs Pierce, enough!"

The force of the police officer's voice took Valerie by surprise and she was again silenced. Just for a moment, but long enough for Detective Inspector Sally Price to take control of the conversation.

"As I said, an experience like the one you had the other night can leave all sorts of unresolved feelings and anxieties. I am taking that into account when considering your present behaviour. I am also aware of your earlier visit to the station and the concerns you had previously raised regarding the accidents involving Mr Cox and Mr Toulson. But I can assure you there is absolutely nothing to link those two deaths. Nor to suggest this latest was anything other than suicide."

"But I predicted this," Valerie responded, and prodded her finger on the table for added prominence. "I predicted this exactly. Three days later. A third death. 9pm. A phone call just beforehand. A victim connected to the *Daily Ear*."

"To be clear," Detective Inspector Price said, "we have no evidence to suggest Mr García received any phone call prior to his death."

"He didn't get a call? Are you sure? Have you checked?"

"Well, the point is we have not been able to find his mobile phone. But, that aside, there is nothing to suggest this was anything other than a very tragic case of suicide."

Just as Valerie was about to respond, there was a knock at the door.

"Come," Detective Inspector Price said.

Valerie did not look up. She assumed at first another officer was just checking if the room was free. But then something was placed on the desk in front of her. A book with a familiar cover, a black and white assortment of salacious headlines and newspaper cuttings sitting behind the silhouette of a man on a telephone. And in large red letters, blood red letters, the words, "Exposé: The Rise and Fall of The *Daily Ear* by Valerie Pierce".

"Thank you, Barnet," the Detective Inspector said, and Valerie heard the door close again behind her. "This is your book, Mrs Pierce, Exposé?"

Valerie wasn't sure where the conversation was now headed but was, again, unhappy at what she considered to be more theatrics. "Clearly. My name is on the cover."

"And this is your account of the downfall of the *Daily Ear* four years ago. The collapse of the Harvey News Group at the hands of the actor, Adam Jaymes."

"Yes."

Detective Inspector Price opened the book and began to flick through its pages. "And in this book, you detail the methods Mr Jaymes used to bring about that collapse. Every three days, at 9pm, he would publish on his website a devastating revelation about someone working at the *Daily Ear*. And, for added dramatic effect, he would call said person just as the story went live. In the book you refer to this as 'phone call night'."

Valerie began to see where the conversation was going and did not like it one bit.

"Here," the Detective Inspector said, finding a page with a turned corner. She removed her glasses once more to read a section of the text: "*I stood with my phone in my hand, being forced into a conversation I had no interest in. I did not want to play any part in his ridiculous games. But I had no choice because Adam Jaymes held the power. He knew something about me, something he was about to expose to the entire world, a story he was about to publish on his website. And I needed to know what it was. And so, powerfully, strongly, resolutely, I spoke to him. 'This is Valerie Pierce you disgusting, cowardly cretin. Whatever you have to say about me, you can say directly to me, right now'. But he took the easy way out, of course. Because at his heart, he is a coward. Rather than speak to me, he read a well-rehearsed line of dialogue. No doubt written for him by someone else. 'Hello Valerie Pierce. This is Adam Jaymes. I just called to let you know it's your turn.' And then he simply hung up. And that was when we knew, when I knew, exactly what his game plan was. Every three days at exactly 9pm, Adam Jaymes would expose a secret about someone who worked at the Daily Ear. And just as he was publishing that story, he would phone his victim to let them know he was about to destroy their life."*

She closed the book and rested it back on the table. "How did this book sell, Mrs Pierce?"

"Pardon?"

"How did your book sell? Exposé? Was it a bestseller? Was it well received critically? I understand you self-published. Were you not able to find a publishing house interested in your story? Or an agent?"

Valerie sighed. "I know what you're doing," she said, the quietness of her voice clearly indicating she was seething.

"And what is that?"

"Suggesting I have imagined a serial killer, who is using the same tactics Adam Jaymes used four years ago. But more than that, you are suggesting I am a failed writer who is taking advantage of the deaths of three of my former colleagues to try to reignite interest in my book."

Detective Inspector Sally Price put her glasses back on and nudged the copy of Exposé towards Valerie. "If it makes a difference, Mrs Pierce, this is my own copy. I brought it in for the station's book club. Personally, I thought it was a thumping good novel. I even gave it a three-star review on Goodreads."

Valerie stood, humiliated and crestfallen. "I would like to go," she said, and the Detective Inspector led her from the room.

"And do let me know if you want to follow up on any of the support services," the officer said. "We are here to help."

CHAPTER 14

"You can't hide from him for ever. He will get you in the end," Lucy said, teasingly, and glanced over her shoulder in Steve's direction.

"I don't know what you mean," he replied, standing flat against the wall of her office so he could not be seen through the narrow glass panel in her door. "I just popped in to say hello. You don't work from your office very often. I thought I would see how you are."

Lucy stopped typing and turned in her chair to face Steve directly. They could both clearly hear Sydney Corrigan passing through the corridor outside, talking to his PA about some lunch plans he wanted her to make. As his voice faded into the distance, Lucy folded her arms. "You were saying?"

Steve looked to the floor, a tone of defeat to his voice. "I just need one big story," he said. "If I can just deliver that, I'll be in a much stronger position with Sydney. I just can't meet with him until then."

Lucy still found it amusing that Steve Gallant was now one of her colleagues. She recalled having something of a crush on him in his hey-day, when he had been a big media celebrity in his own right, regularly popping up on TV or photographed out on the town hand-in-hand with some beautiful pop star or actress.

At the time, Lucy had been a young entrepreneur trying to promote herself as a successful global brand specialist whilst secretly struggling to cover her basic expenses, like utility bills. And yet, years later, they were colleagues at the same newspaper. Only, now, Lucy considered herself to be the *Daily Ear*'s most prized asset whilst Steve, at best, was clinging to his job by the skin of his whitened teeth.

But Lucy's career at the paper had not always been plain sailing. She had run into a few major issues herself, when a few poorly judged columns had somehow offended even the typically unflappable sentiments of the paper's right-leaning readers. She had also learned how easily a few angry posts from lefty influencers on social media could snowball into a powerful call to action for MPs and even, on occasion, for the police.

During those difficult and challenging days, she had suffered a few moments of weakness, albeit fleeting, where she had needed support, someone to speak up for her. And for some reason Steve had always been that person. She had never quite understood why he had taken such a liking to her. It certainly wasn't a romantic interest. But she knew when her back was to the wall, Steve Gallant would rush to her defence.

And now he was in her office, with his back literally to the wall, and Lucy found herself conflicted. Typically, she would have very little sympathy for an underperforming employee, and she could certainly see the many reasons Sydney might have for dispensing with Steve's services. And yet, perhaps a little part of that crush remained. Or perhaps it was some small and uncharacteristic display of loyalty to a colleague in need. But it was one of the few occasions Lucy found herself a willing shoulder to cry on.

"Steve, you cannot keep surviving day-to-day based on whether or not you've delivered a decent story," she said, deciding the best course of action was to offer some tough love. "You've got to get back on your feet. Properly. Permanently."

Steve groaned and relaxed from his rigid position against the wall and then walked forward to take a seat, on her desk, just next to her. "I know, I know," he said and then announced dramatically "I'm pa-the-tic!" But then, in a more subdued tone, he continued: "None of my copy made the paper today. Again. Not the Bake-Off story. Not the Celebrity Painting Challenge. Sydney paid to use agency copy for both, instead of the articles I filed. Agency copy. It's like he is making a point." He slumped forward, face in his hands, and groaned loudly once more.

"You need a strategy," Lucy said. "You need to go to Sydney with a clear strategy. Tell him to invest in you. Set out all the financials. You told me he's cut your staffing to almost nothing. So, show him he was wrong. Show him exactly what you can achieve with greater resources. More staff, more money to pay for stories. He needs to know what you're offering. What your USP would be."

"My USP?"

Lucy began to feel very happy with her advice. It sounded well-informed and intellectual. And the more she spoke, the more animated she became. "Steve, there are thousands of wannabe entertainment journalists out there. All over the internet. Sad, lonely, pathetic individuals, most of them obese, sitting in their bedrooms and searching the internet for celebrity gossip. And then they switch on their video camera and film themselves, repeating what they've read online. And then they put it on their YouTube channel and hope to get more than a dozen views.

"Every single one of them is hoping they might get discovered, to become the new Steve Gallant. And, you know what? *Any* single one of them might be discovered. What makes any one of them any less employable than you?"

Lucy noticed Steve was staring at her as though he did not quite understand what she was saying. She wondered if he was genuinely bemused or simply did not want to acknowledge the truth of her words. "Steve, snap out of it," she said, and surprised him by angrily clicking her fingers in front of his face. "You want to survive? You want to be a success again? Then stop behaving as though you just need *one big story* to get yourself back on your feet. The world has changed, Steve. Everything has changed. What you are doing, what you are offering Sydney, isn't working. So ..."

"So?" Steve chipped in hoping, somewhat lazily, that Lucy would plan his comeback for him.

"So," she continued, thinking on her feet, "so, find out which of the online reporters write entertainment stories. Form them into a single team with you in charge. The *Daily Ear* will then have a proper online showbiz team for the first time. And what if you developed them into a proper entertainment resource? A separate website. With videos of you interviewing people, or talking to camera. Like in the old days when you were invited onto TV shows. An actual interactive, multimedia entertainment resource? Steve, seriously. Every time a celebrity story breaks, that's where people could go to hear the facts, straight to your entertainment website. And you'll be there, streaming live, telling tens of millions of people around the world what you know."

"I... I guess," Steve replied, unconvinced.

But Lucy was delighted with what she had said. She had once unsuccessfully auditioned for Dragons' Den and remembered she had been coaxed by the producers into delivering all sorts of business-speak nonsense for the camera. In her conversation with Steve, she had essentially revisited that audition but felt much happier with the outcome. She had absolutely no knowledge of the entertainment industry or online platforms but had successfully pulled together just about enough stolen words to make it sound genuine. Spent and content, Lucy slumped back into her chair and waved her hand towards her door. "Go on then," she said. "Your future awaits."

Steve responded with gratitude and good manners. And as he left Lucy's office, he pretended to have been inspired by her words and left her with the impression he was going to pursue her plan. In truth, he wasn't, because it had all sounded far too complicated. And, besides, he had no idea how to write a strategy. He wouldn't even know where to begin. Did his future at the *Daily Ear* really hinge on something so difficult and work-intensive? Surely one big exclusive story would be enough.

But he was grateful for her advice and as he returned to his own office it occurred to him that, apart from Lucy, there were few people he could turn to for support or advice. Many in the newsroom were openly unhappy that someone widely considered a deadweight had clung on to his job during the restructure when so many editorial staff had gone. Steve was not liked and knew his sacking would be almost universally welcomed across the company.

It was such a change from when he first joined the paper, the golden boy of showbiz news. Howard Harvey had provided him with a generously sized team of researchers and an almost endless budget. And Steve had quickly grown a posse of celebrity acquaintances (he called them friends) who were all happy to be photographed out and about with him, on the clear understanding any of the more salacious stories he had on them would never be printed.

But gradually things changed. Other tabloids, The Mirror in particular, began to encroach on his territory by poaching his researchers and reporters and setting them up as direct rivals. The increasing popularity of social media also took its toll, its growth throughout the entertainment industry diminishing the need for the press. Suddenly stars and celebrities could bypass the likes of Steve Gallant entirely and reach tens of millions of fans directly with a single post.

As Facebook, Twitter and Instagram expanded, Steve's world shrank. Investment in his column was cut and he soon found himself with almost no staff and having to undertake the sort of mundane chores he had previously delegated to his team. Abandoned, insignificant and depleted, Steve started to fill his column with little more than the content of news releases and the occasional rumour he picked up online. And each day he could feel his time at the *Daily Ear* careering towards an undignified end.

He recalled it had been Javier who had provided him with a path back to success, by persuading him to utilise his secret back catalogue of celebrity indiscretions. For years, Steve had kept many secrets, scandalous stories involving the rich and famous that had never seen print. He had always considered his discretion to be an investment because his public profile relied on being seen out and about with wealthy and famous stars. And what better way to earn their trust than to bury the odd scandal.

But Javier had persuaded him it was time to expose them to the public. "Every star knows there is no such thing as *off the record*," Javier had said, matter-of-factly, "and it's not going to be the worst thing in the world if you chuck a few Z-listers under a bus to get your name back out there again." And so, Steve had done exactly that.

But once he had drained that particular reservoir, he once again felt he had nowhere to go, until Javier had urged him to review his secret tapes and old notebooks, to see what he knew about some of the bigger stars he had socialised with over the years; the better-known celebrities who had so foolishly confided in him. And so, Steve began to offer up some of his bigger celebrity secrets; bigger stories involving bigger names. And once he started, he couldn't stop. The stories kept coming, fast and furious, and Steve wondered why he hadn't done it sooner. His name was splashed over the front page of the paper day after day as he paraded a string of affairs, drug addictions, secret sexual orientations and illegitimate children for the world to see.

For a while everything worked well, and Steve's career enjoyed an unexpected resurgence. But the change in Steve's tactics had been noticed across the entertainment industry and, at some point, he became aware he had been given the nickname *Two Face*. Agents, PR firms and celebrities closed their doors to him, and Steve's reserve of celebrity secrets gradually dried up.

And now he was sat at his desk, depleted, unable to think what the following few days might mean for his job at the paper. He gazed around his office, a shrine to the heyday of his career. His shelves were laden with golden awards for showbiz journalism and dozens of pictures were mounted on the walls, happy images of Steve with a litany of celebrities and stars. But all of it now offered him little more than the cold echoes of success from years gone by.

Steve logged on to his laptop and decided to spend an hour or so perusing the 'entertainment news' inbox. As usual, it was filled with several hundred emails, much of it spam or generic media releases. But every now and again, Steve knew he would be sent a little golden nugget, and he prayed he would find a little treasure amid the daily bombardment of garbage.

As the inbox opened in front of him, an email popped into view at the very top of the list, flagged as confidential with its subject line stating: *"Att. Debbie Braide – interview opportunity"*.

Debbie Braide had been one of Steve's underappreciated former researchers who had been poached by a rival tabloid and now headed the most successful entertainment column in the country, with a hugely popular online version drawing hundreds of thousands of additional views each day. Steve occasionally received information and invitations for Debbie from press officers who had failed to update their press list, and it was often a good day when he intercepted an email meant for her.

The email was already marked as read, which Steve thought was odd as he did not recall having read it. But he clicked it open to see who the mysterious 'you know who' might be.

"Hi Debbie. The SM Club and Private Rooms opening night. The owner (i.e., you know who) wants cool publicity; younger people/woke/monied. She wants discussions about music, theatricality, equality and fashion. Also, a focus on the revisionary transformation of Thameside factory to London's new place to be. All her own design. I have a five-minute slot for you to see her at 10pm. You will need to arrive at 8.30pm. Copy and picture approval only. Absolute confidentiality until printed. Let me know. Sian."

Steve had heard a rumour the world's biggest pop star was planning a new club in the city, and the obvious reference to sadomasochism in the title jumped out at him. "How very 1990s of her," he sniggered. Steve had met *'you know who'* twice over the previous couple of decades and had made a point of always writing positively about her, which he hoped she had noticed.

And somewhere out there, someone called Sian was trying to line up an exclusive with the world's biggest pop star, but Debbie Braide was *not* getting that interview. Steve responded to the email in the hope Sian would be too busy working for her demanding client to realise she had been played.

"*Hi Sian. Steve here. Great to hear from you again. Debbie sends her apologies – on holiday in Greece – but still keen to go ahead. Let me know time and location and I will be there. Happy to agree questions beforehand and, as always, copy and picture approval agreed of course. My contact number below. See you on opening night. SG.*"

CHAPTER 15

Raymond Vaughn kissed Valerie Pierce on the cheek and held her hands with obvious affection. "My favourite ex-wife," he announced loudly and with great enthusiasm.

"My favourite gay ex-husband," Valerie replied, and waited for the roar of ingratiating laughter she had no doubt the patrons of the Old Compton Street restaurant would provide. And indeed, they did. Several even stood to applaud. Valerie knew her audience.

A handsome young waiter collected the pair from the door and led them through the restaurant. Valerie sailed past the other diners as though she did not have a care in the world, when in truth she had dressed for the occasion with the restaurant's specific clientele in mind. She knew one of the main reasons the LGBTQ+ community had begrudgingly accepted her was because of her classic sense of style and signature outfits. Clearly, she thought, it was hard for gay men to continue hating someone who looked so effortlessly fabulous at all times. That day she was wearing a deep purple trouser suit with a watercolour print scarf and a few carefully selected accessories. She knew every single man in the restaurant would be talking about that outfit for the rest of the week.

Ray was strikingly tall and silver-haired with matinée idol looks and a muscular physique that could always be appreciated regardless of what he wore. On that day he sported a pair of smart dark grey trousers, which were particularly tight around his behind, and a black T-shirt skimmed his well-developed chest and accentuated his biceps. No one thought for a moment that he and Valerie were anything but companions, but she enjoyed being seen with him; the perfect finish to her ensemble.

They were led to a more private table towards the back of the restaurant, concealed behind layers of voile fabrics and cleverly positioned mood lighting. It was now routine for Valerie to book a restaurant based on its ability to offer a more secluded setting, particularly when she was meeting a well-known face like Ray.

Their story, once a preciously held secret, was now public knowledge. They had married in their late teens but it had lasted less than 12 months before Ray ran off with his best friend, Pete. There followed a bitter estrangement that lasted more than 30 years before a series of unexpected events brought them back into each other's lives. After several meetings and correspondences, the animosity waned, and they were now publicly reconciled. For the most part, happily so.

They had also become something of a celebrity couple with certain demographics. Valerie was the stylish, sharp-tongued writer and famously reformed homophobe whilst Ray was the reality TV star whose wit and warm nature had won him a legion of fans across the country.

Once seated in their private booth, the waiter handed them each a menu and then poured two glasses of red wine from a bottle, already breathing on the table. Valerie watched with quiet amusement as the inevitable flirting unfolded before her. Ray never missed an opportunity to connect with a good-looking younger man and was quite merciless in the use of his cool, mature charm and Hollywood smile.

He thanked the waiter for getting them a private table. The waiter said it had been his pleasure and if he could do anything else for Ray he just had to ask. Ray cracked a rude joke, a double entendre. The waiter laughed and nudged closer to him. Ray asked if he could recommend anything and looked at the waiter's crotch.

"Young man," Valerie intervened. "My gay ex-husband is clearly enamoured so perhaps you might cut to the chase and give him your number. Assuming, of course, you are into… silver daddies?" She glanced to Ray to see if she had referenced his gay subcategory correctly, and he proudly nodded at her.

"We have a lot to discuss," she continued, "and I need him to be focused on our conversation. And I fear he will be distracted if you hold onto your number until the end of the meal."

Without a hint of awkwardness or delay, the waiter happily obliged and scribbled his number onto a page of his notepad and handed it to Ray before popping the pad and pencil back into the front pocket of his apron.

"Now, I will have the Lobster Benedict from your all-day brunch menu, please," Valerie stated in a clear voice, wishing to remind the young man of his *actual* role at the table, "and do write this down on your pad." She then glanced to Ray. "Call me old-fashioned, but I really don't like it when a waiter tries to memorise the order. They always get something wrong."

With a smile and a nod, the waiter retrieved his pad and pencil and stood ready to take their order. "I will have the Lobster Benedict," Valerie repeated, and watched to ensure the waiter wrote it down, "and I'll have your chardonnay with it, please. A bottle. My ex-husband, I imagine, will have one of your ghastly meat-free concoctions. Ray?"

Ray smiled and looked at the waiter. "The plate of Grains and Greens please," he said. "I follow a strict vegan diet."

The waiter explained that he followed a macrobiotic diet linked to a specific exercise regime. Ray was fascinated and wanted to know more about it. The waiter asked which gym Ray attended. Ray cracked a joke, another double entendre. The waiter laughed. Ray laughed.

"Thank you, that's all for now," Valerie intervened and handed over her menu. The waiter collected Ray's menu too, and then walked back towards the bar, glancing over his shoulder as he went to ensure Ray was checking him out from behind. Which Ray was.

"I assume you were waiting for me to react," Valerie said, with a clear disapproving tone to her voice. "Grains and Greens indeed."

"I am aware your newfound tolerance of other people's lifestyles doesn't stretch to vegetarians or vegans," Ray replied, cheerfully. "You tweet about it enough. What was that last one? The colleague who invited you for Sunday lunch and didn't tell you it was a nut roast?"

"Yes," Valerie snapped, "and she's now blocked on my phone, so that won't be happening again."

Another waiter delivered two glass tumblers to their table and poured them both a sparkling water before leaving them alone once more.

Ray held his glass forward to toast. "Here's to you, Valerie," he said, "to you and your journey".

Valerie clinked her glass against his. "And here's to your divorce," she replied, glibly. But with those throwaway words she glimpsed an unexpected expression on Ray's face. Just for a moment, a flash, but it looked like sorrow.

"You can't honestly be upset?" she asked. "After everything that spiteful little queen put you through?"

"We were together a long time, Valerie," Ray said, with a regretful tone to his voice that immediately annoyed Valerie. It sounded as if he was going to defend his ex-husband, a man Valerie despised.

"You were only married a couple of years," she said. "I don't know. You demanded marriage equality and when you finally got it, you couldn't get divorced quickly enough."

"You keep talking about how short my marriage was," Ray said, a frustrated tone to his words, "but Pete and I would have been married for more than 30 years if the law had allowed it. From my perspective, he and I had a longer and more successful marriage than most people. And, actually, it was mostly wonderful." His voiced tailed off and then he quietly added, "But then we did *Big Brother* and then those other stupid shows. And it all just fell apart."

"It fell apart, Ray, because he was jealous of you," Valerie replied. "You were the handsome one, kind and clever. And with all due respect, Pete was short, bald and fat and proved himself to be quite spiteful. There's a reason you got to the final and he was evicted halfway through. The cameras caught it all."

"He was never like that," Ray replied. "The producers took a few moments, a few seconds, where he was a little mean-spirited and they created a whole narrative about who he was as a person. He was absolutely devastated when he saw it. What they showed was not my Pete."

Valerie placed her glass onto the table. "But what he did outside the house. That was nothing to do with editing. The jealousy. The controlling behaviour."

"He was panicking," Ray said. "He could see how we were being portrayed in the media; the different way people behaved towards me than towards him. We were invited to open a Waitrose in Chelmsford and the crowd booed him. He was actually booed by hundreds of complete strangers! People we had never met in our entire lives but who thought they knew us, knew *him*, well enough to jeer and shout abuse at him."

A few years earlier, Valerie would have likely smiled or even laughed at the idea of Pete being publicly humiliated. She had always blamed Pete for the breakdown of her first marriage, believing Ray might have been able to maintain the facade of a tolerable heterosexual life if he had not been tempted away by another man. And even though she knew in her head that was nonsense, in her heart she had always blamed Pete for taking Ray from her, and her loathing for him had never diminished.

But in recent years she had developed a kindlier relationship with Ray which meant a great deal to her, and she was always mindful of falling into old habits that might dent their friendship. "But he's doing well, isn't he, now? In Boston?" she said, reassuringly. "You're in touch. He's happy. Great job. Great house. New partner. His anonymity restored."

Ray nodded.

"And it's not as if you're living some sad, lonely, celibate life. You're out all the time. And all these handsome young men throwing themselves at you."

Ray sat back in his seat and Valerie was pleased to see the semblance of a smile gently etched on his face. "It does help me while away the lonely nights," he said. "And if truth be told, Pete and I were pretty much running on empty towards the end, even before that newspaper article and all those TV appearances. I think we would have ended up in the same place, but it wouldn't have been such an unpleasant journey getting there."

Valerie reached across the table and squeezed his hand. "No more reality television then," she said. "That's all done. Learn from it and move on."

Ray withdrew his hand and his expression changed to something more akin to a wince. "Ah!" he said. "About that."

Valerie folded her arms. "Oh, for goodness' sake, what now? The jungle? *First Dates*? Celebrity Toilet Habits? Have you really not learned your lesson, Ray?"

"This one is different," he replied. "Very different. It's not strictly speaking reality TV. It's a documentary. A fly-on-the-wall type of thing. The presenter's very well known. He'd follow us around for a few months, live with us a bit. I think it could be interesting. Perhaps even fun."

"Sorry, what?" Valerie replied sharply. "What do you mean by 'us'? I hope you are not including me in any of this."

"It's just for a few months, Valerie," Ray replied, as though asking the smallest of favours. "It would be a boost for both of our careers. They want to call it 'The Odd Couple' or something."

"No," Valerie replied, appalled. "No, no, no. I cannot believe you even thought to ask. Of course, I am going to say no. Darling, no offence, but *I'm* not some trashy reality TV star. That's not me at all."

"But your life is already out there, Valerie," Ray replied. "You write about it yourself all the time, you always have. Your relationship with your mother, your marriage to Jeremy. Most of Alice's childhood played out in your weekly column. And it's not as if you and I have any more secrets left to hide."

Valerie sat shaking her head. "No," she replied again. "Ray, even if I were minded to, and I am not, I have too much going on to even consider it. It just isn't a good time."

Ray huffed and looked crestfallen. "The offer will go away if we don't grab it now, Valerie. It was just an initial expression of interest. They have other options. All those bloody *TOWIE* people for one. What's going on that you won't even consider it?"

Valerie could feel the gentle nudge of her nicotine addiction but knew that would involve going on to the street to smoke and she was enjoying the feeling of safety that came from being cocooned within Balans restaurant, surrounded by plenty of witnesses. "Just something," she replied.

"Is this to do with the other night? When Alice asked me to pick you up, after that suicide?"

Valerie nodded.

"Alice and the girls? Are they OK?" Ray asked.

"Yes, yes. Nothing like that."

Ray was not used to seeing Valerie so reticent and realised something was causing her genuine anguish. "You know you can tell me anything. Trust me. I might be able to help."

"I'm not doing the documentary."

"I don't care about the documentary, Val. Tell me what's wrong."

After a moment to gather her thoughts, Valerie began to quietly recount the events of the previous week only pausing, briefly, when the waiter returned with their meals and drinks. She described the peculiar death of Chris Cox, and the mysterious events at the private stable in Berkshire. She explained, briefly, some of the information she had gleaned from her old police contact and then her meeting with Adam Jaymes. And she ended her story with the subsequent events at the Royal Hotel in Mayfair, something she had predicted.

Ray sat quietly and listened. He was immediately distracted by the news that Valerie had met Adam Jaymes for dinner, and his mind quickly filled with questions. Is he as handsome in person? Was he tall? Did he seem unhappy in his marriage? Are you meeting him again? And he desperately wanted to ask all of those questions, and more. But he knew that was not the point of Valerie's grim story and so he carefully steered his thoughts to more appropriate matters. "The girls are away at the moment, aren't they? In Australia, visiting their dad?"

Valerie nodded.

"Right," he continued. "Then I think you should go away, too. You and Alice. Take Jasper with you. And just vanish. Leave Adam Jaymes to sort all of this out. Keep yourself safe."

Valerie began to move the food around on her plate with her fork, the topic having completely robbed her of any appetite. The idea of running away, of hiding, had weighed heavily on her mind, particularly after Javier died. But she wondered if whisking herself off to some distant, secluded location might make her an even easier target, and if there was anywhere she could genuinely feel safe.

"You know the worst thing about this, happening now?" she said, gazing at her ex-husband. "For the first time in a long time, years, I'm actually happy. Really happy. I'm enjoying my work. I've reconnected with Alice. With you. The girls are an absolute blessing. And this… this is like a great, terrible cloud hanging over me. It's always there, from the moment I wake up in the morning. Always, always there. I just never feel safe."

She dropped her head and, in an uncharacteristic display of vulnerability, looked as though she were about to sob. But Ray immediately moved to her side of the table and embraced her, holding her close so she could cry onto his shoulder if she wanted to. He had no words to reassure her, because he knew Valerie. He knew she was not someone prone to hysterics or delusions. If she believed her life was in danger, he feared she might well be right.

CHAPTER 16

Gayesh Perera sat at his desk, spectacles at the end of his nose, reading through several dozen pages listing every conference, soiree or lunch event he had attended over the previous year. It was a list no one was ever supposed to see, a carefully planned and concealed itinerary that allowed him to claim a lavish salary from the NHS whilst doing very little work.

For Gayesh, it seemed unfair and somewhat peculiar that members of the public felt entitled to ask how he spent his time. He found it even more peculiar that the law facilitated such requests. "And who has demanded this information?" he asked, and then placed the pile of papers back onto his desk and removed his glasses.

Victoria Barrett, the hospital's Head of Communications, sat opposite him quietly seething with resentment; she had no intention of sugar-coating the situation. "The TaxPayers' Alliance," she replied. "They have submitted a Freedom of Information request asking for a full list of every external meeting, event or conference you have attended over the past 12 months in your role as Chief Executive of this Trust."

"I feel I am being targeted," Gayesh said, and offered her an imploring gaze which he hoped would soften her unbending commitment to public transparency. "Do you think this could be racism?" he asked. "I am Indian. Is that the issue?"

"It is not racism," came the reply. "They have submitted the same FOI request to every hospital trust in the country. You have not been singled out."

"But they want to know how I have spent my time?"

"Yes."

"And that is not racist?"

"No."

Gayesh, a short and portly man in his late fifties, shook his head and raised his hands. "It feels like racism. I think we should find an exemption."

Victoria had worked for the NHS continuously for 30 years and had spent the past 10 at Mid and North Kent Hospital Services NHS Trust. Overall, her experience of NHS staff was a set of strongly shared values that included putting patients first and being prudent with public funds. She was not used to working with someone like Gayesh who treated the NHS like it was a personal resource. And, as such, she had very little sympathy for his situation.

"There are no exemptions, Gayesh," she replied plainly, "and please remember we have already had three warnings from the Information Commissioner's Office for failing to provide appropriate responses for FOI requests relating to you."

Gayesh considered her advice and then decided to take a different approach. "I am not sure this is correct," he said, gesturing towards the pile of papers in front of him. "I am invited to many events and they are each put in the calendar, but I do not attend them all. I am not sure this is correct."

Victoria sighed and sat back in her chair. "All of the information was down-loaded from your Outlook calendar and cross-referenced with the data records from your security pass. That information was then double-checked with your PA against your travel and hotel expenses, who confirmed it was accurate."

"My security pass?" Gayesh asked.

"The security card you use to get into this building. Every time you enter or leave using your card it generates an electronic record."

Gayesh stared at Victoria, with a blank expression suggesting he genuinely did not have a clue what she was talking about. She took her own security pass from her trouser pocket and showed it to him. "This," she said. "You have one too."

"I thought it just opened the security gate," Gayesh said, very unhappy to learn he had unknowingly left a data trail proving his serial absenteeism.

"It also records when you enter and when you leave. It means we have live information as to who is in the building in case of a fire or other emergency."

He continued to look at her blankly.

"You did know this Gayesh," she replied, a little exasperated. "It means we were able to double-check whether or not you were here on all the dates your diary suggested you were elsewhere. And, to be honest, a lot of this has been very puzzling. There are many days, a majority of days, when you clocked in at 9am and clocked out a minute later."

Gayesh spent a moment trying to come up with other reasons why the FOI enquiry should be blocked but could not think of any other suggestions. And he was irritated at how overly conscientious Victoria appeared to have been, in ensuring every detail of the information about him had been correctly gathered. And so decided to take a more accusatory tone.

"I feel very uncomfortable that all of this was done behind my back," he said. "I employ you as my Head of Communications. You are supposed to support and protect me from things like this. But I feel as though you have been conspiring against me. This should not have gotten to this stage without my knowledge. Perhaps I need to reconsider if you are the right person to work as my Head of Communications."

Gayesh hoped his words would not sound like an empty threat even though, in truth, he knew he probably did not have a leg to stand on. He came from the "You're Fired" school of management and was accustomed to dispatching underperforming or unhelpful employees quickly and with little care of repercussions. However, he was still relatively new to the public sector and had found it riddled with unions, processes and protections which made it incredibly difficult to steer a clear route through an obstructive minefield of rules and governance.

And Victoria had two teenagers at home and knew only too well when she was being played, and she did not take kindly to it. She also knew Gayesh was making a vague but unpleasant comment about her ongoing employment with the NHS and did not take kindly to that either. "Gayesh, let me make something perfectly clear to you," she said, in no mood to placate him. "I do not work for *you*. I work for the NHS. Ultimately, I work for the public. We *both* work for the public. I do understand you have spent most of your career working for private companies, and I appreciate you are struggling to come to terms with the level of scrutiny and accountability that comes from working for the NHS.

"But, let me make this perfectly clear. It is not, and never will be, my job to cover up for you. Either you can justify how you spend your time, or you cannot. But regardless, I am legally obliged to ensure we respond appropriately to any Freedom of Information request."

Victoria stood as though ready to leave but then, instead, leaned forward onto the desk and looked Gayesh directly in his eyes. "And, to be clear," she said. "I have personally emailed you sixteen times over the past three weeks about this FOI. But due to the time limits we have to adhere to, and your constant non-attendance at the office, I and my NHS colleagues had to take this forward in your absence. We have done nothing wrong. Do not suggest again we have."

Gayesh waited a moment to ensure she had finished speaking and then waved his hand towards the door, a sign Victoria was dismissed. "Leave it with me," he said. "I'll get back to you."

Victoria nodded. "That's fine, Gayesh, but remember tomorrow is our legal deadline. I will send you an email to confirm we had this conversation, so there can be no misunderstandings later." And with that she left.

Gayesh stood and walked across his office to his one window, a chance to take in the view across the hospital grounds. His office did not offer him the impressive, modern design or facilities he had grown accustomed to during his career in the private sector, nor the impressive views he had enjoyed during all his years working in London.

Despite being Chief Executive, the Mid and North Kent Hospital Services NHS Trust offered him little more than a partially obscured, rather bleak view of an outdated 1960s hospital building surrounded by a hotchpotch of temporary units and mobile health vans. It was not how he had hoped he would spend the final few years of his working life. All he had wanted was a big salary to carry him through the next few years before retirement, and a job that could potentially offer the chance to mix with high-level politicians, so he could gently continue his campaign for a seat in the House of Lords.

He had spent the better part of 15 years working at the Harvey News Group, first as Editorial Director and the final five as Chief Executive; a role with enormous benefits but virtually no responsibilities. Throughout that time, he had been able to leave his senior team to run things, including the *Daily Ear*, whilst he had spent most of his time at boozy corporate events or champagne lunches. He knew he had not always been respected or even liked by his directors, but he also knew they rather enjoyed having him out of the way each day so they could essentially run the company without him. He also knew he occasionally had proven enormously useful.

Certainly, whenever the *Daily Ear* had been accused of racism, he had happily allowed himself to be wheeled out to personally deny the accusations. But those halcyon days did not last. One day, completely out of the blue, a ruthless act of nepotism by the news group's owner had left him out of a job and with a tattered reputation that made it almost impossible to step quickly into a similar role.

It had taken an enormous amount of string-pulling for him to land the job at the NHS, and a significant reorganisation of the management team to free himself of the day-to-day responsibilities that would normally come with being the Chief Executive of a hospital trust. He had made dozens of junior staff redundant to create an extremely top-heavy structure that delegated almost all his duties to his directors whilst still leaving the impression he was very much in charge.

If Gayesh could claim to have any business acumen at all, it was his ability to create an environment where he could do nothing. But he had learned a hard lesson, that working in the public sector brought a far higher level of transparency than he was used to. And today, it seemed, that transparency could well be his undoing.

He took some comfort in Victoria's reassurance the same FOI request had gone to all hospital trusts in the country, and he hoped his information would be lost in the 100 or so detailed and complicated responses the TaxPayers Alliance would likely receive. But he did not like the idea his security pass was essentially a device that could spy on his comings and goings. He needed to draw a firm line under that immediately.

He returned to his desk and logged on to his laptop. He thought for a moment about how to approach his predicament, and then emailed the IT team: *"Personal safety issue with security pass data. Please call."*

CHAPTER 17

Alice was preparing a cooked breakfast for Valerie and Ray. She had heard them return from London in the early hours of the morning, giggling and whispering like drunken teenagers before they had staggered up the stairs to their bedrooms. The two had then spent a disproportionate amount of time calling to each other from their bedroom doors, Ray on the first floor and Valerie on the second, professing how much they loved each other, before they eventually closed their doors and went to sleep.

Alice doubted very much either would remember those conversations, and despite being woken by them at some time after 2am, she had still found the whole conversation highly amusing. She decided they would both benefit from a cooked breakfast and had put her mother's ovens to good use preparing sausages, black pudding and bacon in one and the vegan equivalents in the other. She had also splashed some white wine vinegar into a large pan of water ready to poach her mother an egg and had a pot of tea ready.

She had called to them up the stairs several times and even sent them both text messages, assuming they were still slumbering in their rooms. But then, unexpectedly, she heard the front door open and close and Ray appeared in the kitchen wearing shorts, trainers and a vest, fresh from a morning run, a newspaper under one arm.

"Tell me that's not what you were wearing on Old Compton Street last night?" she asked, chuckling slightly.

Ray laughed and shook his head. "No, although I think this would have gone down very well in the Admiral Duncan," he replied. "We detoured to my apartment last night, on the way here, so I could throw a few things in a bag. I hope you don't mind, Alice, but Val's asked me to stay for a few days.

She told me everything that's been going on and I think she just feels safer, having you and me both here, under the same roof."

Alice found Ray's presence oddly reassuring and did not mind at all that he was joining her efforts to support her mother. "How's your head?" she asked, hoping to impress him with her casual use of a smutty double entendre.

Ray laughed then threw the newspaper on to the breakfast bar and straddled one of the seats. And then, almost duty bound, he replied, "I've had no complaints."

"I cannot believe you've been out for a run," Alice said, and poured him a cup of tea. "You were both *completely* stotious. And how are you not dead?"

"Years of practice," Ray replied, proudly. "And to be honest, Val was knocking them back much more than me. I think she needed to get completely blotto, so she could … you know … forget everything. For one night a least. So, I held back a little to make sure she was OK. And we had fun." He smiled at Alice and added: "The Gays of Old Compton Street embrace your mother. She was getting a lot more attention than me. I was getting a little jealous to be honest."

"Oh, dear lord," Alice groaned, as an image suddenly popped into her head of her mother drunkenly dancing on top of a grand piano in some gay cabaret bar. "I hope she behaved herself," she said.

"Oh, she was fine," Ray replied, "but everyone wanted their picture taken with her. You should go on Twitter. She's probably trending. Amazing, really, how her relationship with the gay community has had a complete turnaround. Just a few well considered articles, admitting she was wrong on so many things, over the years, and they've just thrown their arms around her."

Ray had been a revelation for Alice because, until a few years earlier, she had no idea he even existed. Valerie had kept her first marriage a closely guarded secret and it had been a terrible shock for Alice when the truth had been suddenly revealed to her.

After that, for a while, Ray had simply existed as a name, someone her mother had once been married to, briefly, at some point in the late seventies. But then Valerie and Ray had exchanged a few emails, then text messages, and then they had met for a drink. And finally, they had taken an opportunity to talk through what had really happened all those years earlier, when Ray had left her for another man less than a year after their wedding.

Alice could see with each interaction, her mother's hurt and anger began to wane as she and Ray gradually rekindled an important friendship from their younger days. Eventually Ray had been invited to the house where he met Alice, Hannah and Emily. And as his own marriage to Pete collapsed, Valerie and Alice offered him care and support and, on occasion, a place to drink too much and a guest bedroom to sleep in.

Alice had never been one to make relationships quickly, or easily. She had a small but dedicated group of friends and had always felt their companionship was all she needed. But then she met Ray and realised, to her great surprise, that she very much enjoyed his company. There was something inherently kind and decent about him, a calm voice in an often-troublesome world. He also shared her often silly sense of humour and would chuckle along knowingly whenever she would drop a quote from a comedy show into conversation, a line from '*Victoria Wood*', '*French and Saunders*' or '*The Golden Girls*'.

As she poured him a cup of tea, she noticed him gently slide the newspaper to one side, as though trying to push it out of sight. She brought his tea to him, and then sat down next to him and gestured to the paper. "*The Guardian?*" she asked.

"Hmm?" Ray replied, as though the question had been unclear. "Oh, yes. I just thought I'd check through the Arts section. See if there are any new shows I might need to binge watch."

Alice's heart sank, as she realised he was attempting to protect her from the content of the paper. "It's me, isn't it? I'm in it?" she enquired. "The beef burger pictures?"

Ray sighed and nodded.

"Don't worry," she said. "I knew it was going to be printed. They've been messaging me through mum's Twitter account for a few weeks. Asking me for an interview."

Ray's smile disappeared and he gently picked the paper up and unfolded it. "I'm sorry," he said. "I wanted to let Val see the story first. I thought it might come easier from your mum."

"It's fine," Alice replied. "May I see it, though?" She held out her hand, and Ray begrudgingly handed the paper over. The features' banner across the top of the front page included an old black and white picture of Alice as a child, with the headline '*What became of Alice Pierce, the Mad Cow girl?* Inside she found the article which had reproduced the picture in full, a picture she knew very well although she had not seen it for many years. It was a photograph of Alice aged about five or six, she could not remember her exact age at the time. She was stood next to her father outside the old family house in Barnet. And Alice was eating a burger.

She had a clear memory of that morning. Her mother had brought her a new dress especially, a little summer dress with a floral pattern, and then tied her hair into pigtails. Her father Jeremy, smartly dressed in a suit, had then marched her to the pavement outside their house to an unruly pack of reporters, photographers and cameramen, and then handed her the burger and instructed her to eat it.

For Alice, as a little girl, the most exciting part of the whole affair had not been the new dress or being photographed. The most exciting part was the time of day, seven-thirty in the morning; she had been allowed to eat a burger for breakfast. As she reviewed the page she realised, more than 25 years later, those photographs still haunted her.

The article provided a short, potted history of her life, including the shame she had brought on her two upright parents when she had become pregnant at 16, an unwed teenage mother. The journalist then gave a personal view on Alice's estranged relationship with her parents, and even decided to suggest what sort of conversation Alice may have had with her father, at his bedside, as he lost his battle with cancer when she was just 19.

"You really did grow up in public, didn't you?" Ray said. "And I promise, that's not a snide remark about your parents."

Alice closed the paper. "No, it's a fair comment," she said. "I was the daughter of Jeremy and Valerie Pierce: Jeremy, the 'family values' Tory MP who served for three consecutive terms, including a period in Margaret Thatcher's cabinet. And Valerie, one of the most successful and influential journalists in the world, the queen of middle England."

"Did you know they were famous, when you were little? Did you know your life was a bit different from other children?" Ray enquired.

Alice sighed and shook her head. "No," she said. "I was blissfully ignorant. Even now, when I think of my childhood in our old house in Barnet, they are happy memories. Everything I remember about that house is happy, every smell, every sound, every creaking floorboard; Saturday night TV, and

Christmas, and sticky orange squash on hot summer days, and scrap books and sleepovers. Just normal kids' stuff.

"It was only when I became a teenager, I began to realise something was different. Every now and again, one of the other kids at school would bring in a cutting from a newspaper or magazine, stories and articles mentioning me. And it began to dawn in me how little of my childhood had been genuinely private, how many of my birthday parties, Christmases or family holidays had been used as PR opportunities by mum and dad."

Ray frowned. Something Alice had said puzzled him, and so he asked; "Why were journalists writing about you? You might have been a teenager, but you were still just a child."

Alice chuckled, quietly. "Oh, yes, but I was the wrong sort of teenager," she replied. "I had no interest in dresses, or make-up, or highlights. I kept my hair cropped short and pretty much my entire wardrobe consisted of jeans, t-shirts, jumpers and boots. Worse, I dared not to be thin.

"All these articles the other kids would bring into school to show me, they were mostly pictures of me standing next to my impeccably slim mum, looking huge by comparison. I seem to remember one of mum's rival columnist always called me 'stocky'. And that was my teenage years. I was presented as 'just deserts' for Valerie Pierce, the famously sharp-tongued journalist who regularly derided female celebrities for unwomanly fashion choices or for being even slightly overweight."

Alice knew there was more she could share with Ray. The most difficult part of those painful years was neither her mother nor her father had ever defended her, publicly or in private. If anything, Jeremy had occasionally suggested to Alice she could *"do with dropping a few stone"*, and Valerie had regularly tried to convince her to wear make-up or a dress.

And if she were having this conversation with one of her other friends, she probably would have shared more. But although Alice had grown to treasure her friendship with Ray, she still thought of him as *being* Valerie's. And she did not wish to act in a way that might affect his relationship with Valerie negatively. "Anyway," she said, "I got knocked up at 16 and mum and dad couldn't hide me away from the paparazzi quickly enough. So that was the end of that." Although said as a joke, Alice still remembered how abandoned she had felt when she had fallen pregnant. Jeremy and Valerie had quickly moved her to a small two-bed flat in Stratford, a property Valerie had lived in at some point in her life and never sold. And there Alice stayed, quietly raising her illegitimate daughters on her own, hidden away from the media.

She stood, suddenly very quiet, and began to busy herself with preparations for breakfast. And for a moment, Ray did not know what to say. As a rule, he tried to steer clear of conversations about Alice's parents and in particular her father. Although they had never met, he knew Jeremy Pierce had played a pivotal role in many pieces of legislation which had directly impacted on the rights of gay people in the UK. This had included, famously, Jeremy's role in delivering Section 28, a spiteful piece of Government legislation which, for the better part of two decades, had rendered Ray and Pete a 'pretended family relationship', a limbo existence which meant they had no legal right to be recognised as a couple.

But he also knew Alice could not be blamed for the actions of her parents. Quite the opposite in fact. And so, he chose to share some of his own experiences and feelings with Alice, in return for the honesty with which she had spoken to him.

"You know, over the past few years," he said, "I've had my life written about fairly frequently by the papers. It is different, I know, because I'm a grown man and got to enjoy most of my life out of the glare of publicity. And, also, I chose to put myself out there, to be on TV. It was very much *my* choice.

"But there is a sense of helplessness when a newspaper reporter, someone you've never met, writes about you and your life. To see them give an entire opinion about you as a human being, as if they know you. And then to see that twisted version put out there for people to read, and to believe. It's really horrible."

Ray stopped speaking as he realised Alice was looking over his shoulder, looking towards the entrance to the kitchen, and he realised they had been joined. Without turning, he said: "Morning Val."

"Would you like a cup of tea," Alice asked.

"Please, darling," Valerie replied. "I was going to stay in bed a little longer, but I had to get up because my ears were burning."

Alice groaned, just loudly enough to be heard, and then walked back to the counter to pour her mother a drink. "Stop being paranoid. Not every conversation between Ray and me is about you," she said, and gestured to the breakfast bar. "Now sit down," she said, "I'll pop your egg in. You need something to soak up all that booze from last night."

Valerie took a seat next to Ray, who smiled at her. "How's your head?" he asked.

"Darling, it's far too early for smutty humour," she replied, and then kissed him on the cheek. Although Valerie was dressed casually, Alice and Ray both suspected she had been awake and up for at least an hour, preparing herself for the world. The entire second floor of the house was Valerie's suite, a luxurious space including a large bedroom, en-suite bathroom, a writing room and walk-in wardrobe. Valerie would rarely leave the second floor without having spent time dressing and readying for the day ahead, even if she were at home alone.

She lifted the copy of The Guardian from the counter between two fingers, as though handling an infected rag, and asked, "What's this doing here?" an accusing tone to her voice.

"It's Ray's," Alice replied, swiftly. "There's an article about the best shows on Netflix."

Valerie stood and walked to one of the lower cupboards and pulled it open, revealing two bins; one for plastics, cans and glass, the other for card and paper, and she dropped it in. "Still feeding your boxset addiction?" she asked as she retook her seat.

Ray smiled and shrugged. "What can I say? It's a golden age of television."

Alice placed a cup of tea next to her mother, and then dropped an egg into the simmering water on the hob. "Just give me five minutes, and I'll dish up," she said.

"Sounds heavenly," Valerie said. "So, has anything happened in the world today I should know about?"

Alice and Ray looked to each and then, almost in unison, replied.

"No, nothing," Alice said.

Ray shrugged. "Nope. Nothing," he said.

CHAPTER 18

Valerie sat quietly on the chaise longue in her bedroom, reviewing the story in The Guardian, a stranger's version of the life of her daughter. She could see, straight away, how the article had been constructed, in the absence of an actual interview with either Alice or her mother. The journalist had pulled together a series of dates and events, all factually correct, in order to give the impression of insight and accuracy. Those dates and events had been interspersed with the usual quotes from unnamed 'family friends' and experts and then, finally, it had all been linked together with a narrative that relied heavily on the writer's opinions and own experience of raising children. Valerie had to concede that she would likely have approached such an article in a similar way, although she had no doubt her article would have been a far more compelling read.

On her way to the kitchen that morning she had overheard some of what Ray had been saying, and so had suspected the copy of *The Guardian* might have been in the house for a reason. And so, she had waited until she had the house to herself, knowing Ray had an appointment with his publicity agent and Alice had some errands to run at her flat in Stratford. And, once they were both gone, she had retrieved the newspaper from the kitchen bin and retreated with it to her room.

The article read like so many others she had seen over the years, portraying herself and Jeremy as ruthless, exploitative parents who treated their only child as little more than a PR opportunity. Valerie felt terribly sad for her late husband, described in such dismal terms and unable to defend himself.

But as for those criticisms levelled at Valerie, they were little more than water off a duck's back. Indeed, she quite enjoyed being the subject of an article in a national newspaper, regardless of how she was portrayed. She believed all journalists sought some sort of recognition, or fame. Indeed, in her years at the *Daily Ear,* her old editor had accused her on many occasions of "*edging closer to that fine line between valid debate and pure attention-seeking*".

And Valerie had often wondered, in her quieter and more honest moments of reflection, if the reason she had written so critically and often so viciously about celebrities is because she simply envied them. Was that something Valerie Pierce had secretly always coveted, to be famous?

She took a deep breath and, as she closed the paper, realised it was not just the article that had troubled her. She was more perturbed Alice and Ray had attempted to keep it secret, the two of them, working together. And then she recalled how their conversation had suddenly fallen quiet as soon as she had entered the kitchen that morning, almost as if they had indeed been talking about her, despite Alice's strong denial.

And for a moment, she was not sure what it was about their behaviour she found so disconcerting. Did she feel left out? Excluded? Jealous even? Jealousy was not an emotion Valerie ever liked to admit to.

She knew Alice had built a good life for herself in Stratford, and had a loyal circle of friends, many of them people Alice had known since she was a teenager. And Valerie had always taken great comfort in knowing even during those long periods where she and her daughter were estranged, she never had to worry about Alice being alone.

And for many years, Valerie also had also enjoyed the benefits of belonging to a loyal circle of friends. But since her departure from the *Daily Ear* four years earlier, she had lost touch with so many people and her world had shrunk around her. She had begun to feel she had little more in her life than a list of contacts and acquaintances. And now she was worried that, to fill that void, she had placed too much emphasis on her relationships with Alice and Ray.

It was Valerie who had been keen for the two of them to meet, to become friends, to become her own makeshift family; her daughter, her granddaughters and her gay ex-husband. And so, the unexpected feeling of envy, about the friendship between Alice and Ray, confused Valerie. Surely, she should be pleased her ex-husband and her daughter had become such great pals?

But quite often, the two of them seemed to have their own language, a sense of humour Valerie simply did not understand. She recalled one evening when the three of them had dined out together in a restaurant. Towards the end of the meal, Alice and Ray had been discussing whether or not to have a pudding, and suddenly Alice had said: "Is it on the trolley?" in a strange accent, and Ray had not been able to stop laughing.

And then, on another occasion, Alice had been talking about an art club she had belonged to when she was a teenager, and Ray had said: "I bet you can't draw fingers" and Alice had replied: "I can, I can draw fingers." And the pair had laughed for a solid minute.

Valerie simply had no idea what they were talking about much of the time and had to admit to herself she did sometimes feel a little left out. But she did not feel it was right, at such a late stage, to feel envious of her own daughter for liking Ray so much. And so, she decided she would do her best to set aside any nagging feelings of envy and embrace whatever friendship developed between the two.

A ringing noise suddenly filled the air, and Valerie realised someone was calling and, unusually, they were calling on her landline, something she had almost forgotten she had. A vintage rotary phone was quietly nestled between a lamp and an alarm clock on her bedside table, and she crossed the room to answer it.

"Hello?" she said, and at first she couldn't hear anything apart from a quiet crackling sound. Valerie winced, trying to hear any other noises from the other end of the line, but still there was silence. "Hello, this is Valerie," she said.

And then she heard a voice, a man's voice, and she recognised it immediately. "Val. Hi. It's me."

Valerie was at a loss for words. She suddenly felt uncomfortable, almost sick, and wondered why he would think for a moment she would wish to hear from him after all that time.

"It's me," he said again, after Valerie had failed to respond. "It's Jason."

Valerie closed her eyes and shook her head. "I'm sorry," she replied, "but you have clearly dialled a wrong number. Please don't call here again." And with that, she put the phone down, collected the paper, and walked back downstairs to the kitchen to pour herself a glass of wine.

CHAPTER 19

Jason could tell straight away someone had been in his room. A few items had been moved, only slightly. But after his time in prison, spending most of every day in a small cell, he had grown accustomed to everything having its place and had developed a very acute sense of change, knowing immediately when anything had been touched or interfered with.

His first thought was to alert Mrs Warwick, but then he remembered his surprise letter and realised he may already be in possession of some very welcome contraband. He took off his jacket and tossed it onto the end of his bed, and then looked around to see if he could spot any changes to his personal space, any new additions. He quickly noticed his bed cover, usually tightly tucked and flat, appeared to have a slight lump close to his pillows. He gently pulled back his sheets and found a small cardboard box discreetly hidden underneath, with a note attached. *"Jason. Enjoy your new toy. Use it to get up to speed. And prepare yourself for the rest of your life. YM."*

Inside the box was a tablet, strictly forbidden under Jason's terms of release. But more than anything else, Jason needed to step beyond his criminal record and retake his place as the world's most feared paparazzi journalist. Yves Martineau certainly understood the law could be an ass, and he clearly had faith Jason would do the right thing.

As Jason sat on the bed and began to initialise the tablet, he felt something hard under his thigh. He stood and looked again and found a small bottle of Prosecco he had missed the first time. It had a screw cap, so he needn't worry about the loud sound of a cork popping alerting Mrs Warwick to his room. The tablet illuminated, and Jason found it had already been set up under his name and with access to an email account and the internet.

"Sweet," he said. And then he sat back and googled his own name. He lay down on the bed and propped himself up with his pillows, and then began swiping across his new tablet, reviewing a seemingly endless array of news websites and forums where his name was mentioned. During the height of his career Jason's notoriety was second to none, a reputation he enjoyed and, if anything, played to.

But during his time in prison his infamy had clearly transformed into something different, something darker and degenerate. He was no longer the most-feared photographic journalist in the world. Now his name was simply used by campaigners, politicians and every single online know-it-all to further their own agenda, whether that be press restrictions, tougher sentences or curbs on internet porn.

And he hated it. He hated that his name was now little more than the starting point of a discussion about male violence. His greatest successes, the quality and creativity of his work, the stories he had exposed, all now set aside and considered irrelevant. All that mattered to the online masses were his court case and the length of his sentence.

Despairing, he placed the tablet onto his lap and turned to the small bottle of Prosecco sitting on his bedside table. He unscrewed the plastic screw top and took a moment to simply enjoy the aroma of sweet, sparkling wine, and then put the bottle to his lips and downed its entire contents in one. This was not how he wanted to spend the rest of his life, living in hostels and bedsits looking over past successes as though he would never enjoy that sort of success again.

In prison, he had occasionally reached out to some of his old newspaper colleagues, hoping they might throw him a lifeline upon his release; somewhere to stay, a job, a loan. But his letters had all gone unanswered, the nature of his crime apparently ending any expectations of help or support. And it had not just been his work colleagues who had so readily turned their backs on him. Apart from his Aunt Gail his entire family, even his own parents, had disowned him. Jason had gone being from a man who appeared to have everything he wanted, to a man who had nothing and no one. And Jason blamed everyone else for that.

CHAPTER 20

"Mum, you've done all you can. But there comes a time when the kindest thing you can do is let him go to sleep with love and dignity." Alice rarely spoke with such kindness to her mother but, if truth be told, Jasper's failing health had been almost as upsetting for her as it had been for Valerie. She still remembered the first time she had seen him; a beautiful chocolate Labrador pup with big hazel eyes and a tail he never stopped wagging.

She and Valerie had been with Valerie's husband Jeremy, Alice's father, at a private hospice where he was spending his final days after a long battle with cancer. Jeremy had Jasper brought in by one of the healthcare assistants as a surprise for his wife, a wish that she should not be lonely during the dark months that would follow his inevitable passing. Alice remembered thinking what a strange gift it was for a woman who had never had a pet or shown any interest in having one. And yet Valerie had fallen completely and inexplicably in love with Jasper the moment he was handed to her, and the two had been inseparable ever since.

And now, many years later, Jasper's long and happy life was slipping away, his usually large and heavy frame wasted to skin and bone despite Valerie's many and costly attempts to manage his kidney failure. With her mother's permission, Alice had called the veterinary clinic's out-of-hours number and been directed to a clinic that offered emergency appointments into the evening.

Valerie sat on the couch looking down at Jasper's face, his head gently rested on her lap, his breathing heavy and slow and his eyes closed. "I know," she eventually replied to her daughter, struggling to speak through the painful knot in her throat. And when she could not speak again, she simply closed her eyes and nodded her head, tears falling freely down her cheeks.

"Ray's waiting outside," Alice said. "He's bought a bed we can put Jasper in to get him into the car and to the vet."

Valerie nodded again. She looked up at Alice and smiled as bravely as she could, knowing her time with Jasper had finally come to an end.

Alice stood up and for a moment she forgot herself, and she kissed her mother on the forehead. "I'll tell him we're ready. You have a few moments with Jasper." She left the room, knowing she was only a few seconds from crying herself.

Valerie sighed, trying to force out some final words for her beloved Jasper. But her heart was breaking too hard, and her body simply would not allow so much as a whisper to pass her lips. And so, instead, she leaned forward and kissed him on his cheek, a final goodbye to her darling friend. And she realised, suddenly, that she could not imagine what tomorrow would look like without him.

On a table across the room, a small gold pocket watch sat open, tucked between a vase of dahlias and cornflowers and an invitation to the UK Top Women Awards. The watch had been a gift to Valerie's late husband 30 years earlier from Leonard Twigg, a previous editor of the *Daily Ear* who had been a great fan of Jeremy's. Leonard had the watched engraved with the inscription "Jeremy, Keep fighting for Family Values, Leonard Twigg" and over the years Valerie had fondly maintained the watch and, to that day, still used it routinely to keep her aware of the time.

But as she prepared to leave the house, so distracted by her beloved companion, she had completely lost track of the hour of the day. And had she checked the watch, as she so often did, she would have seen it was 9pm.

CHAPTER 21

Jason's trail of thought was interrupted by a faint whooshing sound and he realised something had just happened on his tablet. He picked it up and found a small message window had opened on the home screen, with the words "*YM is typing*". Jason's heart leapt with joy, as he realised Yves Martineau was about to throw him a much-needed lifeline. But then a line of text appeared, and for a moment Jason could not make sense of it. Why would Yves Martineau write such a thing?

"*Hello Jason Spade. This is your murderer. I just called to let you know it's your turn.*"

Jason vaguely remembered those words, or something similar. He was certain Adam Jaymes had said something along the same lines to him a few years earlier, over the telephone. It was the night Jaymes had published his exposé about the contents of an old computer hard drive Jason believed he had disposed of. But Jaymes had outwitted him. He and his team had retrieved the hard drive, reviewed its contents and published the details in a story that had destroyed Jason's life.

And now he was sat on his bed looking at a twisted version of those same words, a message he believed was from the new owner of the *Daily Ear*. He could not work out if it was a joke, or if his new tablet had been hacked. Or perhaps it was a misjudged advert for some online murder mystery game.

He went to raise his hand to the screen, to call up the keyboard so he could respond, but suddenly found his arm would not move. There was a numbness running across his body, a strange sensation that made him feel as though his arms and legs were no longer even there. He watched, helpless, as his other hand gradually relaxed and the tablet fell backwards onto his lap.

"What's going on?" he whispered to himself, almost choking as the words struggled their way from his lips. "I can't move."

He knew if he called for help, he would be found with the illegal device and be thrown back into prison. But as the numbness grew worse, permeating his chest and shoulders, a sudden fear rose within him and he realised he had no choice but to cry out and hope Mrs Warwick or one of her colleagues would hear him. But as he attempted to open his mouth, he realised it was too late. He could no longer speak.

Resting back against the headboard, he could still see most of the space around him and in the darker corner of his bedroom, there was movement. The door to his wardrobe was slowly opening, a gentle creak alerting him to the presence of someone else, someone who had been in the room with him the entire time. Paralysed, Jason watched helplessly as a figure quietly stepped from the wardrobe. A figure in a hood. The light from his bedside lamp was dim, and in the gloom, he could not see who it was. But he knew his life was ebbing away, his heart aching, stinging, and his breathing more difficult. Whoever was in his bedroom did not seem to have any intention of helping him.

The intruder approached the bed and placed a small vial on the table next to him, empty. But with a knowing nudge, it was moved directly next to the empty bottle of Prosecco. The figure, wearing black gloves, pointed between the two, a simple gesture that revealed to Jason he had been poisoned.

Jason looked up as much as he could, trying to see who the intruder was, under the hooded top, and he caught a glimpse of a terrible face underneath, pale and featureless, but with two deep blue eyes staring at him. He wondered if it was a mask, a disguise to hide the intruder's real identity. But in those eyes he could see nothing of humanity, nothing that made him feel there might be a chance he was going to survive that night. The fear that had been building in the pit of his stomach suddenly intensified, and if he could have run screaming from the room he would have. But all he could manage was a quiet wheeze of shock.

The intruder climbed onto the other side of the bed, settling into the narrow gap between Jason and the wall, and picked up the tablet so Jason could see the screen. The message window was neatly uninstalled, and then a browser window was opened. With amazing speed, a dozen search terms were inputted, the results of each opened in separate windows; *Naked female celebs. Stolen celebrity pictures. Private celebrity pictures.* They were the sort of search terms Jason knew people would expect him to be googling, alone in his room with an illegal tablet.

The tightening in his chest grew worse, and Jason realised the paralysing effect of the poison was now beginning to disable his heart and lungs. He wanted to scream, or beg for help, to apologise for whatever wrong he had committed that had so offended the intruder. But all he could do was squeeze out a single tear and watch as the room grew darker around him.

The intruder climbed from the bed and used the pillows to prop Jason up at a more severe angle, to give him a clearer view of what was happening. And all Jason could do was watch, the last moments of his life spent completely helpless, unable to move or speak, as his trousers and underwear were pulled to his ankles and the tablet placed on his chest. The intruder then stood a few metres from the bed, produced a smartphone from his pocket, and began to take photographs of Jason's half-naked body.

CHAPTER 22

"…discovered at 10pm during a routine room check at the Approved Premises, formerly known as a bail hostel. Police say the cause of death is not suspicious and they are not looking for anyone else in connection with…"

How appropriate that #JasonSpade wanked himself to death all alone in some shitty bail hostel.

"…photograph of the scene apparently showing Spade lying on his bed, naked from the waist down, with the illegal tablet lying on top of him. The photograph has already spread across social media and police have launched an investigation into how it was leaked with some suggesting the Met's own computer system may have been hacked…"

After decades of shoving his camera up women's dresses to show rancid #TheDailyEar readers which female celebrities do/do not wear pants, I almost wish #JasonSpade was still alive to finally know how it feels #BabyCarrot #LeakedPhoto

Nah, who am I kidding? I'm glad he's dead

"…literally just shouting and swearing at me in the street. Horrible aggressive, misogynist language often screamed right into my face. And you have to remember he was a big man, tall and very overweight. Physically he was very, very intimidating. Frightening actually. So he would take a photograph of me crying in shock, and then the Daily Ear reporters would write some nonsense about the pictures proving my marriage was breaking down or that my husband was having an affair. I remember Pearl telling me he would do the same to her. He would often reduce her to tears in the middle of the street. But with Pearl the context was different: the Daily Ear would print those pictures as evidence she was having some sort of mental breakdown or was simply drunk and emotional. The truth, though, was she was crying because she had just been verbally abused by Jason Spade."

For years I thought Jason Spade was a massive cock. But now I've seen his tiny little willy and I've realised how wrong I was #JasonSpade #BabyCarrot #LeakedPhoto

@ValeriePierce53 *Supermarkets: don't have your staff offer to pack if they don't know how to. Chucking food items into a shopping bag willy-nilly is an exercise in expediency not customer service.*

CHAPTER 23

"I met him a few times over the years. The last time was here, actually. He was taking pictures of Mum and me for an article. I know it sounds awful, but all I remember was he was incredibly fat. I remember how quickly he would get out of breath, just bending over to use his kit bag or walking up a flight of stairs." Alice sipped her coffee and rested onto the smooth, hard back of the marble bench.

"And now he's dead," Ray said.

"And now he's dead," Alice replied.

It was 7am and the two were sat in their pyjamas and slippers, wrapped in their dressing gowns, on a carved stone seat just outside the French doors leading to the garden from the kitchen. The sky was overcast, and the air still held a fresh scent of overnight rain. They had met minutes earlier, coincidentally seeking a morning coffee at the same moment. But rather than taking their drinks to their rooms and returning to bed, they had joined each other in the garden to assess the events of the previous night.

"Every news report is the same," she said. "No suspicious circumstances. Probably a heart attack. Died alone in a room in a bail hostel with an illegal tablet he wasn't supposed to have. Most likely looking at internet porn."

Ray sighed. "So, basically, a fat man wanked himself to death."

Alice chuckled. "Is it wrong I find that amusing?" she asked.

Ray shrugged. "He was a horrible man, by all accounts," he said, "so it is hard to feel sympathy for him." He sipped his coffee and looked up to the sky, as the dim autumn sun began to gently rise. "But I have no idea how Valerie is going to react. I don't even know if she liked him. Hated him. He's one of the few people from the paper she doesn't really speak about."

Alice raised her brow. "It was quite shaming, wasn't it though?" she said.

"The reason he went to prison. Once you're on the Sex Offenders Register, I can imagine a lot of people you knew would just quietly edit you out of their lives."

Ray wondered how Alice would respond if he voiced a concern he had been pondering for the past few minutes, since she had read him some of the news stories about Jason Spade. He still did not have a complete understanding of the complex relationship she had with her mother and was not sure how she might respond if he offered an alternative suggestion for Jason's death, other than murder. Eventually, he could not help himself and so quietly muttered: "But natural causes."

"Hmm?" Alice looked at him. "Pardon?"

And there was something in her tone, her expression, that made Ray feel he was on safe ground, that she would also welcome a broader discussion about Jason's death. "I was just thinking out loud...," he said, innocently. "You know... another death, and no hint of foul play. And no hint of the police, or anyone – apart from Val – connecting these deaths."

To his relief, Alice did not react with anger, or disappointment. Instead, she nodded, agreeing with the point he was making. "Do you think we were wrong to support this?" she asked. "Do you think we were swept along by it all? Caught up in the drama, a little star-struck at the idea Adam Jaymes was investigating too?"

Ray could tell Alice had left the question hanging in the air, waiting to see how he would respond. And he did not respond immediately. In his typically calm and thoughtful manner he took a moment to consider his reply and then said: "If it wasn't for Val, neither of us would have seen a pattern," he said. "And to be fair, she has been right. Every three days there's another victim, someone connected to the *Daily Ear*."

"But what if the police were right? What they said to Mum?" Alice asked. "What if we are seeing a pattern that isn't really there? I mean, hundreds of people have worked for the *Daily Ear* over the years. Thousands probably. It's a massive company. There are a lot of ex-employees walking about, a lot of them men of a certain age." Alice shrugged and added, "Is it really so unusual, to have a little run of... deaths?"

Ray sighed and then turned to look at Alice. "Perhaps we haven't been helping your mum in the way we should," he said, sadly. "Perhaps we need to be a little more circumspect. Offer her other explanations. She's the toughest woman … the toughest *person* I know. But the fear of this, it's destroying her. I am worried we have done more harm than good."

"OK," Alice said, with a gentle sigh. "But I don't want her thinking we don't believe her. Let's just play devil's advocate a little. Not take everything for granted. Gently cajole her into considering other explanations."

Ray nodded and the two clinked their coffee mugs together to mark their agreement. And then for a moment they sat in silence, admiring the garden, beautifully filled with trees, shrubs and flowers. Ray felt the need to change the subject, to offer Alice something more ordinary to talk about. "This was your nan's place, wasn't it?" he enquired. "Your dad's mum?"

Alice nodded and sighed, quietly expressing an unhappiness Ray had not anticipated would come from such a routine enquiry. "Sorry," he said. "Should I not have asked?"

"No, it's fine," Alice replied. "Nanna Florence wasn't an easy woman to like. I came here many times as a kid. Pretty much every Sunday morning. Absolutely hated it. I had to endure hours of being told to sit up straight, keep quiet and not touch the biscuits because they were for the grown-ups."

"What?" Ray replied, dramatically. "No biscuits for the children? That's child abuse."

Alice smiled and then pointed upwards, towards the top of the house. "Nan had a flat on the top floor. Where Mum's suite is now. It was a completely separate flat back then. She rented out the rest of the house to a couple with two young children.

"Their kids were about the same age as me. But this garden was part of their lease. I used to sit in Nanna's kitchen gazing down onto them for hours on end. I was so jealous when I could see them playing out here. I had nowhere to go. No outside space to play in. I had to just sit there quietly whilst Nan talked to Dad about politics and, well, passively aggressively ignored Mum."

Ray chuckled. "She what?" he asked. "Did she not like your mother?"

"It seems strange now," Alice said, smiling. "Mum being who she was, the perfect middle-class, Thatcherite newspaper columnist. She should have been everything Nanna would have wanted from a daughter-in-law. But I think Nanna just resented a woman, any woman, being in Dad's life. She even resented me, to be honest. She just didn't like having to share her boy."

110

"So, they never got on?"

Alice smiled. "Towards the end," she said. "Mum was very good to Nanna Florence in her later years. She was ninety-something. Completely compos mentis. But frail and desperate to stay in her own home until the end. And Mum made sure she did.

"Dad was off all the time playing politics of course. He made the occasional phone call to 'see how the old bird was doing'. But it was Mum who did all the work. We ended up virtually living here, Mum and me, so Mum could take care of her. And in the end, I think Nanna knew she should have treated Mum better.

"She never apologised to her. Nothing like that. But I remember, and it was only a couple of days before she died, she patted Mum on the hand and said, 'Valerie, I am grateful to you. For helping me retain my dignity'. I think that was the closest Mum ever came to an actual kind word from her."

Ray took Alice's hand and smiled at her. "You know, your mum's not Florence," he said. "She's not old and she's certainly not frail. But we do need to care for her. So, let's help Val keep her dignity as best we can. And not let this situation spiral out of control again."

Valerie had hardly slept. She had spent the night sobbing into her pillow, imagining Jasper lying alone in some clinical storage unit at the vets, waiting to be sent away for cremation. Valerie had paid extra for him to be cremated on his own, because she wanted to be sure that when her granddaughters returned from Australia, and the whole family were together again, they could scatter his ashes on the local beach and they would know it really was him they were saying goodbye to.

But the thought of her beloved pet, by himself, without her, had firmly stayed in her mind until she had finally cried herself to sleep in the early hours of the morning. So many moments of that painful evening had stayed with her. She could still feel the weight of his head on her lap, suddenly limp and lifeless as the injection ran its course.

She recalled the vet using a stethoscope to confirm he was gone, and the kindly, sympathetic way she had then offered Valerie and Alice an exit through the back of the clinic, so they would not have to walk out through the main reception in front of the other customers.

She recalled sitting in the car, sobbing uncontrollably, with Ray embracing her from the driver's seat and Alice sat behind, reaching forward to hold her hand. Perhaps that was Jasper's parting gift to her, she had wondered; two people who had every reason to scorn her but who, instead, had been there to help her through one of the most terrible evenings of her life.

Slowly, she pulled herself from under the covers and sat up, dropping her feet over the side of the bed and onto the floor. She sat there for a moment, trying to decide whether to get up or simply return to bed for the day. She checked her phone and saw she had received a message from Alice. Just two words: 'Come down.' And her heart skipped a beat as she realised it was probably bad news.

And then, as her mind began to turn to other matters, she realised the evening before had been 'phone call night'. With everything that had happened with Jasper, she had completely forgotten. And she realised that was another gift Jasper had given her, one night without fear.

Regardless of whatever she had missed, Valerie was in no rush to be confronted with more terrible news. Instead, she stood and slowly walked to her bathroom to have a shower.

Valerie lit herself a cigarette and stared towards the high windows of her sitting room. "Who?" she asked. She was sat in an armchair, smartly dressed in a mauve suit, and had the appearance of someone who was organised and calm whilst inside her emotions were in turmoil.

"It was the photographer, Jason Spade," Ray replied. "He had a room in a bail hostel. Looks like he had heart failure. Died quietly, all alone."

Instinctively, Valerie gasped. It was not a name she had expected to hear, not one of the many names that had whirled around her mind as she had showered and dressed moments earlier. She suddenly felt wretched, responsible almost. Jason had called her just days earlier, clearly pleading for help, for an old friend. And she had told him not to call her again and then hung up on him. And she realised she could have warned him. Instead of feeling awkward and uncomfortable, she could have simply told him to watch his back.

"Mum, he was a very unhealthy man," Alice said. "You know what he was like. Morbidly obese. That must have put a lot of pressure on his heart. The police believe he suffered heart failure. Natural causes."

Valerie did not like the words Alice had used. It sounded like she was falling in line with the police, and the media; that she was suddenly disbelieving of her. She looked towards her, hoping her daughter would continue speaking, to offer a more cynical take on the details of Jason Spade's passing. But instead, Alice simply stared back with a concerned expression that suggested she had nothing else to add.

Valerie stood suddenly, swept across her sitting room to the window, and stared through the voile curtains at the gloomy day outside. "I see," she said. "Natural causes." She turned and looked at Alice and Ray, her two confidantes who appeared to have suddenly transformed into disbelievers. "And I suppose Chris Cox was an accident, and Derek? And Javier was a suicide?" she asked, irritated by their obvious scepticism. "I suppose all of this has just been in the head of a delusional old fool?"

"No, Mum, of course we're not saying that," Alice replied.

But Valerie was already seething. It was bad enough the police had treated her like some crazy attention-seeker. But now to see her daughter and ex-husband so quickly turned into sceptics as well, that was a stretch too far. Valerie was having none of it.

"There is a pattern," she stated. "Four men dead. All connected with the *Daily Ear*. All killed at 9pm, three days apart. And just because the police are calling this latest death 'natural causes', you are both suddenly falling in line with them?"

"No, no, of course not," Ray said, and stood as though to walk across the room to Valerie to console her. But she threw him a look that made it clear he should just remain exactly where he was, and so he sat down again.

"Mum, you've just been so frightened," Alice said. "If there is a chance we were all wrong, that this has just been a series of unrelated deaths; coincidental, yes, but unrelated, then we must consider it." Ignoring her mother's glare, she stood and walked to her side and gently held her arm. "Perhaps you don't need to be frightened."

Valerie drew on her cigarette and looked at them both. She knew they were simply trying to be kind, to be sensible. But all they had achieved was to make her feel abandoned, as though no one believed her anymore.

"I am tired," she conceded. "Tired of being frightened. Terrified, actually.

But right now, I am more tired of being treated like a silly old fool." She slipped from Alice's hold and returned to her chair.

Ray looked at Alice and, from the expression on her face, could tell her patience was already wavering. He did not want the conversation to escalate into a full-scale row between Alice and her mother, but he knew how quickly she and Valerie could say things they would regret, and then not speak for days or weeks on end. And whatever the truth about Jason Spade's demise, he knew it was not the time for their peculiar little family unit to break apart.

"Valerie, I am so sorry how this has come across," he said. "We're not saying we don't believe you. Of course, there is a pattern. But we just wanted to take a breath, to consider the possibility you've become very frightened and perhaps there is no need. It's just a possibility, that's all, that the police might be right and these deaths are not connected."

But Valerie was no longer listening. Her mind was racing, a dozen different scenarios, and other people. Other people who might have information or a point of view, or who might even have been watching events unfold, and who had been joining the dots in the same way she had.

Surely, she thought, someone else in the country had noticed the same pattern. Perhaps not immediately, after Chris Cox had died, crushed to death under his ridiculously massive television. Or after Derek had been fatally trampled to death in a stable. But perhaps someone had begun to connect the dots after Javier and, surely, after Jason?

Or had people really grown so insular, so self-obsessed and disinterested, they could do little more than vent their delight on social media at the passing of someone they did not like. Had the British people really grown so intellectually lazy they no longer had the capacity, even for a moment, to question whether a series of deaths was really as innocent as it appeared?

And in that moment, Valerie knew she needed to speak to Adam Jaymes once more. He had promised so much help and yet, to date, had delivered nothing. And even though she had coerced him into helping her, she knew he was the only person smart enough, and cynical enough, to see that same pattern as her. Adam Jaymes might turn out to be exactly the ally Valerie Pierce needed.

CHAPTER 24

Denise peered through the blinds at her kitchen window and took a moment to appreciate the view. Her garden was not huge, about 50-foot, but it was her favourite place in the whole world; a secret, hidden oasis in the middle of a busy London borough where outside spaces were considered a much sought-after luxury. Over many years she had lovingly filled it with carefully chosen trees, shrubs and flowers and even embraced the expense of lining it on all sides with a high brick wall for privacy. It was more than a simple indulgence. It was a protective bubble that gave her family somewhere to retreat, to gather their thoughts, to look at the sky and to recover from the hurly-burly of their demanding lives.

At the end of the garden, sheltered from the rain in a small wooden gazebo, she could see her daughter typing on her laptop, the latest module of her university course. Beth had taken to working in the same place each day, somehow finding the end of the garden the perfect environment for quiet concentration and study.

Denise smiled. "A hundred per cent distinctions to date, so we're expecting good things," she said. "Oh, I know it's easy to say when you're not the one studying, facing those deadlines and that horrible cycle of submissions and grades, but Jay and I both know she's going to sail through her dissertation. She'll do fine." She sat down and stared across the kitchen table at her unexpected visitor. "Are you sure you don't want me to call her in, tell her you're here?"

Adam shook his head. "No," he replied. "Best not."

Denise was a GP who worked in one of the most deprived boroughs in London. She had always been committed to her job and was hardworking and principled. And at almost fifty years old, she was now the chair of her local NHS clinical commissioning group and was regularly called upon by national newspapers and academic publications to write on a range of topics from community cohesion to child development.

But she had been careful in selecting the opportunities she would accept. The trappings of fame and showbusiness were not something she had ever been interested in. And she always ensured she did nothing that would draw undue attention to her adopted daughter.

Beth had grown into a clever, determined young woman and introduced other people into the lives of Denise and her husband Jay, including Adam Jaymes. He had been a part of Denise's life since she and her husband Jay had fostered, and then adopted, Beth; the showbiz uncle whose love and loyalty to Beth's birth mother had made him the bridge between the two parts of Beth's life.

And strangely, in Adam, Denise had found a kindred spirit; a young man with a curiously old and bruised soul, someone with whom she could talk for hours about the world, its challenges and injustices and never run out of conversation. Denise's relationship with Adam had always been necessarily secret, a means to keep Beth's identity safe. And she had never felt a need or an urge to brag about him. She simply enjoyed knowing him, those moments when she could sit down and enjoy a cup of tea or a glass of wine with him and they could put the world to rights.

But that day she could tell something was wrong. He was not unfriendly, but he was most definitely preoccupied. And on the few occasions in the past when Adam had been preoccupied during a visit, there was usually a serious issue he was dealing with. "So," Denise said, a neat segue from the polite conversation they had been having. "You are not one to drop in unannounced, Adam. Usually, your visits are planned weeks in advance. Months sometimes. So, what's going on?"

Adam was sipping his tea and appeared content to delay the conversation a little longer, but Denise was having none of it. "This is not a social call," she said. "It is patently not a social call. So why are you here?"

Adam placed his cup onto the table. "I need you and Jay to take Beth on holiday," he said. "Straight away. All expenses paid, of course."

Denise frowned. "Adam, I'm a GP. I cannot just drop all my responsibilities on a whim. Neither can Jay. And Beth's in the middle of her course. This is a critical time for her."

Adam glanced downwards. "I cannot urge you strongly enough to go," he said. "You need to take it as emergency leave, whatever process you have to follow to make it happen. But you must all be out of the country. I have a resort ready for you. Fully staffed. Lots of security."

There was something about the way Adam had mentioned security that alarmed Denise. It made her worry there was more going on than Adam was allowing her to know. "Security?" she asked.

Adam paused, and then he looked up again and stared her in the face. "I am so sorry, Denise, but I cannot accept a 'no' from you. You must go away immediately. You and Jay need to start making those arrangements straight away."

"If this is about Valerie Pierce," Denise started, but Adam interrupted.

"No. No, it's not her," Adam replied. "But there is a situation. I don't understand, exactly, what is going on, but I want you out of the country for the time being."

Denise huffed, loudly. She was used to being in the driving seat and did not like being told she would need to passively accept being told what to do, even by a trusted friend like Adam. "Then we go to the police," she stated, but Adam immediately shook his head.

Denise knew Adam was not a man prone to needless dramatics. Quite the opposite in fact. And if he said there was a serious risk to Beth's safety, and she needed to vanish for a period, then it was up to Denise and Jay to assist. "What will happen?" she asked.

Adam produced an enveloped from his pocket and handed it to Denise. "Be ready to be picked up tomorrow morning, 6am," he said. "You will be gone for at least a month, and so make sure you've made arrangements. If you need help or support with anything, anything at all, let me know and I will make sure it is taken care of."

After Adam had left, Denise returned to the kitchen and gazed down the garden towards Beth. And she wondered just how far Adam Jaymes would go to protect the daughter of Pearl Martin.

The rain was gently tapping on the roof of the gazebo as Beth reviewed the information on the screen of her laptop. From afar it would seem as though she were studiously working her way through her latest essay. But her efforts of the past hour had been far from academic.

She folded her arms, sat back and stared at the headline on The Huffington Post website, unhappy with the information she was reading. *"Daily Ear Paparazzi Pervert Jason Spade Dead."*

CHAPTER 25

"Biraz sürtersen daha fazla ödüyor."

"Sus. Sus!"

"Bana bak, geçen saçını keserken biraz omuzuna sürter gibi oldum adam bana fazladan £15 verdi."

"Sus be!"

Steve could hear the two men talking between themselves, but he did not speak Turkish and was too comfortable and relaxed under his hot face towel to ask what was being said. His weekly visit to his favourite barbers had started with the usual anxious wait. The 'first come, first served' queuing system meant he never knew for sure which gentleman would deliver his weekly wet shave, hot towel, head massage and light hair trim. Of the four chairs, three were staffed by polite young Turkish men who always provided a very agreeable service.

But the fourth was a portly Londoner with poor body odour and penchant for foul language. Too often he would stand with a cutthroat razor in one hand and a mobile phone in the other, loudly giving a blow-by-blow account of the text message row he was having with his girlfriend whilst at the same time tending to Steve's wet shave. It was never a relaxing experience.

Steve much preferred any of the other three barbers who always left him feeling calm and happy, ready for the coming week. The queuing order that day had worked in Steve's favour and a chair with one of the young Turkish men had come free just moments before the Londoner announced he was ready for his next customer.

Now resting in his happy chair, set back and being gently pampered, Steve could let his mind wander while his barber took care of the rest. The hot towel was removed and Eren, a handsome young man with a thick black beard and perfectly combed hair, leaned into his face.

"Was the towel OK?" he asked.

"Yes, lovely, lovely," Steve replied.

"Good, good." Eren then leaned over the sink and started to mix shaving foam in a small round pot.

This was Steve's favourite time of the whole week. It was one of the few moments when he allowed himself the luxury of letting go of all of his worries and concerns, a time when he could step away from his lonely existence and enjoy the quiet company of another person, if only for the hour or so the barber was being paid to take care of him. It was one of the very few occasions where Steve enjoyed any sense of intimacy as he was shaved, massaged and treated with warm oils and hot towels.

Javier's death had impacted on Steve more greatly than he had at first realised. It had made him reflect on his own career, his own existence, and left him with a grinding realisation he had little in his life beyond his job, an expensive Docklands apartment and a small group of friends. But Steve had never been able to maintain longer term relationships and as he considered his current group of friends, he realised most of them were people he had only known a few years.

And as Steve had grown older, the age gap with his friends had grown larger. He still preferred to hang around with bright, young people, mostly in their twenties or early thirties. But he had always suspected many spent time with him for the exclusive venues he had access to, rather than for his company. At 48 years of age, Steve did not believe he had a single genuine friend in the world.

He sank down onto the headrest and closed his eyes as Eren started to apply warm shaving foam to his face. And Steve tried to let his mind wander, to drift into a happier place. But he could not help but focus on all the opportunities he had missed, opportunities to build real and possibly lasting relationships with other people.

Javier García could have been a good friend, he thought. Perhaps even a best friend. And Colin Merroney, one of the *Daily Ear*'s most celebrated former journalists, had often shared a good-humoured pint with him after work. That could have developed into a friendship too, perhaps, if Colin had been a little younger.

Gayesh Perera, the former chief executive of the *Daily Ear*'s parent company, was another missed opportunity. As far as Steve could tell, Gayesh rarely did an honest day's work in the many years he was at the Harvey News Group. But he was always surprisingly good company whenever they had bumped into each other at the various events, launches and exhibitions Gayesh attended instead of going into the office.

Even the great dame of Fleet Street herself, Valerie Pierce, had occasionally uttered a word of praise in his direction. Perhaps she, too, could have become a great pal if only Steve had known then what he knew now.

Steve wondered if he had been too successful too young, a life full of charity galas and venue openings and film premieres and showbiz parties. He had failed to form the basis of any genuine relationship because he had been too busy chasing and propagating the fake ones. And now he was pushing 50, surrounded by people who were as falsely devoted to him as he had been to all the celebrity friends he had eventually betrayed.

And then there was Lucy Strickland, a relatively new colleague, one who had blazed a loud and angry trail across the *Daily Ear* but had somehow made time to develop a quiet and amusing connection with Steve. Despite her often reckless rhetoric, the two had developed the closest thing to a friendship he had known for years. And with a troublesome few days ahead, he found his mind naturally gravitating towards her, the one and only person in the whole world who might be able to offer him a friendly ear.

"I am going to lean in, to give you a really close shave," Eren said quietly.

"OK," Steve replied and smiled. He slipped his fingers over the arms of the chair and relaxed. He felt the reassuring pressure on his skin as Eren pushed against him and as he drifted into his happy place, his mind became focussed on his upcoming exclusive interview.

He had received a text message from the press officer, Sian, asking him to urgently check his messages. But when he had dialled into his voice mail, there had been no message from her. And then she had sent another text, apologising for the confusion and providing a new mobile number he should use as a direct contact with her for the opening night: "*The other number is used by all the press officers here, and that sometimes leads to mixed messages. So, only use this number from now on to contact me. And just to confirm, I had to move the interview forward to 9.30pm. I'll need you outside the venue by 8.30pm. Logistics! Can you please text me back to confirm this is OK with you? Sian."*

And Steve had sent her a friendly text in response. *"Hi Sian. Yes, all good. I will see you on the night at 8.30pm. S xx"*

CHAPTER 26

"Your heart doesn't appear to be in it, Val," Ray said, a little deflated their visit to an exclusive London boutique had not proven more fun. He was sat in the private VIP dressing room, sipping complimentary champagne from a crystal flute, while Valerie remained behind a tall gold screen, with a number of dresses to try on for her attendance at the UK Top Women Awards. "We don't have to go if you don't want to," he said.

"We bloody do," Valerie replied. "If it's going to be another phone call night and I'd rather we were somewhere busy, with lots of witnesses."

Ray placed his champagne onto the large glass coffee table in the centre of the room. "I still think we should just go away," he said. "Alice thinks the same."

Valerie stepped from behind the screen wearing a modest, deep purple bodycon dress with a matching jacket and black shoes. "Plus, I've been asked to present one of the awards," she said, and then turned and looked at herself in the large, full-length mirror on the wall next to her.

"Oh, I didn't know that," Ray said. "Which award?"

"Top Woman Journalist of the Year," she replied. "It will be good publicity for my website. Unless that dreadful Lucy Strickland wins it, in which case I'll be the one committing murder. I hear the awards are quite pointy." Valerie stepped towards Ray and placed her hands onto her hips. "What about this one?" she asked.

Ray pulled a face that suggested he was trying to think of something pleasant to say. "It's not very *awardsy*," he said. "I thought you were going for full-length gown."

Valerie turned and looked at her reflection once more. "It's not the Oscars, Ray," she replied. "You've got to know your awards and dress appropriately. And I think this is the one. The material is gorgeous."

"But it's the first one you've tried on. We've got this room for another hour yet," Ray said, disappointed he would not be able to quaff a few more glasses of free champagne before leaving.

Valerie had found the previous week exhausting, living under the constant fear she could be attacked, and then losing her beloved Jasper. And that awful visit to the police station, where she had been treated as little more than a hysteric. But spending time with Ray, doing something silly like clothes shopping for an awards event, was proving more therapeutic than she had anticipated. She glanced towards the gold screen, behind which she had been provided with two alternative outfits to try, both in the same deep purple. "Very well," she said, and disappeared behind the screen once more.

Ray was puzzled by the suggestion Lucy Strickland might be in the running for an award. "Lucy wouldn't win?" he asked. "Surely!"

"You know these judging panels," Valerie replied. "They do like to be controversial. Gets them noticed."

Ray's route to the position of minor celebrity had been the same as Lucy's; as a housemate on the reality TV show *Big Brother*. All he could remember of Lucy from their time together in the *Big Brother* house was how deeply unpleasant she was. He remembered how intimidated the other housemates had been, living with someone who was constantly on the verge of losing her temper, who wore her anger like a badge of honour, a constant threat of what would happen if she did not get entirely her own way and win every conversation.

But Ray had played his part well during his time in the house; the tired, unimpressed older gay man who had seen it all before and wasn't about to let some entitled twenty-something get away with lazy racism and homophobia on national TV. Whenever Lucy began to air her bigoted views Ray would calmly disagree with her, politely offer facts and then articulate a different perspective in a sensible and logical manner.

Lucy would always react the same way by repeating her well-worn opinion over and over, but louder each time, until she was simply shouting over Ray before resorting to personal insults and, on one occasion, a threat of violence. But Ray would stand his ground, quietly and calmly reaffirming his view that Lucy was wrong and expressing his disappointment that she had yet again resorted to shouting cheap insults.

At the end of week 3, Lucy had left the house to a chorus of boos. At the time, for Ray, it seemed as though the public had made it clear they never wanted to hear from her again. But somehow, over the following few months, her social media presence exploded as her hateful views found a new, eager audience. Ray watched from the side lines, appalled, as her media appearances skyrocketed, and it felt as though in no time at all she was the new weekly columnist on the *Daily Ear*.

Friends would occasionally forward Ray a link to one of Lucy's articles or an extract from her weekly columns and he could never find any intelligence or insight in anything she had written. It also read as nothing more than a rant and, quite often, a racist rant. The idea she could be rewarded simply for being the most famous bigot in the UK filled Ray with anger.

He crouched forward to look at his mobile phone, planning to search his various favourite news websites for any recent information about Lucy, something that might reassure him there was no way she could possibly walk away with a journalism award. But his feed was filled with stories and opinion pieces about Jason Spade and he pondered, for a moment, whether to mention it to Valerie.

They had not spoken about Jason since the morning after he had died, and Ray was unsure if it was a topic that might create tension in the room. But he also needed to know he *could* talk to Valerie about Jason, and so quietly said: "There's a lot online about Jason."

There was a silence from behind the screen, and he wondered at first if perhaps Valerie had not heard him. But after a moment she replied. "Yes, yes, of course there is. None of it good, I would imagine."

Ray scrolled through a few stories, at speed, and could pick out the same key phrases in each of them: 'heart attack', 'died alone', 'internet porn'. He put his phone onto the table and took a sip from his champagne. "You didn't really say… but, was he a friend of yours?" he asked.

Valerie did not reply immediately, and Ray wondered if she was considering her answer. Taking into account the reason Jason was sent to prison, and that his name had most firmly been added to the Sex Offenders Register, he could imagine it was tough for a lot of people to admit a previous friendship with him.

"Not a friend, not really," she eventually replied. "But we were close colleagues. I was always in awe of his photographic talent. And his extraordinary dogmatic commitment to his job."

She reappeared, this time in a fitted, full length, high neck dress with long lace sleeves and a swirl of sequins from her shoulders to the floor, again in deep purple. "And every now and again there was a moment, just fleeting, when I saw a side of him that made everything else fall in place." Valerie looked at her reflection in the mirror and began to turn from side to side to see how the dress would look from different angles.

"Every now and again he would come into my office for a chat," she continued, "and he would ramble on for a bit, about this and that, and I could tell something was bothering him. And so, I would ask how his day had been, and eventually he would admit he had overheard someone in the newsroom make a joke about his weight, or his personal hygiene, and his whole demeanour would change. Just briefly. But all of a sudden, he was like a hurt, fat little boy, angry none of the other kids in the playground would be friends with him. And that's who Jason was. A lonely, angry, fat little boy who had found, in photography, a focus and an outlet for his anger. His photography became his everything."

She turned and looked at Ray, her face slightly flushed, as though she were about to cry. "And I cannot help but wonder if it would have been better if he had stayed in prison."

Ray had many strong opinions about Jason Spade, but Valerie was speaking of him so eloquently that Ray decided it was not the time to air those views. "And Adam Jaymes?" he asked.

Valerie shrugged. "We exchanged a few messages," she said. "I get the impression he's in the middle of it all, his people combing through all the evidence for clues. And, hopefully, with a lot more vigour than the police." She turned and looked at herself in the mirror once more.

"That is a gorgeous dress," Ray said, and put his flute down on the table. "It's much more *awardsy*."

Valerie frowned. "But, perhaps a tad too much for this event?"

Ray shrugged. "You're presenting an award. You want publicity. Why not stand out?"

"Maybe," Valerie replied and then disappeared behind the screen again. "Let's try on number three," she said, a gleeful tone to her voice indicating she was beginning to enjoy the experience.

CHAPTER 27

Lucy had always been an early riser. She enjoyed being up before anyone else. It gave her a sense of ownership over the day ahead, as though she had a greater right to benefit from it than the Johnny-come-latelies who stayed in bed for as long as they could. She had always looked down on them, those people who failed to maximise their time and opportunities by spending too long asleep.

It was a routine she had fallen into as a school pupil, when she had realised she was not naturally smart and would have to work much harder than her peers if she had any hope of outperforming them. But she had reaped the benefits at school, and later found the same routine enabled her to move quickly up the career ladder as a young adult.

And now as a popular newspaper columnist, angry and determined, she used those quiet, dark hours each day to develop her opinions, and rehearse her arguments in her head. She made certain she would go into any meeting knowing exactly what was going to be discussed so she would have an opinion on anything that might crop up. She wanted to impress everyone around her, and mostly she succeeded in that wish. In her heart, Lucy knew she was not naturally clever, but she had learned how to make herself appear smart. And, from Lucy's point of view, that made her the cleverest person in any room.

Even though her job offered flexible working hours, she still ensured she was up and out of bed just after 5am each day. She would get washed and dressed, have breakfast, and then populate those empty morning hours with all the chores she knew she would not have time for later in the day. This was usually a mix of writing, researching, reviewing social media, organising the house or managing her money.

More recently, she had taken to having Radio 4's Today programme playing in the background. She had never really been interested in radio shows, but since she had taken the job at the *Daily Ear*, she had found it would help enhance her image as a well-informed commentator if she could drop into conversation who John Humphrys or Sarah Montague had interviewed. She often imagined herself appearing on the show, promoting her latest thought, and was convinced she would outfox any of the presenters.

That morning, her chores had been somewhat different. Lucy was sat at her kitchen table, with her third cup of coffee, scanning her husband's social media accounts for any signs of activity. But she had found nothing since Alec had uploaded a selfie to his Instagram account, the day before he left for a stag week in Malia with a group of mates.

She did not like it when his online presence faded because she knew, only too well, how much he loved the attention he received from his hundreds of thousands of followers. Alec was handsome and muscular, a talented mechanic with thick blond hair and blue eyes, who had courted an online audience for years, well before Lucy had even met him.

And she knew much of the success of his little empire of car repair centres had come from creating a loyal customer base of lusty women and gay men, mostly of a certain age, who had been attracted by photographs of Alec and his equally muscular and handsome mechanics. Indeed, it had been those images of Alec's handsome face and toned chest that had drawn Lucy to his Notting Hill depot for her MOT several years earlier; Alec's Instagram account was the reason the two had met in the first place.

He had always had particular success on Instagram and would routinely receive tens of thousands of likes and dozens, sometimes hundreds, of comments whenever he uploaded a photograph of himself. He would typically post regularly, three or four selfies a day, in various poses and situations, although mostly they would be pictures of Alec working on a car, shirtless, sometimes with a few beads of sweat or a well-placed smudge of grease.

He would garnish each picture with some mechanical explanation as to what he was doing under the bonnet, but the comments from his followers were never about the car. They were always flirty, naughty and often peppered with emojis; hearts, kissing faces or aubergines.

And, mostly, Lucy had never worried about being married to a man who was the object of desire for so many other people. She didn't even care that online trolls had dubbed them 'Beauty and the Beast', with a clear emphasis Alec was the beauty. As 'showbiz couple' names went, she had heard worse. And even though Lucy had never considered herself pretty, she had learned that a surprising number of men were attracted to the many other qualities she possessed; her confidence, her strong, no-nonsense character and sometimes even her fiery temper. Alec had certainly been one of those men.

He had kept in direct contact with her over the previous few days, sending text messages and the occasional selfie, but she noted none of his pictures included any of the friends he was supposedly on holiday with. The anticipated parade of drunken nights out, dips in the pool or mooning at the other hotel guests never made it to Lucy's phone, and his withdrawal from social media had exacerbated her concerns.

Lucy had taken to stalking his friends on Facebook, but none of them had accepted her friend requests and neither had their wives. It was as if there was a secret club that she was not a part of, an online group that was enabling her husband to vanish.

Worse still, she had begun to align Alec's regular trips abroad with the annual leave booked by his accountant, Janet. Janet was an annoyingly glamorous woman who was older, possibly in her late forties, but who always seemed to be away from the local firm at the exact same time Lucy's husband was on holiday.

Years earlier it had been Lucy who had been Alec's mistress, a part of all the secrets and the deceit, and she had enjoyed the power of knowing another woman was being lied to. But Lucy had gradually started to believe the tables had turned, and perhaps she was now the wife being kept in the dark whilst someone else enjoyed the secrets and the deceits of being her husband's mistress.

It was not necessarily the idea of lies or infidelity that upset her. It was the frustration other people knew or might find out. That others, people who did not like her, might laugh their socks off at her expense and enjoy her humiliation. And she knew no one was going to feel sorry for her, not even her loyal readers at the *Daily Ear*.

Lucy stepped away from her laptop and began to busy herself, tidying a drawer in the kitchen that had become filled with a large number of Waitrose carrier bags. She knew she was procrastinating. She was supposed to have spent that morning finalising her next column and planning her writing for the next few weeks. But thoughts of her husband's adultery had robbed her of the ability to concentrate. And so, instead, she spent the next half-hour clearing out a kitchen cupboard that had been bothering her for months, and then she prepared a needlessly complicated dish in the slow cooker for lunch.

She hoped the distraction might put her in a better frame of mind to plan her work for the coming weeks. She had received an invitation to the UK Top Women Awards and had pinned all her hopes on being named the UK's woman journalist of the year. She desperately wanted to arrive at the awards with a major story under her belt, something that would make it impossible for anyone else to be named, credibly, as the winner.

She had heard rumours of immigrant families entering the UK illegally through marinas on the east coast, places where the better-off moored their yachts for weekend sailing. It would be a great scoop, she thought, the fantastic juxtaposition of wealthy British families quaffing champagne on their yachts whilst illegal immigrants were swimming to shore right next to them.

Lucy was going to win that award by proving the UK was an easy target for unwanted aliens who were a threat to the British way of life. She opened her laptop and started to email a few contacts to ask for help finding a location, where she could confront an immigrant family the moment they set foot on dry land.

CHAPTER 27

Gayesh had convinced himself that everything would work out OK, and that the response to the Freedom of Information request about his comings-and-goings would be lost amid a sea of responses from other NHS trusts around the country. But he had failed to factor into the equation the *Mid and North Kent Shopper*, an aggressive little local paper with a history of railing against almost everything the public sector did in the area, and particularly the local hospital trust and its new boss.

Its chief reporter had painstakingly worked her way through all the information published by the TaxPayers' Alliance and identified Gayesh as being the least hardworking hospital chief executive in the country. In particular, she had highlighted his tendency to "clock-in" to his office each day to give the appearance of being there, even though it was clear he typically spent less than 40 minutes at work before "clocking-out" and heading off to an event somewhere else.

That day's edition was sat on Gayesh's desk, his smiling corporate photograph on the front page framed by the shameful headline: "Is this the laziest hospital chief in the country?" Across three pages, the reporter listed each and every opening, exhibition, conference, launch, lunchtime seminar or black-tie dinner Gayesh had attended instead of his daily duties as the leader of one of the most financially-challenged NHS organisations in the country.

The repercussions of the story had already started to make themselves known. Within a few hours of the advertiser being published, Kent County Council announced it had amended the agenda for its next Health Overview and Scrutiny Committee and Gayesh was now expected to attend to explain the story, in public.

Gayesh had summoned the Head of Communications to his office fully intending to blame her for the whole affair and, if the mood had taken him, to dismiss her from her job. But to his surprise she had wandered through the door accompanied by Alan Thorpe-Tracey, a senior communications manager from NHS England. Alan had a clear, confident manner that Gayesh took an instant dislike to. Alan also showed a complete lack of deference to Gayesh's position as chief executive, and that was something Gayesh disliked even more.

"This is not acceptable," Alan stated, his words leaving a clear indication that more was going to be said.

But Gayesh completely misread the room, and looked accusingly at Victoria, the one person he felt was to blame for the events of that day. "I agree," he replied. "I made it absolutely clear to Victoria that we should find an exemption. That we needed to stop this… this racist paper from targeting me yet again. But not only did she fail to do that, she conspired with this paper to write this story. This is a grave failure, Victoria. And it is on your shoulders."

Victoria did not respond. Instead, she sat back in her seat, crossed her arms and stared smugly at him.

"To be clear, Gayesh," Alan replied, "Victoria is a highly respected communications professional. She followed the law regarding the Freedom of Information request with due transparency and within the correct timeframe. She then offered an appropriate response to the local media when they asked for a statement."

"She did all of this behind my back," Gayesh said.

"Victoria has furnished me with all the email correspondence, Gayesh," Alan replied. "You were kept fully informed. If you choose not to read and reply to your emails, particularly those clearly marked as urgent, then that is your prerogative. But Victoria did her job properly, and she was in touch with me throughout. I have agreed each action with her. Everything Victoria did was signed off directly with NHS England."

"So," Gayesh said, angrily. "You are both responsible. Who is your boss, Alan? Who do you report to? I would wish to speak with him."

"I do not think you understand what I am saying," Alan continued, completely unphased by Gayesh's exasperated tone and implied threats. "Victoria took appropriate and necessary action to ensure this Trust's communications service was able to continue operating even though its chief executive was constantly absent."

Alan nodded to Victoria, who smiled at him and then quietly stood and left the room. Gayesh found her sudden departure unsettling. He could feel the situation slipping away from him, a helplessness he had only suffered once before in his career. Worse, the similarity of the two situations was striking.

Four years earlier it had been the editor of the *Daily Ear*, Leonard Twigg, who delivered the news to Gayesh that his services were no longer required. On paper, the editor of the *Daily Ear* was several tiers lower in seniority than the chief executive of its parent company. But Twigg had connections with the owner of the Harvey News Group and had been personally tasked with removing Gayesh with immediate effect. Twigg had even arranged for security guards to march Gayesh from the building, something witnessed by all the journalists in the newsroom at the time.

And now, once more, Gayesh was sat with a member of staff who, on paper, was several grades lower than him but who was behaving as though he had the controlling vote on what would happen to Gayesh.

"Victoria and I spoke about your conduct," Alan said, "not just your absenteeism, but also the way you behave towards the senior staff. These conversations raised concerns at NHS England and, as such, I had confidential conversations with a number of the directors here."

Gayesh raised his hands in frustration. "What is this?" he bellowed. "Who is this whispering and conspiring against me?"

But Alan continued to speak as though he had not been interrupted. "It is clear, Gayesh, that you have created a culture where staff are unable to raise legitimate concerns about your conduct through fear of losing their job."

Gayesh shook his head. "I expect loyalty from my team. There is nothing wrong with that."

"You expect complicity," Alan responded, crossly. "You ensure no one feels able to question your behaviour or scrutinise your daily routines. You have a CQC inspection coming up, and at the moment I guarantee they will fail this Trust on leadership and likely raise concerns about the culture of bullying that has developed in the time you have worked here. And that will only be the tip of the iceberg."

Alan looked at Gayesh with a disapproving scowl and then lifted his briefcase from the floor and pulled from it a number of typed A4 sheets of paper, held together with a blue plastic folder. He handed the folder to Gayesh.

"I have prepared your letter of resignation," he said, curtly. "It sets out clearly that you have enjoyed your time here, that you have made a great contribution to changing the culture and transforming care and services, and that you have spent much time promoting the Trust to organisations around the country. But in light of recent newspaper stories, you do not wish to become the focus of negative publicity that could impact on the improving reputation of the Trust and so you have chosen to move on to new opportunities elsewhere."

Gayesh declined to open the folder and, instead, folded his arms and leaned forward slightly in his chair, ready for a fight. "And what, pray, is that new opportunity?" he asked.

Alan shook his head. "No idea," he replied, a slight chuckle in his voice, "but I can assure you it won't be with the NHS. To be clear, Gayesh, if you do not resign, you will be removed. Publicly. The choice is entirely up to you."

With that Alan clicked his briefcase closed and he stood. "It would not look good if you resigned immediately so your letter is post-dated for next week," he stated. "This will give Victoria time to work on the external and internal communications, and for NHS England to agree your exit package. I will contact the chair of your trust in seven days to ensure she has received your letter of resignation. If she has not, NHS England will remove you." With that, and without any pretence of pleasantries, Alan stood and left the office.

Although the room was silent, Gayesh had a sense that it was still filled with words; accusations and untruths left hanging in the air that could unfairly relieve him of his high salaried job. And he wondered why these things kept happening to him, why no one could see the value he brought to each organisation by being an ambassador at countless events across the country, and sometimes the world.

After being fired from his position at the Harvey News Group he had attempted to negotiate an improved exit package, believing he had been simply the victim of circumstance, replaced as chief executive by a member of the Harvey family. But he later discovered his personal calendar had been leaked to the company's owner, and that his daily absenteeism had played a significant role in the decision to replace him.

On that occasion, he thought, at least those facts had been kept from the public domain. His hurried departure from the Harvey News Group was widely considered to have been nothing more than a ruthless act of nepotism. But this time he knew things were different, and the way he had spent his days at the Mid and North Kent Hospital Services NHS Trust was very much public knowledge. If he were to lose this job in those circumstances, he knew he would find it almost impossible to get another.

And so Gayesh decided it was time to fight for what he felt was rightfully his. Undefeated, he quickly assumed a course of action to protect his position. He arranged a personal one-to-one with the chair of the Trust, someone who had eagerly accepted many offers to be his plus-one at countless exciting excursions in London and, on two occasions, abroad. Each time he had carefully created the illusion that his attendance at such events and conferences were of great benefit to the NHS. He was sure he could convince her to issue a public statement in support of him, which would immediately compromise any attempts to remove him.

He then printed a number of confidential documents that showed weaknesses in other local NHS organisations which were not currently public knowledge. In particular, a report into a local mental health trust that was failing on teen suicides and a damning internal review about a rival hospital that raised serious concerns about the treatment of frail, older patients. He placed both into an anonymous brown envelope and addressed it to the chief reporter of the Mid and North Kent Shopper, trusting her to attack those stories with the same vigour she had attacked him that week.

Gayesh trusted NHS England would be quickly overwhelmed by a storm of publicity and no one would remember the small matter of his resignation. And he had no misgivings about throwing a few senior NHS colleagues under a bus to distract attention from himself.

And then he turned his attention to the bane of his existence, the security pass that had so readily provided evidence of his "clocking-out". If he was to continue in his role at the Trust and continue coming and going as he pleased, he had to close down the digital trail that could so easily betray him once more. He opened his emails and sent a message to the IT team, with the subject: "security pass: personal safety issue." He then started to plan how and when he would fire Victoria.

CHAPTER 28

Valerie liked to see Ray in a tuxedo. It was nice for once to see him make the most of his classic Hollywood good looks rather than turning up at an event wearing smart casual, yet again. That night, as she entered the ballroom on his arm, she had rarely felt prouder and was pleased she had opted for the full-length purple gown he had been so keen on. The venue was already half full, everyone else dressed less formally; the men in suits and ties and the women in smart evening attire. No one apart from Ray and Valerie had gone 'full-on Dynasty' (as Ray had called it), and for once Valerie was pleased that she had not allowed the event to dictate her choice of clothes.

She noted the many people who turned and acknowledged them with smiles and nods, as though two stars had just entered the room. And for a moment she allowed herself the luxury of wallowing in the attention. After years, decades, of writing about celebrities, Valerie felt she was being treated as though she were one herself.

Across the ballroom, fifty tables had been beautifully adorned with silver cutlery, crystal glasses and fresh cut flowers. A simple stage area at the far end had been created, which included a table for the awards themselves and a podium for the announcements. The walls of the ballroom were brightly lit in hues of purples, pinks and blues and waiting staff ensured there was a constant supply of champagne.

Valerie knew the ceremony was not being televised but could see that a small camera team had set up in various locations around the venue.

"It's being livestreamed on YouTube," Ray said, as though to reassure her, and make her feel especially safe.

Valerie had been given clear instructions for the handing over of her award, and as she had always been comfortable speaking to large crowds, she knew she could simply enjoy the whole evening. Yes, it was phone call night, but she had positioned herself in one of the busiest venues in the city where events were expected to be watched live by tens of thousands of people across the country. She doubted anyone sane would attempt to attack her there.

"Well, well, well. If it isn't Raymond Vaughn and Valerie Pierce. The organisers of these awards are really scraping the barrel if you two are on the guest list."

Ray turned at the sound of a familiar voice to find Lucy Strickland stood next to them, a glass of champagne in her hand. She was dressed in a business-like way, a black trouser suit and her red hair pulled tightly into a bun. "You both look a little overdressed," she commented. "Attention seeking as usual?"

Valerie declined to acknowledge her and instead continued to look across the ballroom at the other guests, occasionally waving if she recognised someone. But Ray looked at Lucy and frowned sadly. "Oh, Lucy. Name-calling so early in the evening? Shouldn't you be posting racist comments on some far-right website?"

"An interesting choice of date, Raymond," Lucy replied, deliberately ignoring his comment. "Your fat ex-husband must be thrilled to know you're back with your ex-wife. Still, I guess Valerie's the only person desperate enough to put up with an arrogant wanker like you as a date."

Ray sighed and then chuckled to himself, as though both disappointed and amused by Lucy's conduct. He had heard it all before, during their time in the *Big Brother* house; the needless aggression and the hateful words that always suggested she was on the cusp of losing her temper. The other housemates had found Lucy intimidating and would typically back down from any conversation where she appeared to be getting cross, but Ray never did. He always continued speaking to her, calmly explaining his point of view whilst allowing Lucy's behaviour to spiral out of control for all to see. "I see you still haven't grown up," he said. "Still rude and throwing temper tantrums at the drop of a hat."

"I am very successful *actually*," she replied, anger becoming evident in her tone. "I have become a powerful and influential woman. What have you done with your life since *Big Brother* apart from dump your fat husband and let Valerie Pierce wear you around town like a big gay accessory?"

Ray smiled to show her comment had not troubled him, and then he coolly replied: "Lucy, the simple truth is that you hurl cheap insults at people because you are neither intelligent nor articulate enough to be witty. As much as you like to pretend that your success is a result of talent or intelligence, you are simply peddling poorly written, racist and homophobic material to morons." He then turned to Valerie and asked, "Shall I get us some drinks?"

"Please," Valerie replied.

Ray smiled, kissed Valerie on the cheek. "I'll be right back," he said, and walked towards the bar.

"Such a dull housemate," Lucy said, furious to have been dismissed in such a condescending manner. "I made more of an impact on the public in three weeks in that house than he made in 12. It makes me sad to think how he's still chasing around for TV opportunities. Makes him look *so* desperate. Old and desperate."

"Oh Lucy, Lucy, Lucy," Valerie replied, still staring across the ballroom as though only half paying attention. "Are you still so upset with Ray because he proved how quickly your barely coherent opinions unravel in the face of just a few salient facts?"

"My opinions have made me rich and famous," Lucy replied. "And I happen to be working on a major exclusive story as we speak. In fact, I have been named one of the most influential journalists in the country."

"Yes, you have," Valerie said, a patronising tone to her voice. "By your own newspaper. And how's it going at the *Daily Ear*? Still haemorrhaging readers?"

Lucy was not happy that Valerie continued to speak to her but not look at her. She was not used to being treated with such an obvious show of indifference, and so attempted to engage Valerie's attention with a few simple brags. "We remain the biggest selling daily paper, our website is the most read news website in the world, and I have almost half a million followers on Twitter."

Valerie knew she had four times as many as Lucy but was not going to play tit-for-tat with her. "Well," she replied, "I suppose you being on Twitter is a price society has to pay, if it keeps you too busy to sleep with any more married men."

Lucy gurned and groaned, as though Valerie had just made the most boring and predictable comment imaginable. "As I have said many times before,

Valerie, I wasn't married. He was. He cheated on his first wife. With me. But I was single. I did not cheat on anyone. I did nothing wrong."

"And I'm sure the very conservative women who read the *Daily Ear* would agree wholeheartedly with your view," Valerie replied, sarcastically. "I'm absolutely certain none of those readers would consider you to be little more than a cheap tramp. Screwed him standing up behind a petrol station, didn't you?"

"We were being adventurous, Valerie," Lucy replied, brazenly. "You should try it sometime. Assuming you're able to attract any *straight* men these days. But isn't it sad that we're at an awards ceremony to celebrate strong, clever women and yet you would still blame a woman for the adultery of a man?"

"Oh, it's not a matter of blame," Valerie replied, "just genuine concern. How long before he does to you what he did to his first wife? I have always found it fascinating, Lucy, that level of delusion. To steal another woman's husband, to marry a man you know to be a liar and a cheater. But to convince yourself that he would never cheat on you. Because it's different with you. Everything's different. But the truth is, *he's* not different. He's exactly the same man as he was during his first marriage. And as you so eloquently pointed out, Lucy, your husband is an adulterer. So, that question again: how long before he does to you what he did to her? Or is he already cheating on you?"

"You know nothing about my husband," Lucy said sternly, hoping to draw a line under the topic.

Valerie had run out of people to wave at and so had started interacting with imaginary guests, looking directly into open spaces and waving towards them. She wanted to give Lucy a clear sign that anything was preferable to looking at her. "You're right, I don't know your husband," she replied, glibly. "Please, bring him over. Introduce him to me. I'd love to meet him"

"Well obviously he's not here, Valerie," Lucy replied with an exasperated tone to her voice.

"He's not?" Valerie asked. "But surely he would want to be here in case his wife was to win an award."

"If you must know," Lucy said, suddenly feeling the need to justify every aspect of her marriage, "and not that it's any of your business, but he's on a stag week abroad with some of his mates. And that's the level of trust we have in our relationship." From the side, she was sure she could see Valerie Pierce smirking.

"Oh." Valerie eventually replied, softly. "Oh, I see. And yes, yes of course. I am quite sure that's where he is. Lucy, I am quite sure you have nothing to worry about."

Lucy was on the verge of losing her temper but knew Valerie would love nothing more than to stand calmly by whilst Lucy's behaviour descended into that of a screeching fishwife. And so, for once, she pushed her anger down into the pit of her stomach and attempted to match Valerie, insult for insult. "And here you are, Valerie," she said, "parading your queer *ex*-husband for all to see, desperately hoping the gays will love you for it. How humiliating, to save your failing career by pandering to an audience you derided with such hate for so many years."

"Hate?" Valerie scoffed. "And this from a woman who literally punched the air when a five-year-old asylum seeker was found drowned on a beach in Kent."

Lucy scowled at Valerie. "That is a lie," she said. "I did not punch the air. And I have witnesses who will testify to that."

"Oh," Valerie chuckled, "well I hope your husband isn't one of those witnesses, because I fear you may have a rather hard time tracking him down."

"What I said, and what I still say," Lucy continued, as if Valerie had not interrupted her, "is that I do not care that these people are dying. My point is that if a five-year-old asylum seeker drowns on his way to England, then his parents are to blame for his death, for dragging him across open waters to a country where none of them are even wanted. That's not hate, Valerie, it's an opinion. Don't misquote me again."

"Oh Lucy," Valerie scoffed, a pitiful tone to her voice, "to misquote you, I would need to read your weekly, sub-standard attempts at journalism. I only tried it once. All those exclamation marks and words written entirely in capital letters. At first, I thought the sub-editors had accidentally published an early draft. What a shock when I found out you had written it like that on purpose. Still, at the very least I should congratulate you on all of your lovely tweeting. It constantly amazes me that you are able to keep your knuckles off the floor long enough to type 140 characters."

"Oh, for God's sake Valerie, even your insults are out of date. Its 280 characters now."

"Goodness," Valerie laughed, "even more of an achievement. Well done, Lucy!"

Lucy decided to bring the conversation to a close and so leaned forward and said quietly into Valerie's ear, "You'll be eating your words later when you're handing me the award for Top Woman Journalist of the Year."

Valerie leaned in even closer, but still did not look Lucy in the face. "Oh, Lucy. I hope you are not too disappointed, but I only agreed to present this award on the express understanding that you were not on the shortlist. The organisers have assured me I had nothing to worry about. Only proper journalists are in the running."

Lucy's heart immediately sank. She had only attended the event because she had genuinely believed her high-profile weekly column had placed her as the clear frontrunner to be named Top Woman Journalist of the Year. And to hear that dream dashed, so casually, by Valerie upset her more than she could have anticipated. Suddenly, she was at a complete loss for words.

Ray returned with a glass of champagne in each hand. Valerie took one, and then slipped her arm through his and they walked away together. As she left, Valerie turned back and looked at Lucy for the first time, a glass raised in her direction. "Goodbye Lucy. I hope I didn't ruin your evening," she said, with a huge smile on her face.

A change in the lights signalled it was time for the guests to take their seats. Valerie and Ray found they were the last to arrive at the table and the other eight guests, already seated, appeared quite happy to chat amongst themselves. But Valerie did not mind and was more than happy to enjoy a simple evening in Ray's company, without any further interruption. But then, just as she was about to summon a waiter to request more champagne, she heard a voice from behind her say: "Valerie Pierce, as I live and breathe."

Oh, for fuck's sake! Valerie thought, and glanced towards Ray in the hope he had recognised whoever it was standing behind her. But she was met by a baffled expression and so simply turned, smiling, hoping it would not be someone as appalling as Lucy Strickland.

To her surprise, there in front of her, was Gayesh Perera. Her former chief executive; a man she had watched being marched from the *Daily Ear* offices by security guards several years earlier, when he had been sacked on the spot as part of a major regime change. A man she had written about in fairly explicitly derogatory terms in her book Exposé. And even though Gayesh had worked at the company for many years, Valerie recalled that she had only met him face-to-face on a very few occasions, as he rarely seemed to be in the office.

"Gayesh, what a lovely surprise," she said, and leaned forward to air kiss him on either cheek. "What are you doing here?"

"Well, Valerie, you know how committed I have always been to equality in the workplace," he said, "and in light of that commitment I was offered an invitation to this wonderful event, celebrating the important role women play in our society."

Valerie noticed an older, grey haired white woman stood next to him, wearing a deep red dress and awkwardly holding a gold clutch bag, clearly waiting to be introduced. "And is this Mrs Perera?" she asked, with no idea if Gayesh was even married.

Gayesh and his guest exchanged a knowing smile, as though it were a misunderstanding that happened often. "No, no," he said. "This is Maureen Parker OBE, the chair of the NHS Trust where I am chief executive."

"I am a huge fan of yours, Valerie," Maureen said. enthusiastically, and leaned forward to hold Valerie's hand. "I could not believe it when Gayesh said the two of you were friends. And I was so excited when he said he would introduce us."

Valerie smiled politely. Her vague memories of Gayesh were that he knew certainly knew how to work a room, and so she assumed he had a good reason to pretend their relationship was more than it was. But she also knew the importance of maintaining contacts and so decided to play along. "Gayesh has been a great pal of mine over the years, and he has spoken very highly of you Maureen, many times," Valerie said, knowing not a single word was true. "Honestly, it is such a delight to meet you at last. I can finally put a face to the name."

"Oh, he's mentioned me, has he?" Maureen replied, flattered and delighted, and beamed a huge smile at Gayesh.

"Anyway, Valerie, we won't keep you any longer," Gayesh said, not wishing to push his luck. "I understand you are presenting an award this evening?"

"Oh yes, so I am," Valerie said. "Thank you for reminding me, Gayesh. Oh goodness, Maureen, I've been so busy drinking champagne I nearly forgot."

Valerie and Maureen both laughed, and then Maureen let go of Valerie's hand and after the correct, polite farewells, she and Gayesh wandered towards the back of the venue to find their table.

"Who was he?" Ray asked.

Valerie smiled. "An absolute tool of the highest order," she replied.

CHAPTER 29

Nothing could have prepared Steve for how ancient he was going to feel as he stood in the pouring rain on a dark, cold evening, watching hundreds of cool, young, beautiful Londoners queuing to enter a new club. He had convinced himself he would easily fit in, that he would not feel old, tired or overweight.

He had napped for most of the afternoon in preparation for a late night, and then spent more than an hour bathing and shaving, and then styling his hair before squeezing into a men's compression body vest and a dark, fitted three-piece suit. Everything that could possibly have flopped over his belt or wobbled as he walked was now held tightly in place. It was, he thought, the best he had looked in years. But his suit and tie were clearly at odds with the dress code for men that evening, who all seemed to be in variations of the same style; button-up shirts, jeans, leather jackets and trainers. By comparison, Steve felt like he was everyone's awkward, totally uncool uncle.

The club had proven somewhat difficult to find, concealed within a dark and gloomy area of abandoned and derelict factories by the Thames. It was just across the water from Limehouse, one of the few remaining rundown docks in that part of London yet to be touched by the magic of regeneration and gentrification. Steve could see the potential for the area and wondered if the club's owner had purchased more than just the one building that she had transformed into The SM Club and Private Rooms.

Perhaps, he thought, she had bought up most of the surrounding area too and was ready to develop apartments, bars and restaurants off the back of the potentially successful opening of her new club. And he began to wonder if that was her retirement plan, so she wouldn't need to keep touring now that pop stars couldn't make any real money out of record sales alone.

He could see the value in those questions, and the interesting article he could write; '80s Pop Queen turns London Property Tycoon.' But he also knew those weren't the sort of showbiz questions his readers would want from the interview. They would want to know her views on her pop rivals, the state of the music industry and the age at which she thought women should stop wearing leather trousers.

It was a quarter to nine, and so Steve casually made his way to the front of the queue, press card in hand, ready to be checked in against the VIP list and escorted past the bright young people to his private meet-and-greet with the club's owner. But as he tried to manoeuvre through the excited crowd, he found little evidence that any of the gorgeous young people were willing to concede any ground to a latecomer like him. "Excuse me, excuse me," he said, repeatedly, as he slowly pushed his way forward. "Excuse me. I'm on the VIP list. Here to interview the owner."

He steered himself towards the entrance but found himself blocked by a group of young women, all excited and eager to get into the club. He could not understand why they did not simply step out of his way to grant access to an older man who, he felt, clearly had gravitas and money. Instead, they stood their ground as though they felt equally entitled, and that immediately annoyed him: surely for these girls it was just another trashy night out? For Steve, this was the rest of his life.

"Excuse me. Excuse me. I'm Steve Gallant. VIP. Here to interview the owner." Steve held his hands out in front of him, trying to gently clear a path by indicating where he was trying to get to. But the young women were not willing to concede any ground to him and Steve soon found himself blocked by the group, who simply saw him as someone trying to push in.

"Excuse me. Steve Gallant. *Daily Ear*. VIP. Here to interview the owner."

"Fuck off Granddad!" one of them said back at him, with a huge smile on her face. It seemed almost good-humoured but, at the same time, Steve clearly got the message that she was not going to let him push by.

"Yeah, fuck off Tango-man," another said. And the whole group erupted into humiliating laughter. Even in a dark, rainswept street it appeared that Steve's fake tan could be clearly seen.

"I'm not pushing in, I'm on the VIP list. I'm a reporter," Steve responded, exasperated, and attempted to continue his passage through the crowd. But the girls did not move and his outstretched hand inadvertently brushed against the cheek of the girl who had called him granddad. Her expression immediately changed to one of anger, and she slapped his hand away. "What the fuck?" she screamed, and she and all her girlfriends surged forward, fronting up to a man who, it appeared, had just slapped one of them in the face. "Did you just fucking slap me?"

Suddenly Steve was surrounded, an angry crowd shouting and yelling at him, accusing him of assault. "No, no, I was just trying to get by," he yelled. "It was an accident." But there was no lessening of the anger around him, and it was only through the timely intervention of one of the door staff that the situation was quickly resolved. Steve was led out of the queue and away from the entrance, booed and jeered as he went. He was taken back towards the entrance to the narrow street that led to the club.

"No, no, no, no," Steve objected. "I can't leave. I'm here to interview the owner. I'm from the *Daily Ear*," and he showed his press card.

The doorman, a tall solemn man, reviewed it and then checked the VIP list on the clipboard he had been holding under his arm. He ran his finger down the page of names and then shook his head. "You're not on the list," he said.

"But I am," Steve replied. "I was invited by Sian. I was told to be here for 8.30pm. The interview was brought forward."

The doorman frowned but appeared to acknowledge there was some possible truth to Steve's words. "OK, wait here. I'll give Sian a call." And he walked back to the entrance and disappeared through the door.

Steve pulled his mobile phone from his jacket pocket, so he could show the text messages to the doorman as further evidence, if required. But he then saw he had received a further message from Sian.

"*Steve. Are you here? The VIP entrance is around the corner from the main entrance, on Sawmill Alley. You can't miss it. Doorman dressed in traditional sawmill clothing – including dust mask. All sprayed gold. It's hilarious – he looks like an Oscar! Sian x*"

Relieved, Steve quickly located a street sign for Sawmill Alley and hurried away from the main entrance, the noise from the crowd of people quickly diminishing as he turned the corner into the dark lane. There in front of him, about twenty metres away, was a little entrance way with a simple cordon and a lone doorman in bright gold dungarees with a matching gold shirt, boots, clipboard and respirator helmet. The man saw Steve and waved at him, jauntily, as though pleased to finally have some company after an evening stood in the pouring rain by himself.

Delighted, Steve hurried down the alley carried along by a wave of confidence that his evening was not now going to have proven an enormous waste of his time. And the doorman's clothes, gold from head to foot, really did made him look like a life-size award statue which Steve took as good sign.

"Steve Gallant. *Daily Ear*. Here to interview the owner," he said, a little breathless, and handed over his press card once more. He could not see the doorman's face through his spray-painted head gear and pondered the relevance of his golden outfit. He then noticed another street sign, fixed to the wall of the alley above the doorway, "Sawmill Alley" and realised he had completely misunderstood the name of the club. The venue was in an area of old abandoned factories and mills, and the 'SM' in the club's title reflected the fact it was a redeveloped sawmill and was nothing to do with sadomasochism as he had originally thought.

The doorman checked his clipboard and then handed Steve back his card and, without speaking, gestured towards the entrance. Steve was in, and he was thrilled. He stepped forward, "Thank you, thank you," he said, and almost gave the doorman a hug, as he hurried inside.

The entrance hall was dimly lit, with an untreated wooden floor and bare walls. There was an overwhelming scent of damp and oil, and Steve wondered if this was all part of the experience the club was trying to deliver; abandoned, derelict, ungentrified. It was the polar opposite of what he expected from a refurbished and repurposed building. And he could not decide if he thought it was clever and sophisticated or simply pretentious and annoying but decided he would praise the bravery of the design if only to ensure his article would see print.

He walked a short distance to the door to the VIP bar and opened it, not knowing whether to expect more of the same or a more generously decorated environment. Instead, the door opened into compete darkness, the only noise coming from high above, the sound of a rainstorm thundering onto the roof. "Hello?" he called, and stepped slightly forward, increasingly confused. "Sian? It's me. Steve. From the *Daily Ear*. Here for the interview?"

His words gently echoed around him, and he wondered if he had perhaps taken a wrong turn, opened the wrong door. But the entrance hall had been short, tiny in fact, and he was certain this had been the one and only door. "Hello?" he called again.

The depth of the darkness around him suddenly expanded, and he realised the door was closing behind him. He spun around and tried to grab it, but it slammed in front of him, blocking the only source of light. Panicked, Steve pulled his mobile phone from his pocket and switched on its torch function. He managed to illuminate the doorway and could see there was no handle. The door was tightly fitted into its surround and there didn't appear to be any way to prise it open with his fingers alone.

He called out to the doorman hoping for assistance but when there was no response he turned and, holding his phone aloft, began to peer through the dimly lit area around him to see if there was another way out. He realised he was standing on a small raised metal walkway and in front of him there was a drop of a few metres to the factory floor which opened into a huge expanse of old machinery, broken internal doors and empty storage crates. The floor below was wet with large puddles of rain from open holes in the roof above, and old light fittings hanging clumsily from the roof beams as though only moments from snapping their remaining cables and crashing to the ground. This was no club. This was simply an abandoned sawmill.

"That stupid bloody doorman must have set up his stall at completely the wrong door?" Steve muttered to himself, the only explanation he could come up with for being guided so specifically into the wrong venue – not a nightclub, but a dark empty factory.

Metal steps led down to the factory floor, where he hoped to find another route out of the building, a door he could push open or a window he could climb through. It was a few minutes until 9pm, so there was still time to salvage the evening and get his interview. Steve descended slowly, one hand holding his phone above to light the way, the other holding onto the rickety metal banister. He did not want to slip onto his backside and arrive for his interview with a wet patch on his behind.

Suddenly his phone burst into life, a ringtone that screeched around the empty space around him and shocked him so much it almost toppled him from the stairs. His heart suddenly pounding, he quickly answered it, hoping it might be Sian so he could reassure her he was on his way.

"Hello, this is Steve. Don't worry – a bit of an unexpected detour but I'll be with you in a couple of minutes. I think your VIP doorman has set up by the wrong entrance."

He waited for a response, for Sian to laugh or apologise or groan with exasperation and complain about the useless security team they'd booked for the event. But there was a momentary pause, and then a voice joined the call that was not Sian. It wasn't even real. It was low and screeching; an electronic distortion of the human voice, hiding the identity of the caller whilst their words could still be clearly understood. "*Hello Steve Gallant. This is your murderer. I just called to let you know it's your turn.*"

CHAPTER 30

"And, to finish, I cannot stand here with a truly inspirational writer, and an inspirational woman like Valerie Pierce without saying how truly honoured I am to be receiving this award from her. Valerie, you have shown all of us that we should never allow others to define who we are, that we should always be open to new ideas and perspectives and to have the courage to change direction and walk a different path. And for that, Valerie, I salute you."

As Marilyn Murphy held up the Top Woman Journalist of the Year award, every member of the audience was on their feet applauding. She then embraced Valerie, and a huge cheer filled the air. For many in the ballroom, there was something exciting and empowering in seeing two such very different women, generations apart and from different backgrounds, happy to celebrate each other's successes.

Although Valerie had always epitomised the values and views of the middle classes, she had also navigated the sexist, male-dominated newsrooms of the eighties to become one of the most famous and influential journalists in the world. And since leaving the *Daily Ear* she had successfully reinvented and repositioned herself, opening herself to a legion of new followers.

Marilyn was a young working-class blogger from Leeds whose powerful control of the English language and analytical approach to investigative journalism had exposed widescale corruption in government, the power industry and even at a local school. But it was Marilyn's online spats with Lucy Strickland that had mostly raised her profile to a national level and made Valerie even more delighted to hand her the award that night.

A blast of music played across the ballroom, a sign for Valerie and Marilyn to leave the stage, and the two returned to the audience to retake their seats. "That's me done for the night," Valerie whispered to Ray. "Now I can really relax."

"You were superb," Ray replied. "Very eloquent. And what a lovely thing Marilyn said about you too. I bet some of her fans start following you on social media."

Valerie smiled and then sipped her champagne. "What time is it?" she asked. "I want to nip out for a cigarette."

Ray checked his watch and then sighed, as though not wanting to relay the information to Valerie. "It's almost nine," he said.

Valerie had completely forgotten. The charming evening and the excitement of her award presentation had pushed everything else from her mind. But as Ray's words filtered into her consciousness, a coldness spread across her whole body and she could feel a tension gripping her stomach. She should feel safe, untouchable, at the event. But the terrifying reality of her situation caught up with her, and despite the wall of people she had placed herself behind, she suddenly felt very exposed.

"You OK?" Ray asked. "You've nothing to fear. I'm here. We're all here. Hundreds of people are here. Thousands are watching online. Nothing is going to happen."

"What an exciting evening this has been," a voice boomed across the ball-room. The host had retaken the stage, a comedian and TV presenter who had managed to neatly flip the evening between comedy and seriousness with sublime ease. And now she was building up for one final announcement.

"This is the 30th anniversary of the UK Top Women Awards," she said, "and you may not know this but the very first award ceremony was held in this very venue. And over the past three decades we have celebrated the work and successes of hundreds of women, from medicine and science to literature and journalism, politics and human rights to engineering and business."

Valerie could feel her heart beating quickly in her chest as the walls of the huge ballroom appeared to close in around her, trapping her. She could feel Ray holding her hand, squeezing it reassuringly. But at the moment all she wanted to do was leave, to run and hide. Lock herself in a cupboard and stay there. She knew the host was still speaking, but the pounding of her heart was now so loud in her ears that she could barely hear anything else.

She let go of Ray's hand and began to fumble by her foot for her bag, but suddenly there was a roar of noise and everyone around her stood. Valerie looked up and grabbed hold of the edge of the table, wondering if this was it. Was the killer rushing towards her through the crowd? Is that what the commotion was?

But around her were nothing but happy faces, everyone looking at her, applauding. Even Ray. He leaned forward and whispered something to her, but she could not hear his words. She did not understand what was happening, or why everyone in that enormous ballroom was looking at her. Gently, Ray helped Valerie to her feet, linked his arm with hers and began to walk her from the table towards the front of the stage.

Taking some reassurance from the calmness and closeness of her ex-husband, Valerie's panic began to lessen and her brain, once more, was able to assemble the information from all her senses into something like a cohesive picture. From the podium, the host was applauding with her arms outstretched in Valerie's direction, and a few guests reached out from their tables to gently touch her as she was walked past them.

And as she ascended the few steps onto the stage, leaving Ray behind, she was finally able to hear and understand what the host was saying. "Ladies and gentlemen, the UK Top Woman of the Year. The indomitable Valerie Pierce."

As Valerie was handed the award the cheering and applause grew louder for a moment. After so many years of attending that very ceremony, Valerie could hardly believe she was actually being recognised. She looked at it, a circle of glass engraved with her name and the award title, the glass embedded onto a silver stand. And she realised, instantly, that it would prove to be one of the most precious possessions she would ever have.

Now she had to speak, to say something important and worthwhile. But her nerves were still badly shaken and, just for once, she had not prepared a single word in preparation for any sort of surprise win. Gingerly, she thanked the host and then stepped towards the microphone her heart pounding once more, an uncomfortable mix of fear and delight. As the room settled down and everyone took their seats, Valerie closed her eyes for a moment and wished the adrenaline rush away. She was safe, she told herself, and she had won.

"It has been a long journey, for me, to get here," she said, and immediately realised how frail she sounded. She cleared her throat, not wanting to deliver a speech that sounded half-hearted, and started again. This time with a strong voice.

"It has been a long journey for me to get here. A lot of change over the past few years. Not just in my life, but in the way that people access information and share their views. The amazing work Marilyn Murphy has done is a great example of this. A young woman who is taking on the world from her kitchen table, with nothing more than her brain and an online blog. It is a remarkable thing to see, and I would reciprocate most proudly the kind words Marilyn offered me earlier tonight. I was absolutely thrilled to present her with the Top Woman Journalist award."

There was a gentle round of applause, but Valerie could tell the audience were a little restrained, as though hoping for something a little spikier from her. Valerie Pierce was not famous for kind platitudes and compliments. The audience clearly wanted something sharper, less kind. And so, she decided to move onto more obvious topics. "And how wonderful, in particular, that Lucy Strickland wasn't even shortlisted."

That comment was met, at first, with a gasp of surprise but it was quickly followed by screeches of laughter and then a ripple of applause. "But seriously, I would like to offer Lucy my thanks. For leaving early. It really did make the evening much more fun." Valerie could tell she was building a momentum with the audience, the laughter rolling, easier to achieve with each joke. "I imagine she's currently backstage, probably in the kitchen, demanding each of the waiters show her their work visas."

And the audience roared with laughter once more.

"As a woman, I have always been willing to challenge other women on their behaviour," Valerie continued, "and I do appreciate, over the years, the nature of some of my challenges were not always well met. But in these dark times, we need to ensure we not only celebrate the successes of our gender, but also confront those women in the public eye who are acting cruelly or with poor intent."

"Here-here" someone shouted, and the audience applauded. It was clear Valerie's comments were loaded, a deafening critique of her successor's conduct. And in the moment, Valerie realised she owned the room. But as she went to continue speaking, she was interrupted by a faint noise. The sound of a mobile phone ringing. And its familiar tone sent a shockwave of fear through her.

"Is that... is that my phone?" she asked, and the audience laughed, believing it to be a joke. But Valerie looked to Ray, standing quietly by the side of the stage. "Is that my phone Ray?" she asked, her voice sharper and more serious. This time, no one laughed.

Ray raised his hands, signing for Valerie to calm down, and started to hurry back to their table to get her bag.

"Sorry, sorry everyone," Valerie said, her panic now clear for all to see. "But if that is your phone, please could you answer it. Please. If it is your phone."

She could see some of the audience shifting in their seats, checking their own devices. But the noise continued, the hateful ringing of a mobile phone at just before 9pm.

Robbed of all her words and her sense of safety, Valerie had an overwhelming urge to run and hide. She bowed her head, dropped the award to the floor and hurried backstage. She could hear a rumble of conversation from the ballroom, her behaviour clearly having confused everyone. And she was met behind the scenes by a number of men and women she assumed were waiters or part of the technical crew, who were trying to direct her back to the stage. "I need to get out," she said. "How do I get out? I need to get out." Her voice grew louder, shriller.

And then Ray was with her once more, holding her bag, and he walked her through the door at the back of the ballroom, into the kitchen, where staff were busily cleaning up after the evening's meal. "It wasn't your phone," he said. "Valerie, it was not your phone."

But Valerie's nerve was completely lost. Pale and shaking, she simply wanted to escape from the building and run away. "Take me home," she said. "Please Ray, just take me home."

Ray nodded and then looked around the kitchen at the staff, who were all stood quietly watching. "Is there a way out that doesn't involving walking back through the ballroom?" he asked.

CHAPTER 31

Steve remained so committed to the idea of his exclusive interview that his mind simply was not able to link all the events of the evening together. He still believed he had been led into the abandoned sawmill by error. He still believed Sian was waiting patiently for him in the *real* VIP bar. And now, he believed the phone call he had just received was nothing more than a random prank, albeit a deeply unpleasant one.

"Dumb freak!" he said to himself and resumed using his phone as a torch to light his way. He had no intention of using it to call for help. The last thing he wanted was for anyone to know he'd become accidentally locked inside an abandoned factory whilst on his way to interview one of the most famous people in the world. His reputation simply wasn't resilient enough to withstand the humiliation. Instead, he was going to find his own way out.

The windows had been meticulously boarded, and after a few failed attempts to lever them open with his free hand, he decided instead to continue looking for another door that might lead out onto one of the many rainswept lanes or alleys that crisscrossed the area. He shone the light across the factory, its brightness only reaching a few metres but as he stepped carefully forward, avoiding the puddles, he began to get more of an idea of what exactly had been left behind when the sawmill had been abandoned.

Overalls, now little more than tattered rags, still hung from hooks on the wall, and machines including a large and rather grim looking circular blade remained in situ. Steve could only marvel at the grey lives the workers must have led, compared with the fun and frothy career he had mostly enjoyed for the past three decades with all the money and trappings that job had afforded him. And now here he was, on the verge of a fantastic comeback, and his fun and frothy life was about to be kick-started into top gear. If only he could find a way out of the factory.

Behind him, for a moment, he thought he heard a door open and close. He turned and shone his torch in the direction of the sound but its tiny light was overwhelmed by the enormous expanse of blackness around him. "Hello?" he called. "I'm Steve. Did you get routed in here by accident too?"

The atmosphere in the space around him had changed. Something was different. The darkness was no longer motionless, now there was movement within its inky black depths. And there was a soft layer of noise that had not been there before, the suggestion of movement and life; short breaths, perhaps, and also footsteps? And even though Steve did not receive a reply, he had an overwhelming sensation that he was no longer alone.

"Hello?" Steve asked again and reached out to his unexpected guest for some display of camaraderie or possibly just good manners. But, again, there was no reply. "We're both locked in. If we work together, perhaps we can find a way out."

But his words were interrupted by a loud 'clang' and then the sound of an aged piece of machinery growling and then roaring furiously back into life. He spun around, pushing his phone as far as his arm could stretch, trying to locate the source of the horrendous din. And he quickly found it; the enormous circular blade was now spinning angrily within its mount, somehow impossibly working.

For the first time Steve began to feel afraid. The evening, until that point, had appeared little more than a series of misunderstandings and misdirections. But now trapped within an abandoned sawmill with a vicious piece of machinery unaccountably screaming into life just feet away, he finally realised he was in danger. "Who's there? Who's doing this?" he yelled, spinning on the spot from one direction to another, hoping the light from his phone might catch his pursuer mid-act. "Who are you?" he yelled and span around. "Show yourself. This isn't funny. Who are you?"

He turned one last time and suddenly a hooded figure appeared, materialising from within the darkness with a terrifying ease. Steve froze, his outstretched hand just inches from the figure's head, and tried to shout or speak or make some sound from his mouth. But the darkness had consumed his bravery and the appearance of another person had left him too frightened to speak.

Slowly the hooded figure looked up and revealed a horrifying secret to Steve: two clear blue eyes set amid a face of tight white skin, robbed of almost all its features. But it was the smile that destroyed any hope Steve had of getting out of the factory alive; a horrible, cruel grin that exposed a soul filled with delight at the prospect of Steve's death.

"Please," Steve said, the word unexpectedly released from his lips. "I have an interview."

But there was to be no delay in what had been planned. Steve was knocked to the floor, his feet swept from under him with a single kick by the stranger. As he fell, he lost his grip on his mobile phone and it was flung sideways. It landed flatly against an adjacent machine, its dim light shining directly onto the spinning blade.

Before Steve could even try to stand, he was dragged by his collar, face down, across the wet floor, dirty rainwater splashing against his face and into his mouth. He yelled out, not words, but a sound from the back of his throat, a discordant mix of terror and discomfort. And then he was trapped; his assailant knelt hard onto the base of his spine to keep his lower half flat against the wet floor whilst pulling his torso upright. One hand was pushing forward against Steve's shoulders whilst the other was holding up his face by pulling his hair.

Steve blinked the muddy water from his eyes, and suddenly realised where he had been dragged to. The spinning blade was directly in front of him, humming loudly as though calling to him. "No, no, no!" he screamed. "For God's sake no. No!"

But he was powerless, unable to move or shift his body because of the pressure his attacker was putting directly onto his spine. "I have an interview!" he screamed. "Jesus! I've got an interview with Madon—"

The blade made short shrift of Steve's face, slicing quickly through flesh and cartilage, a clean cut from his forehead to his chin, splitting his nose down the middle and peeling his face open from the centre. Blood gushed onto the machine and the floor, and as the blade hungrily ate its way through his skull and into his brain, Steve's final thoughts were not of his career or his lost interview. As his consciousness blinked out of existence, his last thought was an image; Eren, one of the barbers from his favourite salon, leaning over him and rubbing oil into his skin.

CHAPTER 32

"...body was found in the early hours by security guards employed by a local nightclub"

'...locked in the abandoned sawmill after being ejected from the SM Club and Private Rooms for falsely claiming to be on the VIP guest list. Police are considering the possibility that Gallant may have wrongly believed the entrance to the sawmill was a back entrance to the club, and accidentally started the machinery in an attempt to find a light switch. Health and Safety officials have now been contacted to investigate why the sawmill's dangerous machinery had been left in a workable condition..."

"Witnesses say, earlier in the evening, Gallant was involved in a physical dispute with a group of women queuing at the entrance. One witness told me he clearly saw Gallant physically strike a young woman before being led from the club by a member of the security team. Police have yet to say if Gallant's death is being treated as suspicious."

The irony of the most two-faced journalist on Fleet Street ending up, literally, with two faces is not lost on ANYONE #SteveGallant #TwoFace #DailyEar

"...had attempted to steal the interview from rival entertainment editor Debbie Braide. Publicity firm Everywhere PR admitted Gallant had intercepted their invitation to Braide and attempted to take her place at the opening of the club. The firm stated one of their agents had left numerous voicemails for Gallant to explain his ruse had been uncovered and that he should not attend, but despite this…"

"…and yet his legacy appears to be somewhat insipid. Far from being overwhelmed by public statements from grieving celebrity friends, there has instead been a dearth of tributes. Indeed, if one were to visualise the reaction to Steve Gallant's death, it would be a tumble weed blowing across a deserted street."

> *I find it hard to grieve for a man who was best friends with racist, far-right apologist @LucyStrickland. Disgusting! Some people are better off dead. Fuck you #stevegallant*

"…but it became so much more difficult and you either rolled with the punches or you didn't. Entertainment news is a sector overwhelmed by the impact of social media and in particular Twitter and Instagram. Steve Gallant, and I don't wish to minimise any success he had during his hey-day, but he is a terrible example of what happens when you don't keep up with the changing way consumers interact with your product. He simply did not see that people did not want him editing the information they would receive. They wanted to see it, hear it, directly from the celebrities they were following. They had no interest in his personal take on an interview or his angle. And, frankly, why should they?"

"…Strickland, the controversial Daily Ear columnist and social media star, claims judges removed her from the award shortlist after Valerie Pierce threatened to back out of the ceremony at the last minute. Awards organisers have released a statement denying Strickland was ever considered for any of the awards. But the owner of the Daily Ear, British entrepreneur Yves Martineau, has demanded a full investigation…"

> *The YouTube clip is weird. She looks like she's having a nervous breakdown. Why was she going on about her phone? #UKTopWomenAwards #ValeriePierce*

"From Spice Girls to film stars, Steve Gallant appeared to have an appetite only for the most beautiful and high-profile women. But over the years each of his romantic liaisons has happily denied any such connection with the celebrity reporter, claiming he was simply a good friend and a polite companion for film premiers and West End shows. Many have suggested Gallant's narcissism made it impossible for him to be attracted to anyone else, female or male. Indeed, there remains an assumption of asexuality which may be at the heart of Gallant's soulless and career-focussed life".

> *Stealing an invitation from someone else. Hitting a woman. Wandering into the wrong building. Splitting your face open on a sawmill you turned on looking for a light switch. What a twat! #SteveGallant #DailyEar*

"...charismatic and of course very handsome. I just remember feeling that he was a friend. Genuinely a friend. And I think that is why it was such a shock when after years of knowing him, he suddenly turned on me, on my husband, and started publishing stories based on private conversations, the sort of conversations you would only have with a friend."

> **@ValeriePierce53** *The last time I saw an NHS Doctor was in 1996 when she prescribed me a two-month course of antibiotics and told me I couldn't drink any alcohol until I had completed it. It's been private healthcare all the way since.*

CHAPTER 33

"How bad is it?" Ray asked, and slowly took a seat next to Alice at the break-fast bar, almost wishing she would not tell him the truth. Unable to sleep, he had taken himself for an early morning run and had returned to find Alice sat at her laptop in the kitchen, fully dressed. She was diligently sweeping the internet to see if anyone had written about Valerie's strange behaviour at the previous night's award ceremony.

It was just after 5am. Alice had not been up for long and so had only had the chance for a cursory review of Twitter. But it had not taken much effort to realise that videos of Valerie's awards speech were spreading, gaining a far greater audience than the event's YouTube channel would normally enjoy. Someone had even attempted to get the hashtag #ValeriePierceIsAMadOldHag trending.

But Alice had seen worse. The story did not appear to have gained as much traction as she would have thought, and she could only guess that some other major story had broken overnight that was stealing Valerie's thunder. "Well, let's just say it's not career-ending, and leave it at that," she said. She then closed her laptop and went to her mother's expensive coffee machine. "Espresso?" she asked.

"Yes, please," Ray replied. "Well, that's a relief at least," he said. "It was such a shame, though. This was a real moment of triumph for your mum. She had the whole venue eating out of the palm of her hand. And just like that it transformed into a moment of public humiliation. But she was genuinely terrified, Alice. And that's what worries me. With each passing day, it's like fear is gradually… diminishing Valerie's character."

The coffee machine gurgled, and Alice picked up the little espresso cup, now filled with a thick dark coffee, and placed it onto the breakfast bar in front of Ray. And it suddenly occurred to her that it had been 'phone call night', and she had failed to check the news to see if there had been any other deaths. "I didn't look," she said, the words suddenly blurted out.

"Pardon?"

"I looked for stories about Mum, but I didn't check to see if anyone died last night." As she hurriedly reopened her laptop, they were suddenly distracted by the sound of a loud chime, echoing throughout the downstairs of the house.

Ray checked his watch. "What the hell? It's five o'clock in the morning. Who the hell is ringing the doorbell at 5am?"

Slowly, Alice closed her laptop once more. "Oh God, do you think it's the police?" she asked. "If someone did die last night, perhaps they want to speak to Mum about it."

The sound of the chime filled the air once more, a sign they had an impatient guest waiting for the front door to be answered.

"I'll go," Ray said, and stood up.

But Alice was not about to let someone else be brave on her behalf. "I'll come with you," she replied, and the two made their way from the kitchen along the hallway to the front door. There was a dim light shining on the other side of the door's decorative glass panels, and they could see the dark shape of someone stood on the other side.

"Who is it?" Ray asked, keeping his voice calm and deep.

"I'm here to see Valerie Pierce. It's urgent," came the response.

Ray and Alice looked at each other, both of them sensing a strange familiarity about the man's voice. Ray gradually unlocked the numerous security bolts holding the door tightly shut and then slowly opened it.

On the other side, casually dressed in a jacket and jeans, a man stared at them both with a solemn expression on his handsome face. "I am so, so sorry to call at such an hour," he said, "but this is urgent. I'm Adam Jaymes. I need to see Valerie immediately."

Valerie did not appreciate being forced from her bed at such an ungodly hour by an uninvited visitor. She was sat in her lounge drinking a hot cup of coffee, reviewing the bizarre sight of the internationally famous actor Adam Jaymes making polite small talk with her obviously star-struck daughter and ex-husband, each swapping stories about pets they had loved and lost. Valerie was finding the whole situation far too busy and loud, and wanted them all to go away.

She noted that Alice was already dressed, wearing her usual plain grey shirt, black skinny jeans and sandals. This made Valerie suspect her daughter had already been up when Adam had arrived.

She also noticed that Ray was speaking in a physically more animated way than usual, and she wondered if he was trying to draw Adam's attention to his muscular arms and legs. Ray was wearing a tight-fitting T-shirt with shorts and trainers and had obviously just returned from his morning run. And Valerie wondered if Alice and Ray had some sort of secret "5am club" that she had not been invited to.

For once, Valerie had declined to get dressed. Instead, she had made a point of remaining in her black silk pyjamas and had simply pulled her hair back and then slipped on a silk, full length, deep purple dressing gown and a pair of slippers. She considered it a form of silent protest for having been woken so early. She had already guessed the reason Adam had visited and felt she had waited long enough for him to offer the information.

"Why are you here?" she asked, during a short lull in the conversation, her voice still tired and croaky. "I assume someone else has died?"

Alice and Ray were both a little giddy with the excitement of meeting Adam, but Valerie's words had an immediately sobering effect on both of them and they remained silent. Adam's demeanour also changed noticeably, and he clearly looked less comfortable. "Valerie, it might be better if we continue this conversation privately."

Valerie put her coffee cup down and then elegantly lit herself a cigarette. She knew smoking would annoy the three other people in the room but wanted to remind them all it was her house and she could do as she wished. "Alice and Ray are well aware of what was has been happening," she said. "There are no secrets here, Adam."

Unhappy, but compliant, Adam spoke. "After what happened last night, I thought it important we meet. This was literally the earliest I could facilitate a face-to-face."

The room fell silent as Valerie, Alice and Ray all realised Adam was about to name another victim, and a terrible darkness suddenly descended on them all.

"Who?" Valerie asked, and momentarily closed her eyes.

"Steve Gallant," Adam replied.

Valerie immediately breathed a sigh of relief, but Ray interjected with a loud and shocked: "Oh my God!" and then placed his hand to his chest, as though clutching at an imaginary string of pearls. "Steve Gallant is dead? Oh no!"

Adam looked towards Ray; a great sadness etched on his face. "Oh, I'm so sorry," he said, kindly. "You knew him well?"

Ray suddenly felt very silly, as though he had introduced himself into a conversation that clearly had nothing to do with him. "Well, no," he replied awkwardly. "I never actually met him. But, you know, he's been around for years. It's like we *all* knew him, really. Isn't it?"

Alice reached over and patted Ray on the thigh, a broad smile on her face. "No, it's not sweetie," she said. "It's nothing like that. But thank you for participating in the conversation."

Ray shrank into his seat slightly, deflated; he and Alice were both clearly aware he had just made a complete fool of himself in front of an international celebrity.

"But, Val, you must have known him," Ray said.

"A little," she replied, relieved it was just Steve and not someone else. "A familiar face. Someone I said hello to in the corridor or saw at the occasional editorial meeting. Bit of a prat really, if I'm honest. He was at the *Daily Ear* for years. Not nearly as long as me, but he had a good innings."

"How did he die?" Alice asked.

Adam shared the information he had hastily gleaned from various sources about the death of Steve Gallant. All the early news reports suggested it had been a self-inflicted accident by a desperate, deceitful entertainment journalist, but Adam detailed the events leading to Steve's death within a much darker narrative.

"The PR company says they repeatedly contacted Steve to tell him he was not invited," Adam said, "but by all accounts, he turned up genuinely thinking he had an exclusive interview with the owner of the club. And that makes me wonder if his phone and possibly his email had been hacked. Were all those messages deleted before he got to them? And if that is the case, then his death was not the result of a series of misunderstandings. It sounds like someone tricked him into attending, and then somehow misdirected him into the wrong building."

"And a phone call? At nine o'clock?" Valerie asked, when Adam had completed his story. "Did he get a call?"

"I understand that the police are trying to find his phone," he replied. "So, it was likely taken."

For Alice, there was something about having Adam Jaymes in the room, speaking so clinically and factually about the *murder* of Steve Gallant, that felt as though a firm line had been drawn under any further talk of accidents or suicides. And Alice suddenly felt terribly guilty about her conduct over the previous few days, and her attempt to manoeuvre Valerie away from her claims of a serial killer.

Although Alice knew her motives had been good, she also knew how much she and Ray had upset her mother, and how Valerie's very public break-down the previous night could well have been worsened by a sense that nobody, not even her own family, believed her. And so, Alice decided it was time to pitch in with Valerie, one hundred per cent, by offering a very clear display of support.

"So," she said, "we have five murders now. The TV guy. The horse guy. The fake prince. Jason Spade and now Steve Gallant too. That's five. One murder, every three days, and always at nine o'clock. And are we saying they were each murdered because they worked for the *Daily Ear*? Is that the link, the only link?"

"Yes," Valerie responded, a little impressed at the way her daughter seemed to have taken control of the conversation.

But then Adam interceded. "Actually no," he said, gently. "the *Daily Ear* is a part of it. But that's not the reason. I don't believe that's the main reason."

"Then what is?" Ray asked, hoping to reprieve himself from his previous faux pas by asking a more sensible question in front of Adam Jaymes.

Valerie sat back in her chair and crossed her arms. "Good question. Adam?" And then she, Ray and Alice all turned and stared at him, an audience waiting for his revelation.

"It's Pearl," he said. "I think the murderer is obsessed with Pearl Martin. I think he is taking revenge against anyone who hurt Pearl. Either when she was alive or since her death."

In her mind, Valerie could immediately make a connection between each of the murder victims and Pearl Martin. She knew what each of them had done and could see how their deaths could easily be considered an exercise in revenge. But she also knew how unkind she had been to Pearl during her years at the *Daily Ear*, and suddenly Valerie began to feel even more at risk.

"And what makes you think that?" Alice asked. "Why Pearl?"

Adam glanced at Alice, his body language suggesting he would still have preferred to have had a more private conversation. "Well, Chris Cox is obvious," he said. "He used his TV review column not only to attack Pearl as an actor but also as a person. Javier's obvious too."

"Why, what did he do to Pearl?" Ray asked.

Valerie threw Ray a dirty look. "Well, if you had bothered to read my book you'd know," she said.

"Many years ago," Adam continued, "in one of his silly disguises, he lured Pearl to the Royal Hotel in Mayfair. She genuinely believed he was a billionaire philanthropist willing to make a donation to a charity she was supporting. Instead, Javier took advantage of Pearl's addiction issues, got her drunk on champagne and then coaxed her into sharing backstage stories about some of her co-stars."

"I think it's fair to say that Javier's article was the final nail in Pearl's career," Valerie said.

"Yes, she was fired from her job," Adam added, "but there were more human consequences to what Javier did, beyond Pearl losing her job. Her depression grew worse. She became incapable of looking after her daughter, and eventually social services took Beth into care."

"But that's where he died," Alice said. "Isn't it? The Royal Hotel?"

Adam nodded. "Javier fell from the 13th floor of the same hotel where he met Pearl. Possibly even the same floor, the same suite. The murderer seems to be very specific."

Alice leaned forward and adopted a thoughtful pose. Perhaps it was the topic of the conversation, or perhaps it was the presence of a famous actor in the room, but she suddenly felt like a detective in a TV cop show, Jane Tennison or Christine Cagney. "OK, so that's the link between Chris Cox and Pearl, and between Javier and Pearl. But Steve? What's the connection there?"

"Again, it's in my book," Valerie said, beginning to sound a little irate. She then gestured towards Adam, indicating for him to continue.

"Years after she died, Steve wrote a series of articles called *The Pearl Martin Tapes*," Adam said. "They were all based on conversations Steve had secretly recorded, conversations Pearl had believed were private."

"Steve's career was already flagging by that stage," Valerie interjected. "He was doing anything he could to stay in the game." And then she scoffed, "The Pearl Martin Tapes indeed. He made it sound like an archive of lost interviews and confessions, when in truth it was just a rather sketchy collection of short, barely audible recordings he'd captured on his Dictaphone each time he chased her down the street begging for an interview."

Adam shook his head. "The recordings were a little more than that, Valerie," he said. "And it wasn't just about the tapes. It was how he twisted what Pearl had said, took comments completely out of context. He wrote the articles as though Pearl was talking from beyond the grave, and that she was admitting everything the *Daily Ear* had ever printed about her was true. It was sick."

"What about the other one. The one with the horses, Derek Toulson?" Alice enquired, beginning to wish she had a flipchart and pens. Or a wall of photographs she could connect with string and Post-it Notes. "What did Derek do?"

"Did anyone read my fucking book?" Valerie mumbled under her breath. "Derek ran the *Daily Ear*'s charitable arm," she said, more clearly. "And we all genuinely believed it was a purely charitable endeavour. You know, with a bit of good PR thrown in for the paper. Derek travelled around the country, gifting tens of thousands of pounds to local community projects in the name of the *Daily Ear*."

"But in reality," Adam said, "what Derek was actually doing was meeting predominantly Tory councillors to offer them the money but only if they pulled funding from other projects and charities he personally did not agree with. So, anything for a minority group for example. Projects for the BAME community, or the disabled. Derek was directly responsible for the closure of about 100 projects and charities up and down the country, all of which supported some of the most vulnerable communities."

"Yes, but to be clear, once more," Valerie interjected, "no one at the *Daily Ear* knew a thing about this. It was a secret plan Derek devised completely on his own and when the editor found out, Derek was sacked on the spot."

At this point in the conversation, Alice had no interest in who knew or did not know what Derek Toulson was up to. She was only interested in what linked his deaths to the others. "And the connection with Pearl?" she asked.

"Well, as I revealed in my book," Valerie said, "one of the projects Derek targeted was a small charity in East London which supported single parents with mental health issues," she said. "It turned out it was the charity Patricia Martin had set up in memory of her late sister. I have to be honest, to this day, I have no idea if Derek knew of the 'Pearl Martin' connection. I suspect he probably did not or, at the very least, that if he did know he didn't care. I imagine he was more incensed by the idea of a charity set up specifically to help single parents. But as a result of Derek successfully persuading the local authority to pull its funding, Patricia had to close the charity. For a period, at least."

Ray was desperate to pitch in to the conversation, to be more of a presence in the room, to interact directly with Adam Jaymes. He had been waiting for a lull in the conversation, a moment when he could say something insightful, or ask a useful question. And the moment Valerie had finished speaking, he quickly jumped in. "And Jason?" he said. And then forgot what else he was going to say. Instead, he looked at Adam and nodded at him, earnestly, as though he had just made an important and salient point.

Adam smiled, politely, and nodded. "I think most of what Jason did to Pearl came out in the court case," he said. "Abusing her in street to make her cry, taking photographs up her dress at awards ceremonies. To be honest, if the link is Pearl, I would have been surprised if Jason had not been one of the victims."

As he spoke, Adam's eyes wandered from Ray to Valerie, who could instantly feel an accusation in his gaze, as though she were in some way culpable for the way Jason Spade had treated Pearl. Valerie had mentioned Jason in her book, but only briefly. She had covered some of the complaints against him over the years, including what she had described as his 'ongoing feud' with Pearl Martin. And she had also alluded to her personal shock at the nature of those photographs which had ultimately sent him to jail.

But the section about Jason had been necessarily short and to the point. Valerie had always distanced herself from his work, the one part of the operations of the *Daily Ear* she had never felt truly comfortable knowing about. She was aware of the hundreds, possibly thousands, of complaints that had been made against him over the years, the vast majority from female celebrities who had accused him of perverse or threatening behaviour.

But, in her mind, she had always countered these complaints with the knowledge that the senior team at the paper had placed enormous pressure on Jason to keep feeding their readers' enormous appetite for explicit and salacious images. As much as the public had screamed in fury at Jason Spade, they had also rushed out in their millions to buy the *Daily Ear* each day, to see the pictures he had taken. And as much of a monster she knew most people had considered Jason to be, she had struggled to see him as anything other than a lonely, angry little fat boy, who had called her for help just days earlier, only to have Valerie hang up on him.

"It does make some sense," Alice said. "Horrible though it is. It does all make sense." And then her heart sank, as she remembered how very cruel her own mother had been to Pearl Martin. And it dawned on her that if someone was indeed killing to avenge Pearl, then Valerie Peirce would most certainly be on the killer's hit list. She looked over at her mother, her face suddenly drained of colour. "Oh, but mum…" she said, softly.

Valerie knew what her daughter was about to say, and simply did not have the strength for such a conversation. And so, with a show of great bravado, she sighed, stubbed out her cigarette butt in the glass ashtray on the occasional table next to her and then lit herself another. "OK, so let's say this is true," she said, projecting a tone which indicated she was still unconvinced. "Let us say there is a serial killer, because that is what we are talking about; a serial killer. Someone who is murdering people because they committed some offense against Pearl Martin. Who on earth would be doing this? And why now, all these years after Pearl died?"

"With respect Valerie," Adam replied, curtly, "this all came from you in the first place. You came to me. Remember? You were the one claiming there was a serial killer at large."

"And I stand by that," Valerie retorted. "But if Pearl is the link, then who is the killer?" She paused and waited, to see if Adam could offer any suggestions.

But Adam could only shake his head despondently. "There was only one I could think of," he said, quietly. "But he died. Years ago. And so, at the moment, my answer is that I don't know."

"Who?" Alice asked, "Who was it that died?"

Adam did not respond. It was as though he did not want to say the name out loud, a horrible chapter of Pearl's life he wanted to leave well forgotten.

But Valerie realised who he was speaking about. "Stone," she interjected, a long-lost memory suddenly crystal clear in her mind once more. "Guy Stone. Pearl Martin's stalker. Oh, dear lord yes." She turned to Alice and Ray: "An absolute loon," she said, and momentarily crossed her eyes. "But, as Adam said, long since dead. Thank goodness."

Alice and Ray looked at each other, nonplussed, and then both looked back to Adam for an explanation.

"He was just a fan of the show, at first," Adam said, a grave expression on his face. "But as Pearl become more famous, she became his obsession. He decided they were in love, that they should be together. But he was clever, too. Really clever. He kept finding out information about Pearl. We had no idea how he did it, but he knew where she was going to be, who with, what she was spending her money on, who she had spoken to.

"Pearl was terrified. Wherever she went, there he was. He just appeared out of the blue. Once she was in a restaurant, in Florida, and he suddenly appeared at the table next to her. He had tracked her four thousand miles across the Atlantic. He had ordered flowers and champagne for her table. He honestly thought it was a romantic gesture. Pearl kept going to the police, she took out injunctions. She even sent him to prison a couple of times. This went on for years. Nothing stopped him."

"But he's dead?" Alice asked.

"Yes dear," Valerie said. "Killed himself. Not long after Pearl's suicide. A blessed relief for everyone, including his own family, I would imagine."

There was a moment when no one spoke, the only sound was from Valerie drawing on her cigarette. Ray was desperate for Adam to stay, for the conversation to move on to lighter matters, something fun and frivolous. And so, he offered to make everyone a cup of tea, in the hope of prolonging Adam's visit, but to his disappointment Adam declined and said it was time that he left.

"I just wanted to check we were all on the same page," Adam said. And then, he turned to Valerie and said: "You were right, Valerie. All along. And I am sorry I doubted you, that first night, at the restaurant. But going forward, we need to work together to expose who is doing this and stop them." With that, he stood and asked Valerie to walk him to the door.

He said goodbye to Alice and Ray and left them both with a request that, for the time being, neither could tell a soul about his visit to Valerie's house that morning. They both agreed, although Ray was particularly crestfallen as he had hoped for a selfie with Adam to upload to his social media.

As Valerie and Adam arrived at the front door, the entrance hall dark apart from a dim glow from the porch light outside, Valerie felt the need to say something gracious, if only because she was so relieved that Adam was now fully on board with her suspicions. "I should thank you for coming here this morning, to speak to me face-to-face," she said, "rather than over the phone or by text. It was gentlemanly of you. I appreciate that."

Adam slipped into his jacket and donned his cap. "And I'm sorry I haven't been in touch before now," he said. "I had to get a lot of things in place. But my team is back online again, and they are already delivering results. I am hoping we will have a shortlist of suspects relatively quickly."

Valerie shook her head. "I feel like we are doing the job of the police for them," she said, despondently. "It just beggars' belief they are still not connecting the dots. That it's down to people like us to solve a series of murders."

Adam reached for the latch but didn't lever it. "Perhaps that's for the best," he said, quietly.

Valerie was surprised by the comment, and waited for Adam to elaborate, to explain what he had meant. There remained an uneasiness in their alliance, and she could tell Adam was struggling to find a balance between the information he had to share with Valerie and the information he could legitimately withhold.

After a moment of thought, Adam spoke. "Someone broke into… a storage unit I own." He then he stepped back from the door and looked Valerie in the face. "I own a small industrial unit in Suffolk. It was the base for my Project Ear team four years ago. But when that particular project was over, I closed it down and locked it up. It was completely secure. No one could possibly get inside."

Valerie nodded, guessing exactly where Adam's story was about to go. "But someone did get inside," she said. It was slightly perturbing to hear Adam finally reveal some details of how he had delivered his 'Project Ear' campaign, how he had almost destroyed Valerie's career and brought the *Daily Ear* to its knees. But whilst she had a morbid fascination for the details, in that moment she was more concerned as to why Adam seemed happy for the police to continue ignoring the deaths of people connected to the *Daily Ear*.

Adam sighed, deeply. "You have to understand, Valerie," he said, "that when I was in the middle of Project Ear, my team uncovered a lot more about your colleagues than I ever made public. There were other scandals, dozens of other scandals, which never saw the light of day."

Valerie crossed her arms and leaned back against the wall. "I see," she said. "Adam, it sounds very much to me as though you were keeping some things in your back pocket, in case you ever felt a need to launch 'Project Ear part 2'." Adam did not reply, and Valerie took his reticence as a sign she was correct. "And then, someone broke in?" she asked.

Adam nodded. "I went there a couple of days ago to find some materials I wanted to review. And someone had been inside. They didn't appear to have taken anything but, whoever it was, they left something behind. Something they wanted me to find."

He reached into his jacket pocket, and retrieved a piece of glossy paper, folded in two. He opened it to reveal a black and white photograph, an image of Adam and Beth eating dinner in what appeared to be a private hotel suite.

"This would have been taken through the hotel window, from a building across the road," Adam said. "This was Beth's birthday, only a month ago, so it's relatively recent."

Valerie looked at the image; two people happily chatting with each other, without a care in the world, not realising their great secret had been uncovered. "But why would they leave this?" she asked.

Adam folded the photograph and placed it back in his pocket. "I think it is a warning," he said. "Whoever is doing this wanted to tell me that they know who Beth is."

Valerie stopped leaning against the wall and stood up straight once more. "Surely they wouldn't target Beth. If they really are obsessed with Pearl Martin, they would consider her daughter sacrosanct."

Adam nodded. "I think so too," he said. "I sent her away, all the same. And her parents. Abroad. So, I know they are safe. But I need to know who this is. Valerie, it was bad enough when I found out that you had uncovered Beth's identity. But this... a serial killer? That frightens me."

Valerie shrugged. "Adam, I don't know what advice to give you," she said. "But whoever is doing this, they're not exactly functioning on a normal level. It's not as if you could have a sane conversation with them, politely ask them to keep schtum about Beth. You have to prepare for the very real possibility that when the police finally capture this person, all of this might come out in court. Where Beth has been all these years, who she is. And no one would be able to stop that. Not even you."

And then Valerie saw an expression on Adam's handsome face that, for a moment, made her blood run cold. Suddenly his deep brown eyes looked almost black, and his brow furrowed, as though he were considering the darkest of choices. And then, without looking at Valerie again, he opened the door and stepped outside. "I'll be in touch as soon as I have anything," he said, and then strode up the path, a car waiting for him on the road outside.

As Valerie closed her front door and secured all the bolts, she pondered that final exchange with Adam, and she wondered just how far he was willing to go to protect the identity of Pearl Martin's daughter. She took a moment to collect her thoughts, and then returned to her lounge to find Ray and Alice in a loud state of euphoria, unable to believe that they had actually just met *the* Adam Jaymes.

"Well, that's reassuring," Alice said, brightly. "We've got Adam Jaymes on side."

Valerie feigned a smile, and then sat down again. "But I'm not going to sit on my hands, waiting for his secret team to tell us what is going on," she said. "I'm a journalist, for God's sake. A successful, award-winning journalist. I'm Woman of the Year," she said, proudly. "And I will not sit here and wait. I should be investigating this myself."

Ray immediately shook his head. "Val, no, no," he said. "Come on, this is too dangerous. People are being killed. We should leave this to Adam and his people. Or at least go and see the police again, try and get them to review all these deaths. There are five of them now. They cannot still pretend none of them are linked."

Valerie lit another cigarette and quietly replayed in her head the conversation they had just had with Adam Jaymes. And then it occurred to her that perhaps he had been right, and that perhaps the connection between all the murders was Pearl Martin. And if that were the case, she realised who she should speak to first, someone who knew more about the life of Pearl Martin than anyone else.

"Ray, darling," Valerie said, "would you very much mind driving me into London today?"

CHAPTER 34

Lucy was alone in her office, sat quietly in front of her laptop. She had been staring at the screen for more than an hour, which was displaying a story from the BBC News website about Steve Gallant. She had found herself unable to withdraw, to look away from his photograph and the story's headline: 'Gallant killed in warehouse accident.'

> Police believe Gallant, 48, entered the abandoned sawmill by mistake, believing it to be a side entrance to the SM Club and Private Rooms, a new club which was celebrating its opening night. It is understood he suffered fatal injuries from the rotating blade of a large circular saw, and police are looking into the possibility he fell onto the blade after accidentally switching it on.

It was all so dark, so gruesome. The complete polar opposite of Steve and his silly, colourful life. And Lucy simply could not marry the two images; Steve, bright funny and alive – and the lonely, horrific way he had met his death. It sat with her, a gnawing disbelief in the pit of her stomach, leaving her feeling empty and unable to cry.

Lucy had spent most of the day blissfully unaware of what had happened to Steve, following a conscious decision to avoid the news. She had not wished to see any celebratory articles about either Marilyn Murphy or Valerie Pierce. She had left the awards ceremony shortly after her conversation with Valerie: that devastating moment when she had been told so cheerfully that not only had she not won the award but that she had not even made the shortlist.

That moment, that exact moment, had played repeatedly in her head. It had been Valerie Pierce – Valerie *bloody* Pierce – who had delivered the news. Humiliated and angry, she had returned home and taken to Twitter where she had posted a series of claims about the event. What better way to explain her omission from the awards than to undermine the integrity of the whole selection process?

And so, she had dismissed the judging panel as frauds, and claimed her exclusion from the shortlist, and Marilyn's win, had been at Valerie's behest. Valerie, she said, had bragged about it to her face. The only small glimmer of pleasure in Lucy's world, during those solitary, angry late hours, had been Valerie's astonishing behaviour on stage and her quivering screams to the audience about mobile phones. And so in between clearing cupboards and cooking, Lucy had tweeted regularly about that too. She had repeatedly shared the YouTube link of Valerie's bizarre speech and attempted to make the hashtag #ValeriePierceIsAMadOldHag trend.

Lucy had initially decided she would work from home that day, unable to face any of her colleagues. They all knew she had fully expected to return to the office with an award. She had been so sure of her win that she had even planned her entrance; she had intended to walk through the busy newsroom with her bag over her shoulder and the trophy conspicuously poking out at the top. She had wanted everyone to know that she had won, but also for them all to believe that she was incredibly blasé about the whole thing, as though she was just going to stick the award on a shelf in her office and forget about it.

However, with no award to parade through the office, and the crushing embarrassment that came with that loss, she had not wanted to see any of her colleagues. But then she had received an unexpected summons from Sydney, and it was only on her arrival at the *Daily Ear* building that Lucy had discovered the shocking news about Steve.

Sydney had asked to see her privately, to check how she was doing, and if she needed any help or support. But she doubted it was going to be a sincere expression of concern for her wellbeing. More an exercise in due diligence. She knew Sydney, like her, found the modern obsession with compassionate workplaces to be unnecessary and distracting. But she also knew he would need to ensure all the right boxes had been ticked.

And so, she closed her laptop, took a deep breath and then headed to the editor's office. On her arrival, Sydney said all the right things; it was shocking news, he wanted to see how she was, and did she need any support. And then, as Lucy sat down, he retrieved a large Manila envelope from a drawer, placed it onto his desk and slid it across to her.

"What is it?" she asked.

"It's a legal document," he replied. "Lucy, it's a severance package for Steve. I was going to fire him today."

Lucy pushed the unopened envelope back across the desk and scowled at her boss. "What the fuck, Sydney?" she asked. "Do you think that's funny?"

"No, no, not funny," he said. "A reminder of your generosity towards Steve. One of my predecessors had this ready for him a year ago. It has been revised and prepared ready for him on a monthly basis since. But you always convinced the people in charge, including most recently me, to keep him on, give him another chance. If not for you, Steve would have been long gone from the *Daily Ear*. You were a good friend to him. Very likely his last actual friend. And we are all sorry for your loss."

Lucy was not in the mood for Sydney's rather ham-fisted attempt at a compliment, and so she chose to change the subject. "There seems to have been a lot of deaths recently," she said.

"Well, these things happen in cycles," Sydney replied, sounding like a world-weary old man. "Look how many famous people have died this year alone. It's like 2016 is cursed. Our obituaries department has been run ragged."

Sydney appeared to acknowledge that Lucy was not in a chatty mood and so kindly offered her an easy exit from the conversation. "Just keep doing a good job, Lucy," he said, "and don't adopt any more charity cases."

Lucy left the editor's office and slowly made her way back to her own. She did not like it when people accused her of being kind, or thoughtful, or charitable. It wasn't on-brand. Typically, she would have happily dismissed such an opinion directly into the face of the person who had offered it. But Sydney was one of the very few people she had never felt any authority over.

With his predecessors, there had always been an imbalance of power that sat clearly in Lucy's favour. She had been directly appointed by the owner, and her angry weekly rants had struck a chord with the *Daily Ear*'s readers and influenced the entire content of the paper going forward. As far as the *Daily Ear* was concerned, Lucy appeared irreplaceable, and she made certain each successive editor had known that.

But with Sydney, things were different. He had the air of someone who had been everywhere, seen everything and knew where the bodies were buried. He was utterly unimpressed with everyone and failed to show any excitement, even when the *Daily Ear* had a major exclusive. And though he claimed to hate every second of being the paper's editor, he was widely considered its most competent leader since the days of the much-revered Leonard Twigg.

Lucy had no power over Sydney because he, too, had become irreplaceable. Moreover, whilst Lucy would fight tooth and nail to keep her job at the Ear, Sydney planned to retire as soon he could get the owner to agree his exit package. But she knew there was some sort of issue with the pension scheme for long-serving staff, and as a result the likes of Sydney Corrigan had seen their retirement continuously pushed back. Much to Sydney's deep frustration. And it was that perplexing combination of amazing talent mixed with a complete lack of commitment that made it impossible for Lucy not to respect him.

It was also that begrudging respect that meant Sydney's words, his opinions, always resonated with her; the idea that she was, perhaps, off her game because she had allowed herself to be distracted from her core purpose by mundane interruptions, including Steve's failing career.

She reached her office, shut the door, and stood quietly for a moment, her eyes closed, and her head bowed. Still, a well of emptiness sat inside her. There were no tears to be cried, no screams or howls of anguish. All she could feel, all she could allow herself to feel, was a grinding disappointment with Steve. He appeared to have ignored her advice and instead chased one last, big exclusive, and that had been his undoing.

"Well, that's that," she muttered to herself, and tried to convince herself she had drawn a line under the matter once and for all and could now get on with the rest of her day without distraction.

She returned to her desk, opened her laptop and closed all the screens that related to news articles about Steve's death. Lucy needed to focus on her column for the following week. She would deliver a loud, inflammatory article to remind the world that, like it or not, she could still set the narrative for every conversation in the land.

She had already decided that her main focus would be on 'women's spaces'. It was the sort of topic she would usually call feminist claptrap and chuck straight in the bin. But a few weeks earlier, she had confronted someone in a women's bathroom at the *Daily Ear* offices and told them they should not be there. Lucy had realised straight away that it had not been a man, but a woman who identified as butch lesbian. However, it had still annoyed her that a woman who presented herself in such a masculine way should believe she could still use the ladies' loo. And so, she had accused the woman of being a man and then asked her to leave.

To Lucy's great annoyance, the woman had turned out to be incredibly calm and articulate, quickly and efficiently putting Lucy in her place before continuing to use the facilities. Worse still, the woman had then raised the issue as a complaint with the HR department, and Lucy had been sent a letter reminding her of the company's equality and diversity policies.

And whilst Lucy had to concede she had lost that battle, she was most certainly not going to lose the war.

She had tested the waters on social media, sharing a twisted version of what had happed. She had transplanted the incident into the ladies' loo at a restaurant and presented the other person as most definitely a "man in a frock". She had also written as though she had been frightened and intimidated by their presence, and that she had simply been attempting to use the facilities when the other person had started to abuse her.

She had used the phrase 'women's hard-fought sex-based rights'. She wasn't entirely sure what it meant, but during a quick piece of research she had seen it repeated across a number of online chatrooms and decided it sounded intellectual. And she thought it would also likely prove a useful dog whistle to draw attention to her tweets.

And although she had received the usual abuse and anger for her opinions, she quickly found support too; a small but loud group of anonymous trolls, angry people from either side of the political spectrum, whose profiles described them as either anti-woke, flag waving Tories or far-left feminists. It was an odd mix, Lucy had thought, individuals she would normally expect to have completely opposing views on almost everything. And she took it as having been something of a personal achievement to have somehow united such disparate groups through a mutual hatred of trans people.

With the issue successfully tested on social media, she knew that was her article for the week. She quickly came up with a suggested headline for the sub-editors; "It's time women were heard. Keep pervert cross-dressing men out of our bathrooms." And after that, the article pretty much wrote itself.

Lucy knew it didn't take much thought or skill to fashion a piece based entirely on untruths that would feed into the natural bigotry of *Daily Ear* readers. She had already successfully led the country back to the sort of casual racism and homophobia most believed had been left in the past. With great ease and little prompting, Lucy had been able to turn that clock back decades, to tell *Daily Ear* readers it was OK to say those hateful things out loud again. It was freedom of speech, she told them. A middle finger in the face of political correctness and insipid do-gooders everywhere.

And, oh, how grateful her readers had been for it. To be told, instructed almost, that they could say the unsayable once more. For them, it was like every Christmas had come at once: immigrants were cockroaches and spongers, Gay men were perverts who were corrupting the nation's children and confusing them on the topic of gender, black families offered unstable, typically fatherless environments for children, the disabled had too many rights and every Muslim harboured a secret terrorist agenda. It was a catalogue of hateful, forgotten language that Lucy had pushed back into the British way of life. And her readers adored her for it.

Whenever she was challenged and asked to evidence her weekly rants, she would argue she was simply repeating what normal, decent and concerned British citizens were saying. "I don't just spout this stuff," she had argued, on more than one occasion. "I choose my words carefully. Every single word I use is chosen very specifically and I stand by everything I say."

In truth, Lucy knew her words were rarely carefully chosen. Her tirades were always written quickly and angrily and pushed to the sub-editors without a second thought. The subs would then have to unpick her meandering copy, painstakingly correct her grammar and attempt to bring some sense of clear narrative to whichever topic she had focussed on that week. It was a process that had worked, but perhaps too well. Lucy had fallen into a cycle of raised expectations; every week she needed to up the ante once more.

And although she knew her attack on Trans people would land well with her readers that week, her thoughts were already on the following week, and what she could write about.

Her laptop chimed, announcing the arrival of a message. She opened her inbox and watched as all her emails dropped down a place to make way for a new arrival: "*please read: illegal immigrants, east coast.*"

"Oh!" Lucy said, immediately attracted by the potentially racist undertones of the email's subject line.

"*Lucy. A contact passed your details to me. Said you were looking into illegal immigration routes into the UK. I work at a marina in Suffolk. It's worth a visit. I just need to speak to a few other contacts and then will be able to give you an exact time and place. I will be in touch.*"

"Gotcha!" Lucy said, and grinned from ear to ear.

CHAPTER 35

"I see you've given your staff the day off again," Adam said, looking around the empty space. "I'm beginning to wonder if anyone else really works here at all."

Patricia locked the door to her office. "It's called flexible working, Adam," she replied, coldly, and began to switch off the lights in the main room. She was obviously shutting the office down and getting ready to go home.

Adam felt unwelcome, as though Patricia was going to leave regardless of his unexpected visit. "So, you've been keeping track of what's been going on with the *Daily Ear*?" he asked, casually.

Patricia stopped what she was doing and looked him straight in the eyes. "Seriously?" she said, and then with a frustrated tone added: "Are you still caught up in that mad old bag's delusional ideas about serial killers? Adam, seriously, what has happened to that *famous intellect* of yours?"

Adam could tell Patricia would have loved to put air brackets around the words 'famous intellect' and was surprised she had shown enough restraint not to. He had noticed that each time he saw her, particularly of late, the pleasantries and pretence of friendship lessened. His sudden and unforgiveable involvement with Valerie Pierce seemed to have been the final straw.

But he wasn't there for idle chit-chat. He was there for information and so pulled a chair from one of the desks and sat down. "Five deaths in less than two weeks," he said, "every three days. At 9pm on the dot. That's not a coincidence, Patricia. With all due respect, you don't need a 'famous intellect' to see there is a pattern. You just need common sense."

Patricia threw Adam a glare, clearly unhappy at the tone he was using. She showed no signs of sitting with him. Instead, she stood with her arms folded, a disapproving scowl on her face. "I expect, then, Adam, that the police are all over this. I expect it is a matter of public record that a serial killer is at large. Is that the case?"

Adam did not reply. Instead, he sat back in his seat and stared at Patricia with a perplexed expression, unable to understand why she was so closed to the discussion.

"And for the record," she continued, "I *have* kept abreast of the events, if only to celebrate the death of every single one of those bastards who made my sister's life so miserable. And you are wrong. There is no pattern. There is no way you can say they all died at exactly 9pm. There is no way you can even say a single one of them was murdered. They just died. People do that, Adam. So why don't you just stop this bullshit and go home to America. Those of us who chose to continue living in this shithole of a country have our own lives to lead. And some of us are too busy to get involved in nonsense like this."

Adam shook his head. "It's not nonsense," he replied, quietly. "Patricia I am sorry, but it's not. Valerie Pierce was right all along. These deaths are linked. They *are* murders. And you and I are right at the heart of it all."

Undeterred, Patricia put on her coat. "You know, I do sometimes wonder, Adam, if taking that part on *Doctor Who* was good for you," she said. "Monsters in every shadow, an alien conspiracy behind every unexplained event. I cannot help but think it affected your perception of reality."

Before Adam could respond, the door alarm buzzed, and Patricia suddenly shot across the room to deal with it. There was a panel on the wall with a small video screen that would typically show who was at the front door. But Patricia was typing aggressively on the keypad and the screen remained blank. "Oh, for God's sake," she said, "I completely forgot I have a delivery." She fiddled with the controls for a moment, as though seeing them for the first time. "I can never get the hang of this bloody thing," she muttered, and then pressed a button and held it in place. "This is Pat," she said, loudly. "I'm in a meeting so just leave the delivery behind reception. I'll sign for it online. Thank you." And then she pressed another button and waited long enough for whoever was at the door to enter the building.

"This is what I mean," she said, turning to Adam. "Real fucking life. Being busy, and relied on, and having responsibilities. And bills to pay. And services to provide. And deliveries to arrange."

* * *

And then with an unexpected shift in her manner, adopting a gentler tone, she added: "Adam, I know how much you loved Pearl. And believe me, she knew. She absolutely knew how much you loved her. But I also know how much you wish I was more *like* her. But I'm not. I am my own person. And the simple truth, Adam, is that you and I are *not* family and we are not friends. We never have been. We just have people in common. We have a history. But that is all, and I wish you would accept that. I wish you would stop coming to see me, hoping to get some sort of 'Pearl Martin' fix just because I look like her."

All of Adam's words simply vanished. In that moment, all the times he had visited Patricia over the years, his countless attempts to develop some sort of relationship with her, turned to dust. And there was a part of him that ached, as though he had just lost his dearest friend all over again. He looked to the floor and wished it would simply open up and swallow him so he would not need to look at Patricia before he left.

"I promise you," she said, softly. "I am not saying any of this to hurt you. I just want you to stop coming here. To be honest, Adam, I just don't want to see you again."

Adam knew it was time to leave but he was struggling to lift his head, to face Patricia and admit she was right. But then a voice filled the air. A familiar voice, but one that should most definitely never be heard in the same room as Pearl Martin's sister: "Well, Adam. It looks like we both had the same idea."

As Adam looked up, the first thing he saw was Patricia's expression, twisted with anger and surprise. And then he turned to the door where Valerie Pierce was stood with her hands on her hips, impeccably dressed in a stylish raincoat and matching boots. And smiling, as though extremely pleased with herself.

Ray hated driving in London. He hated the narrow roads, the endless junctions, the buses, the taxi drivers, the cyclists – particularly the cyclists – and the aggressive behaviour of other motorists. Life had become much easier since he had bought a decent sat-nav, which had made it less stressful to circumnavigate the busy city streets. But it was still something he would rather not be doing.

He had dropped Valerie at the building she had given him the address for and waited, briefly, on a double yellow until she had been safely buzzed inside. He had no idea how long she would be but had been asked to stay close by so as not to leave her stranded on the pavement once her meeting had concluded. And so, he had started to circle the block, finding nowhere in the immediate vicinity where he could park.

As he turned back into the road for the third time, he could see Valerie had still not returned to the pavement and so hoped her meeting, whoever it was with, was proving productive. The traffic lights outside the building turned red, and Ray sat at the wheel and watched as a small group of people hurried from the nearby street and crossed the road, clinging together to shield themselves from the wind and rain. There were about a dozen of them, mostly young, laughing and chatting without a care in the world, enjoying a day out in the city, albeit a cold, wet day out.

But as the group hurried to the pavement on the other side of the road, one was left behind. A lone figure, wearing jeans and trainers and a top with a low hanging hood, who remained on the crossing immediately in front of Ray's car. And for a moment, an undeniably odd moment, the figure stood completely still, as though pondering what to do next.

"Go on," Ray said, somewhat frustrated by the entire day. "Keep going, sweetie. The lights are about to change."

But then the figure turned, ever so slightly, and Ray's heart skipped a beat as he caught a glimpse of the peculiar face concealed beneath the dark shadow of the hood. It was a face with almost no features, with skin so pale it was almost translucent and two deep blue eyes that stared directly at him. Ray felt he had been recognised, perhaps even acknowledged. But his time on *Big Brother* had given him a certain level of fame, and he was frequently recognised whilst out and about.

"Yeah, yeah," he muttered to himself. "It's me off the telly." He suddenly felt a little ashamed that he had found the stranger's face so disconcerting and wondered if he should wind down his window and offer an autograph or a selfie.

But then the figure turned around and hurried away from the pedestrian crossing and back to the narrow street the group had originally come from. Ray watched, somewhat baffled by the incident. It was as if the lone figure had never been a part of that group and had simply joined it at some point; using a dozen happy day-trippers as some sort of camouflage, a way of crossing the road unseen and unnoticed.

But Ray had somehow provided an unexpected stumbling block. His presence, simply sat in a car at a pedestrian crossing, had been enough for the hooded stranger to lose purpose and be left with no option but to rush away in the opposite direction.

"I've said it before and I'll say it again," he said to himself, "this city is full of freaks."

The traffic lights turned green and Ray continued his journey, ready to circle the block until Valerie had completed her meeting.

For a moment, it was as if time had stopped. Valerie was stood in the doorway, smiling as though oblivious to the extremely cold welcome she had received. Patricia, by comparison, wore an expression that was halfway between confusion and anger. She appeared so perplexed by Valerie's audacious entrance that she had been momentarily robbed of the ability to speak. And Adam Jaymes was stood between them, if only to create a physical barrier in case Patricia attempted to reach out to strike Valerie.

Eventually, Patricia was able to articulate her feelings. "How dare you," she said, her voice deep and quiet, a tone that alluded to an anger that had sat within her for many years. "How dare you come here."

"Desperate times, Patricia," Valerie replied. "It is, in fact, quite literally a matter of life or death."

Valerie spoke with a casual familiarity that Adam found quite perplexing. "Valerie, this isn't appropriate," he interceded, hoping to swiftly conclude the conversation and lead Valerie from the building before she caused any further damage to his relationship with Patricia. He gestured to take Valerie's arm, but she gently flicked his hand away.

"Then why buzz me in?" Valerie asked. She took a seat, crossed her legs and began to remove her gloves, clearly making herself at home.

"I didn't know it was you," Patricia replied. "Believe me, if I had known, that door would have remained firmly closed."

"Valerie let's go outside and talk," Adam said.

Valerie raised her hand. "Adam, dear, it obviously isn't you I came to see," she said. She then fixed her gaze on Patricia and smiled at her. "I came to see Patricia," she said, lightly, "and I am not leaving until we have spoken."

Despite Valerie's friendly countenance, it was obvious to Adam that Patricia's anger was not fading. "I don't know how you have the gall to come here," Patricia said. "To think any member of Pearl's family would want to see you, speak with you, after everything you did to her."

Adam knew that, over the years, Valerie and her colleagues at the *Daily Ear* had been blamed or implicated in Pearl Martin's suicide many times and by many people. And Patricia had been one of her most vocal accusers.

"We all have our crosses to bear, Patricia," Valerie said, with an oddly glib tone that Adam found puzzling. "But people are dying," she continued. "Right here, right now. And it occurred to me that you might hold the key."

With those unexpected words, Adam turned to face Valerie full on and shook his head. "Valerie, what on earth are you talking about?" he asked, both exasperated and baffled. "How on earth would Patricia know anything about this?"

Valerie did not like speaking to Patricia through Adam, and so looked at Patricia with the air of someone who was in complete control of the proceedings and who was not going anywhere until she had some answers. "Guy Stone," she said and then raised her brow, as though she had proven a point.

Adam watched, unsure of how events would unfold. In that moment he could only see two outcomes; either Patricia would slap Valerie, or she would tolerate a brief conversation if only to take the opportunity to tell Valerie exactly what she thought of her.

But he was proven wrong. With unexpected calm, Patricia sat down opposite Valerie and then quietly spoke. "My late sister's dead stalker," she said. "Please tell me, Valerie, why you wish to speak to me about him. Why you want me to relive those years of absolute hell."

"Because as much as I hate to admit it, I think Adam was right," Valerie replied. "When all of this started, I thought someone was targeting people connected with the *Daily Ear*. But Adam suggested the connection was far more particular, that this *someone* is targeting people who had in some way offended your sister, either during her lifetime, or since her death."

Patricia glanced towards Adam, and he felt as though her eyes were coldly taking a measure of him, assessing how deeply embedded he had become with the enemy. And he suddenly felt the need for full disclosure, to reassure Patricia that he had nothing to hide, had done nothing wrong.

"If we have linked these deaths correctly, Patricia," he said, quietly, "there is a killer who is showing all the signs of having been obsessed with Pearl. With her memory. Someone who believes they are showing their love for her, their undying love for her, by seeking revenge, all these years later. On anyone who wronged her either during her life, or in the years since she died."

Valerie and Adam looked to each other, to acknowledge their consensus on what had been said, and then they both looked to Patricia to see how she would respond. And after a moment, she sighed loudly and sank into her seat as though defeated.

"You're still going with this serial killer nonsense?" she asked, "and are now assuming it's one of Pearl's stalkers?"

"So, there were others?" Valerie asked, attempting to stifle a triumphant tone in her voice that would suggest she had been proven right.

"Oh my God, Valerie, of course there were," Patricia replied. "You know this. You *must* know this. For pity's sake, look it up on Wikipedia. There's probably an entire page dedicated to Pearl's legion of fucking stalkers."

Suddenly Patricia's expression and tone changed once more, reverting from indifference back to accusatory. "And when you do look it up, Valerie, just remember the role you played in creating that level of fanaticism towards my sister. You and your friends at the *Daily Ear*. It was *your* obsession with Pearl, the endless stories and photographs. You created Guy Stone. You created the others too. Every single one of them was created by you and your rancid colleagues."

"Honestly, Patricia," Valerie said, a lightness in her voice that belied the hostile nature of the conversation, "is there anything you don't blame me for? Like it or not, your sister made a choice to become an actor, and a choice to take a role in a big TV show. I did not make Pearl Martin famous. That was something she did herself. And unfortunately, as we know, people in the public eye can attract all sorts of lunatics and undesirables."

The room fell silent and Valerie's comment was left hanging in the air. Adam remained puzzled by her overly familiar behaviour towards Patricia and wondered if it was a poorly judged tactic; an attempt to lighten what was always going to be a challenging meeting. "I think we have our answer," he said, and gestured to take Valerie's hand. "We need to go."

And when Valerie accepted his hand and stood with him, Adam knew in his heart that Patricia would have seen that gesture as proof that he had chosen a side. Quietly, he and Valerie left the office and walked down the stairs back to the front door.

"What was all that about?" he asked, trying to prevent his frustration from becoming too pronounced. "All that between you and Patricia? You were clearly baiting her."

Valerie spotted Ray driving towards her and waved him down, clearly uninterested in debating her behaviour with Adam. "I was perfectly polite," she said, "and at the very least, Patricia has confirmed that Guy Stone was not Pearl's only obsessed fan."

Adam sighed. "Yes, but we already knew that. There was absolutely no need for you to come here today. If I hadn't been here…"

Valerie smiled at him. "Oh, Adam, I promise you. If you hadn't been here, I would have had an entirely different conversation with Patricia. Now, what next? I'm not going to have you vanish on me again."

Adam nodded. "I'll get my team to look into it," he said. "We'll get a list, see who's still alive, who's not in jail. Perhaps one of your police contacts might consider looking into it if we do the groundwork?"

"Fine," Valerie said. "And I will do a little investigating of my own. You need to remember, Adam, I am a journalist too. I have my own skills and contacts. And I need to start putting them to good use."

As they stepped onto the pavement, Ray pulled up next to them. "May I offer you a lift?" Valerie asked, "I'm sure Ray would be thrilled to drive you pretty much anywhere you wanted to go."

But Adam had already donned his hat and glasses, his low-key disguise for walks through the streets of London. "I'm good," he said, "but I'll stay in touch." And then he left.

Valerie climbed into the car, knowing the journey home would now be one long whinge from Ray that she should have done more to convince Adam to accept the offer of a lift.

CHAPTER 36

"I don't understand what I am looking at," DI Price said, making very little effort to conceal the irritation in her voice. It was only 10am and she had already had to deal with a plethora of complaints and accusations ranging from institutional racism to financial misconduct. She had even had to deal with a reporter from the *Daily Ear* demanding she explain why police officers were allowed time to take part in the annual London Pride parade, rather than keeping to their normal duties.

Detective Constables Barnet and Sly were not her favourite officers, either, having proven themselves to be deeply incompetent and generally quite irritating on more than one occasion. But they had assured her they had uncovered something concerning about the night Steve Gallant had died and wanted to share it with her.

"It looks like Facebook," she said, staring at the computer monitor, and shrugging. "Why are you showing me Facebook?"

"It's a page that's been set up by the SM Club and Private Rooms," Sly responded, moving the mouse slightly to scroll up and down on the page. "These are pictures that have been posted by people who had tickets for the opening night."

"The night Steve Gallant was killed," Barnet added, attempting to punctuate the conversation with some gravitas.

DI Price nodded. "And is he in some of the pictures?" she asked.

"No, he's not," Sly replied, "but my son was on this page last night, and he showed me something he thought was a bit... well... creepy." The officer isolated one of the pictures, a selfie taken by a young woman surrounded by friends, all laughing and smiling at the camera. "This one was taken at the junction with Sawmill Alley. You can see down the alley, just a little, over the girl's shoulder. And if I zoom in a bit...."

DI Price watched as a detail in the background become enlarged, clearer; a lone figure dressed entirely in gold, wearing some kind of face mask or helmet, and standing at what appeared to be the entrance to another club. "And that is?" she asked.

"That," Sly replied, "is the entrance to the wrong building. That is the wrong turn Steve Gallant took that night."

"We had been working under the assumption that he had been turned away from the main entrance and tried to find a back door," Barnet added. "But this looks like someone had set up an entirely separate VIP entrance. We've checked with the club and this was nothing to do with them. And none of the buildings down that alley are in use. They are all abandoned."

"One of those illegal one-off raves?" DI Price asked.

"We don't think so," Sly responded.

DI Price was unhappy. Her constables were bringing a problem to her, a suggestion that a simple industrial accident might have actually been something far worse, something planned. But she also knew that if there was something unexplained about the gruesome death of Steve Gallant, she would need to make sure it was resolved.

"Visit the scene again," she said. "Take some pictures of your own, and make sure you are certain that's the door Gallant used to enter the building. And then have another look around inside." She went to leave, but then noticed her two officers were exchanging looks, as though they were plucking up the courage to tell her something else. "What?" she asked.

"There's one other thing, and it may be connected," Sly said. "The post-mortem examination on Jason Spade. There was a toxin, in his blood. They've not identified it yet, but it does seem as though it was not a simple heart attack. More likely he ingested something that caused his death. A poison."

DI Price shrugged. "So, a suicide rather than heart failure," she replied, with a tone that indicated the matter was concluded. "To be clear, I want your focus to be on the nightclub, and what happened down that alley." She pointed at the image on the computer monitor, a ghostly golden figure stood in the middle of a shadowy, rainswept street. And then she turned and walked away, having had quite enough of conspiracy theories for one day.

CHAPTER 37

Sat in her kitchen with a large glass of merlot and a small plate of cheese, bread and olives, Valerie opened her laptop; she had work to do.

The death of Steve Gallant and her brusque encounter with Patricia Martin had placed her firmly into reporter-mode, a state she found both calming and absorbing. It was in those moments that she found her fear mostly subsided and she was simply a journalist investigating a lead on a story. And that was a very comfortable place for Valerie to be.

She had painstakingly searched the *Daily Ear*'s website for stories about celebrity stalkers but had found the site's new search engine a very poor substitute for what had been there previously. She had been unable to search by date or using Boolean search phrases and regularly found herself looking at lists of stories that had little, if anything, to do with what she had actually searched for. And even when she appeared to find a relevant article, the page would load with half a dozen videos and animated adverts splashed in front of the text with no obvious way of closing them down in order to read the article underneath.

Valerie knew the paper's current owner, Yves Martineau, and she did not consider him to be a man with any concept of quality. She had watched with dismay as he had driven the paper's print and online versions into the gutter to squeeze as much dirty cash out of them as quickly as he could. For Valerie, the fact he had hired Lucy Strickland was proof in itself that quality was not something Yves Martineau aspired towards.

But her frustrations that morning had not simply been through the obvious drop in quality of the *Daily Ear*'s website. She had also had to face the brutal reality that decades of her work had never made it online: more than 30 years of columns, comment pieces and exclusives – her journalistic legacy – were nowhere to be seen. And beyond her hurt pride, she had a strong feeling the answer to many of her questions about the recent deaths of so many of her former colleagues would be within one of those long-forgotten articles. In the end she had used Google but, even then, she had only been able to find images of many of the *Daily Ear*'s most salacious front-page articles:

"He's NOT Your Father! Celebrity DNA Shock Exclusive by Colin Merroney"

"Gay TV Star's Affair with US Tycoon Exposed; World Photo Exclusive by Jason Spade"

"Drunk Soap Star's Expletive-Filled Lunch Shocks Diners; Explosive Showbiz Exclusive by Steve Gallant"

"Singer's Terror After WE Reveal Her Soccer Star Ex is HIV+. Exclusive by Debbie Braide"

Behind each salacious story was a reporter Valerie had known, had worked with, for years. And it occurred to her just how many people she had instantly lost touch with the fateful day she had walked out on her job and turned her back on the *Daily Ear* for ever. So many people she had not seen since, and after the events of the previous few weeks, some were people she would never see again.

Her cursor hovered for a moment over one name, *Colin Merroney*, and she wondered whether she should contact him, to warn him that his life might be at risk. He had once been a force to be reckoned with within the UK newspaper industry; the *Daily Ear*'s much feared 'king of the kiss-and-tells'. But he had also been a dear friend, and her closest ally during the many trials and tribulations that came with working at one of the world's most controversial newspapers.

Colin had also left the *Daily Ear* under something of a cloud, not long after Valerie. He and Valerie were estranged at the time, and so she had quickly lost track of him. She knew all of the contact details she had for him were out of date, and she was not entirely sure where he was or what he was doing. She had a vague notion he might be in Scotland, editing some regional paper, or possibly travelling the world feeding stories to the tabloids under a nom de plume. But she hoped whatever he was doing, and wherever he was, his closely kept low profile would keep him safe.

She wondered if Colin had read *Exposé* and, if so, what he had thought about it, because several chapters had been dedicated to Colin and his obsessive reporting on Pearl Martin. There were others, too, dozens more named and shamed in Valerie's book for what they had done to Pearl. There was Gayesh, of course, a man who had provided the editorial team with a near endless resource to pursue their stories.

And then there had been Howard Harvey, the infamous media mogul who had bought the *Daily Ear* as a failing and feeble copy of the Daily Mail and turned it into the world's most successful tabloid. The success of the *Daily Ear* had been a major building block in Howard's media empire, and many considered his path to billionaire status had been paved by the invasion and destruction of the lives of hundreds of celebrities, such as Pearl.

And then there was Howard Harvey's ex-wife Audrey, a lady from an old money family whose tendency to gossip had initiated the *Daily Ear*'s obsession with Pearl Martin in the first place, after the two had a misfortunate encounter at an awards ceremony. There were several board members who had used their power and influence to prevent numerous press watchdogs from censuring the *Daily Ear*'s coverage of Pearl.

And there were politicians too, some now in the Lords, who had manoeuvred around parliamentary debates and votes to ensure there were no changes in the law which might offer celebrities, like Pearl, greater protection from press intrusion or bigger pay-outs for defamation.

And each of them with their very own section in her book. As she reflected on Exposé, Valerie felt it somewhat strange that the final version of the book was so different to the story she had originally set out to write. When she had first sat down to research and plan the content, she was focussed solely on Project Ear, an insider's account of Adam's crusade against the world's biggest selling tabloid.

But she had quickly realised how Pearl's tragic story was intimately entwined with the lives of almost everyone at the paper. And so, Exposé became more than just a first-hand account of *Project Ear*. It became an investigation into whether Adam Jaymes had been right to blame so many people at the *Daily Ear* for Pearl's death.

Her suicide was a topic Valerie had only occasionally addressed publicly and when she had addressed it, she had relied on a script provided by the *Daily Ear*'s PR department. It was a tightly edited form of words which sought to exonerate the *Daily Ear*'s coverage whilst implicating the actress's own lifestyle and addictions.

However, in the quieter years after leaving the *Daily Ear*, Valerie spent some time considering how she may have contributed to the destruction of Pearl's life, a young woman she knew had struggled with addictions and mental health problems. She had also learned so much about the life of Pearl's daughter, Beth, and it sat heavily on Valerie's shoulders, to think that her actions may have contributed to a girl losing her mother to suicide at such a young age.

To a degree, Valerie had found the writing process for *Exposé* cathartic, a way to publicly renew herself, to dissolve the old Valerie Pierce and seek recognition of the many changes she was making in both her life and herself. But although she had found it easy to recount the drama and scandals of *Project Ear*, and how the actions of others had destroyed Pearl's career and then her life, she had found it impossible to attribute, in writing at least, any blame on herself. And so, Valerie was not one of the many people named and shamed in *Exposé*. Instead, she had allowed herself a more distanced role within the narrative; a commentator, reviewing and considering the guilt of others.

Valerie closed her laptop and sipped her wine, and her mind immediately re-focussed on the reason she had attempted the search through the online archives of the *Daily Ear*; to identify anyone who might have killed so many of her former colleagues to avenge Pearl Martin.

But as she reflected on those suspicious deaths, she realised all of the victims, in varying degrees, were mentioned in her book. And she wondered, once the murderer was finally revealed and brought to justice, would thousands of new readers purchase Exposé simply to choke down the gory details of the destruction of Pearl Martin's life? And within its dark pages, would they find sympathy for the actions of the killer? Perhaps, just perhaps, they would consider Exposé a justification for each and every murder. And perhaps, Valerie thought, the murderer had already done exactly that.

What if her book had provided the killer with his motive? Perhaps some still-grieving, deluded Pearl Martin fan had read Exposé and decided Adam Jaymes had not gone far enough with his campaign, four years earlier. Perhaps someone had decided the people named and shamed in Exposé should die.

Valerie stepped down from her stool and walked briskly to her office, a small room on the ground floor where she did most of her writing. She quickly located a copy of Exposé on one of the wall-mounted shelves and quickly returned to her seat in the kitchen. She then began the arduous task of speedreading through all 356 pages and highlighting everyone named in the book, named in a way that could provide a motive for murder.

"Is this a late lunch or an early supper?" Ray asked, joining Valerie in the kitchen. He helped himself to an olive, dropped down onto the stool next to her and kissed her on the forehead. "How are you getting on? Have you solved the case yet?"

Valerie gestured to her laptop, and with a frustrated tone replied: "None of it's there," she said. "Online. I can't find a thing. And I know we covered it at the *Daily Ear*. I know all the information, every sick detail of every sick individual, is in the print editions. But none of it made it onto the website."

"But there'll be a library at the *Daily Ear* won't there? Back copies. They might even have scanned them, made digital records."

Valerie shrugged. "Yes, of course. But I can't just wander in. There'd be uproar."

Ray shrugged. "So, ask a friend," he said. "Someone you know who still works there. Someone you can trust to be discreet. There must be someone who owes you a favour?"

Valerie thought for a moment, her mind suddenly whizzing through name after name until she settled on someone who fitted that exact criteria. "Yes, there is. I'll drop him an email," she replied. "But there's something else too. Something else I have worked out. Do you know what he's done?" she asked, a tetchiness to her voice.

"Who? Adam?" Ray asked.

"No. The murderer. He's used my book. My book! To plan and execute his killings."

Somewhat bewildered, Ray sat back and tried not to look shocked. "That really wasn't what I was expecting you to say," he replied. "What on earth makes you think that?"

Valerie moved the book across the worksurface and showed her highlighted sections to Ray. "They are all in here, all of them. Chris, Steve, Derek, Javier, Jason. And not just their names, but what they did to Pearl Martin. The role they played in the destruction of her career, of her life."

Ray gently folded back the pages of Valerie's book and could see other names highlighted too. "Val, I honestly don't think you should start to blame yourself for anything of this. Nothing that is happening here is your fault."

Valerie groaned. "Oh, I know that," she said. "I'm not taking responsibility for some crackpot's murder spree. But it might give us an idea of who else is at risk. I could take this back to the police. They might listen now. See the connection. What do you think?"

Ray had speed read Valerie's book when she had first released it, mostly out of a sense of obligation, and he vaguely recalled an extensive roll call of characters. And whilst Ray could see some logic in what Valerie was saying, he also knew the reality of their predicament.

The police had already laughed her out of the station, and Ray was concerned she now ran the risk of even more people laughing in her face. And not just laughing at her but, perhaps also, taking to social media to talk about Valerie Pierce's mad suspicions. They might even suggest her actions were nothing more than the attention-seeking efforts of a failed author, using the deaths of her former colleagues to gain publicity for herself.

Gently he closed the copy of Exposé. "Val, there are dozens and dozens of people named in your book. Honestly, I think you should stick to what you were doing originally. Don't look for more victims. Look for the killer. You can't warn everyone."

Valerie glanced downward, and her expression suddenly changed, as though she were wincing in pain.

"Val, you OK?" Ray asked.

"Jason," she said. "I could have warned Jason."

Ray did not understand what point Valerie was making. "You didn't even know he was out of jail. How could you have contacted him?"

She lifted her head and stared Ray in the face. "He called me, here," she said, "Reaching out, hoping someone from his old life would help him start over. But I pretended not to know him. I told him he had the wrong number and not to call here again. And then he was dead. I could have warned him, Ray. I could easily have warned him."

Ray sighed, and then nodded. "I get it," he replied, quietly. "But what happened to Jason Spade was not your fault, in any way. I understand why you feel you could have done something, but this is not your fault." He gently tapped the copy of Exposé on the breakfast bar in front of them. "But if this book is the key, Valerie, then what you are talking about… it's a needle in a haystack. There is no way you can possibly know who the killer might or might not be targeting."

Valerie shrugged. "There's Gayesh," she said. "I could have told him at the awards the other night. He's in the book."

Ray shrugged. "I guess so," he said, "But do you think he would have believed you?"

Valerie's face suddenly lit up, and she clicked her fingers, as though Ray had just made a great suggestion. "Well, let's find out," she said. "I'm going to visit him, tomorrow. Test the waters. See if I can get just one person to believe me."

CHAPTER 38

Alice stood at the entrance to the cemetery, a grating sense of hypocrisy stopping her from walking any further. She had not visited her father's grave in many years. More than 10, she supposed. She had never found peace or solace talking to a gravestone and, in her day-to-day life, had few fond memories of him. There appeared no way she could reconcile years of resentment towards Jeremy Pierce when he was not there to hear her words.

But over the previous few weeks, she had begun to feel guilty about the depth of negative feelings she had for him. She was not sure where her guilt had come from. She had wondered if it was because she had developed such a close friendship with Ray, her mother's first husband. Or perhaps it was because she had made efforts to rebuild her relationship with Valerie, whilst making no effort to rethink her feelings towards her father.

And she had wondered, what if Jeremy had lived? What if he had survived his cancer and lived? Would they have grown closer? Would he have accepted he had failed her as a parent too many times, and needed to make amends? Would he have ever said sorry?

In her heart, she knew she would find no answers at the cemetery that morning. But she hoped placing flowers on his grave, and spending a few moments sitting and reflecting on his life and death, might ease some of the guilt she had been suffering. At least it would feel like she had tried. And perhaps her mother was right. Perhaps Jeremy truly had adored his daughter but had simply lacked the skills or emotional intelligence to know how to show it.

Alice took a deep breath and finally managed to step forward, through the rusted iron gate. She was wearing a thick purple coat and matching scarf (borrowed from her mother) and carried a small bouquet of flowers from the local florist, already deposited into a plain grey vase to be left the gravestone.

There was a swirling damp mist in the air which had reduced visibility to just a few metres, but Alice had a clear memory of the various footpaths to her father's grave and was able to make her way there with little fuss.

As she neared the corner of the cemetery, where she knew she would find the final resting place of Jeremy Pierce MP, the mist grew thinner and she was surprised to see someone was already there, kneeling and tending the plot with a trowel. "Oh, hell no," she whispered under her breath, angered that some arrogant local Tory party member had taken it upon himself to interfere with her father's grave.

It was a man, in his late fifties or early sixties, who was wearing a thick coat over a suit and tie and seemed too smartly dressed for someone who was digging soil in a damp cemetery. He was balding, and slightly overweight, and had enormous bags under his eyes, like someone who was permanently tired. And as Alice stomped forward, she caught the man's profile side-on and recognised him. A vague recognition, perhaps, but definitely someone she had once known and, she felt, someone she had liked.

"May I help you?" she asked politely but with a clear tone of entitlement to her voice, to make it clear that he was imposing on her territory.

The man stopped and turned, squinting at her through the early morning gloom and the mist. "Good lord, Valerie?" he asked, and stood up immediately, leaving the trowel in the soil. "It's been so long." But then, as his eyes focussed more keenly, he realised his mistake. "Oh, I am so sorry, I thought you were someone I knew."

Alice stepped forward, her mind trying to place the voice and the face but without success. "I think we do know each other," she said. "I'm Alice. Valerie and Jeremy's daughter."

The man smiled. "Well, of course you are," he said, suddenly friendly and familiar, like an old uncle she had not seen for years. And Alice suddenly felt a great warmth and knew that if it wasn't for the vase and flowers she was holding, she would almost certainly have hugged him. And that was before she had even recalled who he was.

"It's been so long, Alice, I'm not surprised you don't recognise me. I've aged terribly. I'm Sydney. Corrigan. Remember? I worked with your mother for years at the *Daily Ear*, but I knew your father very well too. Yvonne and I came to many of the parties at your house."

Alice's memories of Sydney suddenly slotted into place, and she recalled the many times he and his wife had joined various dinners and soirees at the old family home in Barnet. Despite being a relatively lowly member of staff at the *Daily Ear*, her parents had always made sure he was invited and involved. She recalled Valerie once saying that Sydney had influence well beyond his rank, although she had never truly understood what that meant. But what Alice did know is that unlike all the other guests at those endless parties, Sydney and Yvonne always took care to bring Alice a small gift each time they visited and were always very nice to her.

"But goodness Alice, I haven't seen you since you were, what, about 13? 14?"

Alice smiled. "I was 16," she replied, factually. "I was about to become an unmarried teenage mum, and so mum and dad banished me from their social circle and moved me to a flat in Stratford."

Sydney chuckled. "You don't just look like your mother, you talk like her too," he said. "To the point, no nonsense."

Alice knelt and placed the vase of flowers on her father's grave, and then stood and gave Sydney a brief hug. "It is nice to see you," she said. "I never got to say how sorry I was, about Yvonne. She was always... well... she was always just very lovely."

Sydney smiled fondly, and then looked to Jeremy's grave. "I suppose you are wondering why I am here and what I am doing?"

Alice chuckled. "Well, it was a bit of a surprise to see you here, in a suit, tending to Dad's grave," she said.

Sydney looked back to Alice, and although he was still smiling, the warmth was suddenly missing. "A promise I made your father. Well, that a few of us made your father, during his final days."

"What promise?"

Sydney picked up the trowel, wrapped it in a small plastic bread bag and then dropped it into a leather satchel he had strapped across his chest. "Are you in a rush?" he asked. "I've a few hours spare this morning. I'd really like to catch up. Hear how your mother's doing. May I buy you a coffee?"

Alice knew most of the more pleasant tea rooms would not be open at that time in the morning and so was not surprised when she and Sydney ended up in a nearby café that was popular, she assessed, with 'white van' types tucking into various versions of a full English, and commuters who were grabbing a hot drink and a bacon sandwich on their way to the station.

The café was small and busy and only offered half a dozen tables, but they were able to find a couple of seats close to the door and quickly settled there. Sydney went to the counter and ordered two coffees and two bacon butties and returned to the table. "Terry's going to bring them over," he said, and sat down.

"Terry? You're on first name terms?" Alice enquired, somewhat surprised. The café, with its plastic chairs and steamed-up windows, didn't seem the sort of venue that a highly paid national newspaper editor would choose to patronise.

"Of course," Sydney replied, as though surprised by her question. "I'm virtually a regular. I'm here a couple of times a month."

Alice shrugged. "The café next to my dad's cemetery is your regular?"

"Well… yes," Sydney replied. "You could say that."

Terry delivered their drinks and food, and Alice sipped her coffee. "So, this might be the right moment to tell me about this promise you made Dad," she said, "on his deathbed."

Sydney quickly demolished his bacon butty, a skill he had picked up after decades of fitting meals around heavy work schedules and tight deadlines. "Alice, your dad was loved by millions," he said, "a true-blue Tory who promoted traditional family values at a time when many voters across the country wanted to see family values restored to the heart of British politics. The media loved him, and party members gave him a standing ovation at every conference."

"I know," Alice said, a softness to her tone as she felt a twinge of regret that she had never adored her own father as much as the Tory faithful obviously had.

"But," Sydney continued, "as in all politics, when you have a man so beloved by one party, he was always going to be hated by the others. And Jeremy *was* hated, deeply, by the left. And to be honest even by the centre. He was routinely accused of being racist, homophobic, anti-NHS, anti-benefits, anti-women, anti-poor, anti-northerners. And he lived under a constant threat of being attacked. The security on your home had to be increased to pretty much 'James Bond' standards, and the local police had to boost foot patrols where you lived, and their intelligence operations to keep you all safe."

Alice put down her mug of coffee and looked around the café, to try and distract Sydney from her surprised expression. She didn't want anyone to feel they knew something about her parents, about her own life, that she did not.

"You … you did know all of this, didn't you, sweetheart?" Sydney asked. "I hope I'm not speaking out of turn."

Alice shrugged. "Fortunately, my father suffered a long, painful and humiliating death which appears to have kept most of his haters broadly satisfied."

Sydney leaned forward, as though through kindness he felt a need to contradict and reassure her, but Alice gestured with her hand for him not to bother. "Honestly, Sydney, it's fine. I've had people, complete strangers, tell me to my face how thrilled they are that my father died, that cancer finally got the right person, that they hoped he suffered and was in great pain at the end."

Sydney sat back and shook his head sadly. "I'm sorry you have had to deal with comments like that," he said. "Politics aside, he was your father."

"I learned to be pragmatic," she said. "Sometimes the haters aren't just abusive. Sometimes they will share their story with me, explain to me why they hated my dad so much. They offer me a glimpse of where their venom came from. I've had people tell me they lost loved ones too, husbands or wives, or children. And they tell me it was due to cuts in benefits, or cuts to the NHS, or changes to mental health services. All changes my father implemented when he was in government.

"And as vile as they are to my face, I can understand why their anger has lived on even after my father died." Alice looked back to Sydney and smiled. "What I am saying, Sydney, is that you don't have to walk on eggshells around me. I am more than tough enough to deal with whatever you have to tell me."

Sydney gazed at her with a bright expression, as though enjoying the similarities between Alice's character and her parents'. "Your father is buried in a public cemetery," he said, "and his grave is desecrated. Regularly. Jeremy knew this would happen and asked me and a few other trusted individuals if we would maintain his plot to ensure you and your mother would never see any of it. He felt you had been through enough during his life and did not want you to deal with the repercussions of his political career after his death."

Sydney's words did not upset Alice. More than anything else, she simply felt irritated that other people thought they had the right to do *anything* to her father's grave, whether it be lay flowers or spray graffiti. But she knew that for all of her father's critics, he had an almost cult-like following among the party faithful and was not surprised he had been able to convince a few of those fanatics, including Sydney, to keep his grave clear of any nonsense.

"That's very kind of you," she said. "Very kind of *all* of you." She did not ask who else was involved. She was not interested. And she decided in the moment that she would not visit her father's grave again and would instead leave it to Sydney and his other followers. If they loved Jeremy Pierce so much, they could bloody well have him.

"How is your mother?" he asked. "I do miss her. She cut herself off from all of us when she resigned from the Ear. She seemed to forget she had some good friends there. Some very good friends."

"She's fine," Alice replied and started to eat her bacon roll. "She's getting a lot of work. In fact, we're at the stage now where we're turning down about half of what she's offered. She wanted to prove she could still be a major player in the media without a weekly newspaper column and I think she has proven that."

Sydney chuckled. "She certainly has," he replied. "Although I'd have her back in a shot if I thought she'd agree."

"Oh God no," Alice replied, and laughed. "There's no way she'd share a paper with the likes of Lucy … thingamajig. What's her name?"

"Strickland."

"Lucy Strickland. That's her. Could you imagine?"

Sydney sat back and raised a brow, as though considering something important. "Well, you know," he said, sounding as though he wasn't quite sure where he was taking the rest of his sentence. "Lucy filled a gap in our paper when we needed someone after your mother left. But her cards are marked. She won't be around for much longer."

"Really?" Alice asked, surprised at his candour. "She's very good at presenting herself as being a crucial part of the new *Daily Ear*. I don't think anyone would expect her to leave."

Sydney shook his head. "To a degree, you can certainly argue that she has kept the *Daily Ear* relevant, talked about. But she's costing a lot in legal fees and our resources generally. There was a bit of an HR cock-up when she joined, so she's on one of the old contracts, with all the old terms and conditions. Including membership of the old pension scheme."

Alice shrugged. "I am assuming that's bad?" she enquired.

Sydney nodded, "Oh yes," he said. "It means we are legally responsible for everything she writes, and that includes social media. And her social media is a minefield of defamation cases and accusations of inciting racial hatred. She's an absolute fucking nightmare, if I'm honest."

"The old contracts?" Alice asked, puzzled by the phrase. "Is that like the contract mum had with the *Daily Ear*?"

Sydney nodded. "In those days, we had so much money. The paper was an absolute gold-plated cash cow. So, whenever Howard… you know, the old owner… whenever he hired someone he thought had talent, he would give them this gold-plated offer. They were all on those contracts, the old guard. The people he considered to be his top talent. Your Mum, of course, and Colin Merroney. Chris, Jason, Javier, Steve. And not just the front of house staff. The back-office people, too. People like Gayesh Perera. I think that moron, Derek Toulson, had even managed to wangle himself an enhanced deal."

"It must have cost an absolute fortune," Alice said, "I mean, if they were all earning the same as Mum."

Sydney chuckled, as though Alice had just made an enormous understatement. "The old pension scheme alone is, well, frankly unsustainable," he said. "But the rest of it, well, at the time, in the good old days – before Adam Jaymes – we could afford to be generous. But after all that 'Project Ear' stuff, we took a massive financial hit that we never recovered from.

"And if you think about the legal protection… That was all designed in the days before social media. Back then, all we had to worry about was the print edition and then, eventually, the online version. And we had a team of sub-editors triple-checking everything before it was published. But these days, we've got the likes of Lucy bloody Strickland posting whatever she likes to her Twitter account without a second thought, and the *Daily Ear* is financially liable."

"How did she, Lucy, how did she end up with that contract? She's only been there a couple of years, hasn't she?"

Sydney nodded and smiled. "Our new owner was in a rush to get Lucy signed up exclusively, and the HR team was harangued into sorting it out within 24 hours. I can only guess someone pulled an old contract out of a file somewhere and just said, 'This will do'."

"It makes sense though," Alice, replied. "The contract itself, I mean. I know Mum always felt very protected when she was at the paper. I remember she would regularly have long phone conversations with the on-call lawyers to establish what she could and couldn't get away with. And they usually got it right."

"Yes, but that's because your mother was thorough; into the detail of everything. She was sensible enough to check her facts before her story was published. A proper journalist. Lucy's the exact opposite; shoot first and ask questions later. She's just not smart enough to think about the repercussions of what she's doing."

Alice doubted very much that her mother would wish to return to the daily grind of working for the Ear, but knew she was obliged to at least enquire. "And if Mum were interested in coming back?" she asked.

Sydney shrugged. "There are plans in place to relieve the *Daily Ear* of Lucy Strickland's services without being in breach of her contract."

"It would make quite a big splash, though, don't you think?" Alice asked, "Lucy getting fired and Valerie Pierce reinstated?"

"Oh yes," Sydney replied, almost smirking at the thought of it. "I bet your mum would love that."

"But you know she would be working for you differently?" Alice said. "She has a lot else going on. A successful website, articles for international publications and magazines, TV and radio slots. She wouldn't be working for you exclusively like she was before."

Sydney nodded. "Right now, anything could be on the table. I am very open to it," he said. "So? Will you talk to Valerie about this, open the negotiations? Confidentially, of course."

Alice smiled. "I can't promise anything, but I'll certainly put it to her," she replied.

"Well," Sydney said, clearly a happy man, and raised his cup of tea to Alice, as though in a toast. "Wasn't it fortuitous that we met?"

CHAPTER 39

Valerie did not wish to be diverted from the task at hand but knowing Alice had slipped from the house early that morning to visit her father's grave was proving too great a distraction. The evidence of her daughter's secret outing was clearly displayed on the 'friend finder' app on her phone; Ray was at his flat in Walthamstow, no doubt, Valerie thought, recovering from his late-night date with the waiter from Balans. But, to Valerie's surprise, she had found that Alice was also in London and, on closer inspection, at the cemetery where Jeremy Pierce was buried.

For years, Valerie had tried her best to ignore the many oblique references Alice had made about her late father. She knew, of course, that her daughter had not had an ordinary childhood. And whilst there had been many benefits to Alice of having a successful politician as a father and a high-profile journalist as a mother, Valerie had learned to accept that, from Alice's point of view, there had also been many drawbacks.

She had hoped that as Alice had grown older and wiser, she may have begun to focus more on the benefits than the drawbacks. But it appeared the opposite was true. Alice now had a clear, uncompromisingly negative narrative for her childhood, one that Valerie could only hope would never see print. But it made Alice's visit to Barnet Cemetery that morning all the more puzzling.

"I am sorry Mrs Pierce, but he's been held up in traffic. He sends his apologies but is going to be here shortly." Valerie looked up as the receptionist spoke to her.

"Thank you dear," she replied, courteously. She remembered that Gayesh was rarely ever on time for anything, and so was not surprised he was already half-an-hour late for their meeting.

"May I get you another tea?"

Valerie declined politely and handed back her mug. "Thank you, though, that really hit the spot," she said. As the receptionist returned to her station, Valerie looked around the entrance lobby and was struck by how much money had been spent on it. Her route from the car park had taken her through an endless parade of busy, cramped and outdated waiting rooms and corridors, and she had expected the Trust's management block to be along the same lines; small, dingy and antiquated.

Instead, the entrance lobby was modern, white and almost entirely devoid of people; a clinical white space with high-tech security barriers and wall-mounted information screens. The shining reception desk had hidden lighting and chrome rails across the front as decoration, and there was a small waiting area with expensive leather seats next to a security desk with monitors and a guard.

The security gates which led to the NHS offices upstairs were three-quarter length panels of hardened glass, attached to a metal framework that allowed them to swing open in either direction, depending on whether the card holder was coming or going.

Valerie wondered how much public money had been spent on that one space, an entrance hall for a small group of NHS managers, which could have been spent elsewhere. And then she remembered who was in charge of the Trust, her old chief executive, Gayesh Perera, a man she knew full well would happily spend a small fortune giving himself a posh entrance hall even if it meant closing an entire ward.

"Valerie, Valerie, Valerie," Gayesh said, as though greeting an old and dear friend.

Valerie looked up from her phone to find him stood in front of her wearing a large, damp raincoat and carrying a briefcase. His rounded features were shining, wet from the rain outside.

"I would give you a hug, but I'm soaking," he said.

Valerie stood and air kissed him on both cheeks. "It is good to see you, Gayesh. Thank you for finding the time at such short notice."

"Not at all. For you, Valerie, I always have time. Please, follow me to my office."

Beyond the entrance hall, through the barriers, the corridors and lifts quickly lost their sheen and Valerie found herself transported back to (she supposed) the 1970s, when those parts of the building had last been decorated. Under her feet was a highly patterned vinyl floor, and the walls had been adorned with some sort of textured wallpaper to give the impression of wood panelling. It had not aged well and was peeling.

"This will all be upgraded in phase 2," Gayesh said, waving his hand at the surroundings and appearing somewhat embarrassed. Valerie could not help but remember how Gayesh had renovated the old headquarters of the *Daily Ear*. He had spent a small fortune to replace all the equipment with the very best hi-tech facilities, and then commissioned a huge amount of structural work which had included replacing many of the internal walls with glass partitions. He had introduced sophisticated mood lighting across the building which changed throughout the day and installed three towering TV screens which hung over the newsroom. The executive suite on the top floor was reached by a glimmering silver lift.

His new offices were obviously quite a step down for Gayesh, and she could see why he was making such great efforts to replicate the opulent environment he had enjoyed in his previous role.

"You were very mysterious on the phone," Gayesh said as they reached his office. "It is of course a delight to see you again, Valerie. And so soon after our last encounter. But I am a little puzzled."

Valerie surveyed Gayesh's office, a grim small space with a poor view of the hospital grounds and began to appreciate just how far his career had dipped since his days leading the Harvey News Group. "Well, it is a sensitive issue, Gayesh. One that I really did not think was best communicated over the telephone."

Gayesh hung his raincoat on a hook behind his desk, and then sat down without opening his briefcase. "Would you like another tea?" he asked.

Valerie sat down opposite him and shook her head. "No, I'm fine," she replied.

Gayesh paused for a moment, and then smiled at Valerie. "So, how may I be of assistance?" he asked. He noted she looked uncomfortable, as though anxious about the conversation she was about to instigate. And that was a surprise for Gayesh. He remembered Valerie very much as a woman happy to say just about anything to anyone.

"I just need to ask that you keep an open mind, Gayesh," Valerie said, tentatively. "What I am about to tell you might seem somewhat… fantastical. However, there is a lot of detail and evidence to show that I am right." But before she could continue, there was a knock at the door.

"My apologies, Valerie. I will just see who it is," Gayesh said, and then called, "Come in".

Valerie was sat with her back to the door and did not turn. She had always felt it was a bit common to turn her head or hoist herself around in a chair just to see who had entered a room. Instead, she would wait to be informed and introduced by her host. And so, she sat and watched Gayesh's expression change, and was taken by the somewhat theatrical way he responded to the unexpected interruption, as if it was not unexpected at all. "Oh, my goodness, Maureen. What a surprise," he said.

Valerie realised Gayesh was using her visit to gain favour with the chair of his Trust but decided that, under the circumstances, it was best to play along. She stood and smiled and shook Maureen's hand. "How lovely to see you again, Maureen. I hope you don't mind but I am just borrowing Gayesh for a short meeting. You can have him back very soon."

Maureen beamed, clearly delighted that Valerie had remembered her from their brief encounter at the UK Top Women Awards. "Oh, there's no rush, Valerie," she replied with a familiar tone as though they were now old pals. "And I hope you are feeling better," she added, with a cheeky wink. "All that champagne."

Valerie suddenly felt very foolish, as she suddenly remembered both Maureen and Gayesh would have witnessed her very public meltdown at the awards ceremony. And she knew, if her conversation with Gayesh was going to be successful, she had to present herself as being sane, stable and in control. "Oh, my goodness, yes," she said, and smiled, and then told a complete lie. "I have to be honest, Maureen, my doctor had prescribed me a course of medication for a back issue I have. And I completely underestimated how strong the medication was. Turns out, drinking alcohol was a bad idea. Still, lesson learned."

Maureen squeezed Valerie's arm. "I don't think anyone really noticed," she said. "And congratulations on the award. I was thrilled you were finally recognised." Maureen then gestured with her hand at the open door and a portly, bald man entered the office, wearing an old-fashioned dark green suit and looking somewhat wide-eyed and overwhelmed by the situation. "Valerie, this is my dear friend Cllr Mel Travis. He chairs the County Council's Health Overview and Scrutiny Committee. He just popped in to discuss the agenda for the next meeting."

Before Valerie had the chance to acknowledge the new arrival, Cllr Travis lunged forward with his hand outstretched. "An absolute pleasure, Mrs Pierce," he said, his voice a higher pitch than usual due to a sudden bout of nerves. "I'm a huge fan of your writing. Huge. Have been for many years. And obviously had enormous respect for your late husband. I was in Blackpool. In 87. For his famous 'family values' speech. It was a defining moment in my life. Made me decide to go into politics. So, this truly is an honour to meet you."

Valerie had met hundreds of *Maureens* and *Mels* over the years, the adoring true-blue brigade who were wedded to a version of the Tory party she knew simply did not exist anymore. Her late husband, Jeremy, was spoken about with reverence, as though he were some sort of deity, and Valerie was afforded the undying love and respect that came from having been his loyal wife for so many years.

"Thank you," she said. "I am glad so many people remember him so well."

"And with great affection," Maureen said.

"Yes, yes. Enormous affection," Cllr Travis added.

There followed a short and uncomfortable pause, as though the cast of an am-dram production had forgotten their lines, and so Gayesh intervened in order to help the conversation run its course.

"Did you perhaps have something you wished to speak to Valerie about, Cllr Travis?" he asked.

With a clear prompt, Cllr Travis remembered his mission and clapped his hands together loudly, excitedly. "Yes, yes I do," he said, with great enthusiasm. "Mrs Pierce. Our local Conservative Party Association is holding its annual winter fundraiser in December. It has just occurred to me, just this minute, that you would make a wonderful after-dinner speaker."

"Oh, what a wonderful idea," Maureen said, and looked hopefully towards Valerie. "My goodness, we would need to book a bigger venue than last year, I would think," she said. "And I am sure the association would be happy to pay your standard fee."

Valerie had no idea how her diary looked so far in advance but did not recall booking anything that could not be rearranged, and so agreed. If nothing else, she thought, it might at the very least put Gayesh in a good mood and perhaps leave him more open-minded on the topic Valerie wished to speak to him about. "And please, I am happy to waive my fee," she said. "I am sure it will be an enjoyable evening. Just send the details to me via my website, and my manager will be in touch to confirm arrangements."

"Oh, that is just wonderful," Cllr Travis replied. "I cannot wait to tell the fundraising committee." And after a few brief farewells, he and Maureen went to leave the room, but before they did, Gayesh intervened once more.

"Cllr Travis, before you leave, could you please confirm the agenda for the next Health Overview and Scrutiny Committee?" he asked. "I have some vague recollection that at some point I was being asked to attend. But I'm not sure that is still the case."

Cllr Travis's bright expression dimmed slightly as he recalled the price he had to pay for his introduction to Valerie Pierce. "Oh, no, no," he replied, as though it was not an important topic. "I cannot imagine what that was about. But the agenda is very full already so there's absolutely no need for you to attend."

Gayesh nodded. "I thought that was likely the case," he said, and then gestured to the door with his hand and both Cllr Travis and Maureen left the room, their excited voices echoing from the corridor as they headed to the lift.

"That was very kind of you, Valerie," he said, as they both took to their seats once more. "I hope it is not an imposition."

"Oh, not at all. I've done dozens of Tory fundraisers. They're usually quite good fun, to be honest. All I need do is throw in a few Thatcher anecdotes and they'll be eating out of the palm of my hand," she replied. "And the wine is usually very good."

They both smiled at each other, and then Gayesh said: "So, this fantastical issue you wanted to share with me?"

Valerie took a deep breath and went to tell her story but was interrupted by another knock at the door.

"My apologies, Valerie. The life of a chief executive!" Gayesh said. "Come in!"

Once more, Valerie did not turn but instead watched Gayesh as he performed another startling rendition of 'man pretending to be surprised'.

"Timothy, what on earth on you doing here today?" he asked.

A young man appeared next to Valerie's chair. He had long hair and was wearing clothes that were clean but scruffy; corduroy trousers, a red and white striped shirt and woollen tank top. She wondered if he was one of those tiresome young people who believed it was stylish to be ironically retro.

"I am just pulling together the staff e-bulletin for this month and I heard you had a visitor," Timothy said, and then turned and looked directly at Valerie with a smile that failed to conceal his obvious embarrassment. He then looked at Gayesh again and said: "I wondered if I could take a photograph of you both together? It would make interesting reading to let everyone know you used to work with Valerie Pierce."

Gayesh raised his hands, as though helpless to control the constant stream of interruptions. "Valerie, I am so sorry. This is such an imposition."

"Oh, let's get it over with, Gayesh," Valerie replied, pragmatically. "It's only a bit of internal comms."

Nervously, Timothy guided them into position; Valerie in her chair and Gayesh perched on his desk next to her, both looking informal and happy. He used his own phone to take the photographs and asked that they chat to each other rather than look at the camera. He wanted to capture an image of two old pals, former colleagues, caught unawares as they talked over old times.

As she posed for what felt like an endless succession of pictures, Valerie recalled another occasion when she and Gayesh had been photographed together. It had been a few years earlier, during one of the many periods when the *Daily Ear* had been accused of racism. She had been asked to interview Gayesh, as it always helped to deflate such accusations when the Harvey News Group was able to wheel out its Indian chief executive. And it was certainly one of those occasions when Valerie had known the headline (*'My paper is NOT racist', says Gayesh Perera*) and the pictures would be the critical components, not her copy.

And as the memory became clearer in her mind, she recalled who the photographer had been on that occasion. Jason Spade. And she felt a little flutter in her chest, her heart skipping a beat as she remembered that Jason was dead.

Timothy completed his work and he and Gayesh exchanged some pleasantries before he left, then Gayesh and Valerie were alone once more. Gayesh retook his seat opposite Valerie and smiled at her.

"Now, without any further interruptions. How may I be of service, Valerie?"

Valerie decided she had earned more than enough brownie points from Gayesh to deserve a fair hearing. "May I smoke?" she asked. "I know it's probably not allowed, but on this occasion?"

Gayesh reached into a desk drawer and pulled out a large glass ashtray, which he then placed on the desk in front of Valerie. "I never did agree with the smoking ban," he said.

Valerie chuckled and produced her lighter and a gold antique cigarette holder from her handbag. "I assume you still do not smoke?" she asked, and Gayesh shook his head. "Well, it's very good for you to keep an ashtray for your guests who do."

"I would be a very poor host to ask my guests to go outside," he said. "Damn the hospital smoking policy."

With her cigarette lit, Valerie sat back in her seat and felt slightly less anxious, but she still did not know how her story would land with Gayesh. It would require a leap of faith and she was not sure Gayesh had it in him to do anything which did not result in an immediate opportunity or benefit. "Do you remember Derek Toulson? He worked with us at the *Daily Ear*?"

Gayesh thought for a moment, leaning forward onto his desk and staring into space. "Toulson?" he repeated, quietly, and then looked at Valerie. "The PR man?"

"Yes. I assume you didn't know him well?"

"Not particularly," Gayesh replied. "Why do you ask?"

Valerie drew deeply on her cigarette and then exhaled, politely, to one side. "He died, recently. An incident at a stable. He was trampled to death by a horse."

Gayesh's expression changed from indifference to bafflement. "My goodness. How awful," he replied, confused as to why the news was in any way relevant to him.

"The police are calling it an accident," Valerie said, her voice clear but quiet. She did not feel it was the time for grandstanding, or excited commentary. To win Gayesh over she would need to be seen as calm and analytical, not hysterical. "I, however, believe it was the result of foul play. There are a lot of conflicting details, but if you put them all together-"

Gayesh raised his hands. "Valerie, I don't understand," he said. "I am sure this is terribly sad, but in all honesty, I barely remember the man. Why did you travel all this way to tell me this in person?"

Valerie stubbed out her cigarette in the large glass ashtray and looked Gayesh directly in the face. "I need to explain the whole story," she said. "You see three days before Derek died, Chris Cox was killed in an apparent accident. And three days *after* Derek, Javier García died in an apparent suicide. Three days after that, Jason Spade. And three days after that, Steve Gallant. All dead." Valerie could sense that somehow, impossibly, in spite of her dramatic tale, she was losing Gayesh's interest. He seemed fidgety and distracted, as though suddenly wishing their meeting over.

"Did you know Steve?" she asked, hoping that perhaps Gayesh had more of an emotional connection to Steve than he had Derek.

"To some degree," Gayesh said. "He spent a lot of money. Too much, to be honest. I gave all of you very extravagant budgets to pursue your stories, but Steve overstepped the mark many times and, in the end, I had to put a stop to it. He acted like I had given him a blank cheque book. And it wasn't."

Valerie smiled, and enjoyed a moment of fond memories of Steve and his faux glamorous lifestyle. "He was a silly one, really," she said. "Silly Steve."

Gayesh nodded. "Yes, I read about that. And, also, Javier. The Fake Spanish Prince. Very sad for their families."

"And Jason?" Valerie continued. "The police claim he died of an apparent heart attack."

Gayesh shrugged. "Well, he was extremely fat," he said. "I cannot say I am surprised."

"No, no. You're missing the point," Valerie said.

But Gayesh shook his head, a sudden solemn expression on his face which did not fill Valerie with much hope that he was taking her concerns seriously. "No, Valerie, I don't believe I am," he said. "Your repeated use of the word 'apparent' makes it obvious that you believe there was foul play in *all* of these deaths. Correct?"

Valerie could tell Gayesh was either not interested or not convinced, or both, and she began to feel her trip may have been a waste of time. But she did not want to leave until she had given Gayesh the fair warning she felt he deserved. He was, after all, one of the people named and shamed in her book.

"Think about it, Gayesh," she said. "Five men, all linked to the *Daily Ear*. And each of them dies in strange circumstances, with exactly three days between each death. And each death was at 9pm. That is not coincidence, Gayesh, it is a pattern."

Gayesh tried to maintain his neutral expression, but he was deeply unhappy with what Valerie was telling him. He wondered why she would bring such an unwarranted and unnecessary drama to his door, particularly when he was trying to navigate such a complex situation of his own. Why on earth would she consider that he would even care? "You are saying someone murdered them?" he asked. "A serial killer?"

"Yes," Valerie replied, decisively. "Without a shadow of a doubt."

Gayesh curled his bottom lip and shook his head. "I do not recall seeing anything about a police investigation when I read about Javier. Or Steve. The police seemed quite sure there were no suspicious circumstances. With any of them."

Valerie shrugged and then, stumbling over her words, replied: "Well, the police… they aren't… so when I met with them, they… I mean, they haven't yet linked all the evidence as I have." And that was the moment she realised she had lost Gayesh entirely. She sounded like a paranoid conspiracy theorist, and nothing else she said would have any credibility.

Gayesh looked at Valerie with an expression of kindness and concern. "Is there a reason you came to see me?" he asked. "You had other colleagues at the paper who might be more… curious about your concerns. People you were much closer to. Because, to be honest, apart from the other night, we haven't seen each other for many years. Since I left the *Daily Ear*."

Valerie began to subtly collect her things together in preparation for her departure. "I do understand your reluctance to believe me," she replied. "I honestly do. But I think someone is targeting people who used to work at the *Daily Ear*. In particular, people who may be in some way accountable for the death of Pearl Martin. And Gayesh, to answer your question very simply, I came here to warn you that I believe your life may be at risk."

Gayesh felt oddly flattered that, of all the people Valerie could have travelled to see, she had chosen him. But it did not diminish a strong desire not to be involved. He had spent too much time over the previous week unpicking the harm caused to his reputation and career by the local press. He had no wish to be distracted by someone else's drama. "I will alert our security company," he said. "Thank you for the warning."

After an uncomfortable farewell, Valerie left the office and made her way back through the gloomy corridors of the main hospital building and then to the car park. She carried with her a grim sense of finality as though, in her heart, she did not expect to ever see Gayesh again.

CHAPTER 40

"Because of the weekend's derailment, we have dodged a bullet. There's nothing in the local media regarding the outcome of the Adult Safeguarding Review. Mid and North Kent Shopper, BBC Kent and Kent Advertiser all missed the report, distracted by the train story and subsequent injuries. We seem to have gotten away with it (again)."

Gayesh had nudged his reading glasses to the very end of his nose to offer himself a touch of added gravitas as he read from the front page of the local paper. He imagined he looked very much like a grumpy head teacher who was about to permanently expel a pupil. "Are you saying you did not write this email?" he asked and placed the week's edition of the Mid and North Kent Shopper on to his desk, ensuring its headline could still be seen: *"We got away with it" – gloating email of hospital manager on death of great-grandfather.*

Victoria Barrett sat quietly on the other side of his desk, her complexion was grey, her hands rested limply on her lap. Every aspect of her being reflected a state of complete devastation and defeat. After a moment, she replied: "I don't understand how the reporter got my email. I sent it to two members of my team. I have known them for years, trust them completely. Neither of them would do this."

"Then perhaps you accidentally copied in the reporter yourself?" Gayesh suggested and placed his glasses onto the desk.

"No. I've checked, and double-checked. I had IT look, too. The email only went to my two colleagues, no one else. And neither of them sent it on to anyone. I just don't understand."

Gayesh sighed and sat back in his chair, thoughtfully knitting his fingers together. "I think you are focussing on the wrong issue," he said. "No one is asking how this email was leaked. That's not the reputational crisis. The crisis is that our head of communications wrote an email in which she bragged that a report into the death of one of our patients was missed by the media because, luckily, all of our local reporters were distracted by a rail accident that left a dozen people badly injured. That, Victoria, is the crisis. And I am afraid it has already become much worse."

Victoria looked up, tears beginning to form in her eyes. "What? How?"

"Your colleagues tell me the story is now on the *Daily Ear* website. And the *Mail, Sun, Mirror.* They've even had a call from ITN. You've just gone national."

Victoria dropped her face into her hands. "Oh God. Oh my God. I'm finished."

Gayesh nodded. "Yes, yes, I rather think you are," he said. "Victoria, we are going to formally investigate this matter. I will have to suspend you during the investigation, and I promise the investigation will be fair and transparent. But you have admitted to writing this email, and it is the content of your email which is the issue, not how it ended up as an embarrassing international news story. Your email suggests a very negative culture within our communications department, a department *you* lead. And therein lies our issue."

Victoria wiped her eyes and nodded. "You don't need to investigate, or suspend me," she said. "I will offer you my resignation. You can have it in writing before the end of the day."

Gayesh considered his options. He had quite looked forward to firing Victoria. Ultimately, though, he considered her departure to be the true win and so he nodded and agreed to accept her resignation. "Funny, really," he said. "Last week I was on the front page of the Mid and North Kent Shopper and was threatened with the sack, this week it's you on the front page, and you are resigning. But I am still here. You are leaving, today, but I am still here."

Victoria shrugged. "I don't think that's at all funny," she said. "Why would you say such a thing to me?"

Gayesh shrugged, not wishing to reveal his hand any further, and instead gestured to the door. "I will let our HR director know what we have agreed," he said. "Goodbye, Victoria. I wish you all the best for the future."

Frail with stress and nerves, Victoria stood and went to leave. But as she reached the door, something drew her attention back to Gayesh and she turned and looked at him, her expression now dark and angry. "You did it," she said, her voice unexpectedly strong and clear. "You asked someone in IT to give you access to my emails, didn't you? You did this to get rid of me. Because I wouldn't cover up for you. Cover up the fact you're never bloody here."

Gayesh was conflicted. On the one hand, he simply wanted Victoria gone as quickly and cleanly as possible. But on the other, he desperately wanted her to know he had outmanoeuvred her. For a very long time she was going to be sat at home, unemployed and unemployable, all because she had tried and failed to outfox Gayesh Perera. And he wanted her to leave his office knowing it, that she had taken on a man well out of her league and had lost, badly.

But he also knew that if NHS England suspected he had leaked the email to the local media it would almost certainly put his job at risk once more, and so he chose to deny all knowledge. "Don't be ridiculous," he replied. "You are an important and respected member of my staff. A great loss to this trust. And I will personally see to it that we financially compensate you as much as we can within the rules and governance of the NHS. I wish you well, Victoria."

Victoria did not appear convinced, but she was not in a strong position and so, for the time being, she accepted his words and quietly left.

Gayesh then spent a few moments writing a memo to the head of HR asking for Victoria's resignation to be processed quickly, and for her three-month notice period and outstanding annual leave to be paid in full. He followed this with a memo to Maureen Parker, chair of the Mid and North Kent Hospital Services NHS Trust, in which he congratulated himself for resolving Victoria's situation on good terms. He explained he would quickly appoint an interim Head of Communications and would personally oversee a full review of the communications department and its 'toxic culture'. He copied Maureen's email to Alan Thorpe-Tracey at NHS England, partly for professional reasons and partly to remind Alan how quickly people's situations can reverse in the hectic world of the NHS.

Happy and spent, Gayesh went to close down his emails for the day but noticed one with the subject:

'Re: Re: Re: Security Card: Central Register Bypass.'

His secret contact in the IT team had already proven useful in accessing Victoria's emails, sourcing a particularly salacious message and forwarding it to the chief reporter of the Mid and North Kent Shopper in a manner that could not be traced. And now his secret contact appeared ready to resolve the outstanding issue of Gayesh's security pass. Gayesh read the email with glee, excited that so many of his problems appeared to be concluding on the same day.

"Gayesh. I have now resolved all the issues with your new pass. As requested, I have not shared this project with any other member of IT. Your new pass will record your entry into the building only, not your exit. I will have your new pass ready later this evening. Apologies for the delay but I can only do this once my colleagues have gone home for the day. The different programming does also take some time.

"I will leave it in an envelope with the security guard at reception for collection at 8.55pm. It is essential you use it as you leave the building this evening so I can check in the morning if it worked. Our IT systems are being upgraded tomorrow and so this evening is the only opportunity we will have to try it out. Hopefully it will work first time. Regards, YM."

CHAPTER 41

Valerie poured herself another glass of Rioja and reclined in the armchair. She realised that, through sheer force of habit, her left foot had remained flat on the rug, as though Jasper was still with her, dozing on the floor next to her chair, his head rested on her shoe. The Portman Square private club was one of the few which allowed dogs and over the years, since the death of her husband, Valerie had rarely attended without Jasper.

She had been a regular at the club for almost 30 years. It offered its members privacy and security, a traditional, old-money retreat from the outside world. It had a famously opulent entrance hall with an enormous sweeping, grand staircase which led to a never-ending rabbit warren of lavish rooms and historic architecture.

She and Jeremy had been regulars throughout their marriage and had been beloved by the other members; the dashing Tory cabinet minister and his young but influential journalist wife. After Jeremy's death, Jasper had become her companion and quickly won himself something of a fan club among the members, all of whom knew the story of how Jeremy had gifted him to Valerie on his death bed.

Amidst the countless drawing rooms, libraries and bar areas was a small lounge that counted as the building's unofficial smoking room. And at some point, during the previous decade, it had become Valerie's retreat. She had never requested the room be reserved for her, but no one else used it and there now appeared to be an unwritten agreement that it was for Valerie's sole use.

That day she found herself missing Jasper, missing his actual physical presence; the weight of his head and the fresh smell of his doggy hair, always clean through a strict routine of baths and brushing. For a moment, she allowed herself the illusion he was there. She dropped her arm to the side of the chair, as though reaching down to stroke him, to touch him. To reassure herself that everything was as it had been, and her darling Jasper was still a companion at her side, through thick and thin. But she knew, of course, that her fingers would find nothing but empty air, and so she withdrew her hand and rested it on the arm of the chair once more. "Silly," she said to herself. "Silly me."

Her difficult meeting with Gayesh had left her feeling somewhat hollow. She had discussed the encounter with Alice, who had tried to reassure her that she had done the right thing, regardless of how Gayesh had responded. But Valerie was used to being listened to, taken seriously. And she felt there had been too many people, over the previous few weeks, who had ignored her concerns and treated her as little more than an annoyance. And it was that feeling of being powerless that she hated the most.

"Your guest is here," a voice announced, and the club's elderly porter appeared in the doorway. "A young gentleman, Lewis Greene."

"Thank you, Arthur. Please show him in."

Valerie stood, and allowed a broad smile to cross her face as Lewis entered the room. And in that curious moment, she realised she was genuinely pleased to see him. He had not changed much over the previous few years. He was still a sharp dresser; a good suit and expensive shoes. His hair was slightly shorter, and there was the hint of stubble on his face which suggested he had given in to the recent fashion for beards on British men (Valerie didn't approve of the beard craze; too many men hiding weak chins). But overall, he was the same young man who had supported many of her campaigns in the latter years of her time at the *Daily Ear*.

"Lewis," she said, and kissed him on both cheeks.

"Mrs Pierce, it's really lovely to see you again," he replied.

"And you. Please sit down. And would you like a drink? We have everything."

"Oh well," he replied, "I'm not driving and I'm not on call, so I wouldn't say no to an Old Fashioned, if that's OK? I hear this club has a reputation for its whiskeys."

Valerie liked a man who knew his whiskey. Jeremy had been something of a whiskey connoisseur and had a particular fondness for the club's Old Fashioned. "Arthur, would you mind?" she asked.

The porter nodded. "I'll have it sent up," he replied and left the room.

Valerie and Lewis sat down, and she could not help but reach over and squeeze his arm. "It really is lovely to see you," she said. "I'd ask you how everyone is at the *Daily Ear*, but I fear I wouldn't have a clue who any of them are these days."

Lewis chuckled. "There has been a lot of change," he said. "Howard Harvey took some of his favourites with him when he sold the paper. Others just moved on. Sydney Corrigan's the editor right now, although I think he'd retire in a shot if he could."

Valerie smiled and rolled her eyes. "Oh Sydney," she said, fondly. "He was already talking about retirement when he was your age, Lewis. It's all he's ever wished for."

"And I suppose you heard about the accident. Steve Gallant."

Valerie withdrew her hand from Lewis' arm and sat back. She hadn't intended to react so dramatically, but she had forgotten, for a moment, that it was 'phone call night' and when the image of Steve Gallant's brutal death flashed before her eyes, she had suddenly felt the need to pull back into her seat.

"Oh, I'm sorry," he said. "You must have been close after all those years working together. I shouldn't have brought it up."

Valerie tried to regain her posture. She shook her head and offered Lewis a smile. "No, no," she replied. "Steve and I were very much work colleagues. Just people who saw each other at the office each day. We never socialised. He was always too busy seeking out bright young things in the office to take to showbiz parties. I'm surprised he never invited you. As I recall, you would have been very much his type."

Lewis grinned quizzically. "His type?" he asked.

Valerie felt she had crossed a line. Although she had spent much of her career as the purveyor of gossip, she did not wish to be seen as a woman who actively gossiped in routine conversation. But she had spent years trying to put Steve Gallant into a box. She had never believed any of his celebrity relationships were genuine and had noted how often he would loiter around the newsdesk, instigating conversations with the many young men who had worked there over the years. And as Steve had gotten older, the young men remained young. But now he was gone, and Valerie did not wish Lewis to think she was idly 'outing' a dead colleague.

"Oh, you know," she said, clutching for a sentence to dig her back out of a hole. "All those young trendy people who work at the Ear. Steve didn't like socialising with men or women his own age. I think we made him feel old. A young colleague like you would be far more likely to be invited to one of his famous celebrity bashes."

"Well, sadly not," Lewis said. "I clearly wasn't trendy enough for him."

Valerie patted him on the arm. "I doubt you missed much," she said.

One of the bar staff brought Lewis his drink in a heavy cut glass tumbler, and for a few moments he and Valerie chatted about some of the projects they had worked on together, and some of the people they both remembered. And once again, Valerie allowed herself the luxury of forgetting. But eventually she knew she would have to address the matter at hand, and so turned the conversation to the point of his visit. "Lewis, I appreciate I haven't given you much time," she said, "but did you have any luck finding the articles I asked for?"

Lewis placed his drink onto the nearby occasional table and clicked open his briefcase. "Yes," he said. "I have printed a few for you to look at tonight. The rest are on this memory stick." He handed Valerie a small silver and black flash drive, and then a folder containing a number of press articles. "The memory stick has three folders: Guy Stone; other people accused of stalking Pearl Martin; and then other celebrity stalkers more generally. I managed to find about 100 articles in all. There are more, but I only had access to the library for a couple of hours so tried to focus on certain key words. But obviously if you need more, just let me know and I can have another look."

Valerie reviewed the first two of the articles Lewis had printed up. The first was a picture exclusive by Jason Spade: Guy Stone confronting Pearl at a restaurant in America. She recalled that Jason had been dispatched to follow Pearl and her sister covertly whilst they holidayed together in the States. He had spent the better part of a week secretly photographing the two of them, but none of the pictures had been interesting enough to print. Until, out of the blue, Stone had appeared at a restaurant where Pearl and Patricia were having dinner. From Jason's point of view, Stone's unexpected entrance had been pure luck which delivered an astonishing exclusive for the paper.

The second article was a court case that resulted in Guy Stone going to prison for 18 months, a rare legal victory at the time for a victim of stalking but one that set a precedent which Valerie knew had helped other victims in the years that followed.

"May I ask, Mrs Pierce, is there a reason for this sudden interest? Are you working on a new book?"

Valerie did not want Lewis to know the truth, and so shrugged and said, "Possibly. I am looking at a few different topics at the moment." And she suddenly felt the need to impress him by pretending she had a publishing deal in the works, and so added: "My manager is talking to a few publishers. I think they like the idea of me sharing my recollections on a particular subject, like celebrity stalkers. But we've not agreed a topic just yet."

It occurred to Valerie that time was ticking by, and soon it would be 9pm again. 9pm, three days after the death of Steve Gallant. And although she felt safely tucked away at her club, she found Lewis' presence oddly reassuring. He seemed like an important person, someone that had a bright future full of achievement and success. A future, she felt, that did not include some gruesome dinner party story of how he sat by and watched helplessly as the legendary Queen of Fleet Street was bludgeoned to death in front of him by some lunatic serial killer.

"Have you eaten?" she asked.

"Oh, well, actually no," he replied. "I'm going to grab a kebab on the way home."

"Why not join me for dinner here? I'd love to catch up a little more. Talk about a few things that have nothing to do with work."

From the subtle change in Lewis' expression, Valerie could tell the offer had taken him by surprise. But then he enthusiastically accepted.

"And please, it's Valerie. Mrs Pierce was my mother-in-law and she was a bloody awful woman."

CHAPTER 42

All the pieces had fallen into place. Victoria was gone, the chair of the Trust had offered her full backing, his enforced resignation had been withdrawn and the digital paper trail of his comings and goings was about to be deleted for ever. Gayesh had won.

And the future looked even brighter after the chief officer of a neighbouring Trust had announced her departure, and Gayesh had thrown his hat in the ring to be named interim joint CO whilst a formal merger was designed. He had no doubt he was going to cruise into retirement with a gold-plated NHS pension to add to all his other pensions. He would want for nothing.

His glum little office with its limited space and poor view no longer seemed good enough for the interim joint chief officer of two hospital trusts. He had his eye on one of the areas on the first floor, where A&E staff could take a break and relax during shifts. It was a large room with a nice view of the nearby woods. And he had found a pot of money he could use to renovate the whole space and give himself the sort of office he felt he deserved with a leather seating area, a widescreen wall-mounted TV and grand wooden desk. And perhaps even a secret personal bathroom.

He switched off his laptop, logged out of his phone and collected his things together. It was rare for him to be at the office so late in the evening, but he had a good reason that night. And the extra time had given him a chance to plan his next move and reflect on the successes of the previous week.

He caught the lift to the ground floor and made his way through the narrow corridors that led to the lobby, an entrance area only for staff and their visitors that led to the NHS offices in the floors above. During the day it was a busy thoroughfare with staff coming and going, but early in the morning and late in the evening the lobby was mostly empty, save for a single security guard.

Even though the security gates had cost a significant amount of money, they served an important purpose as Gayesh had wanted to ensure commoners could not accidentally wander into his office suite. But now, when he looked at them, all he could see was an oversized tally counter, clicking and recording his comings and goings on a daily basis.

"Is there an envelope for me?" he asked the guard, who was sat at the security desk on the other side of the barrier. That evening it was a woman called Helen who Gayesh remembered from an incident a few months earlier, when she had successfully prevented a small group of 'Save The NHS' demonstrators from entering the building. They had disguised themselves as junior doctors and Helen, a slight but commanding woman in her late fifties, had recognised some of the protesters on her security monitors as they approached and had quickly locked the main doors to keep them from entering. Gayesh had been so grateful and impressed he had personally visited Helen to congratulate her.

Now, as he peered through the glass and watched as she rifled through the tray on her desk, he hoped her skills as a security guard would not include an ability to realise he was about to use a bogus security pass.

"Here you are, Mr Perera," she said, and used her own card to open the glass gates. She then held out a Manila envelope. "This was left in my tray for you."

Gayesh took the envelope from her. "Thank you, Helen," he said, but then realised she had left her card in the slot and was waiting for him to exit. And he remembered what his secret contact had told him; this was the only chance they would have to test if his new card worked.

"We had an engineer here at three in the morning performing maintenance on the gates," she said. "But they've been a bit clunky ever since. So, it's best if I let you out."

It was an awkward situation for Gayesh. On the one hand, he desperately needed to test his new security pass. But, on the other, he did not want to announce to another member of staff, particularly a security guard, that he *had* a new security pass with special properties he needed to test.

Then, as if by some miracle, Gayesh's phone began to ring and he stepped backward from the security gates. "Apologies. I've been waiting for this call," he said and, coyly, turned and walked back into the building, just far enough that Helen could no longer see him. He answered the phone, and then jammed it between his shoulder and his cheek so he could open the envelope at the same time.

His hands gleefully ripped at the seal and he quickly extracted his new security pass. It was a plain white plastic card without the usual NHS logo, staff photograph, name or job title. But it was the same size and shape as a normal pass, and so he assumed it would fit the same slot.

"Hello, this is Gayesh," he said, only just remembering that he was in the middle of a phone call. At first there was silence at the end of the line, and Gayesh took the opportunity to put the envelope into a nearby bin. "Hello?" he said again. And when the person on the other end of the phone finally spoke, Gayesh was so shocked he found himself frozen to the spot.

"Hello Gayesh Perera. This is your murderer. I just called to let you know it's your turn." The final few words were screamed down the line; a voice deep and distorted, crackling with electric undertones and shattering Gayesh's already-frayed bravado.

"I … I beg your pardon?" he responded. "What did you say?" But the line cut off, and the light on his mobile phone disappeared. It could, of course, just be some silly prank. Perhaps one of the 'Save the NHS' campaigners had somehow gotten hold of his personal number and decided to put the frighteners on him. But then he remembered his conversation with Valerie Pierce, and her insistence that his life might be in peril. That a serial killer had been targeting staff from the *Daily Ear*.

And that voice, that screaming, deranged voice, and those hate-filled words did not seem like a prank. They had left him shaking and feeling exposed and scared. And then he remembered that Helen was just a few metres away, with her imposing demeanour and calm ability to manage almost any security issue. And he suddenly needed her to keep him safe.

He hurried back to the lobby and almost sprinted to the security gate. "Helen, Helen I need your help," he shouted, "I have just been threatened."

Helen was sat behind her desk again, keeping an eye on the security monitors, but quickly rose to her feet. "I'm coming, Mr Perera," she said, and started towards the barrier.

But Gayesh reached it first and hurriedly pushed his new security pass into the slot. Immediately, all the overhead lights dimmed and Helen span around to see what was happening. Across the entire entrance hall, every electrical item either went dead or dipped in power; the wall-mounted information screens went black, and the security monitors on her desk switched off entirely. The ceiling lights glowed brighter for a moment, almost too bright, and then dimmed again. And throughout it all, she could hear a buzzing sound that grew louder and louder.

"What the hell did that stupid engineer do?" she muttered under her breath. And then she realised Gayesh's pass hadn't worked and the security barrier had remained closed. "I'm sorry, Mr Perera, let me open that for you," she said. But as she walked towards the security gates, she noted a pungent burning smell was heavy in the air. The lights dipped and then lifted and then dipped again, and she could see Gayesh stood on the other side of the gate, his hand still rested on the slot where he had inserted his pass. "Mr Perera? Are you all right?" she asked, his form silhouetted in front of her. "Gayesh?"

The lights overhead flickered brighter just for a moment, offering her a brief glimpse of Gayesh's face. And in that moment, her heart pounding in her chest, Helen realised he was already dead. Somehow, impossibly, the barrier had become electrified and thousands of deadly volts were now flowing through the last person to use it.

Calmly, she reached for her radio and called for help. "The lobby, main building. I need medical assistance," she said. There followed a loud bang and every light in the entrance hall went out. And the silence that followed was interrupted briefly, just once, by a dull thump as Gayesh's burnt, lifeless body dropped to the floor.

CHAPTER 43

"…apparently confirmed reports that just seconds before he died, Perera claimed he had been threatened…"

"…suggesting the security barrier had undergone regular inspections and, indeed, had been reviewed by an engineer just 24 hours before the accident. However, I've spoken this morning to the company that maintains the trust's security barriers and they say no one from their staff has visited the hospital building since the last maintenance check three weeks ago"

The most shocking thing about his death is that Gayesh Perera was apparently at the office, working late. Well, working at all #SaveTheNHS

"…was famously lazy. One version of events is that he was fired as Chief Executive of the Harvey Media Group after its owner, Howard Harvey, was accidently emailed a copy of his work diary and saw that he was barely ever at the office. Cut forward a few years, and an investigation by a local newspaper uncovered the exact same pattern of behaviour in Gayesh's new role as Chief Executive of a hospital trust in Kent. A man who clearly enjoyed the trappings of highly paid, senior roles but had no interest in fulfilling the duties and responsibilities that came with those roles…"

"…have taken all similar security barriers offline until a full investigation has been carried out to establish how a piece of equipment installed to keep staff safe ended up killing the trust's chief officer…"

"…security guard reportedly told police that Perera took a phone call moments before his death, after which he appeared quite panicked and complained he had just been threatened. Police have yet to confirm this but, if correct, it might throw doubt on the current assumption that Perera's death was an accident caused by a faulty security gate…"

My condolences to Gayesh's wife, children and family at
this sad time @THEhowardharvey

"…named in Valerie Pierce's book, Exposé, as one of the key players in the Daily Ear's obsession with the late actress Pearl Martin. The book states: 'Gayesh was incredibly generous with the paper's money in part, I believe, to appease the senior editorial team and so prevent anyone questioning his constant absenteeism from the office. Gayesh was lazy, unquestionably so, but with him in charge of the money, we were endowed with an almost endless financial resource; a resource which meant we could source and investigate any stories about the rich and the famous which held even a remote chance of being true. And it was money well spent because the more we spent, the better our exclusives. And the better our exclusives, the more papers we sold. We could outmanoeuvre and outbid any other newspaper. In all honesty, much of the success we had over those years was down to Gayesh Perera'. It is doubly ironic that Perera's death follows so closely the demise of a number of other grandees from the golden era of the Daily Ear including…"

@ValeriePierce53 *"May I get you anything else?" asks the*
waiter, delivering my 'rustic' steak and chips on a wooden
board. "Yes" I replied, "a plate." #restaurant #restaurantfail

CHAPTER 44

Lucy was not used to being summoned to the editor's office, particularly on a day when she had no plans to be in the city. She did not appreciate the gesture, the second time in only a few days, a suggestion that she was at Sydney's beck and call and no more important than any other member of staff at the *Daily Ear*. She had only attended because his PA had impressed upon her it was an urgent matter that could not be discussed over the telephone, and this had piqued her curiosity.

However, she still intended to firmly put Sydney back in his box. Lucy was not the same as every other employee. She had been hand-picked by Yves Martineau himself, personally installed by the owner of the newspaper. And perhaps it was time she reminded Sydney of that.

She stomped down the corridor that led to his office and could hear the voices of two men in conversation. One was Sydney, but the other was not so recognisable. It sounded like a young man, a junior reporter perhaps. And as she approached the door, she instinctively quietened her footsteps and slowed to a complete stop. There was a tone to the voices, as though they were discussing something secret or conspiratorial, and it drew her attention enough that she paused and began to eavesdrop.

"You were right to bring this to me, Lewis," Sydney said. "I cannot have something like this being sent to every member of staff. It will certainly leak, and how will that make us look? An absolute fucking laughingstock."

"I thought it could be shared on a 'need to know' basis," Lewis replied. "The senior management team only?"

Lucy had a vague memory of a young man in a lift called Lewis, something to do with communications, or internal communications.

233

"No. Not even that. Leave it with me. If anyone else needs to know, I will tell them," Sydney replied.

"But we don't know how widespread the problem is," Lewis said.

And with that, Sydney's tone changed, and became less affable. "Lewis, it's a no. And when I say no, I don't expect to be sat here debating it. Have I made myself clear?"

There was silence, and Lucy could only assume that Lewis had nodded as a response. The two men then had a quieter discussion that Lucy could not clearly hear, and then the door opened unexpectedly, and Lewis was stood in front of her, looking somewhat surprised to see her.

"Oh, hello," Lewis said, awkwardly, and then glanced back into the room at Sydney, who was stood by his desk with his arms folded. It was obvious to both men that she had been listening at the door.

The two men quietly exchanged a look, which made Lucy feel somewhat foolish, and she would not allow anyone to make her feel foolish. "I'm a journalist," she replied. "Of course I was listening. You both sounded like you were up to no good."

Sydney chuckled, enjoying the shamelessness of her reply and then gestured with his hand to Lewis, giving him permission to leave.

"Nice to see you again, Ms Strickland," Lewis said, a bright smile on his handsome young face, and then he left.

"Come in, come in Lucy," Sydney said, and returned to the expensive leather seat behind his desk. "And please close the door."

Lucy did as she was asked, and then took the seat opposite Sydney, a plain wooden chair. "So, what are you keeping a secret?" she asked.

Sydney smiled. "Well, if I told you that I'd have to kill you," he replied. And without waiting for a response, added: "Are you planning to be at the seniors meeting this afternoon?"

"I wasn't planning to be here at all today," Lucy replied, sharply. "I'll be leaving straight after our conversation. So no, I won't be at the meeting."

Sydney noted a pronounced lack of respect in the way Lucy was speaking to him and assumed it was because she had not liked being summoned to his office. But he knew how the conversation was likely to unfold, and that it would not be a pleasant experience for Lucy, and so he chose not to mention her tone of voice.

"Strictly between us, Lewis believes our IT system has been compromised," Sydney said.

Lucy nodded, keen to display a thorough understanding of IT security issues. "Our emails, you mean?" she asked.

"Everything," Sydney replied. "Emails, phone systems, electronic files, HR records. You name it. If it's something you plug in and switch on, chances are its content has been stolen."

"Are you going to alert the police?" Lucy asked.

Sydney's expression darkened and he shook his head. "Absolutely not," he said. "Lewis is going to come back to me with evidence and, if he's right, we will find who's doing it and ask what they want. We need to keep this out of the public domain at all costs. No police."

Lucy was not surprised by Sydney's reluctance to inform the police. A few years earlier, during Adam Jaymes' campaign against the paper, she had seen the *Daily Ear* publicly stripped of its dignity, reputation and many of its secrets. And despite the crushing impact that scandalous period had on the paper, she had always assumed Jaymes had barely scratched the surface.

She tried to settle back into her chair, but it had an uncomfortable wooden frame and no cushion. It was the perfect piece of furniture for Sydney, a man who would never want anyone to outstay their welcome. "So, you are saying there's been a security breach, but you don't know exactly what has been stolen, or why?" she asked.

"No," Sydney replied. "I am saying that a relatively junior member of staff believes there has been a security breach," he said. "But, to be on the safe side, you may want to look back through your emails and files and see if you can find anything that looks wrong."

Lucy nodded. "Yes, I will," she replied. "And is that it, are we done? Is this why I was asked to meet with you?"

The pause that followed unsettled Lucy. Sydney's demeanour changed, notably. His face had a sudden, more serious expression, and his body language was different. He sat more rigidly, as though about to begin a more formal conversation. He reached into his desk drawer and pulled out a large brown padded envelope which he held in both hands for a moment, as though unsure that sharing its content with Lucy was the right thing to do. But then he placed it onto his desk and gradually slid it across to her.

"Oh, for fuck's sake, Sydney," she said. "Another envelope? I told you last time. Whatever's in there, I'm not interested."

Sydney gestured to the envelope. "We had to buy the content from a freelance photographer," he said. "It cost us a lot of money. And I mean a lot. But we had to avoid a bidding war, and she was willing to make a deal directly with us as long as the cheque had enough noughts."

In an uncharacteristic display of restraint, Lucy did not immediately snatch up the envelope and open it, because in her heart, she already knew what it would contain. "I see," she replied. "And can we trust her?"

Sydney nodded. "Yes, I know her. And she signed a watertight NDA too. The content of that envelope will never see the light of day."

Lucy lifted it from the desk. She assessed its weight and decided it was just about heavy enough to contain a dozen or so photographs. And her thumb was pressing on a small hard object that was most likely a flash drive.

"I can give you a moment if you like," Sydney said, "but once you have reviewed the content, we will need to discuss and agree what happens next. You and me." He leaned forward on his desk, ready to push himself from his chair and leave the room.

But, with a voice that was unusually timid, Lucy interjected. "No, no. You're fine," she said, and gestured for Sydney to retake his seat. She pulled open the paper flap of the envelope and slipped the photographs onto her lap. The top picture was innocuous; her husband Alec walking along a bright sun-drenched beach in a pair of tight-fitting black trunks, against a colourful background of palm trees and wooden cabins that could easily have been lifted direct from a brochure for a paradise island getaway.

She placed the envelope onto the desk and tentatively made her way through the rest of the pile, waiting to see if her suspicions were correct. And just three photographs in, a familiar face appeared – Janet, Alec's accountant, a woman whose annual leave always seemed to coincide with Alec's 'boys only' trips abroad.

But the next few pictures confused Lucy. She had met Janet's husband a number of times; a thick-set, shaven-headed Londoner with multiple tattoos and a chubby red face. And there he was, with Janet and Alec, happily drinking cocktails on what increasingly looked to be a private beach. And for a moment, she was concerned her husband had become a holiday sex toy for some middle-aged couple's midlife crisis or, worse, that he was now one third of a 'throuple'.

It was only as she looked through the remaining images that everything fell into place. A fourth person appeared in the pictures, a beautiful, raven-haired young woman with bright green eyes and a flawless smile. In some of the pictures she was walking hand-in-hand with Alec on the beach. In others, they were laying together on the sand, kissing or laughing. But in every image, the young woman gazed at Lucy's husband with an undeniable look of love. And Alec looked at the young woman in the same way. Lucy's heart sank as she realised he had never looked at her with such obvious affection.

"The older woman is your husband's accountant," Sydney said.

Lucy nodded without looking up. "Yes, I know her. And the bald man is her husband. I've met them both. But the young woman?"

"Their daughter," Sydney replied. "Your husband has been having an affair with her, we think, for at least a year. And, it would seem, with the blessing of her parents."

Although Lucy's marriage had never been perfect, it had been empowering and, at times, great fun. At the very least she had trusted Alec to never do anything that would embarrass her. And yet here she was, being informed of his adultery by her own editor and told that an entire group of people outside of her marriage, including a paparazzi photographer and her husband's accountant, knew of it before she did.

Lucy did not wish to appear shaken. She would not allow Sydney to see her weakness. And so, she slipped the photographs back into the envelope and looked him in the eyes. "How much do I owe you?" she asked and placed the envelope back onto the desk in front of him.

"Well, nothing," Sydney replied, a little puzzled by the question. "This was a business transaction on behalf of the newspaper. Pictures like this would damage your reputation and, by default, our reputation. Lucy, have you any idea how many people were just waiting for your husband to cheat on you? For you to get your just deserts for breaking up his first marriage?"

"Oh Sydney," Lucy replied, tersely. "You cannot break up a happy marriage, and besides I wasn't-"

"Yes, yes. I know. I've heard it before, Lucy," Sydney said, crossly. "*You* didn't commit adultery because *you* weren't married. Alec was the cheater, not you. But, believe it or not, most people… most of our readers… don't see it like that. They don't see you as the innocent party. They see you as a marriage-wrecker and will be delighted to see another woman now wrecking yours."

Lucy wanted to regain some control of the conversation, to make it clear she would not be rushed into a major, life-changing decision simply because it was expedient for the company she worked for. And so, she sat forward and prodded Sydney's desk. "I don't care what other people think," she said. "This isn't anyone else's business."

Sydney's reassuring demeanour evaporated right in front of Lucy's eyes. He fixed her with a dark, hard stare that she found somewhat disturbing. It was a look of contempt, of a parent disgusted by the ungrateful behaviour of a misbehaving brat.

"Now you listen to me, Lucy Strickland," he said, "the content of that envelope makes your marriage my business. Your excessive salary, your expense account, your gold-plated pension, the endless legal costs this paper incurs because of you. All of those things make your marriage my business. Your brand and this paper's brand are indelibly linked, and that makes you as much a liability to me as it does an asset.

"I have just spent a small fortune buying paparazzi pictures of your worthless, cheating husband with his mistress. Photographs that would create a storm of negative publicity around you. They would remind our readers that you had an affair with a married man, and there will be an army of haters in other papers and online, revelling in the destruction of your life. And that would go on for weeks, if not months. Everything you write from that moment on, every opinion you offer on any subject, will be countered by thousands of other people ridiculing you. We cannot take a reputational hit like that. Not at the moment.

"So, it was in the best interests of the *Daily Ear*, the newspaper you work for, that we had to keep these pictures out of circulation. Do not give me some bullshit story that you want to give Alec a second chance, and that the two of you are going to try and fix your pathetic mockery of a marriage. He'll be back with his mistress before you know it, and I'll be sat here with another load of photographs to buy. And that is not going to happen."

Lucy tried to find some strength from deep inside herself, some anger she could draw on to tell Sydney to stuff his job and go to hell. But in that moment, she realised she was impossibly lost. More so than she ever thought she could be. Her husband's betrayal was not completely unexpected. On some level, she had always believed he could cheat on her, from the moment they first got together. He was an affair just waiting to happen.

And, for some reason, it had been bearable when she believed he had been enjoying nothing more than a series of meaningless one-night stands. And even when she suspected he was having an affair with an older married woman, she had believed she would be able to cope with it, with the absurdity of it. She would have enjoyed the opportunity to confront him, to throw his affair in his face and make all sorts of vindictive, demeaning jokes about Alec having a grandmother fetish. And she was certain he would have ended the affair and come home to her.

But instead, she was presented with a far less tolerable scenario; her husband was in a committed, long-term relationship with a single, younger woman who was as beautiful as Alec was handsome. And the woman's parents had embraced Alec as one of their own. The photographs were not of a man having an affair, they were of a family holiday.

Lucy's humiliation was overwhelming. And now Sydney, her editor, was losing patience with her, insinuating that her job could be at risk if she did not commit, there and then, to ending the problem once and for all. And perhaps Sydney was right. Perhaps attempting to fix her marriage would prove a fool's errand. If she forced Alec into a make-or-break choice, she had an awful feeling he would choose his mistress without a second thought. And so perhaps it was time to show her loyalty to Sydney, to the paper, and quickly resolve an issue that could easily become a reputational crisis.

"I'm tough," she said, wanting at the very least for Sydney to acknowledge that.

"I know," he replied, choosing a tone that was far less irate.

"I want to finish this conversation and get home," she said. "I have several wardrobes of designer suits to shred."

Sydney smiled. "Of course."

"So, from your perspective, what next?" Lucy asked.

"OK. There are two clear phases," Sydney said. "But we will need to act swiftly. First phase, you call your husband. Today. You tell him you know about the affair, you have photographic evidence of the affair, and that if he doesn't do exactly as he's told you will take him to the cleaners. He will lose every penny, the shirt off his back, including that collection of car repair centres he's so proud of. You get him to agree to a quick divorce and a gagging order. But you make it clear the gagging order is for him only, not you. You get to say whatever you like."

Lucy shrugged. "But I thought the whole point of this is to keep the photographs secret. To keep his affair secret. How can I threaten to use them if the whole point of this is to bury them?"

"It's a bluff, Lucy," Sydney replied. "You call him today, and you offer him one course of action, and only one. No reconciliation, no arbitration. He has one option, and it is the option you are giving him. Or he loses everything."

Lucy sighed, and shook her head. "I can't speak to him until he gets back," she said. "Whenever he goes on one of his 'boys only' holidays… well, what I *thought* was a 'boys only' holiday… he goes completely off the radar. His phone is switched off."

Sydney dipped into the envelope and withdrew a sheet of paper, which he then slid across the desk to Lucy. "Already sorted," he said. "If you look at that, you will find the direct telephone number for his cabin on the beach. You can surprise him. He'll pick up the phone thinking it's room service, and instead he'll get his wife calmly calling him from London to discuss his adultery and a divorce."

Despite her annoyance at Sydney, Lucy quite liked the idea of ruining the remainder of her husband's holiday. How satisfying to know Alec would be marooned on his paradise island for four more days, anxiously pondering what vindictive actions his wife was undertaking back home. "And phase two?" she asked.

"Phase two," Sydney said. "We take control of the public narrative. Once Alec has agreed to keep schtum, you announce your separation in your weekly column and the reason for it."

"And what are my reasons," Lucy asked, "if we are burying the affair and the photographs?" She began to draw a strange reassurance from the conversation. It was strange because she was being handed, on a plate, a process to quickly and cleanly resolve her mess of a marriage, a process with a clear beginning, middle and end. And as ruthless and, perhaps, even heartless as Sydney appeared in that moment, Lucy found herself oddly grateful for what he was doing.

"Oh, I don't know," Sydney said. "You can come up with something, can't you? Something empowering for you. Boredom, perhaps? You're an incredibly intelligent woman and you married a … what's the word … himbo? You know, great sex. For a while. Lovely to turn up at events with him on your arm. But at home, when you tried to engage your husband in a conversation about politics, or something, he was always too busy doing push-ups or styling his hair. Or watching TOWIE."

Lucy was not sure that would work. Alec was actually a clever, well-educated and cultured man who just happened to be a mechanic. But she also knew most people had made sweeping judgements of their marriage based purely on his handsome face and her perceived wealth and showbiz lifestyle. All in all, Sydney's twisted version of their marriage would probably land pretty well with their readers; 'dumb husband fatigue' would be a very believable version of events.

"So," she said, calmly. "My column next week. Don't marry a younger man for his looks, because once the sex becomes routine, you'll have nothing to talk about."

"Sounds good," Sydney said. "And really push the angle that he was thick. Come up with some anecdotes. You know, like you told him you were cooking ratatouille for dinner and he asked if you had removed the tail."

Lucy surprised herself by laughing, and with that laughter the tense atmosphere in the office lifted. She stood, leaving the envelope on the desk. "But please keep the pictures," she said. "I really don't want to see them again."

Sydney returned the envelope to his desk drawer. "Take my advice. Call him today and then check in with me later to let me know how it went."

"Yes, I will," Lucy replied.

"And be calm on the call. Really calm. That will unnerve him. Be specific and targeted in what you say. Do not raise your voice, not even once. And no name calling, not even about his mistress. Pace the way you speak and hold something in your hand that you can squeeze to stop yourself losing your temper."

Lucy nodded. "Oh, I will," she said. "Nothing scares a man more than an angry wife who keeps her cool." She looked at the piece of paper listing

Alec's cabin phone number, before tucking it into her jacket pocket. "Thank you," she said.

"You've had a tough few weeks, Lucy," Sydney replied, "what with Steve's death and now this. Don't let it defeat you. Keep fighting."

Lucy smiled at him and then quietly left. She stood outside Sydney's office for a moment, feeling a strange combination of hollowness and contentment. She knew the house would seem all the emptier upon her return now that Alec would never live there again. He would visit to collect his things, perhaps sign some papers. But it was no longer his home.

In some ways, however, it was as if a weight had been lifted from her shoulders. All of the uncertainty and the suspicions about her husband were now gone. She would no longer need to pursue her obsessive investigations of his life for any clues about an extra-marital affair. She would no longer scan their joint bank account for any evidence Alec had accidentally used the wrong debit card for an incriminating purchase. She would no longer cyberstalk him and his friends on Facebook in case one of them carelessly uploaded a picture proving Alec's affair. And she would not need to gently quiz him on his return from his holiday, to seek any inconsistencies in his story.

She now knew, without a shadow of a doubt, that Alec was cheating on her and, by the looks of the photographs, was planning at some stage to leave her. And as she made her way back along the corridor to the lift, she wondered why he had stayed for so long, why he had prolonged the misery of the deception when he appeared so happily embedded in someone else's family.

"Oh, we meet again," came a man's voice.

The lift doors had opened, and Lewis was stood inside, smiling at her. Lucy stepped in and pressed the button for the ground floor. And as the lift doors closed in front of them, she turned to Lewis and said: "You seem to be involved in a lot of things, Lewis. I get the impression you are more than just a communications officer."

He shrugged. "I suppose you could say the remit of my role is broader than what you'd find in my job description."

"So, were you involved in securing those photographs? Of my husband?"

At first Lewis looked puzzled, but Lucy could tell straight away he was feigning ignorance and she wasn't going to tolerate it. "Were. You. Involved?" she asked, more assertively.

Lewis' expression cleared to something far more neutral, and then he nodded. "I was the go-between, essentially," he said. "I've done a lot of that sort of work since Sydney was put in charge."

"Why?"

Lewis shrugged. "I guess he trusts me. I must have one of those faces. A lot of the senior staff have over the years. I couldn't begin to tell you some of the jobs Leonard Twigg used to send me out on."

"And how are you paid for this extra work?"

"Oh, just expenses and overtime claims. Nothing much. But I see it as good experience, you know, long-term. For my career."

Lucy's irritation with Lewis suddenly evaporated as she realised she might be able to put his additional skills to good use. She had wanted to spend the next few days arranging her story about the marinas on the east coast, but knew she was going to be too distracted with Alec and his mistress to make a good job of it.

She didn't want to delay the story, however, particularly as her secret correspondent was due to report back with a time and location, and so she would need some help. "I have something I would like you to do for me. Can you assist?" she asked.

Lewis nodded. "Sure, I'd love to. What is it?"

"A story I am working on. A millionaires' playground. Yachts, marinas and illegal immigrants. What do you think?"

CHAPTER 45

Alice had not always thought so kindly of Ray. When he and her mother had unexpectedly rekindled their friendship a few years earlier she had suspected the worst, that an attention-seeking reality TV star would exploit his relationship with the infamous Valerie Pierce to continue his pursuit of fame.

And so, she had kept an eye out for clues that she might be correct. Whenever Ray and Valerie went for dinner, she scanned the papers the following day to see if anyone had tipped off a photographer as to where they would be eating, and when. She had monitored certain chat rooms and gossip websites for any rumours that Valerie had renewed her romance with her first husband. And she had quietly but steadily questioned Ray about his life and his career, for any clues that he might be hiding his true intentions.

But, to her great annoyance, her suspicions proved unfounded, and Ray showed himself to be kind and decent, someone who had made mistakes in his life but who worked hard to always do the right thing. More than 30 years after his divorce from Valerie, Alice could see the hurt he had caused still weighed heavily on his conscience. And now she knew his guilt must be even greater with the knowledge that he had betrayed Valerie's trust once more by failing to maintain his support as she attempted to uncover a series of terrible crimes.

"Hospital boss killed by security barrier," Alice said, reading the main headline from the front page of the Mid and North Kent Shopper's website. She tutted and then looked over the screen at Ray, who had busied himself on the other side of the breakfast bar, chopping onions.

"Have you read the whole thing?" he asked. "It's bloody grim. The last thing he said before he died was that he had been threatened. And then, zap! A million volts. Right in front of a security guard. Ugh, can you imagine the smell?"

Alice closed the laptop and folded her arms. "Gayesh is the one Mum went to see. She went to warn him, tell him she thought his life was in danger. And he couldn't get her out of his office quickly enough. He made her feel as though her attempt to save his life was an imposition. Idiot."

Ray paused what he was doing and looked at Alice. "Sweetie, you and I are hardly in a position to criticise him for that. Your mum absolutely relied on us to be the ones who believed her, believed *in* her. And yet the first opportunity we had to back out and say none of this was real, we did exactly that. Both of us."

Alice leaned onto the counter and sighed. "Oh, I know, I'm just projecting," she said. "It's insane though, isn't it? This whole situation. Six men are dead, and that's just the ones we know about. But where are the police? Where are the public appeals for information? There's a serial killer out there somewhere, and my mum could be next on his hit list. And no one is doing a bloody thing to protect her."

Ray looked down and continued to chop the onions as Alice looked at his face, sullen and grey.

"I am guessing this is part of your apology," she said, gesturing towards the assortment of meats, vegetables and sauces he was preparing. "Looks complicated."

"My famous Ragù alla Napoletana," he replied, allowing himself to adopt a more affected tone as he spoke. "It was Pete's favourite. I used to make it at least once a month. This is the quick version. There's another version I cook overnight. But, you know, needs must."

"You sure you shouldn't stick with something more basic, like a spag bol?" Alice asked, with a chuckle. "Less chance of it going wrong."

"Oh, wash your mouth out," he replied, smiling, but then his expression changed, saddened, and he said: "Sometimes we should invest in our apologies."

Alice smiled, sadly. "So, Ragù thingamajig it is," she said. "You know, you've never really talked to me about Pete."

Ray shrugged slightly but didn't say anything.

"So, now I know his favourite meal," she continued, her curiosity getting the better of her. "You were with him a long time. Mum said you two were together more than 30 years."

Ray nodded. "Pete's not a great topic of conversation for me, sweetie," he said.

"Oh, I'm sorry," Alice replied, unhappy that she had caused an uncomfortable moment between the two of them. "It's just that, you're such an important part of the family now, but everything I know about you, I mostly know second-hand from Mum. But I didn't mean to upset you. I am sorry."

Ray put his chopping knife down and exhaled deeply, releasing a little groan as he did. "No, it's fine," he said, quietly. "The truth is, Pete and I were very happy for a long time. Muddling along in our little cottage. Gardening, DIY, dinner parties, our annual holiday to Provincetown every July. And then we had a little taste of fame, and one bad decision led to another. Before we knew it, Pete was the nation's most hated man and I was being offered a load of appearances without him. And our happy little marriage just couldn't stand the strain of it all. Pete left the country and I ended up clearing out our cottage and selling it. It's not a great story, but that's it in a nutshell."

Alice was not quite sure how to respond. Ray had condensed the very public collapse of a 35-year relationship into a short tale that sounded more like a glib elevator pitch for a film producer. He hadn't offered much by way of detail; a sign perhaps, Alice wondered, that he was still grieving for his relationship with Pete. "Have you heard from him? Since he left?"

"Oh yes," Ray replied, a slightly more positive tone to his voice. "Quite a few times. We check in with each other every now and again. To be honest, Alice, at first, he blamed me a lot for what happened. He said I was so busy being the 'nice guy' on *Big Brother* that I was happy to make him look like the bad guy. But we're past that now. I think we're in quite a good place. We can both see that circumstances just got the better of us. Neither of us did anything intentionally to hurt the other."

"And is he happy? Settled?"

Ray shrugged. "He says he is, but I'm not sure. He didn't leave the country by choice. It was just impossible for him to stay. Everywhere he went he was abused, or had names shouted at him from across the street. And I could tell he just didn't want to be around me anymore. He couldn't stand it when he would see me get the complete opposite reaction from people."

"And America wasn't for you?"

"I wasn't invited," Ray replied. "When Pete decided to leave the country, it was very clear he was leaving me behind. But, as I say, we're good, now."

Alice didn't know Pete. She had never met him and, as she didn't watch reality TV, she wasn't familiar with the time he and Ray had spent in the *Big Brother* house. Before meeting Ray, the only version of Pete she had known was the one offered by her mother, and that had hardly been a complimentary description of the man. But she did know Ray, and she struggled to believe he would have spent most of his life with someone as awful as Pete was often accused of being.

She looked at the digital clock on the cooker which showed the time as 18:03. "Right," she said, "and on that bombshell I think you and I deserve a glass of wine. Red or white?"

"Yes please," Ray replied, eagerly. "Red for me, but white's good, too, if you'd rather."

Alice reviewed her mother's extensive collection of wines, stacked almost to the ceiling in a tall, wooden 64-bottle holder that stood next to the doors to the garden. Alice was no connoisseur, and so after pulling out and replacing a number of bottles, she simply picked the first that had a label she liked the design of.

She returned to the breakfast bar. "It's a chianti," she said, hoping that meant something to Ray, and quickly removed the cork and poured them each a large glass. "I'd offer a toast but I'm not sure what we would be toasting right now."

They both tasted the wine, and then Ray put his glass down and continued to prepare the food. "Anyway, what about you?" he asked. "Have you heard from the girls?"

Alice retook her seat and continued to drink her wine. "Ah, my turn," she said.

"It's only fair," Ray said. "Come on. What's happening with the girls?"

Alice had never been one to wear her heart on her sleeve; she had never been particularly demonstrative. She had a small number of good, practically minded friends, but mostly she had enjoyed her own company and committed the better part of the past 17 years to raising the twins on her own. In comparison, Ray exuded warmth and kindness, and there was something about his presence that often-persuaded Alice to let her guard down and speak more freely. "The girls are doing very well," she said. "They are getting to know their dad, they like his wife and their kids. They're loving Sydney. They love the house. It has a pool, as they keep reminding me. They're having the time of their lives, by all accounts."

"And their dad… Christopher, wasn't it? What's he saying?"

Alice took a large swig of wine and then shook her head, as though suddenly very sad. "He thinks I've done a great job raising two fantastic young women. He now wishes he had been a part of their lives all along. And he's really pleased Hannah and Emily are getting to know their brother and sister. It sounds very much like happy families all around." She finished her wine and immediately refilled the glass.

"It does sound like there is a 'but' coming at some point," Ray suggested.

Alice smiled, but it was not a happy smile. "I was Skyping the girls yesterday," she said, "and Emily mentioned, just in passing, that some of their friends from college are taking a gap year before university. I knew what she was going to suggest straight away, and I just couldn't cope with having that conversation, so I just quickly changed the subject and ended the call as soon after that as I could."

"You think they were going to ask about staying out there for longer?"

Alice nodded and then, with a great sternness in her voice, said: "If they don't come home, if they take a gap year and stay with their dad, then I think in six months' time Christopher will be on the phone talking about university courses in Australia."

"Don't be daft," Ray said, casually, "their entire life is here. Their friends. You, Val. They're just enjoying their holiday. And it must be nice for them to get to know their brother and sister. It's a big adventure for them, but they'll be home soon."

Alice rested her chin in her hands and grimaced slightly. "They've suddenly got this charming, charismatic Dad, his amazing house with a pool. All of these new relatives, everyone so pleased to meet them for the first time. It is such a huge adventure for them both. And how can I compete with that, Ray? How can I compete with him, if he wants to keep them?"

Ray put his knife down again. "You're serious, aren't you?" he said. "You're genuinely worried."

Alice nodded. "Don't tell Mum I said any of this," she said. "She's got enough to worry about."

"But they're children. And you have custody, don't you? It's not even their decision."

"They're 17 going on 18," Alice replied, "and they've always wanted to travel, the pair of them. And they've clearly fallen in love with Austin. And his big house with the pool. Did I mention he has a pool?"

Ray did not have an easy answer for Alice, and so he busied himself with his food preparation. But after a few moments of silence, he lifted his glass and tipped it towards Alice, as though toasting her. "Sweetie, thank you for sharing," he said.

Alice lifted her glass and returned the gesture. "You too," she replied. Before they could enjoy any more wine, they were interrupted by the chiming of the doorbell. "I'll go," Alice said. "I'm guessing Mum's still in the bath. So, you keep chopping and I'll go and see who it is."

"OK," Ray said. "But if its Adam Jaymes again, give me a warning signal so I can go change into something more tight-fitting."

Alice quietly made her way to the front of the house but remembered the new security protocols she had agreed with Valerie and so checked all the security locks before she called out: "Who is it?"

"Detective Inspector Sally Price," came the reply. "I am here to see Valerie Pierce."

Alice opened the door and looked the police officer in the face. "Nice to meet you," she said dryly. "But I think you might be a few murders too late."

CHAPTER 46

Valerie's bedroom had become something of a sanctuary over the previous few years. As part of the remodelling of the building, she had knocked three rooms on the second floor together, creating a large master bedroom with a walk-in wardrobe and en-suite bathroom. It had been tastefully decorated in shades of pale green, was gently lit by standard lamps and included a comfortable seating area for Valerie to relax and read when she did not want to use the rest of the house.

Her bath time had become part of her evening routine; a long soak in a double-ended slipper bath where she could drink wine and listen to her favourite music piped through to the Bluetooth speakers she had so proudly learned to master. Her choice of music was limited, singers like Elkie Brooks or Rod Stewart, voices that echoed from her past, which could transplant her to younger, simpler times. Most of her favourite singers had threatened legal action against her at one time or another, but she was still able to enjoy their music all the same.

That evening, her quiet time had been interrupted by an unexpected visitor. Alice had summoned her from her bath to let her know Detective Inspector Sally Price was waiting for her in the sitting room. But Valerie was in no rush to see her guest. Instead, she sat at her dressing table, brushed her hair and pondered how to handle the meeting.

Alice had brought her a fresh glass of wine, just in case she needed to settle any nerves before speaking to the police. But Valerie was not nervous. She was more than ready. She'd had enough of being frightened, of being discounted and ignored.

"I didn't have a good impression of Sally Price," she said. "The last time I saw that dreadful woman she essentially accused me of exploiting Javier's death to sell more copies of my book."

Alice was sitting next to her mother on an antique chaise longue they had bought together from a second-hand store in Leigh-on-Sea. "But more people have died since then," Alice replied. "I'm not being funny Mum, but you even guessed Gayesh was a likely target. You went to warn him. That's more than the police have done, and I doubt they would want that getting out."

The mention of Gayesh's name angered Valerie, and she began to brush her hair with more vigour. "Stupid man," she said. "I've known him for years, but he still couldn't be bothered to listen to me. He treated me no better than that stupid woman downstairs."

She placed her hairbrush onto the dressing table and sighed, immediately regretting how she had spoken about Gayesh. She turned to Alice and said, more gently; "But then, why would he have believed me? With no police investigation, why *should* he have believed me?"

"You did all you could, Mum," Alice replied.

Valerie stood, crossed the room and entered her closet, a room filled with clothes on hangers or folded onto shelves; outfits for all occasions and almost all in various hues of purple, Valerie's signature colour. She had already decided what she was going to wear. It was time to bring back some of the *old* Valerie Pierce, the powerful and feared Queen of Fleet Street, a woman who could end the career of any high-flying Government minister with just a few choice words. Valerie wanted to make it clear that, on this occasion, Detective Inspector Sally Price had bitten off more than she could chew.

"Have you thought about phoning Adam?" Alice asked. "Might be useful to agree what you're going to say. The last thing either of you want is for the police to think the pair of you have been up to no good."

"Oh, dear God no," Valerie called out, as she peered through her closet for one particular outfit. "Adam only has one priority. He doesn't want anything to happen that would lead the police or the media to Pearl Martin's daughter."

"And, is that likely? If the police start to investigate?" Alice asked.

Valerie paused what she was doing and recalled her own desperate threat to expose the whereabouts of Beth Martin, if Adam had declined to help her. It felt like a lifetime ago, that initial conversation with Adam, in a restaurant that seemed designed for secret meetings. In retrospect, it had not been

251

Valerie's proudest moment and it was certainly something she feared would appal her daughter.

"I don't know," she replied, quietly. "I do believe, however, that Adam was perfectly happy that the police did not believe me. As long as they are out of the picture, Adam feels in control and can protect Pearl's daughter. But I think he forgets that he's just an actor. He's not *actually* a superhero or masked vigilante solving crimes."

"So, what if the police tell us they believe you now?" Alice asked. "What if they announce they are investigating? It's going to be completely out of his hands."

Valerie stepped from her closet and, to Alice's great delight, she had dressed for battle. She was wearing Alice's favourite outfit, a fitted purple trouser suit. It had been a mainstay of her wardrobe throughout the past 30 years. But after she had left the *Daily Ear*, she had put it away and mostly forgotten all about it. For a long while, the suit had become symbolic of a person Valerie simply did not wish to be any more.

But now, in that moment, Alice could see that her mother needed to draw some energy from the powerhouse journalist she used to be. And dressing in her old clothes seemed to do the trick.

"What I think, darling, is that we leave Adam's name out of this entirely, for now. I will call him later if I need to, just to keep him in the loop. But if the police are finally taking this seriously then, for us at least, that's a good thing. Adam's priorities are different, and he will need to manage that himself."

"OK," Alice replied. "I'll pop down and let DI Price know you are on your way. And I'll quietly let Ray know not to mention anything about Adam Jaymes."

Alice left the room, and Valerie took a moment to consider her reflection in her full-length mirror. "That's more like it," she said, and then smiled to herself.

CHAPTER 47

"Is your mother going to be much longer?" DI Price asked. "I would like to speak to her with some urgency."

Alice and Ray were sat opposite her, not speaking, just staring at her disdainfully.

"Urgency?" Alice replied. "An interesting use of the word, wouldn't you say, Ray?"

"Yes, I would, Alice," he replied.

"Perhaps the police have a different definition of the word," Alice continued. "I always thought 'urgent' meant you had to something quickly, not casually saunter through the door after half a dozen murders."

DI Price returned the disdainful look and then said: "There really is no need for either of you to be here. I have come on my own to have a one-to-one conversation with Mrs Pierce. You may both leave."

"It's my house, officer," Valerie interjected, "and my daughter and ex-husband are more than welcome to stay exactly where they are."

All heads turned to the door where Valerie had appeared, glass of wine in hand. She crossed the room, and gracefully lowered herself into the armchair next to Alice and Ray. She then sat back and crossed her legs, placing her glass on the table next to her. "You said something about an urgent matter?"

"Yes, but it really would be best if we spoke alone, Mrs Pierce," the police officer replied.

"I believe I have already addressed that topic. So please continue."

Ray and Alice both smiled, somewhat smugly, at DI Price, and then both sat back and crossed their legs, mirroring Valerie's position.

"Very well," DI Price said. "I want to be clear, Mrs Pierce, that this is not a formal police interview. I simply wish to follow up our conversation from earlier in the month and update you on a few matters. I hope, also, that you might assist me with some additional information."

Valerie simply nodded, and then lifted her glass and casually sipped her wine.

"May I ask when you last saw Gayesh Perera?" DI Price asked.

"Yes," Valerie replied, brightly. "The last time I saw Gayesh was on the day he was murdered."

"And what was the nature of your meeting?"

"To warn him that he was going to be murdered," Valerie said, factually.

DI Price did not reply immediately. Instead, she stared at Valerie with a puzzled expression, as though attempting to assess her mood. And after a moment of contemplation, she asked: "You had evidence to suggest Mr Perera was in immediate danger?"

Valerie did not like the inference that she had failed to alert the police of an impending crime. "No," she replied, curtly. "As you know, DI Sally Price, I have been concerned for some time that somebody was targeting people with connections to the *Daily Ear* newspaper. And since the police have done nothing about it, I took it upon myself to visit Gayesh and warn him myself."

DI Price knew she was being baited but did not feel she was in a position to rise to it. And so, instead, she calmly continued to ask questions. "But did you have cause to consider Gayesh was at particular risk?"

Valerie shook her head. "No," she replied. "I bumped into him at an awards function a few nights ago. It occurred to me he could easily be at risk and so I made an appointment to visit him and warn him. Well, I thought someone should, bearing in mind you were doing nothing."

"You will admit, Mrs Pierce, that it is quite a coincidence," DI Price said. "Out of all the people you could have gone to warn, you happened to pick a man on the very day he died."

Valerie fixed the detective with a steely glare. "Unlike you, DI Sally Price, I'm not a believer in coincidence," she said, coldly. "Six men are dead. Six. All connected with the *Daily Ear*. They each died at 9pm, three days apart. And I would propose once more that they each received a phone call just before they died. If you are still, *still*, refusing to see a clear pattern in those deaths, then frankly you are an utter waste of public funds. Perhaps you should consider an alternative career better suited to *whatever* skills you *claim* to have. I believe the last time we met we discussed a career teaching French, didn't we?"

After a moment, DI Price leaned forward in her chair and appeared to speak to all three of the disapproving adults in front of her. "The last time we spoke I had no reason to suspect any wrongdoing," she said. "Since then, there have been a number of deaths, and other information has also come to my attention which has suggested at least one of these was the result of malicious intent."

"Malicious intent?" Alice blurted, loudly. "Oh, for goodness sake, you can't bring yourself to say murder. All of these men were murdered, Detective Inspector. Each and every one of them."

Whilst she was very pleased to see her daughter speak so strongly in agreement with her, Valerie wanted to hear what DI Price had to say. And so, she raised her hand, a sign for Alice to be silent, and asked: "Which one? Which death do you now believe could be the result of malicious intent?"

DI Price paused and then said: "We will be releasing a statement in the morning confirming we are launching a murder investigation into the death of Gayesh Perera. That's mostly the reason I am here; to give you forewarning that this is going to be in the public domain."

"Why Gayesh and not the others?" Valerie placed her glass of wine back onto the occasional table next to her, a sign that DI Price was now getting her full attention. "As my daughter has said, it would be useful to know what has changed your mind about that *one* death."

DI Price relaxed back in her seat again. "Most of this will be in the media briefing tomorrow, but it must not be released before the briefing. I hope you can agree to that, Mrs Pierce. I have colleagues speaking with family members at the moment, and it is important they have the opportunity to absorb the information before we go public."

Valerie nodded.

"You are aware that, just before he was electrocuted, Gayesh Perera told a security guard he had been threatened."

Valerie nodded. "Yes. I imagine he was threatened over the telephone. I did tell you that was part of the pattern."

"We are still working at the scene to unpick exactly what happened," DI Price said, "but we do know the security barriers had been modified. We still don't completely understand the modifications. But it would appear the moment Mr Perera inserted his security pass into the card reader, both the reader and the metal walkway he was standing on became electrified."

Valerie glanced at Ray and Alice, who both looked away from DI Price at the same moment, and directly to her, with expressions of total commitment. There was no hint of dissent from either of them, and Valerie realised she *had* the room. "And you are satisfied it wasn't simply botched maintenance work?" she asked and looked back to the police officer once more.

"Yes," DI Price replied. "The modifications that were made to the barriers were very specific and highly technical. Because of the expertise that was required, we believe we are dealing with someone quite extraordinary, and I am not using that word as a compliment."

"That's all rather gruesome," Ray said, unsettled at just how elaborate the killer's ploy had been in order to kill Gayesh. "But why electrify a security barrier? Why not just shoot him, or run him over in the car park? There are easier ways to kill someone."

Ray realised the other three people in the room were staring at him and appreciated his comment had sounded somewhat callous. "Well, come on, there are," he said, a defensive tone to his voice. "I'm just stating a fact."

"Actually, you do raise a good point," DI Price said. "We are building a profile of the killer, and we believe they are someone for whom the planning and the execution of this murder was as important as the murder itself. We don't yet know why he or she chose this particular method to kill Mr Perera, but we believe he is trying to make a point." DI Price then turned and looked at Valerie. "Mrs Pierce, have you any other information about the death of Mr Perera you are able to share with me? Did he say anything to you on the day to suggest he felt his life was at risk?"

Valerie shrugged and shook her head. "No," she replied, despondently. "When I told him of my concerns, he didn't believe me for a moment. And to be absolutely clear, DI Price, I blame you for that. Without even the hint of a police investigation, there was absolutely no reason he should give any credence to my concerns."

DI Price sat back in her seat once more, unhappy at having been chastised in front of members of the public. "As I have previously stated, Mrs Pierce, we are acting on new information that we did not have when we first spoke."

"But what about the others?" Alice asked. "Are you telling us that you are still treating them all as accidents?"

DI Price checked her watch, and suddenly appeared ready to leave. "I am not in a position to divulge any further information at this point in time," she replied.

"Oh, for goodness sake," Valerie said, becoming irate. "May I just point out that I might actually be able to help your investigation if you could at least tell me what you believe may have happened to some of my former colleagues. And, clearly, no one in this room is going to leak any of this information. We want you to find this killer. We aren't going to jeopardise your investigation for some tawdry online article. I don't need to grab for attention, I can assure you of that."

DI Price exhaled loudly and shook her head as though unable to decide what to do. And then she began to speak, but quietly, as though sharing a great secret. "We are continuing to investigate the death of Steve Gallant" she said. "We are reviewing the scene of his death and in particular the entrance he used to access the factory where he was killed. But we are hampered by the area itself. We are struggling to find who owns most of the buildings, and obviously there is no CCTV. And the eyewitnesses... well, it's fair to say they were somewhat intoxicated. So, it is proving tricky to establish the facts. Mrs Pierce, may I ask when you last had contact with Mr Gallant?" DI Price asked.

"Oh, years ago," Valerie replied. "When I left the *Daily Ear*. He wasn't a great friend or anything like that. Just someone I worked with. It is still terribly sad though."

DI Price nodded in agreement, and then asked: "And what about Jason Spade? When was the last time you had contact with him?"

The mention of Jason's name took Valerie by surprise and, for a moment, she let her guard drop and could only look to the floor, as a sudden wave of guilt and grief passed through her. If DI Price was reviewing Jason's death, she was clearly considering the possibility that he had also been murdered. And suddenly, Valerie could only imagine how frightened and alone Jason must have been in his final moments, paralysed and unable to call for help.

And then she recalled their brief phone call, shortly before he died, that dreadful, awkward moment when he had clearly reached out to speak to someone he considered to be an old friend, but instead Valerie had simply put the phone down on him. She did not wish to complicate the conversation with some pointless digression relating to Jason's vain attempt to speak with her, but she also had no intention of lying either.

"Val, are you OK?" Ray asked and leaned across to touch her hand.

Valerie looked at him and smiled. "I'm fine," she said, and patted his hand.

"I'm sorry Mrs Pierce. I'm sure none of this is particularly pleasant. But I do need you to answer my question. When was the last time you had contact with Jason Spade?"

"The last time I saw Jason was about four years ago, on the night he was the victim of Adam Jaymes' exposé," she said. She had chosen her words carefully. The statement was completely true, she had simply omitted to mention the more recent phone call. "We were all in the newsroom at the *Daily Ear* when the story broke. I remember I looked at Jason and said something like: 'You'll never come back from this'. And then Leonard... the editor, Leonard Twigg... he had Jason rushed from the building in the back of a van. I didn't have the chance to see to him again after that."

DI Price shuffled in her seat, as though preparing to stand up. "Mrs Pierce is there anything else you can share with me, anyone else you think I should speak with?" she asked.

After a pause, Valerie gently shook her head. She had decided that Adam Jaymes' involvement was something only Adam himself should divulge to the police. After all, he had only become involved as a direct result of Valerie's request. It would be, if nothing else, impolite to now hand his name to a murder inquiry. But she did feel it only right that his theory about the killer's motives be shared with the police.

"The only other thing I can offer you, Detective Inspector, is just an idea," she said. "If you are finally, truly open to the notion that I was right, that there is someone out there targeting people connected with the *Daily Ear*, then what if the connection is not just the *Daily Ear*? What if the killer is someone obsessed with Pearl Martin? Someone who is taking revenge on anyone who hurt Pearl during her life, or who has in some way damaged her legacy since her death."

"A crazed fan, you mean?" the detective asked.

"Yes," Valerie replied. "Pearl did seem to attract many of the nation's loonies. And it is all set out in my book, Detective Inspector. Each of the victims is named in Exposé, and if one of Pearl Martin's obsessed fans were to look for a motive for each murder, then I am very much afraid they will find it right there, in black and white. In my book."

DI Price said nothing to suggest she was either convinced nor sceptical of the theory. And then she stood up and brushed herself down. "This has been most enlightening," she said. "I will most definitely follow up some of your suggestions. But, as I said, I hope I can count on your discretion?"

"Yes of course," Valerie replied, and she looked to both Ray and Alice who nodded in agreement.

"Thank you," DI Price said, "and I will be in touch again if I feel you might be able to assist further."

Valerie saw the police officer to the door for a polite but expeditious farewell. Both women had something they wanted to do: Valerie wanted to return quickly to her lounge so she could discuss and analyse the conversation with Alice and Ray, whilst DI Price had a sudden urge to drive to the station and see if she could unearth her copy of Valerie's book.

CHAPTER 48

Lucy had agreed with Alec that he would not return to the house once his holiday was over. Instead, she would have his possessions moved into storage where he could collect them once he had found somewhere else to live. A removal firm had delivered a number of crates the night before, and she had spent the dark and lonely early hours of the morning gradually filling them with his belongings, willy-nilly. She wanted every last bit of Alec out of her house as quickly as possible and had little interest spending her time organising the content of each crate in a logical manner. He would simply have to sort through the chaotic content after he returned from his luxury paradise island.

She decided to take a break and so settled at the kitchen table with her laptop. She wanted to continue researching information for her exclusive story about illegal immigrants at the millionaire's yacht club. She had set her colleague, Lewis, the task of finding as much negative data as he could to support her angle that those arriving on English soil were aiming to do little else than commit crimes, claim benefits, hoodwink free treatment from the NHS and likely set up terrorist cells.

But, to date, he had been unable to find any supporting data. All the evidence suggested other countries – France, Spain, Germany and Greece in particular – had much higher rates of asylum applications than the UK. And there was no official data to suggest immigrants had any impact on crime rates, benefits, the NHS or council houses. If anything, it suggested immigration benefitted the UK. And that was not what Lucy had wanted to hear.

Her entire exclusive had been built around the idea of a dramatic confrontation: a group of newly arrived illegal immigrants would climb from their boat and come face-to-face with their most famous accuser. But that alone would not be enough, not on this occasion. She had wanted to expand her exclusive to include a plethora of facts about the impact boatloads of asylum seekers were having on the quality of life for decent, hard-working British families. Those facts would provide the context for her confrontation: the brave, well-informed journalist facing unwelcome foreigners who were putting the whole British way of life at risk.

Lucy wanted to convince her readers that EU bullies had created a bottle-neck which had forced asylum seekers across the Channel to England. She was going to enrage her readers with suggestions that those entering the country were all muggers, rapists and terrorists but who were still awarded huge benefit payments, hand over fist, and pushed to the top of every council house waiting list. But without any supporting data, Lucy wasn't sure where to take her story beyond her usual dog whistling.

She was not used to early morning visitors and so was perplexed when, at 7am on the dot, her doorbell chimed. She was unhappy that her routine was being disrupted and so stomped to the door and called out, sharply: "Who's there?"

"Lewis Greene, reporting for duty," came the response.

When Lucy had asked Lewis to assist with her article, she had assumed they would liaise by email, or phone. She had not expected an early morning visit to her house. And under normal circumstances, she would have sent him packing with a flea in his ear. She had opened her home to work colleagues rarely and, even then, only for those in senior positions who might benefit her career. The likes of *Communications Officer Lewis Greene* most certainly did not fall within that category.

And although her initial instinct was, indeed, to send him away, this quickly subsided. Lewis held an ambiguous role within the company; a young professional in a relatively junior position, but with inexplicably strong links with the executive team, and very much the editor's right-hand man. And although he was in a junior position today, she guessed he would move up the corporate ladder very quickly. Lewis Greene might be a useful addition to Lucy's circle of influential contacts. And so, she opened the door and offered him a happy smile. "Good morning," she said, as though pleased and unsurprised to see him.

Lewis, as always, was perfectly turned out. He wore a fitted black duffle coat, and under that a suit and tie. A leather laptop bag was strapped over his shoulder and he carried two lidded paper cups and a white box made of card. "Coffee and pastries," he said. "I thought I'd come prepared."

On some level, Lucy begrudgingly admired his gall. She invited him in and then led him through the long hall to the kitchen at the back of the house, closing doors to all the other rooms as she went. She did not want Lewis to see the turmoil created by her efforts to remove all trace of her husband from her house.

They set up a workstation at her kitchen table and sat facing each other, laptop to laptop. And after a few moments of casual conversation about the cold weather and the darker mornings, Lewis set about the task at hand, gathering negative data and information about asylum seekers and illegal immigrants for Lucy's exclusive article.

Lucy made an effort to look as though she were equally busy, but she was distracted by her young colleague and could not help but observe him as he worked. She remained somewhat perplexed by him; a bright young man, always smiling, polite. Someone who exuded warmth and good manners. But increasingly she believed that was all a façade.

Surely behind that cute smile and those sparkling eyes there must be a coldness, a steeliness. The secretive jobs he completed for Sydney were likely to be highly unethical, possibly illegal. So how else could a decent young man like Lewis undertake such tasks unless he was not the decent young man he pertained to be? She recalled their meeting in a lift a week or so earlier, when he so happily announced he was attending a party to celebrate the death of a former colleague. At the time she had found the idea amusing but, in retrospect, it was unsettling. Who was Lewis Greene, she wondered, who was he really?

"I hope you don't mind me asking," Lewis said, cautiously, looking over the top of his laptop at her, "but how did the phone call with your husband turn out? Was he surprised when you called him? I only ask because I was the one that got the number for you."

Lucy sat back in her chair, folded her arms and, with one eyebrow clearly raised, looked Lewis up and down. His role in securing the photographs which had proved Alec's adultery seemed to have left him feeling he was entitled to enquire about a private phone call. An audacious act, she thought, but for some reason she rather liked him for it.

With Alec out of the picture, and Steve gone, Lucy didn't have anyone to talk to, to express her anger to. There were very few people she considered friends, and none she would trust to confide in. She had yet to speak to her parents about Alec's affair, and had no doubt they would blame her. They had both adored Alec and would most likely explain away his adultery by suggesting Lucy must have failed, in some way, as a wife.

And so, over the previous few days, her big empty home, her pride and joy, had become little more than an echo chamber for her feelings of betrayal, amplifying her anger as each solitary day passed by. And although she knew little of her current companion, discretion was certainly at the heart of everything he did. He appeared very capable of keeping matters private, and Lucy really needed the chance to vent.

"You appear to have an interesting skill set," she said.

"Well, I've learned to make myself useful," he said. "Apologies. Have I spoken out of turn?"

Lucy shook her head and relaxed her arms. "No, it's fine. Let's be honest, I wouldn't have been able to speak to Alec at all if it hadn't been for you. The conversation went pretty much as I expected. He was calm, didn't even seem surprised. Said he was relieved it was out in the open, at last. Told me how happy he was with 'Gemma'. Said he hoped I could find the same happiness with someone else."

Lewis curled his face slightly. "Ooh, no" he said. "That's shady. He shouldn't have said that. What a tosser."

"Thank you!" Lucy replied with a loud, positive tone to her voice, happy that her own feelings had been validated. "And you know what, Lewis, on the surface, everything he said was tick-box perfect. He said sorry. He said it was all his fault. He said he would agree to anything I wanted. He would fully take responsibility. But I knew, I just bloody knew, he was being a dick. And I am sure 'Gemma' was sat next to him during the whole call. I could hear it in his voice, as though he was playing to an audience. And I was the butt of their fucking joke."

As she spoke, Lucy could feel herself growing angrier. She could feel an entire well of hatred and rage bubbling inside of her, one that she knew would need some release.

"Has he agreed to the divorce? And the gagging order?" Lewis asked.

"Oh yes, yes," Lucy replied. "And I think he was actually quite thrilled when I told him I would keep his affair secret. The truth about Alec is that he loves attention. He absolutely lives for his social media. Most nights he would post a picture of himself, usually shirtless, and then sit there for the rest of the evening counting the likes and reading the comments. Most of them filthy. He's addicted to it, couldn't live without it. But he has seen what happened to other men who cheated on their wives, you know, famous rugby players or TV chefs. They instantly lose their entire fanbase. Even the Gays abandon them. And Alec couldn't last a day without his bloody gays."

"So that's it? Quiet divorce. All amicable. It's done?"

Lucy smirked. "Well, not entirely," she replied. "I've changed all the locks to the house and am moving all of Alec's possessions into storage. There's a removal firm coming this afternoon. I told him on the phone I would be doing that. I don't want him to have any reason to come back to the house. I don't want to see him. And he agreed to it."

"Seems fair," Lewis replied.

"But… I have done something I did not agree with Alec over the phone," she said. "My pièce de résistance. Yesterday I sold his car. His treasured 1966 Austin Healey BJ8 mark 3. I advertised it online and sold it within an hour. For a pound."

Lewis chuckled. "A pound?" he said. "Classic."

"But it's not enough," Lucy said, with a frankness that surprised both of them. Once said out loud, she decided she might as well expand. "I want him to suffer," she said. "I want him to suffer now. I want to ruin his fucking holiday. I want him stranded there, miserable, worried. Unable to concentrate because he doesn't know what's going on back home."

Lewis was silent for a moment, quietly pondering Lucy's predicament. And then he reached over and gently tapped the top of her laptop. "This isn't your work computer, is it?"

Lucy shook her head. "No, it's my own," she replied.

"Did he ever use it? To access his social media, or his bank accounts?"

"No, not really. Not since he gave it to me."

"So, it used to be his?" Lewis asked.

"It was originally. He let me have it when he upgraded, but he deleted all his files."

Lewis gestured with his hand for Lucy to move it over to him. "Anything on there you wouldn't want me to see?" he asked.

Lucy shook her head. "Nope. Nothing," she replied, beginning to have an inkling of what Lewis was going to do.

He slid his laptop to one side, and manoeuvred Lucy's across the table and in front of him. "Let's see what sort of cyber trail he left behind," he said, and wriggled all his fingers. "Is this yours?" he asked and hovered the cursor over a small icon on the internet browser.

Lucy leaned over to see the screen and then shook her head and shrugged. "I don't think so. What is it?" she asked, settling back into her chair once more.

Lewis smiled. "It's an extension on your browser, a password manager. You've never used it?"

"No, I've never needed to. Is it useful?"

Lewis flashed his eyebrows. "I think Alec may have overlooked it when he was deleting his files," he said. And then, with startling speed and ease, he accessed all of Alec's social media accounts and changed the passwords and security settings to lock him out of each of them. He then accessed Alec's bank accounts, including a few Lucy had known nothing about, and cancelled all of his credit and debit cards by reporting them all stolen, before changing the passwords and security questions to lock him out of those too. And then, as a final flourish, he accessed Alec's mobile phone account to report his phone stolen and imposed a temporary block to prevent the phone being used.

He then moved the laptop back to Lucy. "Sorted," he said, and smiled. "No social media. No credit or debit cards. No money. No phone. Now that's what I call stranded."

Lucy was at a loss for words at first. She was thrilled with the technical brilliance her colleague had demonstrated and knew she would likely make good use of his skills again in the future. But she was also somewhat surprised at the gleefully malicious way Lewis had quickly executed the task. It had been unexpected, particularly from a young man who presented in such an unassuming and well-mannered way.

"Thank you," she said, realising she owed Lewis a show of gratitude. "That was… quite something."

"All in a day's work," he replied, and then returned his focus to his own computer.

"It's not that I don't appreciate your help, Lewis," Lucy said, "but why *did* you do that? It's not part of your job. And to be honest, we barely know each other. I mean, I'm very happy that you did it. But *why* did you do it?"

Lewis sat back in his chair and his bright, young face suddenly looked less bright. "To be honest, I have very little patience with guys like your husband," he replied. "My dad treated my mum the same. They weren't married, like you and Alec, but they were in a long-term relationship. Lived together. Had me. Bought a house. But when I was about seven, mum found out he was having an affair."

"How did she find out?"

Lewis took a deep breath, and then leaned forward onto the kitchen table, as though sharing a darkly kept secret with Lucy. "My dad worked in sales and was away from home a lot."

The moment the words left Lewis' lips, Lucy knew she wanted to roll her eyes or groan: 'worked in sales', 'away from home a lot'… The words screamed 'adulterer'. But she was intrigued by her unexpected companion and so chose to rein in her usual behaviours.

"He didn't earn much but luckily Mum was really good with money, always squirrelling it away into savings," Lewis continued. "I don't know how she did it, to be honest. But there was always plenty of money when we needed it. So, we had a nice house and Mum was at home full-time. But then one day, when Dad was supposed to be away on a business trip, Mum found out he was actually tucked up in some Travelodge with a woman he worked with. It had been going on for years, apparently."

"What happened?" Lucy asked.

Lewis shrugged. "Mum phoned Dad and told him she knew about his affair, and then Dad just… well, he didn't come home again," he replied. "Straight away, he moved in with the other woman, started a new life for himself. Without Mum, without me. And Mum just got on with it. Took over the house, the mortgage. Paid all the bills. Did it all single-handed. I've no idea how she did it. She just found the money from somewhere. But she was never the same again. It was like she just closed off a whole part of herself, anything that exuded warmth or love. Towards anyone, even me. She was just … cold, from that day onwards."

Lucy was finding it difficult to relate to Lewis' story. She was angry about Alec's affair, but she certainly wasn't devastated. There was no way her entire life would fall to pieces because of his adultery. But she knew, in situations like this, it was important to show interest if not empathy, and so asked: "What happened to your dad?"

"Oh, he's fine," Lewis replied, an edge to his tone that revealed a great unhappiness with his father. "He moved on with his life very quickly. Married his girlfriend six months later. They had a couple of kids. But he did the same as your husband. He tried to present himself as being magnanimous. He let all our family and friends know that he had wished Mum the best, and hoped she would move on, meet someone else. He even invited Mum to his wedding."

"He did what?" Lucy blurted out, the information resulting in an unexpected spasm of anger. "He invited your mother to his wedding? His wedding to his mistress? I assume she said no."

Lewis nodded. "Oh yes, of course. But it was all part of Dad's plan. He wanted everyone to think we were all happy about it, that he and Mum had separated amicably and were going to be mates. So, when mum said she wouldn't go to his wedding, he got really nasty. Started slagging her off to anyone who would listen. Tried to screw her over financially. In the end, she got to keep the house. But we mostly lost touch with him after that. I think his girlfriend wanted him to focus on *their* kids and didn't want me to be a part of their life." Lewis smiled at Lucy, knowing he had revealed a great part of himself to her. "So, that's why I helped you," he said. "Your arsehole husband reminded me too much of my arsehole dad."

Lucy had not expected him to share such a personal tale and wasn't entirely sure what to say in response. But she could certainly see the parallels between his dad and her husband, and the comparison had done little to quell her anger. "I'm sorry to hear that," she said. "But I promise you, that is not going to happen to me. Alec can have his mistress and his divorce. I will move on, too. I guess, if I'm honest, I was never as reliant on Alec, or as in love with him, as your mum was with your dad. It's going to be easier for me. Although ruining Alec's holiday really fucking helps, so thank you again for that."

An unexpected pause followed, and Lucy realised Lewis wished to ask her something else but appeared to be gathering his nerve.

"Tonight," he said, eventually, "I hope you don't mind, but I'm going to come back and drive you to the marina," he said.

Lucy gurned slightly and shrugged. "No need," she said, "I'm quite capable of driving myself."

"Oh, I know, I know," Lewis replied immediately, clearly wishing not to cause any offence. "To be honest, I'm on a photography course and I've been trying to convince Sydney to give me some on-the-job training. I thought if I got some good shots tonight, he might give some more thought to it."

Lucy looked blankly at Lewis. She had been so busy jealously guarding her scoop she had not even thought of booking one of the *Daily Ear* photographers to go with her. And she realised Lewis had offered her both a problem and a solution in a single breath.

"I can bring my equipment with me, to get some good shots for your piece. I won't interfere, I'll keep out of sight. You won't even know I'm there."

Lucy raised her hand. "Yes, yes, OK. That's fine," she said, as though graciously conceding to his wishes. "But I will drive. And I will cancel the booking I've made with the photographic department. You can be my photographer for the night. Just don't fuck it up."

"I won't, I promise," he replied, with a huge smile on his face. "Thank you."

CHAPTER 49

As Valerie's taxi pulled up outside the restaurant, she gazed at its vague, nondescript exterior – another of Adam's carefully chosen haunts – and it occurred to her just how much thought and planning someone with Adam's level of celebrity must have to put into a simple, everyday task like booking a table.

"Are you sure this is it?" Alice asked, looking quizzically at her mother. "It's just… well… it's just a door. It doesn't look like the sort of place you'd expect an international star to be hanging out."

Valerie slipped some cash through the money slot in the glass screen and thanked the driver. She then collected her things, buttoned up her coat, and ushered her daughter from the taxi. "Don't do that again," she said, once the car had pulled away.

"Do what?" Alice asked, and zipped up her raincoat.

"Mention anything about who we are meeting in front of Joe Public," Valerie replied. She gestured with her hand towards the battered red door, made notable only because of a small sign above it decorated with the words 'Red Door'. "Places like this can only exist if ordinary people don't know about them."

Alice looked around the quiet, dark and windswept street, dimly lit by streetlamps, and felt as though the whole of London was a million miles away. They were only a stone's throw from the West End, but it felt like one of the most isolated locations she had ever visited. "Yes," she replied. "Sorry."

"And remember," Valerie continued, "whatever or whoever we see behind that door, do not give any indication that you are impressed. At the end of the day, it's just a restaurant. If any of the staff get snotty with you, put them in their place."

"And how do I do that?" Alice asked, beginning to find her mother's conduct a tad irritating.

Valerie took her daughter by the arm and marched her forward. "Oh, I don't know. Order something and then send it back," she suggested.

The red door opened onto a quiet, intimate restaurant, separated into booths and partitioned by screens, offering privacy and comfort as much as fine dining. Valerie could imagine it was the sort of venue where Harry had romanced Meghan beyond the gaze of the press, or where endless ministers had conducted their affairs. And all within an agreed understanding that what happened in the restaurant stayed in the restaurant.

She glanced at her daughter who was stood with an expression which, annoyingly, looked like awe and Valerie certainly was not having that. "What did I just tell you, Alice? Close your mouth and stop looking so impressed," she said, quietly but sternly. "It's a restaurant, not the Sistine Chapel."

Alice shook the expression from her face. "Sorry," she said, humbly. "I think I just saw David Beckham and it threw me for a moment."

Valerie took a deep breath. "Oh God, not the bloody Beckhams," she groaned. "The amount of times they've sued me over the years, I'm probably paying for their bloody dinner."

The maître d', a handsome middle-aged man with a neatly trimmed beard, and perfectly turned out in a dark blue suit, approached them from his station. "It's Ms Pierce and guest?" he enquired.

"Oh, that's *Mrs* Pierce," Alice interjected, politely, before her mother could reply less politely. "*Mrs* Pierce and guest."

The maître d' smiled. "Yes of course. The other member of your party is already seated," he said. "Please follow me."

As he led them through the restaurant, Valerie whispered to Alice. "Don't look at the other tables," she said. "Let them look at us, but don't look at them."

Alice was struggling to understand all the rules of dining in a celebrity venue but managed to follow her mother's advice by fixing her gaze on the maître d's surprisingly pert bottom as he showed them to their table.

As they approached a darkened booth towards the back of the restaurant, Alice could see Adam Jaymes already stood, waiting to greet them. She had forgotten how dazzlingly handsome he was, even more so on this occasion, turned out in a dark burgundy three-piece suit with the top two buttons of his shirt open and his thick hair swept back from his face. And for a moment, a brief but telling moment, her stomach turned over as she came face-to-face with one of the world's most famous actors once more. Even under such awful circumstances, she couldn't help but thrill with the excitement of meeting him again.

"Your guests," the maître d' said to Adam.

"Thank you, Fred," Adam replied. "We're fine for now. Perhaps fifteen minutes?"

The maître d' nodded, took Valerie and Alice's coats and promised to return later to take their orders. Adam then gestured to the seating within the booth, and they all took their seats.

"I ordered some wine," he said. "I trust I can pour you a glass without having it instantly thrown in my face?"

Valerie smiled, broadly. "I'm not making any promises," she said.

Adam poured them each a glass and then sat back in his seat. "I wasn't sure if you would wish to undertake some small talk before the meal, or just dive straight into the business at hand." He then noticed that Alice had already finished her glass of wine and so, smiling gently at her, he poured her a second. "Good stuff, isn't it?"

Alice grinned and nodded. "Sorry. I don't get out much" she said.

Adam returned her smile, and then looked towards Valerie once more. "I saw the news reports about Gayesh. It seems the police have realised at least one of these deaths is suspicious. Our killer is getting sloppy."

"The point," Valerie replied, sternly, "is that it's phone call night. And after all these deaths, we are still no closer to stopping… whoever it is that's doing this."

Adam frowned, puzzled by something Valerie had said. "Phone call night?" he asked.

She nodded. "It's what we called it, back at the *Daily Ear*. During your campaign to bring the paper down. Every three days, at just before 9pm, you would call someone to let them know you were about to publish some terrible and dark secret they had been hiding. We started to call it 'phone call night', because whoever received your call, well, we knew their life would change. And not for the better."

Alice knew the story well but struggled to connect the man in front of her with the one who had so ruthlessly brought the *Daily Ear* newspaper to its knees just a few years earlier. And as she gazed at his face, expressionless at that moment, she could not help but wonder if she could see a slight hint of a smile; gratification or perhaps even pride.

"And you are still frightened that you may receive a call?" he asked, calmly.

"I believe I am as likely a target as anyone," Valerie replied. "Gayesh is being treated as a one-off, at the moment. Although I get the impression they are reviewing the circumstances around Steve's death. But right now, Gayesh is the only one that's led to an actual murder investigation. And, I must say Adam, with all your resources, you don't appear to be bringing much to the table. I thought we'd have this solved by now and this maniac would be behind bars."

Adam sipped his wine, and then asked: "How do you know that? What you said about the police looking into Steve?"

"Mum saw Gayesh the day he was killed," Alice replied, feeling the need to project some warmth into the conversation, as she could see her mother and Adam were taking their corners, ready for a potentially unpleasant fight. "So, we had a visit from the police, to ask Mum a few questions."

"It was exasperating," Valerie interjected. "DI Sally Price. She would not concede anything. Still the same old nonsense, refusing to so much as consider any links between all these deaths."

"That is probably a good thing," Adam replied. "At this stage, we don't want the police upscaling their operation. They'd only get in the way."

Valerie and Alice exchange puzzled looks and then stared at Adam in surprise.

"I… I beg your pardon?" Alice said. "Adam that is *exactly* what we want. We want the police to launch a full murder enquiry. For all of these deaths. You… you do understand that, don't you?"

For a moment, the conversation stalled. Adam did not answer, leaving an uncomfortable impression that he was calculating the pros and cons of a number of different responses. And it seemed to his two dinner guests that he had done something he so rarely did: the famously private superstar had accidentally revealed a great secret. Far from working, with Valerie, to prove to the police a serial killer was at large, Adam Jaymes had an agenda entirely of his own.

"Adam, how did you think this was going to play out?" Valerie asked, anxious to understand whether Adam had been working against her the whole time. "What do you think you are going to do if you track this man down? What exactly is your end game?"

CHAPTER 50

"It doesn't look like much," Lucy said, as she stepped through the darkened walkway from the parking zone and looked around the marina. About thirty luxury yachts of various sizes were moored, but all of them were covered and locked down. The marina was enclosed by half a dozen newly developed apartment blocks, some six storeys tall, others higher. But all were completely unlit and served as nothing more than a wind tunnel for the howling gale that was blowing in from the sea.

Beyond the dock, Lucy could see little but a rolling expanse of black, the restless dark sea beaten by the wind, carrying sprays of seawater into the air and onto the slippery cobbled walkways, fresh and newly laid.

Lewis joined Lucy and buttoned up his coat, feeling a dip chill after leaving the warmth of the car with its heated seats. He held tightly to the strap for his camera bag, to stop it straying in the breeze. "I know all the apartments have been sold," he said. "And it looks like the owners have started using the marina for their boats. Do you think there's been a power cut or something?"

Lucy sighed, somewhat disappointed. "I imagine they've all been bought on spec, and no one can move in until all the pipes and electrics are completed. It's not going to make for great pictures. I was hoping to have some wealthy families quaffing champagne in the background."

They surveyed the grim scene before them, and then Lucy turned to Lewis and said: "I think it best you wait in the car, to begin with. My contact isn't expecting anyone but me and I need to tell him you are here before he sees you."

Lewis scowled and shook his head. "Lucy, I'm not sure that's a good idea. We've just had all our safety training at work and there's a whole section about lone working and…"

Lucy raised her hand and silenced him. "Lewis. I'll be fine. As soon as I've spoken to my contact, I'll send you a text to let you know it's OK to join us. But, for now, car!" Sternly, she handed him her car keys and pointed him to the dark recess that led back to the parking zone.

Lewis nodded and did as he was told and quickly disappeared into the shadows. Lucy watched him leave, and then set about trying to find the boat where she had arranged to meet her contact, described as a medium-sized yacht called *The Ocean Pearl*.

"Hello? Is someone there?" Lewis called. He clicked a button on the keys and Lucy's car momentarily lit up to confirm it had been unlocked. Amid the darkness and the sound of the howling wind, Lewis thought he had caught sight of something, out of the corner of his eye; a fleeting glimpse of someone, perhaps in a hoodie, rushing from the dimly lit, empty car park into the darkness beyond. "Hello? Are you here for Lucy?" he shouted into the air.

"I'm… I'm Lewis. I'm her photographer. She's just gone to meet you at the boat."

He waited for a reply and began to think that perhaps his imagination was running away from him. Perhaps the ghostly wailing of the wind and the creeping darkness around him was getting the better of him. But as he listened more intently, he was sure he could hear something. Footsteps, quick paced, as though someone were running, trying to move with such speed that Lewis would not be able to see them.

Unnerved, he moved more quickly towards the car, planning to call Lucy the moment he was inside with the doors locked. But as he approached, the car unexpectedly lit up once more and he heard the unsettling clunk of the doors locking him out.

"What the hell…?" he quietly asked himself, and then held the keys before him and began to repeatedly press the button that would normally unlock the doors. But the fob appeared dead in his hand, no longer having any effect.

Desperate, he hurried to the driver's door and began to pull on the handle, pressing the key fob again and again. But nothing happened. He was locked out. And as the interior light gently faded into darkness, Lewis could just make out his own reflection in the car window and realised someone was stood behind him.

Slowly, he turned, and found himself facing the hooded figure, the one he had seen out of the corner of his eye. "You… you've done something to the car, haven't you? To stop me from getting in," Lewis said, nervously.

Gently, and without speaking, the figure nodded, and reached out to show Lewis a small black device in the palm of his hand.

"You were blocking the signal from my fob," Lewis said, quietly, and the figure silently nodded once more. And then, with a sudden, savage punch, Lewis was knocked to the floor. Shocked and frightened, he tried to recover and get back to his feet, to run away. But his assailant was too quick and rained down a series of hard blows to Lewis' head. Lewis tried to call out, to scream for help, but the wind was too loud and easily overwhelmed his terrified cries, cries that diminished with each attack.

Still and silent, Lewis lay on the floor, his eyes closed, his arm outstretched under the car. His hand fell open and the keys to Lucy's car tumbled from its grasp and onto the cold stone floor. His attacker stood astride him, taking a moment to look at him in the dim light from a nearby streetlamp; the young man's pale complexion, bloodied by a deep cut to his forehead.

The attacker knelt and gently stroked Lewis' hair from his face, as though suddenly conflicted by what had happened between them. After a moment, he picked up the keys to the car and pressed the fob. The car lit up and clicked open, and Lewis' lifeless form was lifted from the ground and placed inside the boot.

Once more, the attacker took a moment to stroke the young man's face, before reaching inside Lewis' pocket to retrieve his mobile phone. Once unlocked, using Lewis' thumb print, the phone was used to take a series of photographs of his beaten and bloodied face.

CHAPTER 51

"There are things you don't understand," Adam said, quietly. "There are… complications. Things I need to take care of."

His dinner guests remained silent, waiting for him to expand on his comments, to offer an explanation, a reasonable and believable explanation, as to why it was best the police were not involved in trying to track down a serial killer. But moments passed, and it became clear the actor had concluded his statement and did not feel the need to explain further.

Alice shook her head. "No, no, no," she said. "Absolutely not. There are *no* complications. Nothing at all that would prevent us handing any evidence or information we have to the police. What on earth is wrong with you, Adam?"

Valerie reached across the table and gently squeezed her daughter's hand. "Perhaps Adam can explain what he feels these other priorities are," she suggested, and then turned her gaze to Adam himself. "Although, I do have an inkling what… or rather *who* this complication is."

Adam stared back at Valerie; his bright sparkling eyes suddenly darkened. "I'm sorry, Valerie. But she's my priority. She always has been. You know that."

Valerie quietly sipped her wine and did not respond. She was suddenly cautious of the conversation, worried of what Adam might say, in front of Alice.

"There was a time when almost every journalist in Fleet Street was trying to find her," Adam said, "to get that exclusive interview with the only child of one of the world's most famous women. And even today, all these years after Pearl's death, the world still wonders what happened to Elizabeth Martin. And I have to protect her from that."

"Oh, that's a bit of an exaggeration, surely?" Alice said, a hint of derision in her tone. "She's hardly disappeared. She was adopted. Why should anyone expect to know where she is now?"

Adam smiled. "Because people, like your mother, feel entitled, Alice. Entitled to know anything about anyone. The idea of privacy, or someone's right to privacy, does not exist. For people like your mother."

Alice realised she had stumbled, and had inadvertently handed Adam an opportunity to attack her mother. She felt a sudden need to defend Valerie, and so replied by saying: "I think that's very unfair, Adam. Even if Mum knew who and where Beth Martin is, she wouldn't tell a soul. And apparently, it would be the exclusive of the century. But she *wouldn't* do that. So clearly you don't know her as well as you think."

Adam raised his brow, and for a moment looked as though he were about to reply. But Valerie did not want that part of the conversation to develop, for her daughter to know the threat she had made to Adam to secure his services. "The point, Alice, is that clearly whoever this lunatic is, he apparently has found Pearl's daughter. And that, I assume, is the issue." She turned and stared directly at Adam. "You want to shut him up, don't you? You want to ensure that whatever happens, he won't be in a position to expose Beth Martin."

Adam did not reply.

"And how exactly are you intending to do that?" Valerie asked. "We're talking about a serial killer, Adam. It's not exactly the sort of person who's going to be open to negotiation, or bribery."

Again, Adam did not reply.

"Or, perhaps, that isn't the point," Alice said, softly, beginning to feel a sickening sensation in the pit of her stomach as Adam repeatedly failed to reply to the conversation. She stared into his dusky brown eyes, which seemed to have lost their sparkle. Now, they just seemed dark, as though a shadow had fallen across his face. "Perhaps you're planning to ensure he is never found," she said, "that this becomes another of those unsolved mysteries. Who was the *Daily Ear* killer? We'll never know. Because he took his secrets with him to the grave. Adam Jaymes made sure of it."

CHAPTER 52

Lucy was determined that the night would be a success. She needed that success. She needed to break a story, a big story that would gain traction in the national press, on social media, perhaps even internationally. Thanks to Donald Trump's election campaign and his promise to build a wall, illegal immigrants had become a hotly argued issue once more. And Lucy wanted a piece of the action.

And if that night was a success, and her article became a national talking point, perhaps Trump might even share her story with his 12 million Twitter followers. Her name as a hard-hitting British journalist could begin to gain recognition in the States. And what a magnificent platform that would offer Lucy. Elevated way beyond her boring peers, to an entirely different level of stardom, of notoriety.

And whilst she was whizzing around the world taking part in conferences and TV interviews, speaking at Republican conventions and advising Trump on immigration issues at the White House, she would become the must-have guest for every news and current affairs programme on every channel and station in the UK. All those arrogant producers who repeatedly declined to book her for their shows would suddenly find she did not have time for them, because she would cherry-pick only the very best offers. And her cheating husband would be sat at home with his dull girlfriend, wishing he hadn't thrown it all away. Lucy would have the sort of fame Alec could only dream of. And she would love knowing how jealous he would be.

As she marched up and down the dock, trying to find *The Ocean Pearl*, she was already planning her questions for the family of asylum seekers she was about to confront. They would climb from their vessel, exhausted and desperate, but receive a far from warm welcome. Rather, Lucy planned to harangue them, to demand they justify their decision to leave a safe country like France to travel to England in such a reckless fashion.

She already knew how her copy would read. She would paint a picture of a situation that was spiralling out of control, of dangerous and deceitful foreigners swarming across the Channel like cockroaches, to infest the British mainland with their non-British views and customs and claim benefits meant for hard working British families.

And it suddenly occurred to her that she might have a bigger success that night than she had anticipated. Perhaps, if she were aggressive enough, she might repel the invaders, turn them back to sea. Perhaps Lewis would photograph her, heroically forcing the immigrants back onto their boat, single-handedly denying them free access to British soil. She could become a national hero, at least for those as determined as she to protect the British way of life.

Thrilled by her own ingenuity, she wondered if the local council would consider erecting a statue in her honour, right there in the marina, showing her with her hand outstretched, as though saying "No more" to the rolling seas. It would only take a little prompting for her army of Twitter followers to begin crowdfunding. And her name, and her bravery, would become indelibly linked to that stretch of water.

As her mind began to wander into the realms of fantasy, she stopped at a yacht and saw it had 'The Ocean Pearl' painted along the side. It was one of the less impressive vessels, with a faint light in the cabin and a small dinghy moored to the side. But she was now too excited to care. The yacht had its stern butting the walkway, and a low bathing platform, offering Lucy easy access onto the boat.

She hastened on-board and made her way to the cabin door, but found it locked. She knocked and called loudly, to make herself heard over the roaring sea and howling wind: "This is Lucy. I believe you are expecting me." But there was no answer, and after a few moments of silence, she realised no one was there.

Frustrated, she decided to investigate the rest of the boat, and edged around the starboard side, clutching the handrail tightly for support until she reached the bow. And for a moment she simply gazed out across the enormous, roaring expanse of water in front of her. And she wondered how anyone could be so desperate they would risk their lives travelling in such conditions.

As she began making her way back to the bathing platform, she felt her mobile phone vibrating in her coat pocket and wondered if it was her contact, letting her know why he wasn't there yet. It was almost nine o'clock. He was definitely late. She suddenly worried that perhaps he was cancelling, phoning to tell her everything had fallen through and she would have to come back a different night. And she had no time for that. She needed the story to happen there and then, that night.

"Hello. This is Lucy," she said, and began to carefully edge her way back towards the stern of The Ocean Pearl. At first all she could hear was the sound of the wind, somehow captured by the phone and broadcast back to her through the earpiece. And then a voice came on the line, a terrible, soulless voice stripped of all humanity and recreated electronically. Loud and angry, it screamed down the line at her; "*Hello Lucy Strickland. This is your murderer. I just called to let you know it's your turn.*"

Lucy stopped, frozen to the spot. "I'm… I'm sorry?" she replied. "Who is this?" There was no reply. The line was dead, and her phone gradually lost its glow and went dark once more. She was suddenly very frightened and aware of how alone she was, stood by herself, not even on dry land. And then she remembered Lewis was only a short walk away, safely locked in her heated car. And as an unfamiliar sensation of panic began to rise inside of her, she realised all she wanted to do was jump in the car and drive away.

She put her phone back in her pocket and began to edge her way forward once more, but as the wooden jetty came into view, she realised she was no longer alone. A dark figure, hooded and still, was at the stern of *The Ocean Pearl*, only just visible in the darkness around them. Without thinking, she prepared to call out, to ask for assistance. But she quickly gathered her thoughts and realised she had no idea who the figure was, and there was a very real risk he might have been the person who had just called her, threatened her.

Instinctively, she edged back to the bow of the ship and crouched down, hiding. She wanted to call Lewis, to ask him for help, but she was worried she might be heard, or that the light from her phone would alert the man on the jetty to her location. She needed another option. And as she looked around her, she noticed something metal was hooked over the railings next to her. She leaned forward and looked downwards, and saw it was a boarding ladder, connecting directly to the dinghy next to the yacht. And that was her escape.

With the punishing, freezing wind still blustering around her, Lucy was overwhelmed by the need to flee, as quickly as possible. She quietly climbed over the railing, trying to ensure the ladder did not clatter against the side of the boat. The darkness grew even more intense as she entered the shadow of *The Ocean Pearl*, and onto the dinghy.

It moved beneath her feet, far less stable in the water than the larger vessel it was attached to. But there were two oars laying on the floor and even though Lucy had never rowed before, she was confident she would have enough natural skill to take herself from harm's way, perhaps out to sea a little, just far enough that the man on the jetty could not reach her, and she could safely call Lewis.

The rope holding the dinghy in place was easy to untie, and then she sat back and manoeuvred the oars into the water and began to row. With reassuring speed, the dinghy moved quickly away from the yacht, away from the jetty and into the expanse of rolling black water that led to the sea beyond the marina.

Once there was enough distance from the land for Lucy to feel safe, she drew the oars onto the boat once more, lay them on the floor and took out her phone to call Lewis.

Not far away, on the other side of the empty apartment blocks, the faint sound of a mobile phone ringing began to emanate from the boot of the only vehicle in the darkened car park.

"Come on, Lewis. Pick up, pick up, pick up," Lucy said. But after a few more rings an electronic voice offered Lucy the opportunity to leave a voicemail. Her heart sank, and she realised her only option was to call the police instead.

As she began to dial 999, there was a roar from the darkness beyond her dinghy. A load, growling, mechanical roar. She peered through the darkness in the direction of the sound, and another boat suddenly lit up in front of her, about ten metres away. It was a small vessel, something more along the lines of a motorboat, and it seemed unnecessarily well lit, as though someone was trying to draw attention to it.

Lucy dipped down in the dinghy and stared ahead, a desperate hope that this was someone who could assist her. But as a figure came into view, waving at her, directly at her, any hope or sense of safety was immediately stripped from her. It was the same hooded figure she had seen on the jetty; he had a boat of his own and he knew exactly where Lucy had escaped to.

Panicked, she realised she had to get back to shore as quickly as she could and so scrambled for the oars. As she did, the motorboat began to move in the opposite direction, away from the land and out to sea. Suddenly, the dinghy lurched backwards, throwing Lucy onto her stomach and as she tumbled, she lost her grip on her phone, which slipped from her grasp and disappeared over the side of the boat and into the hungry black water beyond.

She felt the dinghy tip up slightly at the front as it started to move in the wrong direction, away from the land, somehow following the motorboat, its speed growing. For a moment, in her confusion, she thought the dinghy had simply been caught in an undercurrent created by the larger vessel and was following in its path simply because of the amount of water being churned and displaced in its wake.

She pushed herself up, holding tightly onto the plastic grips on the side of the dinghy to prevent herself from slipping down to the foot of the boat, and realised a light was being shone directly at her from the other vessel. It illuminated sprays of water either side of the dinghy as it began to pick up speed, taking her quickly away from the marina and out to sea.

Lucy was helpless, unable to move, clinging on simply to stay within the boat as it moved quicker and quicker. For a moment, she was able to lift her head, just enough to see the front of the dinghy, and realised there was a second rope, tightly pulled, connected to the motorboat in front, dragging her out to sea. The dinghy had not been her escape. It had been a trap.

CHAPTER 53

"You are both being ridiculous. I am not planning to kill anyone," Adam said, quietly but sternly, to draw a line under the suspicions that were being voiced in front of him. "And I give you my word, I am not holding back any information. The truth, Valerie, is that we have found nothing. Whoever this person is, they are smart. Really smart. They've not left a data trail, nor any physical evidence, not a spit of DNA. Their only slip up to date was giving Gayesh the opportunity to call for help before killing him. If it had not been for that, there is every chance the police would be treating his death as some mechanical accident, not murder. Another accident to add to the list of all the other accidents."

"Fine," Valerie said. "So, you aren't withholding evidence. But that is not the point is it, Adam? You still want to find this man first, before the police."

"Yes," he replied, flatly.

"But why, Adam?" Alice asked, gently. "What good will that do, apart from placing you in danger, incredible danger? This man is a killer. Do you honestly think you can barter with him, get him to agree to… to retract his threat to expose Pearl's daughter?"

Adam sipped his wine, as though trying to buy a few extra moments to assess whether to share his thoughts with Valerie and her daughter. He placed his glass back on the table and released a deep sigh. "If truth be told, I am not sure if the threat to expose Beth is real or not," he said. "If we are dealing with someone who is obsessed with the memory of Pearl Martin, I struggle to believe they would willingly destroy the life of Pearl's only child. But a threat was made. It was clear and targeted. And so, I need to take it seriously."

"But how exactly are you hoping to buy his silence?" Valerie asked. "I fully appreciate who you are married to, and the resources you have available to you. But sooner or later this man will be caught, and he will go to prison. For the rest of his life. And all the money in the world is going to be worthless to him when he's behind bars."

Adam shook his head and then replied with a surprising candour. "Not money. I am not going to offer him money," he said. "But he is obsessed with Pearl, which *does* give me room to negotiate. There are things I can offer him. Things no one else in the world has. Things no other fan in the whole world has ever seen. Letters Pearl wrote; private letters to me. Other things, gifts she gave me, had made for me. A music box that plays 'Thank You for Being a Friend'. A one of a kind."

"The *Golden Girls* theme song?" Alice asked.

"Yes," Adam replied, and then smiled fondly. "It was our song," he said. "She had it made especially for my 18th birthday. And, I believe, it is something this man would want."

Valerie had a clear memory of Adam and Pearl singing 'Thank You for Being a Friend' on *Children in Need* many years earlier, when Adam could have only been fourteen or fifteen. It was that night the nation truly fell in love with Adam Jaymes, a handsome teenager in a suit with a surprisingly powerful and beautiful voice. The public reaction to the performance was so overwhelming that the BBC quickly recorded and released the song, which made three times more money than the show's official charity single that year.

"But it's not as if you can pop in for a quick chat once he's in police custody," Alice said. "Everything you are talking about is dependent on you finding him before the police. And apart from the fact that it is going to be incredibly dangerous, I just don't understand how you are going to manage it. By your own admission, your people haven't found a single clue."

"And I'm sorry, Adam," Valerie said, "Getting you a private audience with this lunatic is not our priority. Our priority has to be helping the police find him. We must put him behind bars. Someone could be killed tonight, another innocent victim. Stopping this is our priority."

Adam's expression changed, became more serious, and Alice wondered if it was because her mother had used the phrase 'innocent victims'. She doubted very much that Adam would consider any of those who had died to be truly innocent. "Mum's right," she said. "That has to be our priority. I think it is time we spoke to the police again and, this time, you need to come with us, Adam. The police clearly think Mum's a complete loon, but I think they will have a tougher time dismissing you."

Despite the insinuation in her daughter's words, Valerie nodded and agreed. "We have an opportunity now," she said. "I hate to admit it, but Gayesh's murder is the opening we needed."

Adam shook his head. "No, I'm not speaking to the police. Not until I have spoken to him."

Alice went to reply, to plead with him to change his mind, but Valerie raised her hand to silence her.

"Adam Jaymes, that is utterly irresponsible," she said, an anger beginning to harshen her tone of voice. "People are dying, being murdered. Beth Martin's privacy is not our priority."

"But it is mine," Adam replied, bluntly, and appeared unexpectedly heated by Valerie's words. "I am sorry, but she is, and always will be, my priority. You know that. The only reason I am involved in this at all is because *you* threatened to expose her if I did not help you. And you did that because you knew full well what buttons to press. I will do anything to keep her safe."

Adam's words arrived like a great and terrible wave, sweeping all other issues from the table, and leaving Valerie and Alice in very different places.

"You... you said what?" Alice asked, hoping she had misunderstood the comment. She turned her head and looked her mother directly in the face, suddenly overwhelmed by a deep and sickening sense of loss, as though her transformed mother was nothing but a lie, a fraud. "You threatened Pearl Martin's daughter?"

Adam fell silent and sat back. He did not consider it his place to cause friction in other people's relationships and had not intended to create it between Valerie and her daughter.

Valerie, at first, was flummoxed, and struggled to find the right words. "That's... that's not quite what happened," she said. "Alice, you must remember how frightened I was. I am. How desperate I was when the police kept sending me away. Adam was my only hope, and I would have said anything to gain his assistance."

But a familiar feeling settled onto Valerie, a feeling that her daughter was not truly in the room with her, that she was already absent. Any warmth

Alice had tried to bring to the conversation evaporated. Her face became flushed, and her body language shifted, became more rigid.

"I honestly thought you had changed," Alice said quietly, no longer looking at Valerie and avoiding any eye contact with Adam. "I told you, Mum, what you did to me, how you *ruined* my childhood. You and Dad. Using me like you did. To this day, I am still ridiculed. Those bloody pictures of me eating that mad cow burger or wearing that hideous Shirley Temple dress to the Royal Variety Performance."

Valerie did not reply. She knew there was no point. She had reached this moment with Alice so many times in the past, and she knew even the grandest, most heartfelt apology would make no difference. A wall had reappeared between them, and it would take a long time before it was gone again.

"I thought you had listened to me, Mum. I mean *really* listened to me. But now, here we are, and you would happily chuck another young woman under a bus. To ruin her life, like you did mine." Alice quietly collected her things together, and without another word she left the table and walked towards the exit.

Valerie remained seated, knowing any attempt at a conversation in that moment would only make matters worse.

"Are you not going after her?" Adam asked, softly.

Valerie shook her head. "No," she replied. "We have reached this same precipice too many times in the past and I have learned, at a great cost, that Alice will need time alone to process her thoughts before she will be in a place to speak to me again."

"I did not intend to cause an argument between you and your daughter," Adam said. "I am genuinely sorry."

Valerie nodded. "Not a great night for any of us, was it?" she asked.

Adam shook his head. "Probably not," he replied.

Valerie sighed. "Adam, I want to say, to make it clear," she began, suddenly feeling propelled to make a confession to him. "When we first met, that dreadful night Javier died. What I said about Beth, the threat I made. It was an empty threat. I would never have done it. But now, I'm sitting here feeling just terribly ashamed of myself, and I want you to know the truth. I would not, and will not, ever, expose her identity. To anyone."

After a moment, Adam nodded. "I did not believe for a moment you would do anything to harm Beth," he said. "And to be honest, I am not entirely sure why I agreed to help. It certainly wasn't under duress. I suppose, on some level, I was intrigued enough to investigate it. And then, when I woke up the next morning and heard what had happened to Javier, it became clear you were onto something."

Valerie smiled, ever so slightly, and then picked up her wine. "Thank you," she said.

"I'm sorry I have not been as forthcoming with my intentions," Adam continued. "And to be clear, I'm completely committed to capturing this person and putting them behind bars. I was simply seeking a way to do that and protect Beth at the same time. I can appreciate how those two objectives might appear incompatible."

Valerie shrugged. "So, what do we do?" she asked. "We've gotten nowhere. Even with all your resources, we're no closer to finding out who this man is."

Adam gently pushed his wine glass with his fingers, forward and back. "Valerie, we are missing something," he said. "It is staring us in the face, something obvious. I can feel it."

Valerie checked her watch. "It's after nine," she said. "No phone call. Looks like I dodged a bullet again."

CHAPTER 54

It took a moment for Lucy to realise that the motorboat had stopped. Her dinghy was rising and falling on the cold, black waves beneath, but it was no longer being dragged out to sea. Lucy had clung on as hard as she could and managed to keep both oars within the dinghy by wrapping her legs around them. They would be her only chance of getting back to shore.

Frightened and cold, she carefully pulled herself forward as much as she could, to peer over the side of the dinghy and across the rolling waters, to try and judge the distance back to the marina. She had no idea how far she had been pulled by the other vessel; how far out to sea they had travelled. It had felt like an eternity, tightly clinging to the handles while the velocity of the speeding vessel had almost forced her out from the bottom of the dinghy and into the sea.

The spotlight from the other boat lit the monstrous moving ocean around her, waves crashing and roaring amid the freezing wind. The darkness beyond that light was overwhelming. Lucy had no idea where she was. And she wondered if this was it, that the other vessel would now turn tail and leave her behind, with only the oars to help her back to shore.

But then a particularly high wave raised the dinghy into the air, and dropped it suddenly back down, lifting Lucy momentarily from the boat. She screamed, terrified she was about to be washed overboard, and clung on to the plastic handles as hard as she could. But as the dinghy settled again, she looked down and realised the oars were gone. "Oh no, no," she cried.

The light began to grow brighter, and suddenly Lucy could see the side of the motorboat drawing parallel to the dinghy, like a great white sea monster lurching towards her.

Lucy struggled on to her knees, still holding tightly to the grips, hoping desperately that this was the moment it would all be revealed as some terrible prank. Some idiot with a camera phone would appear, live streaming her terror for the world to see. And then, once he had his stupid little victory, he would grant her access to the motorboat and safe passage back to shore.

She could see the rope adjoining the vessels being pulled in, the larger of the two, still brightly lit, looming down at her. A shadow fell across the dinghy as the hooded figure appeared, looking over the side of his boat directly at her, and Lucy squinted to see if she could identify her assailant. But he remained silhouetted, just a shape.

"Who the hell are you?" she screamed. "What the hell is this about?" Her words were strong, angry, a vain attempt to conceal her terror, to force herself to feel tough and empowered, even adrift and alone in the middle of the sea. But as moments passed, the crushing reality of her helplessness pushed down onto her. No one was there for her. No one was looking for her, not at that precise moment. Lewis had probably fallen asleep in her warmly heated car as he waited for her call. Alec was still abroad, living it up with his trollop girlfriend. Sydney wasn't even aware of her trip down to Kent. And Steve... and Steve...

As an image of her dead colleague unexpectedly appeared in her mind, Lucy suddenly remembered all those other conversations she had overheard about people who had died, people who were connected to the *Daily Ear*. At her very first meeting with Lewis, he had been heading off to some mock wake for the paper's former PR director. And then there had been Javier, at about the same time. And Jason Spade, the paparazzi guy who went to jail. And Steve, of course. And more recently, some Indian bloke who used to be chief executive or something.

So many deaths, in such a short space of time, in less than a couple of weeks. And now here she was, tricked and kidnapped. And she wondered, with a grinding tension in the pit of her stomach, if this hooded figure had been responsible for them all. Had this madman killed Steve, and all the others?

"Did you do it?" she yelled, wanting to ask a question but not wanting an answer in case it was an affirmative. "Did you murder my friend? Did you murder Steve Gallant?"

The figure seemed to lean forward, although it was tricky to know for sure with the two vessels moving about so aggressively in the sea. But as she peered through the lights and the spray from the water, she could see, she could most definitely see, the figure nod.

"Oh my God," she whimpered, realising all hope of a safe passage to shore was now gone.

The figure moved suddenly, and Lucy narrowed her eyes to try and understand what was happening on the boat. And then she saw it, a knife. Large and shining in the lights, her assailant's hand tightly gripping the handle.

She shuffled as far from him as she could, as far into the dinghy as was possible. And she wondered if he was going to climb aboard, to attack her there in that stupid little inflatable boat. But he made no such movement. Instead, he reached down, as though pointing at the dinghy with the tip of the knife. But he kept leaning down, until the tip was in contact with the dinghy. And then he kept pushing and pushing. And in that moment, completely alone and knowing not a single person in the world was thinking of her, Lucy realised her fate.

The knife created an indent in the thick rubber shell of the dinghy, and the harder the man pushed, the more the rubber stretched until finally, it yielded, and the knife slipped through the shell, creating an enormous puncture. And then the hooded figure withdrew the knife and made a second cut further along. And then another, and another, being sure to hit all the inflation chambers inside. Lucy realised he wasn't even looking at what he was doing. With each stab of the knife, he was looking directly at her, as though wanting to see her fear, her desperation. He was enjoying this.

"You're insane," she said, but her words were lost to the howling wind and the roar of the sea. She watched, paralysed, unable to move, as her assailant untied the rope binding the two vessels together and wound it back onto the motorboat. Then with a cheerful wave, he disappeared from view.

Already, Lucy could feel the tightly pulled plastic of the dinghy beginning to crumple beneath her, and the side of the boat punctured by the knife was rapidly deflating. The lights shining around swung away, and there was a growl from the other vessel as it suddenly twisted away from the side of the dinghy and roared into the blackness beyond.

Darkness fell around her. Lucy could barely see a thing. But she could feel the dinghy collapsing beneath her. Freezing water splashed against her side, and then the PVC vessel disappeared completely. She grabbed out, thrashing against the sea that engulfed her, her panicked mind thinking the dinghy might still be there, might still have enough air to provide a float, something to cling to as she tried to swim back to shore. But as her coat tangled around her, the hungry, angry sea pulled her downwards. The surface was gone, now somehow impossibly far above her, and her arms did not have the strength to fight her way back to air.

She could feel blood pumping furiously behind her eyes, as her lungs filled with water. Images flashed through her mind; Alec, his girlfriend. Her beautiful house. And as she began to lose all sense of where she was, and what was happening to her, her mind focused on the despicable realisation that she had not thought to change her will; *they* would get her house, *they* would end up living in her beautiful house. Alec and his floozy.

And then, as the crushing, freezing blackness around her finally squeezed the last oxygen from her helpless body, a vision appeared before her. A little immigrant child, like the one who had drowned in that very same stretch of water, reaching out to her, to help her home.

And in that moment, the final moment of Lucy Strickland's angry life, she wished more than anything else that child was really there; to drown in the sea, instead of her.

CHAPTER 55

HM Coastguard scrambled a search and rescue helicopter after receiving an emergency call from a member of the public that a woman was seen in a dinghy heading out to sea in stormy conditions. The rescue helicopter was deployed along with two RNLI lifeboats to try to find the missing vessel.

"...is thought to be Daily Ear journalist, Lucy Strickland, whose car was found abandoned at the marina. The news comes amid rumours that Ms Strickland's marriage to entrepreneur and social media star, Alec Matthews, had recently come to an acrimonious end."

> *I am currently waiting with bated breath for #LucyStrickland*
> *to be washed up on a beach so I can punch the air. Does*
> *that make mea bad person?*

"...is flying home from a private holiday retreat this morning, where it is reported he had been relaxing with family friends following the breakdown of his marriage to Ms Strickland. Mr Matthews, a prolific Instagrammer, had been notably absent from his social media accounts over the past few days..."

"...was Lucy's increasing far-right views, something I know Alec struggled with. You have to remember he's a modern young man with a very broad fan base. And he told me, many times, how upsetting it was when he was targeted for online abuse because of something his wife had written for the Daily Ear..."

All I'm getting from this #LucyStrickland story today is that #AlecMatthews is now officially single again and might need a cuddle.

"…blamed for contributing to a resurgence of racism and homophobia in the UK. Last year, the Labour Party published data from the police which pertained to show a direct correlation between spikes in complaints of racist abuse and the publication of Strickland's articles in the Daily Ear. The lesbian, gay, bisexual and transgender (LGBT) rights charity, Stonewall, had also publicly called-out Strickland for regularly deadnaming trans celebrities in her weekly tirades and promoting hatred against trans people…"

Javier García, dead. Jason Spade, dead. Steve Gallant, dead. Lucy Strickland, missing and hopefully dead. It's been a bad few weeks for #TheDailyEar, but Satan must feel like he's won the fucking lottery!

Sickened by weak, woke snowflake lefties demeaning #LucyStrickland's work today. She had more balls than all of them put together, and was the only one brave enough to speak up for white British people who are sick of coming last #RIPLucy #BritishFirst

"…has confirmed that the body of a woman has been found."

@ValeriePierce53 My local Tesco Extra has gone from "May I help you pack?" to "You're alright packing, aren't you love?". I'm not sure if it's the reduction in service or the overly familiar tone but, either way, I won't be going back.

CHAPTER 56

Sat alone at a table for two in full view of dozens of other people, Valerie felt very conspicuous. Moments earlier, as the waiter had walked her through the restaurant to her seat, she had noted how many heads had turned her way, how many conversations had suddenly become excited and hushed, a clear sign that she had been recognised by some of the other diners. And she was increasingly anxious that the better informed among them might also recognise Sydney when he arrived.

It was a great shame, she thought, as she had spent days looking forward to their lunch, a chance to catch up with an old colleague, an old friend, after far too long. But now, in front of an audience of the wealthy and connected, she wondered what they would make of Valerie Pierce having a seemingly clandestine meeting with the editor of the *Daily Ear* just a day after the prized role of weekly columnist had so suddenly been vacated.

The previous day's news had turned everything upside-down. Although she had no time for Lucy, the details of her grisly demise had been a great shock. And even though the media had once again reported it as another accident, another journalistic venture gone wrong, Valerie had no doubt Lucy had been the latest victim of the *Daily Ear* killer.

It was barely twenty-four hours since her body had washed up on a beach in Suffolk and Valerie did not want anyone to think, even for a moment, that she was taking advantage of the situation, that she had swiftly arranged a meeting with Sydney to negotiate her return to the world's biggest-selling tabloid newspaper. She had even suggested they postpone, or even cancel, their lunch appointment. But Sydney had insisted they still meet.

Valerie tried her best to filter out the prying eyes and whispered comments by focusing on her mobile phone. She had taken to checking her emails and messages regularly, hopeful for some gesture from Alice, some suggestion that her daughter was moving past the events which had unfolded during their meeting with Adam Jaymes. But, again, there was nothing.

The day before, Ray had kindly confided that Alice had contacted him to check how her mother had coped with the news of Lucy's death, and to enquire if Adam Jaymes had been in touch with any information. But she had not contacted Valerie directly, and while Valerie would usually afford her daughter the time and space she needed to move past her latest issues, on this occasion she did not feel there was any time at her disposal. The next 'phone call day' could be Valerie's.

"Hello Val, my dear," came a familiar voice, gravelly and reeking of tiredness.

Valerie slipped her phone into her bag and looked up to find Sydney stood next to her, the waiter helping him from his raincoat. "Sydney," she said, smiling, and enjoyed a moment of genuine warmth at being reunited with a long-lost friend. He kissed her on the cheek and then the waiter pulled out his chair and he took his seat.

"Blood awful day," he said. "Bloody awful couple of days."

"Yes," Valerie replied, and tried to see out of the corner of her eye if any of the diners had reacted notably to Sydney's arrival. But judging by the lack of interest at the other tables, it would appear no one had recognised him. "To be honest, I am surprised you didn't cancel. I would have totally understood," she said.

Sydney shook his head. "God no," he replied. "This is the one thing I have been looking forward to. And I don't look forward to many things these days, believe me. Cancelling this was not an option." Unexpectedly, he reached across the table and squeezed Valerie's hand. "I've missed you," he said, "and I'm sorry I've not been in touch."

Valerie smiled and patted his hand. "Don't be daft," she said. "You had more than enough going on, becoming editor, and then Yvonne. I sent her a few letters, you know. Included some old photographs I had found. I don't know if she received them."

"Oh, she did. She did," Sydney replied. "And they meant the world to her. Honestly, the absolute world to her. But she just didn't want to see anyone at the end. Cancer took almost every dignity from her, and that's not how she wanted to be remembered. I know you will understand that."

Valerie took a deep breath, recalling her late husband's final days, and suddenly felt a great remorse that a dear friend like Yvonne had suffered in a similar way.

Sydney withdrew his hand and smiled at her. "You know, when I met Alice, at Jeremy's grave, and we had a chance to chat and catch up… I don't know, it all came flooding back to me. All those years, all those dinner parties and soirées. And all that time we worked together, too. Golden days, really."

Valerie smiled and nodded. "Yes," she said. "I must admit, I do sometimes feel a little pang of sadness that I'm not with you all anymore. But I don't regret walking away when I did. And against all the odds, I've made a success of it since."

"Oh, I know, I know," Sydney replied. "And it's not the same, anyway. Too many of the greats are gone. And the new offices are crap. And the new owner's an arsehole. Honestly, Val, you got out at just the right time."

Valerie chuckled at Sydney's familiarity. There were only a few people she had ever allowed to call her Val, but Sydney had done it from the first day they had met and, for some reason, she had never minded. "Well, if your plan was to ask me to come back, you're not exactly selling it to me," she said.

Sydney raised his brow and nodded. "Oh, I had great plans," he said. "But I think we can agree the timing isn't right."

Valerie nodded. "No, absolutely," she said. And her heart sank a little. Although she was far from certain she would have agreed to return to the *Daily Ear*, she suddenly found herself bereft that the offer was no longer on the table.

"In the past week, I've had two members of staff die," Sydney continued, "another's gone AWOL. And, between you and me, the police are now reopening Steve Gallant's death because they've decided there may have been foul play after all. And we've had a massive systems breach. All our emails, private files, the works. I just don't know what the fuck's going on."

The mention of Steve made Valerie's heart skip a beat. "Sorry, what was that about Steve?"

"Oh yes," Sydney said. "Turns out—"

They were interrupted by the waiter, who took their order and then began to busily ensure they had the correct cutlery. By the time their wine had been delivered, and poured, Sydney had lost his trail of thought entirely and so Valerie quickly nudged him back in the right direction.

"What were you saying about Steve?"

"Oh yes. Steve Gallant," he said. "God, that man was a dick. But, anyway, yes, turns out the police now think he didn't wander into that factory by mistake. They reckon he was tricked. It all sounds really grim. I mean, if it's true, someone must have really fucking hated him."

Although it had not been her intention, Sydney's talk of Steve suddenly made Valerie realise her lunch could prove a source of useful insight. But she knew she had to be careful. She did not wish to prompt Sydney into a trail of thought that might send him back to the office with a whole new way of looking at so many recent deaths connected to the *Daily Ear*.

"I am sure it will all come to nothing," she said. "Granted, Steve was a bit of an idiot, but I cannot imagine he did anything so bad someone would actually want to kill him," she said. "Especially not recently. His glory days were well and truly over."

Sydney nodded in agreement. "Yes, you're probably right," he said. "Anyway, what are you up to at the moment? Alice said you've had some stuff in the *New York Times*."

Valerie sipped her wine and then smiled. "Oh yes, reaching across the pond. I approached them with a series of articles about Thatcher's close relationship with Reagan and why people shouldn't expect the same of May and Trump. The Americans absolutely lapped it up. I was even on CNN and Fox."

"You've really found your niche outside the Ear," Sydney said, with more than a hint of admiration in his voice. "And any more books? The last one was an absolute cracker."

"Really?" Valerie replied, surprised. "You read Exposé?"

"Of course I bloody did," he replied. "I wanted to see if I was in it. Sadly not. Everyone else was. But I didn't even get a fucking mention!"

Valerie almost slipped, almost told Sydney that if her suspicions were correct, *not* being in her book may well have saved his life. But she quickly gathered her thoughts and moved the conversation on. "Well, I am researching my next. A bit different this one. Celebrity stalkers."

Before she could continue, their starters were delivered to the table. Sydney had spicy meatballs in a thick tomato sauce with bread, while Valerie had marinated artichoke with a watercress velouté. Sydney had not eaten all day, and rapidly tucked into his meal. But Valerie had not finished with the topic, so she quickly restarted the conversation, "Anyway, where was I? Oh yes, my next book. Celebrity stalkers."

CHAPTER 57

Ray was trying his hardest to appear nonchalant, but Adam Jaymes' unexpected visit was proving highly stimulating. The actor was sitting at the breakfast bar in Valerie's kitchen, wearing tight blue jeans and a fitted white shirt, displaying every detail of his toned physique. In particular, Ray found that his eyes kept wandering to the bar stool and Adam's muscular bottom. The air was scented with a subtle, attractive fragrance; a gentle, spicy scent of lime, nutmeg and vanilla. He assumed it was from Adam's own gender-neutral line and was trying to think how he could enquire without seeming like a dirty old man who went about sniffing much younger men.

Adam had arrived without warning and asked to be invited in, even after being told no one else was at home. And now Ray was enjoying an entire fantasy where Adam admitted his marriage was a sham and that he always had a thing for older, silver-haired men in their fifties.

"I hope you don't mind me imposing?" Adam said. "I was hoping to see Valerie and I sent my driver away to get his lunch before I checked she was home. And, well, it would be a bit tricky to just go for a walk or order a cup of tea in the local café while I wait."

"No problem!" Ray said and realised, in his excitement, he had over-enunciated the words. And he hated himself for it. He cleared his throat and then, more quietly, said again, "No problem at all. I was about to make some lunch if you haven't eaten? Or a glass of champagne? There are always a few bottles chilling. Or a cup of tea?" Ray deliberately gestured to one of the kitchen cupboards, in the hope Adam would acknowledge the muscles of his outstretched arm.

"A black coffee would be perfect, if that's OK?" Adam replied. "And please, instant's fine."

"Oh, OK," Ray replied, a little surprised that Adam Jaymes even knew what instant coffee was, and then busied himself filling the kettle and organising mugs. "Are you absolutely certain I can't tempt you with anything else?"

Adam shook his head. "No, thank you," he replied, politely. "I fast for sixteen hours each day. So, it's pretty much sparkling water and black coffee until 2pm."

"Oh, I've heard of that," Ray said, "does it work?"

Adam shrugged. "I've been doing it for years now. I never deviate from it, and it has helped me keep in shape."

Ray joined Adam on one of the stools while he waited for the kettle to boil. "You know, I read all the fitness magazines and websites. I've never once seen any mention of you fasting."

Adam sighed. "I try not to bore people with it, to be honest," he replied. "Exercise and healthy eating have always been a part of my life. But that's not the case for everyone. And there have been too many occasions when pictures of me have been used to body shame other people. And that's not how I want my image to be used. So, I just quietly do my own thing and hope other people are happy and healthy doing their own thing."

"I follow a strict vegan diet," Ray said, his go-to topic whenever health and fitness were being discussed.

"And does that work for you?" Adam asked.

Ray stood up and lifted his arms. "You tell me?" he said, and did a little turn, his desperate sexual attraction making him lose any sense of subtlety. And for a moment, he just stood there, with Adam looking at him, seemingly unsure what to say next.

"Well, you… you do have a fantastic physique," Adam eventually replied.

Ray was thrilled with that response and wondered if it might to lead to something more, what with them being two attractive gay men, alone in a house with multiple bedrooms.

But then Adam continued. "I wish my dad would exercise more," he said. "He's in his fifties, too. And, I will say, he looks great. But a lot of that is because he's naturally slim, so he's never really bothered with exercise, and his diet is terrible. I do worry he's got a lot of health problems waiting in the wings as he gets older. You know, things like visceral fat."

Ray was mortified at being compared with Adam's father, and was grateful when the sound of the kettle boiling gave him a neat opportunity to change the topic of the conversation. "You are very welcome to wait here of course," he said, and poured their drinks. "But I am surprised you haven't just summoned your driver back."

"No, of course not. He has to eat," Adam replied, as though appalled by the suggestion.

"Oh, I know, I know," Ray replied. "But I just thought, you know. The lifestyle you must lead now. I mean, you have a really successful career anyway. But you're married to one of the world's richest men. It's just easy to assume all you have to do is click your fingers and everyone jumps to it."

Adam frowned. "Well, I – I don't click my fingers at people, Ray. I hope you know that's not the sort of person I am."

Ray nodded. "Of course. Sorry. I just haven't met someone like you before, Adam. You know, super-rich, super famous. Sorry. I'm making assumptions."

Adam nodded, and then chuckled slightly. "To be honest, I know a lot of super-rich, super-famous people and there are some who do behave very badly."

"Ooh, feel free to name names!" Ray replied, with excitement and brought their mugs of coffee to the breakfast bar and sat down once more. He hoped that perhaps 'celebrity gossip' might prove to be the much-needed common ground to enable some sort of relationship to blossom between the two of them.

But Adam shook his head. "No, that's not my point," he replied. "Ray, I've not always had money. This is all still relatively new to me. I grew up in a little two-bedroom cottage in a small village in Essex. My mum's a music teacher at the local school and my dad writes books about musical theatre. They really never made much money, but between the two of them they earned enough to pay the bills and put food on the table. And I never went without. I had lovely birthdays and every Christmas was magical. You don't need much to give your kids a magical Christmas. And each year our family holiday was a week in Margate. Always at the same family-run hotel."

Ray knew some of this from his years of Googling about Adam Jaymes. But he hadn't known about the annual trip to Margate and, in that moment, that little unexpected piece of information encapsulated Adam's childhood more than anything else; a working-class couple and their little boy staying for a week in a cheap B&B in a windy seaside town.

"My point," Adam continued, "is that we didn't have money. But I had a lovely childhood and was raised with manners and a sense of respect for others. And although my life has changed enormously since my childhood, my values remain the same."

Ray smiled. "I'm actually really pleased to hear that," he said. "I know gay men can sometimes get caught up in these stories about the diva-like demands of the world's biggest stars. You know that story about the princess who stubbed out her cigarette on someone's hand because there wasn't an ash tray. Or the singer who had to be carried into a hotel because the managers forgot to cover the floor of the lobby with rose petals for her arrival. And we adore them for it. To a degree. We act like it's hilarious. But, in truth, if you love a celebrity, you just want to know they're a decent human being more than anything else."

"And do you think I am a decent human being?" Adam asked, a little smirk lifting one side of his mouth. "Valerie might disagree with you, if you do."

"Valerie has changed a lot since she left that newspaper," he said. "And I think the past few weeks, and the help you've given her, the support... I think she is struggling to dislike you. But don't tell her I said that."

Adam shook his head. "Wouldn't dream of it," he replied. And then, in a more serious tone, he said: "May I ask how you are? The news about Lucy Strickland must have been a shock for you. I understand you were in the *Big Brother* house together a few years back."

It was a question Ray had not expected. Even Valerie hadn't asked him how he had felt, and he had not had the opportunity to consider his own feelings. And so, he paused for a moment, and tried to think how he had reacted to news of Lucy's death. "I hadn't really thought of it, to be honest," he said. "I mean, you might know that I didn't like her. I know you aren't supposed to speak ill of the dead. But when we were in the *Big Brother* house together, I just found her angry and rude. All the time. A bit of a bully, if I'm honest. And, since then, the way she's abused her position on social media and in that paper to promote racism, homophobia, transphobia... it really shocked me; disgusted me."

"You're not obliged to like everyone, Ray," Adam said, in a reassuring tone. "Just because someone has passed away, you don't have to pretend to like them, either."

"Oh, I know, I know," Ray said. "But I suppose what was strange, now I think about it, when we heard the news that her body had been found, I remember that my heart skipped a beat. Not just because I know it probably wasn't an accident, and that she was tricked or trapped and then killed by some lunatic. But I *was* sad, because I can picture her at the end, and I think about how lonely and scared she must have been, out there on her own, with no one to help her. And as awful as she was, it's still a really upsetting thought."

For a moment the kitchen fell into silence, the two men sat at the breakfast bar, warming their hands on their mugs of coffee. And then, completely out of the blue, Adam leaned over and squeezed Ray's wrist, staring him directly in the eyes as he did so. It was one of the most erotic moments of Ray's life.

"Please don't be awkward around me in future," Adam said. "Right now, the four of us, you and me and Valerie and Alice, we are the only people in the world who know what is really going on. And we have got to be true to each other. And not just to keep each other safe, but to do our best to make sure Lucy is the final victim."

"Yes of course, of course," Ray replied, hoping Adam would keep hold of his wrist for as long as possible. "I'm sorry, I didn't realise I was being so obvious."

"It's fine," Adam replied. "I get this sort of reaction a lot. I'm used to it. But this is a very specific set of circumstances and we can't allow anything to get in the way of us working together."

Ray nodded and watched sadly as Adam withdrew his hand and sat back in his seat once more.

"And Ray," Adam continued, sounding uncharacteristically awkward. "I don't think I have read this wrong and please accept my apologies if I have. But I do need to make clear that I am a happily married man. And no matter what you may have read on gossip websites or in gay chat rooms, my husband and I do not have an open marriage. We are monogamous. I know you are single at the moment, but I am not. I did feel I needed to say that."

Ray realised Adam, twenty years his junior, had just laid out the parameters of their relationship. He suddenly felt like a silly old fool.

"So, are we OK?" Adam asked.

Ray took a deep breath and then groaned. "I'm so sorry," he said. "I don't know what it is, but I always make myself look foolish whenever you are in the room. You know, most people consider *me* to be the calm one, the person who could always be relied on to keep a level head. But there's something about you, Adam, that turns me into a babbling idiot."

Adam chuckled. "Believe it or not, Ray, I do know what that is like. I was introduced to Madonna at a party a few years back and could barely get a word out. She was being really great, really interested and conversational. And the best I could manage was to tell her Borderline is one of my favourite songs. The conversation ended quite soon after that. And I have regretted that moment every day since. Oh my God, it still burns with shame when I think of it."

Ray had achieved some level of fame for himself over the previous few years, but Adam had become a household name as a child and had blossomed into a handsome, international star. There was something enigmatic and endlessly attractive about him, something that just drew audiences to him as though, as a fan, you could never know as much about him as you would like.

And yet here he was, Adam Jaymes, sitting in the kitchen, chatting about himself in a way that created the impression of a normal human being. And Ray began to feel ashamed at having created such an awkward moment. He wanted to reassure Adam that he was quite capable of acting in an appropriate and responsible manner.

He stood and pulled his wallet from the back pocket of his jeans. He opened it and produced two cards. "Listen, I want you to have these," he said, and handed them to Adam. "One is my business cards, the other is for Alice."

Adam surveyed the information on the cards. The first was black and glossy, with gold lettering that read: 'Ray Vaughn (He/Him), Public Speaker and Reality TV Star'. The second was simpler, just black text on a matte white card: 'Alice Pierce MCIPR (She/Her). Accredited PR Practitioner and High Performing Social Media Manager'.

"I am just concerned that one day you might need to get hold of Val urgently, but she might be busy or unavailable," Ray said. "If that happens, call Alice or me. We should know where she is."

Adam smiled and nodded. "This is very useful, Ray. Thank you." And with that, he tucked both cards into his trouser pocket.

Ray left his wallet on the breakfast bar and retook his seat. "So, how do we make sure Lucy is the last?" he enquired. "Valerie seemed to think your team wasn't making much progress."

Adam nodded. "Yes, but I think we may have turned a corner," he said. "I think we were right about this potentially being one of Pearl's obsessed fans. We are just trying to locate as many as possible. Guy Stone aside, there are four we have on our radar now. And any one of them could be behind this."

The mention of Guy Stone made Ray remember something he had meant to ask, a missing detail from Valerie and Adam's conversation the previous week. "How did he die?" Ray asked. "Guy Stone."

"He committed suicide," Adam replied.

"Yes, but how?" Ray enquired.

Adam's expression darkened, as though remembering something deeply unpleasant hidden at the back of his mind. "Oh, I thought you would know the story. I thought everyone did," he said.

"I honestly don't," Ray replied. "I remember Pearl dying, of course. That was everywhere. It was all over the news for months. But I don't remember the story about Guy Stone."

Adam nodded. "Well, please remember this man was incredibly clever. Really clever. He seemed able to gain access to anywhere, at any time. It was one of the reasons Pearl was so terrified of him. No matter where she was, there was always a chance he might appear out of nowhere. But then Pearl, the woman Guy Stone was obsessed with, she took her own life. And I suppose he had nothing left to live for. And the way he killed himself. It was such an angry way to go. And right there, in front of everyone, at Pearl's funeral. It was like he felt we all needed to be punished, one last time, for keeping Pearl from him."

Ray's eyes widened with shock. "He committed suicide, at her funeral? Oh my God. Was her daughter there?"

Adam shook his head. "No, no, thank God. We had a private service with Beth days later. This wasn't the family service. It was more for the public, to give her friends the chance to speak, to say how the media had destroyed Pearl's life."

"And what did he do? I mean, I hope you don't mind me asking. But how did he actually kill himself?"

Adam took a deep breath and closed his eyes. "I remember the smell.

That's the first thing that alerted me, all of us, that something was wrong. A sudden overwhelming stink of petrol."

Ray sat back slightly in his seat, realising the grim conclusion Adam's tale was heading towards.

"And then we heard him screaming, shouting. And it was so confusing, because the security was supposed to be watertight. But there he was. He had found a way in, bypassed all the security barriers and staff. Guy Stone was right in the middle of the chapel, in the aisle, telling us all how he loved Pearl more than any of us did, and how he was going to be with her. How he could have kept her safe and how we had all failed her. And then, that was it. He lit a match and exploded into flames, right there in front of us all. The security people, well, they leapt into action straight away. They had extinguishers all over him. But he was soaked in petrol and there just wasn't anything they could do. We were all rushed out the doors. And that was that."

As Adam's story unfolded, Ray could feel his blood run cold as a memory resurfaced, a memory of a recent event that had seemed strange, a little disconcerting, but not something that at the time had warranted any discussion or conversation. But now, hearing what Guy Stone had done at Pearl Martin's funeral, it was an event that suddenly appeared to have far more significance; a figure, in a hood, with a strange look, a face stripped of almost all its features. A figure on a crossing, outside an office owned by Pearl Martin's sister.

"Adam, may I ask," he said, "are you absolutely certain Guy Stone is dead?"

CHAPTER 58

"The funny thing is, I wasn't even thinking about writing another book. And then, and this was completely out of the blue, I was talking to a friend about some of the most shocking stories I've ever covered, and it got me to thinking about Pearl Martin and that dreadful man who stalked her all those years."

"Oh yes," Sydney replied. "What was his name? Stone? God, that takes me back. What an absolute fucking nutter. So, is that the idea, then? Celebrity stalkers? Sounds a bit, well, sounds like it could be a bit salacious, and I thought you had higher ideals these days."

Valerie chuckled. "I just need something to keep the old noggin working," she replied, tapping herself on the forehead and attempting to sound casual and slightly indifferent, as though not completely sold on the idea. She did not want Sydney to become suspicious that she may have other reasons for raising the topic. "But it won't be salacious. My aim would be to really get inside their heads, to find out how a person can get to that stage in their life, to become so completely obsessed with a celebrity that they would go to prison for them or even, perhaps… commit murder."

Sydney nodded. "Are you planning on interviewing any of them?" he asked. "Because that's where the money is. People are sick of hearing from the victim. They want to hear from the criminal. That's where your publishing deal will be."

Valerie put down her knife and fork, and then sipped her wine. "I will, if I can trace any of them," she eventually replied. "Stone's probably the best known, but I can't interview him, of course. Not without a clairvoyant, and I refuse to co-write my next book with anyone called Doris."

Sydney frowned, as though Valerie had said something objectionable, and then carried on eating his lunch.

"What was that?" Valerie asked. "That look. What was that about?"

Sydney shrugged. "I'm just not sure you'd need a clairvoyant," he replied, casually, and continued chewing.

"For Guy Stone? Of course I would. He's been dead for years."

Valerie was surprised when Sydney shook his head and said: "I don't think so, Val."

None of the words from Sydney's mouth were making sense. Valerie knew, absolutely knew, that Guy Stone was long dead and did not understand why Sydney was contradicting a known fact. "Syd, he killed himself at Pearl Martin's funeral. There were about two hundred witnesses," she said. But once more, to her great confusion, her friend shook his head.

"Val, he *attempted* suicide at the funeral. As far as I know he's still alive. A complete fucking state, I would imagine. And hopefully still locked up. But as far as I know, he's not dead."

"But we reported it, in the *Daily Ear*, at the time. All the papers did."

Sydney put his cutlery down onto the table and stared at Valerie. And she knew that look. She had seen it many times over the years they had worked together. It was the same expression he always had, whenever he had sneaked into her office to tell her something he knew he was not supposed to tell her.

"You know Val," he said, "I've always had a theory, that every truly great journalist has at least one truly great story that they keep secret."

Silently, Valerie feigned a smile and nodded, but she was suddenly extremely anxious at what she was about to be told.

"You remember that Stone came from money?" Sydney asked. "And you know who his family is?"

Valerie nodded again.

And with that, Sydney continued: "Well, for years, Guy Stone's behaviour brought shame and scandal on his family. He was having a huge impact on their name and reputation. And they all wanted him to disappear. So, after he tried to barbecue himself at Pearl Martin's funeral, they took advantage of his... condition, and quickly had him relocated to a private facility. It was all under the guise of getting him the very best care that money could buy. And then a few days later the family issued a public statement, you remember the one, telling the world that very sadly he had passed away from his injuries."

"And in truth?" Valerie asked.

"In truth," Sydney said, "they locked him up and threw away the key. They were true to their word, though. They did get him the best care. Top plastic surgeons, psychiatrists. But he was never seen or heard from again."

Valerie gasped. "So, they killed him off?" she asked. "I mean, not literally. But they 'vanished' him. Made everyone think he was dead?"

Sydney nodded.

"And we never reported this?"

Sydney groaned and sat back. "Val, we were in the eye of the storm, sweetheart. You must remember what it was like," he said, with a sorrow in his voice that betrayed just how unhappy those memories were. "When Pearl Martin committed suicide, the whole world came down on us. Everyone blamed us, even the other papers. The police were under pressure to arrest members of staff, MPs were demanding the *Daily Ear* be closed. Advertisers were leaving like rats from a sinking ship. And this went on for months. Months and months. We had death threats made against us, we had protesters at the gates. Our cars were pelted with bricks and shit, literally shit, on a daily basis. It's not really surprising that no one was interested in double-checking what really happened to Guy Stone. His family said he was dead, and that was the end of that. We were all too busy scraping the shit off our windscreens."

Valerie nodded. "Yes, yes, I remember," she said. "Of course, I remember. But how do you know this? And why haven't you ever told anyone?" For a moment it looked as though Sydney might be smiling, slightly, but Valerie wasn't sure if he had found something amusing or was trying to quietly pass a belch out of the corner of his mouth.

"Well, Yvonne and I were close to the family," he said, "and when she was first diagnosed, they were very generous. Got her the best treatment. I honestly think we had an extra ten years together because of that. Because of them."

"And now?"

Sydney shrugged. "Let's just say their generosity wasn't as altruistic as I thought. They've called on me to kill a lot of stories over the years. Too many. And now Yvonne's gone, well, they don't have as much sway as they used to." He then raised his glass to Valerie. "So, even though I cannot currently offer you a job with the *Daily Ear*, I hope this little titbit of information will help you with your next book."

Valerie smiled, and tried to pretend she was grateful rather than frightened.

She could feel her stomach churning but did not want Sydney to be in any way suspicious. She knew she had to complete their lunch as though nothing untoward had happened. "Stone just faded into obscurity, didn't he?" she said, thoughtfully. "And to be honest, I think that's what he deserved. I always felt he got some perverted pleasure from being splashed over the newspapers, even if he was being named and shamed as a stalker. A criminal. He seemed to love the attention. Perhaps the best punishment was that everyone just stopped talking about him."

"But it would make a great few chapters in your book," Sydney replied, "especially if your readers also thought he was long dead."

Valerie nodded. "Yes, yes," she replied, softly, and then added: "I wonder what happened to him, though?" as if casually pondering out loud.

Sydney frowned. "God. Probably hasn't had a great life. Endless surgeries. Locked up for all those years. No one to stalk."

"But he was clever," Valerie said. "More than clever enough to get out, if he wanted to. And Guy Stone was his nom de plume. So, any legal documents, or panels or judicial hearings… they would have been under his real name. No one would have realised who they were about."

Sydney shrugged. "I suppose," he said, and then picked up his cutlery and began to eat his lunch once more, clearly no longer interested in the topic. "But listen," he said, chewing, "we could always talk about a serialisation deal on your book when you're close to finishing it. It sounds like a great combination: Guy Stone and the *Daily Ear*. Yes. Sounds like a winner."

Adam Jaymes sat quietly on the back seat of his chauffeur-driven car. The darkened windows shielded his famous face from the passing pedestrians, as he was driven through the streets of Southend-on-Sea and back towards London. His conversation with Ray had left him feeling unsettled as he realised he had unfinished business that he needed to attend to urgently.

A noise distracted him from his train of thought, and he realised his mobile phone was vibrating on his lap. He picked it up and saw the letters 'VP' flashing on the screen. He quickly pressed the answer button and held the phone to his ear. "It's Adam," he said, sharply.

"He's not dead," Valerie replied. "Stone. He's alive."

Adam felt his heart skip a beat. "Are you sure?" he asked.

"Yes," she replied. "I just had lunch with Sydney Corrigan. He confirmed it. I've been a bloody fool. How could I have missed this?"

"If that is true, Valerie, then we all missed it," Adam replied, attempting to sound reassuring. "But I just came to the same conclusion as you. I was at your house, just now. I wanted to talk to you. And your ex-husband, Ray, he said something that worried me."

"Ray?" Valerie asked. "What on earth could he know?"

"That day we were both at Patricia's office and Ray was outside waiting for you in the car. He said saw someone, loitering, behaving very strangely. A man, wearing a hoodie. But he saw his face, just briefly. And the way he described him. It sounded like a man who had undergone a lot of plastic surgery. Perhaps for burns."

There was a silence at the end of the line for a moment, and then Valerie replied: "Dear lord. You think that was Stone? Do you think he is stalking Patricia?"

"I'm going to call her," Adam said. "Or at least try to. She's not particularly receptive to me at the moment."

He heard Valerie sigh. "That's most likely because of me, isn't it?" she asked. "She thinks you are on my side. But that's not important, Adam, not right now. Stone is insane. She could be in terrible danger. You have to make her listen to you."

"Yes, I know. I will get hold of her somehow. And I will check in on Beth too." On the other end of the phone, Adam could hear Valerie's breathing had become ragged.

"Are you certain Beth is safe?" she asked, her voice trembling.

"Yes," he replied. "She's far away, surrounded by security." But as the words left his lips, he knew how unjustified that claim was. Stone could find anyone, anywhere. And if he knew who Beth was, he would know how to find her. "I have to go," he said. "I'm heading back to London now. My people are already on the case, trying to confirm whether Stone is alive and, if he is, where he's been all these years. I will let you know as soon as I hear from them. Stay safe, Valerie."

He hung up and dropped the phone back to his lap. With a deep groan, he released all the air from his lungs and sank into his seat. He knew he would have to call Patricia, but in that moment his priority had to be checking that

Beth and her family were safe. He scrolled through his contacts and found Denise's number.

"Adam, how did you know?" Denise said, without even offering a 'hello'. "I was literally about to call you."

"Know what?" Adam asked. "I'm just checking in."

"Oh, dear lord," Denise whispered, and Adam suddenly became aware of a tension in her voice that he had not heard before. "Beth's gone," she continued. "Packed a bag, grabbed her passport and headed to the airport. She's been gone all day, we think. She's probably on a plane back to London as we speak. She might be there already."

Adam's heart skipped a beat, and he was almost too fearful to ask any further questions. But he knew he had to understand exactly what was going on. "Was she taken? Is there any sign of a struggle?" he asked.

"What? No, of course not," Denise replied. "With the security you've given us, a fly couldn't get through. No, she's packed her stuff and taken her passport. We've been out for the day, walking, but she didn't want to come. We didn't think anything of it. She does like her own company. But when we got back, she was long gone."

"I don't understand," Adam said. "Why would she run off without telling you?"

"I don't know," Denise replied. "She was on the phone a lot, with her cousin Ben. Something was going on between the two of them. And then yesterday she seemed really upset about something. She wouldn't talk about it, but I am sure I could hear her crying in her room. And now, well, she's probably already back in England. Adam, you said there was a real danger. You have to find Beth."

"I will," Adam replied. "I will find her. Don't worry. I will keep her safe."

CHAPTER 59

"So, this is where the little monster grew up," Valerie said, and stared at the gloomy, forbidding building in front of her. Most of the house was lost under a dense layer of ivy, and the few windows Valerie could see had been boarded up many years earlier. Even though it was dark she could see gaping holes in the roof, leaving the inside of the property exposed to the elements.

Despite its dilapidated state she could tell that, once, it would have been the most expensive and exclusive home in the area; a twenty-room, detached property set well back from the road at the end of a winding gravel drive, the entire grounds surrounded by seven-foot iron fences.

But now, its once proud visage was decayed and menacing, hidden from the outside world by a thick, unforgiving boundary of overgrown trees, weeds and prickly bushes. Fortunately, Ray had been able to find a way through the brambles, already trampled flat, no doubt by some of the kids from the neighbourhood daring each other to visit the local haunted house.

They had both been expecting the worst, and so had dressed accordingly; jeans, thick jackets and boots. Valerie had shortened the strap on her handbag, so it pulled tightly against her side, and complemented her outfit with a subtle purple scarf. Ray had ensured his leather zip-up jacket was skin-tight, so as not to hide his physique, just in case they bumped into eligible young men during their outing. They had both brought torches and switched them on as they approached the area at the front of the house where they felt it most likely they would find the front door.

"You were certainly right about the money," Ray said. "And this isn't even the family home?"

Valerie shook her head. "Just their London town house," she said. "The family estate is in Norfolk. But this is where Stone spent most of his time. I believe he adopted it as his main home, mostly because the rest of the family disliked him so much. It gave him his own space."

Ray slipped on a pair of gloves from his jacket pocket and pulled at the vines growing across the entrance. He quickly revealed a pair of thick set, wooden double doors, one slightly at an angle to the other, ajar. He brushed a metal plaque attached to the brick wall next to the doors and revealed the inscription *Grosvenor House*.

"It really would have been something, once, this place," he said. "I cannot believe it's been allowed to just sit here and rot. This is a millionaires' row. You'd have to be a multimillionaire just to afford the smallest house in the neighbourhood. You'd have thought the other residents would have complained to the council, had the house knocked down or sold. Or something."

Valerie shrugged. "It's set back, hidden behind iron gates and a mass of trees and bushes. And it does have a lot of infamy because of Stone."

Ray pushed hard against the door that was slightly ajar, and found it had distorted, and was sticking to the floor. He nudged it with his shoulder, and then again, and then again, managing to push it back a few inches each time, until it was open just enough for them both to step inside.

The entrance hall was not quite as grand as he had expected. It was fairly narrow, with a staircase to the left and a selection of doors leading to the ground floor rooms. Most of the floorspace was taken up by the metal frame of what he assumed was once a grand chandelier, with all of its glass prisms removed. Now it looked like little more than an enormous metal ball, with a large spike extending from the top which, at one time, would have fixed it to the ceiling.

"Very '*Phantom*'," Valerie said, and began to direct her torch around the hallway, its beam capturing the peeling wallpaper and exposed plasterwork. There was an overwhelming smell of damp, and the sound of dripping water was all around them.

"So, the plan is, we get some pictures, and then we go," Ray said. "Adam and his team can track down Guy Stone, while you get exclusive photographs of his old house."

"That's the plan," she replied. "It's about time Adam and his team did some actual work."

Ray stood at the foot of the stairs, the light from his torch catching a few shreds of fabric on some of the steps, the remnants of what would have been a carpet. "I have a horrible feeling this is going to be a waste of time," he said. "If the hallway is anything to go by, we're not going to find anything interesting. It's just a big old empty rotting house."

He turned at the sound of a creaking door, and saw Valerie disappear into one of the ground floor rooms.

"Anything in there?" he asked.

There was a pause, and then Valerie replied, her voice echoing in the darkness, "No. Empty. No furniture. No light fittings. No rugs or carpets, paintings. Nothing." She reappeared and shrugged. "Someone cleared this place out. A long time ago."

"The family?" Ray asked.

"Possibly. Or burglars. Squatters. But they've taken everything. Ripped up the carpets, removed the wall lamps. But let's keep looking. And then we can go back to the car and get the camera equipment. It's still going to make for some good pictures, especially if I can source some images of what it looked like in its heyday."

She crossed the hall to a door at the foot of the stairs and pushed it open. To her surprise, there was a light on the other side, a dim blue light that gently lit the room beyond the door. And as she peered through the gloom and shone her torch across the dark expanse in front of her, she realised this room was not empty. Far from it.

There were chairs, a table and desk, and all arranged in a way that suggested the room was still used. On the desk there was a piece of electronic equipment, the source of the light, and after a moment she realised it was a computer. It was humming, still very much alive and in a working condition. And beyond it, a wall filled with photographs and newspaper articles.

Instinctively, before she could stop herself, she had crossed the room and was looking at the pictures that had been pinned to the wall, all of them faces from her past, many from the glory days of the *Daily Ear*. She noted that all the pictures appeared recent, and taken secretly, as though part of a sinister surveillance operation.

Chris Cox was there, sat in what appeared to be a pub, alone at a table, with a pint of ale on the table in front of him, reading the *Daily Ear*; a peaceful image of a man enjoying his retirement. Jason was stood outside the gates of a prison, perhaps only just released. He looked bewildered and lost. Gayesh was in a restaurant, eating a gourmet meal with two people Valerie did not recognise, but she had no doubt it had been a freebie and that Gayesh had not picked up the tab.

Javier was in an exclusive tailor's shop on Savile Row, and it looked as though he was being fitted for a suit. Clearly, she thought, he had believed money would be coming to him. Steve was leaving a barber's shop, and Derek had been photographed stood waiting next to a sign that said, 'Kenley Common'.

And as Valerie allowed the light from her torch to move across the wall, she found an image of herself, with Ray, out and about somewhere, casually dressed. And for a split second she lost her nerve and looked away. She could have no doubt, now, that she was most definitely in the killer's eyeline.

"You OK Val?" Ray asked, now standing by her side, staring at the wall, and trying to take in everything he was seeing.

She nodded. "Yes, I'm good," she said, and then turned back to the wall to see what else the killer had included in the sinister collection of pictures and cuttings. The photographs were surrounded by articles from the *Daily Ear*, all of them about Pearl Martin and some written by Valerie herself.

"Drunk soap star takes a tumble at TV awards"

"Hysterical star breaks down in street: exclusive pictures by Jason Spade"

"Pearl Martin reveals the explosive behind-the-scenes row on Britain's biggest soap'. Exclusive by Javier García"

"Drunk soap star in home alone disgrace. Exclusive by Colin Merroney"

"Star 'high on drugs' as daughter taken into care"

"Sacked! BBC FINALLY takes action on shameless soap star"

"Soap star dead"

"Valerie Pierce: Pearl Martin was a shameless and reckless television star and we should not mourn her"

"The Pearl Martin Tapes: Star speaks from beyond the grave and reveals all. Exclusive by Steve Gallant"

The most recent, from a few months earlier, had been written by Lucy Strickland: *"Pearl Martin was a selfish drunken yob and a bad mother. Why do so many young women today still idolise her?"* And as Valerie scanned Lucy's article, she could see much of it had been directly lifted from comment pieces Valerie herself had written many years earlier.

"Bloody cheek," she muttered quietly to herself, trying to make herself feel less scared, just for a moment, by focussing on Lucy's barefaced plagiarism.

Interspersed between the pictures and the articles were pages ripped from a book. And as she peered more closely, she realised they were pages from her book, Exposé, with sections highlighted in yellow, sections which linked so many of her colleagues with the events which led to Pearl Martin's suicide or actions after her death that impacted on her memory and legacy.

There was a section in which she had described the blank chequebook Gayesh Perera had provided to the editorial team, to pursue their stories, many about Pearl. There was a section in which she commented on Derek Toulson and his secret project that led to the closure of many local services and charities, including one set up in Pearl Martin's memory.

There were other sections too in which she had reflected on the tactics so many of her colleagues had used to chase their exclusive stories, and so many of those stories had been about Pearl Martin. And with a terrible sense of regret, Valerie realised she had been right; her words had directly contributed to the deaths of many of the people whose pictures were pinned to that wall.

"I think we have found his nest," Ray said, and Valerie turned to find him stood next to her, shining his torch across the wall. "We should phone the police," he said, and began to wander slightly away from Valerie, to the pictures and newspaper clippings on the far edge of the montage, those Valerie had not yet seen.

She nodded. "Yes, but not straight away. I want to get our photographs first. Let's get the camera equipment out of the car." She noticed Ray was squinting, looking at something on the wall, a photograph.

"Who's this?" he asked. "I don't recognise her."

Valerie stepped sideways to look at the photograph, and her heart sank as she saw it was a picture of Pearl Martin's daughter, Beth, taken from afar as she wandered casually down a street with a friend. Valerie reached forward and removed the drawing pin holding the picture to the wall, and then took the picture, folded it several times and slipped it into her bag.

"You can't do that," Ray said. "This is a crime scene. That's evidence."

"Believe it or not, Ray, I am doing exactly what Adam Jaymes would want me to do. I am protecting someone who has nothing to do with this and should not be involved." Valerie turned and shone her torch back towards the door and started to walk away. "Come on, let's stick together."

But as she reached the door, she realised Ray had remained where he was, fixated by the gallery of pictures and press cuttings. "Come on Ray. Camera!" she said.

"This... this doesn't make sense," Ray said, quietly. "Val, there's a picture here, but it... it can't be... it's not possible..."

Valerie shook her head. "Ray, nothing here is going to make sense. But the police will—"

"No, Val... there's a picture here of you. I mean, of us. The two of us."

"Yes, I know, I saw it," she said. "It's hardly a surprise, Ray. At this stage I'd be quite disappointed if I wasn't on the wall."

"No, no," Ray replied, an alarming urgency beginning to sound in his voice. "Did you look at the picture closely?"

Valerie shrugged, not wishing to admit she had been so frightened at seeing the photograph that she had looked away immediately. "No, not really," she replied. "I was busy looking to see who else was up there."

Ray's agitation grew more pronounced. "It's a photograph of us," he said, "but just now, outside on the pavement when we were trying to find a way in. Someone took this picture, printed it and put it on the wall in the past few minutes."

It felt as though a coldness had suddenly wrapped itself around Valerie, and for a moment she was unable to move, or speak. She looked across the dark room at Ray, now stood facing her, his torch pointing to the floor, and she realised they were both in great danger.

A noise suddenly cut through the silence, an electronic beeping, and Valerie realised her mobile phone was ringing. She wanted it to be silent as quickly as possible and so pulled it from her bag and went to answer. But just as she was about to press the bright green button on the screen, she hesitated as a terrible realisation struck at her very core. "It's nine o'clock," she said and looked across the room at Ray. "Its nine o'clock." She pressed the green button, and the silence that fell onto the room no longer made Valerie feel safe. It was a frightening, imposing silence that demanded she speak to her caller.

"This is Valerie Pierce," she said, her eyes tightly closed.

"*Hello, Valerie Pierce,*" a man hissed, hatred spewing from the back of his throat. "*This is your murderer. I just called to let you know it's your turn.*"

There was a strange echo in the room, as if the man's voice had somehow left the phone and reverberated through the darkness, bouncing against all the walls and screeching through the air. Her eyes flew open as she switched off her phone and thrust it back into her bag. She shone her torch at Ray. "That was him. It's my turn. Let's go," she said.

But then she realised something about Ray looked odd, out of sorts. The expression on his face was not one of fear or concern, but of shock. His eyes were wide, and his lips trembling. It seemed at first as though he were looking at something behind Valerie, and so she spun around and shone her torch at the open doorway. But there was no one there.

Her heart pounding, she turned back to Ray. "Darling, come over here to me," she said, softly. She moved her torch slightly and noticed something unusual. Ray's shadow remained static behind him. As Valerie moved the torch, she expected the shadow to move too, but it remained where it was, motionless and solid. "Come here Ray," she said once more.

"Oh, Val," he gasped, breathlessly, tears forming in his frightened eyes. "Run."

Ray dropped to his knees, and fell forward, flat to the floor. And his shadow remained where it was, stood behind him.

Shaking, Valerie lifted her torch and shone it directly at where Ray had been standing and its beam revealed not a shadow, but a dark figure, his face concealed by a hood. In one hand he held a long knife, the blade dark and wet; the blood of her beloved friend.

"What have you done?" she asked, her voice trembling. "What have you done to Ray?"

With his other hand, the figure pulled back his hood to reveal himself, his face now little more than a suggestion of the man he once was. Years of surgery and healing had robbed him of most of his features, but his cold blue eyes remained.

"Now," he said, his voice deep and rasping, "I am going to cut out your lying tongue." Suddenly, he was moving, quickly forward, towards her, the knife in his hand ready for its next victim. Valerie screamed, turned and ran through the door and back into the hallway. Her mind could not let go of the image of Ray and the horrible expression on his face; the shock of knowing he had just been murdered.

In her panic, she ran first towards the front door but realised immediately it had been closed, perhaps even locked, and without thinking or considering what to do next, her feet simply carried her in the opposite direction and up the stairs. She screamed again as she heard Stone stumble into the hallway and then angrily stomp up the staircase behind her.

She reached the landing, a balcony overlooking the hallway with too many doors to choose from and all of them closed. She could hear Stone beneath her, grunting with rage and crying out. She looked down to see one of the stairs had given way beneath his weight and he was trying to retrieve his foot from within the splintered wood. The house was rotting beneath their feet.

She had no idea where to go, no idea how to get back to Ray, to see if there was a chance he might still be alive. But then she saw motion on the staircase and realised Stone was on the move once more, so she ran at the middle door and opened it. Inside, an old metal key was still in the lock and she quickly slammed the door behind her and wrenched the key as hard as she could until she heard the reassuring sound of the lock clicking shut.

She looked around and found herself in a bedroom, plain and almost empty apart from a single bed and a pile of clothes on the floor. The windows were boarded shut, but the room was not completely dark, instead it was gently lit by two candelabras. Of all the doors she could have chosen, Valerie realised she had blundered into Stone's inner sanctum.

Within seconds, she could hear him pounding at the door, roaring angrily. But she realised she was not completely helpless. She had her phone, still, and could call the police.

She quickly retrieved it from her bag and dialled 999. A woman answered with a reassuring speed. "Please help," Valerie said, her panic forcing the words from her mouth far more loudly than she had intended. "He's trying to kill me. Guy Stone. He's killed my husband. Please help, he's got a knife. It's Grosvenor House in Bishops Square, north London."

The woman's voice was stern and reassuring, asking her questions, clarifying her situation. But Valerie was suddenly distracted by the silence. Stone had stopped banging at the door, and he was no longer yelling and shouting. "Wait," Valerie whispered. "I think he's gone."

The woman was saying something to her, but in the absence of any other noise Valerie was too frightened to speak. Slowly, she stepped forward, towards the locked door, the floorboards creaking beneath her feet screaming her location just inside the entrance to the room. As she reached the door, she leaned into it and pushed her ear against the wood to try and hear any sounds that would indicate what was happening on the other side.

And there were noises, but not made by any human. There was the wind, whispering through the many cracks and holes in the aged property. And the crumbling walls and floors were creaking and groaning, as though the decaying house itself was ready to finally crumble away.

Valerie stepped back from the door and held her phone to her ear. "He's gone," she said, quietly.

Another noise suddenly filled the air; a loud thump, followed by the sound of something being pounded quickly, but not the door. Her eyes became focussed on the wall adjoining the next bedroom. It seemed to be moving, vibrating, clouds of plaster dust tumbling from the ceiling above. And the pounding grew louder, and faster, and then stopped. And for a moment, a brief moment of respite, there was silence again.

But then the wall exploded in front of Valerie's eyes. Plaster and scraps of wallpaper and splinters of rotted wood filled the air, and a terrible growl surrounded her, as though the house had screamed in pain as a massive hole was forced through its structure. The air was filled with dust and for a moment the cloud was so thick it almost extinguished the light from the candles. As it settled, and the candle light was able to transcend the darkness once more, Valerie could see the wall had almost entirely disintegrated, leaving a large pile of wood and mortar on the floor in front of her.

She pushed herself backwards, against the wall behind her, knowing that

Stone had broken through, that he was going to appear at any moment, and step through the hole he had so furiously created. Frozen with fear, unable to move or speak, she stared at the yawning hole and the blackness beyond and waited for Stone to make his ghoulish appearance.

But he was already in the room. A noise in front of her drew Valerie's gaze to the pile of rubble on the floor, and she realised it was moving. A hand reached up from beneath the broken wood and mortar and began to push the debris to the side. And soon she could see him fully, Stone, clambering to his feet, covered in cuts and dust. But still, he held that bloodied knife.

He turned on the spot as he tried to establish where Valerie was standing, and when he saw her, cowering against the wall, he smiled.

Throughout her life, all Valerie ever had was her keyboard and her opinions. And as she stared Stone in the face, she knew she had to force some words from her mouth, just something to keep him occupied. Because at that exact moment, her words were the only defence she had.

"The police know it's you," she said, her voice trembling but her words clear and loud. "We proved it. Adam Jaymes is with the police right now. He's telling them everything."

Stone's empty face failed to offer any hints as to what he was thinking, or if he had even heard Valerie's words.

"Did you really think you would get away with it?" she asked, trying to claw a response from him. "All that death. And why those people?"

"You know why," he responded suddenly, his voice deep and hoarse. "For her. It was all for her. For everything they did, that *you* did to her. It was all for Pearl."

"And you think you're the hero in this?" Valerie asked, trying to keep the conversation going. "Pearl Martin hated you," she said. "You terrified her. And she would be appalled at what you have done."

"You know nothing of my relationship with Pearl."

"Oh, for God's sake, you didn't have a *relationship* with her," Valerie snapped. "Is that what you're still telling yourself, that it was love? Unrequited love?"

Stone did not move. He stood amid the ruins of his bedroom, lit only by candles, and stared Valerie in the face. "She wasn't well," he said. "She didn't always understand what she was doing or saying. But I understood.

I always understood. I was the only one who could protect her. Everyone else failed her."

For a moment, Valerie thought she heard a noise, something from beyond the room, perhaps from downstairs, beneath the creaking floorboards under her feet. A sound of something being scraped or moved. But it was fleeting, gone almost as soon as it started, and her focus quickly returned to Stone.

"Why them?" she asked. "Why those people in particular? There are hundreds of reporters who wrote stories about Pearl Martin, and most of them negative. Why did you pick those victims?"

Stone then made a strange noise, and at first Valerie wasn't sure what it was. And then she realised he was chuckling, but it was a sound that was so deep and guttural she had almost thought he was choking. "What's so funny?" she asked.

"Your book," he responded.

"*Exposé*? You read my book?" And for a moment, Valerie was almost flattered.

"Yes," Stone replied. "It was terrible."

"Oh."

"Page after page of poorly written, self-absolving drivel. Just awful."

Valerie frowned and tilted her head. "Well, I think 'awful' is a bit of a strong word," she said. "Perhaps we can agree on 'challenging'?"

"No," Stone replied. "I'm happy with awful. It really was one of the worst books I've ever read. I mean, honestly, what was chapter seven all about?" He shrugged, and then paused, as though waiting for a response.

But Valerie felt she had received more than enough critical feedback for one conversation. "Well – well, let's not get off topic," she replied. "I asked how you picked your victims, and you said my book. How so?"

Stone took a deep breath, and tilted his head slightly to one side, and for a moment Valerie feared he may have realised what she was doing: just trying to keep him talking in the hope the police might arrive to save her.

Suddenly very afraid again, she could feel every muscle in her body stiffen with fear. But then, once more, there was a sound from outside the room, but this time closer, as though someone were creeping along the landing behind her. And she wondered, she hoped, that perhaps it was Ray, not dead, just injured, coming to rescue her. She knew she had to keep him talking for just a few minutes longer.

She remembered the Guy Stone of old. She recalled so many stories from colleagues who had written about him, Pearl Martin's infamous stalker, and how he appeared to enjoy the attention that came from his notoriety. One colleague had even speculated Stone wanted to be famous because he believed that would make him Pearl's equal, a celebrity peer she could finally fall in love with; it did not matter to Stone how he became famous, as long as he was as well-known as Pearl.

Valerie could see how deeply his delusion was embedded, even after all these years. Stone simply could not appreciate how other people saw him, not even Pearl. But she also recalled conversations with some of the reporters who had covered Stone's many court appearances, and how they had described the great pride he had taken in his own cleverness; hacking computers and tracking passports, how he could easily trick bank staff into revealing financial transactions, airports into revealing travel plans or hotels into confirming bookings over the phone. And she guessed it would only need a bit of nudging to do the same now and have him brag about how he had planned and executed so many murders.

"Come on, Stone, be honest," she said, trying her hardest to sound strong and unafraid. "You clearly want someone to know how you did it. All the planning, the picking and choosing. Tell me, how did my 'awful' book have anything to do with this?"

"Your awful book," Stone repeated back to her, and chuckled once more. "It was like a shopping list, Valerie. You told me who deserved to die, and even gave me pointers as to *how* they should die. It had to make sense, you see. They couldn't just drop dead. There had to be some relevance. A connection between what they did to Pearl and how they met their own end. And, of course, you even gave me a pattern to follow. One murder, every three days, at 9pm. With a phone call just beforehand to the lucky victim. Me letting them know it was their turn."

"Yes, yes, and I am sure Adam Jaymes will be thrilled to know that, too," Valerie said. "But specifically. Each victim. Chris Cox was first. Why him?"

After a moment, Stone replied, his tone deep and quiet, thoughtful, as though he wanted Valerie to consider the complexities of his thought process, rather than sound as though he were simply bragging. "Of all the newspapers that ruined Pearl's life, I knew the *Daily Ear* had led the pack," he said.

"You were the most to blame, and your book told me everything I needed to fill in the blanks."

"Such as?"

"I had forgotten how cruel Chris Cox was to Pearl," Stone replied. "But your book reminded me about the little cartoon pints of beer he used each week, to rate her performance, depending on how drunk he claimed she was. If he considered her performance was OK, he would give her one pint of beer out of five. If he decided it was bad, he would give her five pints out of five. He publicly ridiculed her every week and, according to your awful book, found it hilarious.

"But your book also mentioned that his retirement gift from his colleagues at the *Daily Ear* was an enormous television, one that was as big as an entire wall. Nice and heavy too, it turned out. When I dislodged it from the wall, it caught him at an odd angle, shattered his spine and crushed his internal organs. But he didn't die straight away, Valerie. I got to sit with him and watch as his lungs filled with blood. And the whole time he was staring up at me, begging me to help him, spitting blood from his mouth. He really was quite the coward at the end."

Valerie tried not to hear his words. She did not want to imagine the grotesque picture his words had painted, of a former colleague spluttering blood as the life gradually ebbed from his broken body. All she needed to do was keep Stone talking. She did not have to listen. "Derek was next. Why him?"

"Your book told me how Derek had abused his position at the *Daily Ear*, to force the closure of dozens of charities across the country he did not approve of, by getting the funding withdrawn. Your book told me one was the charity set up in Pearl's memory. He had it closed simply because it was a mental health charity aimed, specifically, at supporting single parents. And Pearl, as we know, had been a single parent."

"And the horses?"

"Oh, come on Valerie. You know that story. That's also in your book. Derek's hilarious faux pas, closing a horse sanctuary because he wrongly believed it was some lefty refuge for gay horses. So, I catfished him. Lured him to a stable in the middle of nowhere, locked him in and then whipped the horses into a state of panic until they trampled him to death. Oh, and the noise that made, Valerie. The satisfying crunch as the horse shattered his skull."

"And… and Javier?"

"Oh yes, the Fake Spanish Prince himself. Royalty no less. To be honest, I knew an awful lot about him already, how he had entrapped Pearl and ruined her career. But it was your book that told me that fateful meeting had taken place in Javier's favourite suite at the Royal Hotel in Mayfair. And so, what better place for him to take a fall? I contacted him as soon as he was out of prison, pretended to be a rich media mogul hoping to put him back at the top of his game. It didn't take much to lure him to that hotel. And then I just played a few tricks with the lights to frighten him. He ran straight out onto that wet slippery balcony."

"You knew it was going to rain?" Valerie asked.

Stone shook his head. "No, of course not," he said. "The thunderstorm was a bonus. It really added to the atmosphere. All that wind and rain and lightning. It was superb. But I'd made plans to make sure he took a fall. I'd pulled a wire across the floor of the balcony. He tripped the moment he stepped outside. Of course, I didn't just let him fall. I grabbed his ankles and pretended to save him. Only for a moment, but it was fun. His final few seconds spent dangling over the edge, thirteen storeys high; thinking, praying right until the last second that perhaps it was just a joke gone wrong, that I was going to pull him back to safety. And he was a real screamer. I could hear him all the way down. Right until the sound of him smacking onto the roof of that car."

Valerie recalled the scene; Javier's face, moments after his death, his broken body lying atop a crumpled car. And the delight with which Stone relayed his stories filled her with horror. But she knew she had to keep asking, keep the conversation going. And Stone, at least, appeared to be enjoying himself, distracted by his own cleverness once more.

"Jason, of course," Stone continued, clearly enjoying his own story, bragging about his cleverness, and no longer needing Valerie to prompt him with the name of each victim. "The hypocrisy of the *Daily Ear*. I was vilified for trying to protect Pearl from men like Jason Spade. If you want a real villain, Valerie, there he is. Your friend. The paparazzi king. A man who spent his time following Pearl down deserted streets. He would shout and scream at her, make violent threats, sexual threats, to make her scream and cry in fear. And then he would take photographs of her, and sell the pictures, claiming they were evidence of Pearl having a breakdown in public."

"He wasn't my friend, he was just a colleague," Valerie replied. But then remembered once more the last time she had heard from him, a lonely voice at the end of a telephone line. And amidst the terror of that moment, she found a small part of herself that grieved for Jason Spade.

"But your book told me, Valerie," Stone continued. "You told me how Jason had shown no remorse for any of the attacks he had made on Pearl's privacy, that he actually felt entitled to take those disgusting photographs of her. All those times he laid down on the pavement, trying to take pictures up her dress. Pretending it was in the public interest to know whether or not she had underwear on.

"So, I gave him a taste of his own medicine. I tricked him into drinking a toxin that caused paralysis and then suffocation. He was helpless, just like Pearl had been helpless to protect herself from him. And once he was paralysed, as his breathing started to become heavy, more difficult, I removed his pants and trousers and took photographs of him naked. Just like all those pictures he had taken with his long-angled lens. And then I posted them on the internet. So, in death, people could see the paparazzi giant for the little man he really was."

Behind Stone, in the dark void beyond the enormous hole he had created in the wall, Valerie was sure she could see movement. Out of the corner of her eye, she thought she could see something, perhaps someone, standing just inside the shadows. Perhaps it was Ray. Or a police officer. Someone waiting for the right moment to strike. And if that was the case, she knew she had to keep Stone talking.

But Stone did not need any encouragement. He was describing each of his murders and clearly enjoyed sharing the gory details. "And Steve, of course," he said. "That wasn't an accident. Of course, it was not accident. Steve Gallant pretended to be a friend to Pearl for many years. But your book reminded me that, after she died, he betrayed that friendship to try and claw his career back from oblivion.

"He used recordings he had secretly made of phone calls with Pearl. Conversations she thought were private, between friends, and he abused her trust, her memory, to get himself a cheap exclusive. How very two-faced of him. So, I hacked his email account, hacked his phone. Pretended he had been invited to a gala event and then deleted all the emails and voice mails from the organisers telling him he wasn't invited."

"You make it sound so easy," Valerie said.

"Oh please," Stone replied. "I've been hacking computer systems since my parents bought me my first ZX Spectrum. How do you think I siphoned off so much of their money after they thought they'd cut me off?"

"So, what happened?" Valerie asked, although she did not really want to hear the answer. "The night he died. What happened to Steve?"

"I diverted him to a pretend VIP entrance. It was particularly good fun, that one. I got to dress up. I led him into an abandoned sawmill and then I locked him in. It was very Scooby-Doo. I had been there a few days earlier and found one of the old circular blades was still operational. Perfect, really. I left him literally two-faced. And you know what? He died doing what he did best. Name-dropping."

Valerie had been certain another person was nearby, hiding in the darkness, but no one had charged forward to save the day. And she began to believe that perhaps she had been wrong; that perhaps she really was all alone, facing Stone entirely by herself. And all she could think to do was to keep talking.

"Gayesh was in my book, of course," she said.

"Ah yes, Gayesh," Stone replied. "So, what did I learn about Gayesh Perera from your awful book? Well, of course, that he was the laziest man in the land. You told me that he was the one who funded everything you did, and generously so. He gave you cash, hand over fist, so no one would ever confront him with the fact that he was never actually at work."

"It wasn't like that," Valerie said. "That's not what I said in my book."

"Really?" Stone replied, his rasping voice suddenly tinged with an air of sarcasm. "Because I'm sure I was paraphrasing, Valerie. And it's too late to change your narrative now. You have to take responsibility for what you wrote. Gayesh funded your campaign against Pearl. You, Chris, Jason, Steve, Derek, Javier. All of you, awash with money and resources, able to do anything, go anywhere, buy *anything*, pay off *anyone*. Gayesh funded the destruction of Pearl Martin's life. And that is why he went on my list. Gayesh Perera is dead because of what you said about him in your awful book."

His tone was changing, becoming less humorous, more serious, angry. The more he spoke about Gayesh, the more irate he became. And although Valerie knew she had to keep him talking, she also knew she had to keep him calm. And so, she quickly interjected, to offer him the adulation he was so clearly seeking.

"But it was so complex, so technical,'" she said. "I mean, honestly, how on earth did you manage it?"

Stone nodded in agreement. "I did have quite a complex plan for Gayesh," he replied, "and I knew a key part of that was making him trust me. So, I posed as a member of his IT team. I cloned an NHS email address and managed to hack into all sorts of files and networks at the hospital. It was the least secure network I've ever hacked. But you know Gayesh, he was far too busy spending money on refurbishments to bother with investing in something as tedious as IT security."

"And his trust? How did you win his trust?"

"Oh, we swapped a few messages. He was having trouble with one of his managers, so I leaked a few of her emails to the local paper that were so damaging she had no option but to quit her job. Gayesh was really happy about that. Thrilled, in fact. And afterwards, he was putty in my hand. He was doing the same as he always did of course. Coming and going as he pleased, delegating all his work to other people so he could spend his days at conferences and lunches, quaffing back champagne and stuffing canapés into his briefcase for the train journey home. But his security pass was recording it all. There was an actual digital record of his laziness. And I offered to help him end it."

"But it wasn't all done by email," Valerie said, beginning to find herself oddly fascinated by Stone's ongoing story, and the undisputable ingenuity he had shown in planning and then executing Gayesh's murder. "You rewired a security barrier to electrocute him. But how did you know for sure it would kill him, and not someone else?"

"Well, if you could let me finish and stop interrupting, I'll tell you," Stone replied, curtly. "I provided him with a new security pass. I told him it would make him a ghost, able to come and go as he pleased and never leave any sort of digital trail. What it actually did was send me a signal, to tell me when he was using it. I had been inside the building, days earlier, pretending to be a technician giving the security barriers an overhaul. But of course, I was doing much more than that."

"So, when Gayesh used his new security pass it sent you a signal, and that's when you electrified the barrier?"

Stone shrugged. "Now you're the one making it sound easy, Valerie," he replied, with a strange tone to his voice, as though offended by her simplistic version of events. "It was highly complex and technical. I just make it sound easy. And it was a shame, because Gayesh was the only one I wasn't there for, in person, at the end. I did it all remotely."

Valerie tilted her head and realised an odd rhythm had begun to form in her conversation with Stone, as though she had adopted the role of journalist and he, the interviewee. And she wondered if, unintentionally, she was fulfilling one of Stone's long held fantasies; to be interviewed by the Queen of Fleet Street. "Why weren't you there for it?" she asked. "I would have thought you would have enjoyed the spectacle of it all."

Stone did not reply. Instead, he stood, motionless and silent, staring at her. And Valerie suddenly recalled the more graphic details of Gayesh's grisly death that had been shared online; the smoke and terrible stink of burning flesh. And she wondered if that would have been too close to home for Stone; that even within his distorted version of reality, the memory of his own fiery attempt at suicide was something he now struggled with. So much so, that he could not bring himself to watch Gayesh's murder, the one victim he did not see die.

But she knew she could not allow the conversation to stall. She needed to keep him talking for as long as possible. "But not Lucy," she said. "Lucy isn't in the book. You can't claim her death had anything to do with me."

Stone nodded and gave the impression that he had raised his brow even though there was no way of knowing for sure. "True," he said. "Lucy brought herself to my attention, with that vindictive article, calling Pearl a drunken yob. A bad mother. She should have known better. I added her to my list quite late in the day and had to plan quickly for that one. It wasn't as slick or perfect as I would have liked. But it was certainly a just conclusion to her rancid existence."

Stone's demeanour suddenly changed, and the anger in his voice lessened. "You owe Lucy some thanks, Valerie," he said. "Did you guess that I had planned that to be *your* 'phone call night'? And I had such an elaborate evening prepared for you, Valerie. A complex night of mishaps and misdirections that would have left you abandoned and alone, exposed, in the middle of nowhere. Without your ex-husband, or your daughter, or Adam Jaymes to hide behind. Easy pickings for me. Would you like me to give you some clues as to what I had planned for you?"

"No," Valerie snapped, horrified at the idea that she should have met her end three days earlier, as part of some grisly scheme. "Tell me about Lucy," she said. "Why like that, out at sea? Why drowning?"

Stone paused again, and Valerie knew she was snared in a cycle of diminishing returns. Every time she tried to elongate the conversation, he seemed more aware of what she was doing, more likely to decide it was time the talking should end. But he had a few final stories to tell, a few more elaborate schemes to brag about. And so, he began to speak about Lucy.

"Pearl was a decent and kind person," he said. "She worked so hard for so many good causes, often behind the scenes, never seeking publicity or praise. She worked with the British Red Cross, to support vulnerable refugees and asylum seekers coming to the UK. Pearl's great-grandparents were immigrants, who came here after the war, to make a better life for themselves, for their children. Pearl had spoken about them many times; their bravery, their fight to survive.

"But Lucy Strickland disgraced their memory. She demeaned all immigrants. She called them cockroaches, terrorists, rapists. She used her column at the *Daily Ear* to spread lies and hatred. She didn't even care when children were drowning. She said so herself. She didn't care. There were children washed up on our beaches, dead, and she didn't care. She wrote one article that directly attacked Pearl's memory, and another that attacked her heritage, too."

"So, you tricked her into going to that marina?"

"Yes," Stone replied. "She thought she was onto the scoop of her career. She thought she was going to confront a family of immigrants as they rowed to shore. It turned out to be a tricky one, though, because I hadn't anticipated that she would bring…" Stone's words suddenly ended. He seemed to have meandered into a part of his story he had not intended to share. Stone keeping something secret.

"What?" she asked. "What had you not anticipated? What did Lucy bring with her?"

After a quiet moment of thought, Stone lifted the knife and pointed it towards Valerie's hand. "I think they've got everything they need, Valerie," he said, his voice hoarse and deep. "Time to end the call."

Valerie tightened her grip on her mobile phone and hoped she had said enough, and loudly enough, for the emergency services to be on their way. She lifted her phone, held it up so Stone could see it, and then pressed the 'end call' button on the screen. "There," she said. "Ended." She put the phone back into her bag. "I assume you wanted them to hear all of that, otherwise you would have asked me to end the call sooner."

Stone muttered something under his breath. Valerie could not quite hear all the words, but she could tell it must have been an insult, most likely directed at her.

"They will have a recording of my confession, Valerie, and I am grateful you enabled that," he said. "Could you imagine how angry I would be if the police continued to say this had been nothing more than a series of unfortunate accidents? All my work, all of it in Pearl's name. My undying love for her, my tribute to her memory. And because the police were so deeply incompetent, and missed all the clues I left for them, no one would ever know what I did? I wasn't going to have that. No, no, I wasn't. After tonight, one way or another, they were going to find out the truth. Everyone was. This seemed as good a time as any."

"But one final question," Valerie said, hoping against hope that by bringing the conversation to a conclusion, that if someone were hiding in the shadows they might finally leap into action. "Why that pattern? Every three days, at nine o'clock. A phone call just beforehand."

"You know full well that's what Adam Jaymes did, all those years ago, when he brought the *Daily Ear* to its knees," Stone replied, as though perplexed by the question.

"Yes, but what was the point? Why bother to copy Adam Jaymes?"

Stone did not speak immediately. Instead, he appeared to lean back slightly, as though taking in an evening breeze. And then, without moving, he replied: "Why don't you ask him yourself?"

Valerie did not understand what Stone had said. How on earth could she do that? Was he suggesting she should call Adam Jaymes, on her mobile phone? But before she could ponder any further, Stone spoke again.

"Adam. It's time to step out of the shadows and tell Valerie the truth."

There was movement again, from the other room, within the darkness. A sound, slight at first, but this time it was not so discreet or elusive. Someone was there, definitely there, beyond the yawning hole in the wall. And after a moment, Stone was joined by a second man. And they stood, almost side-by-side, staring directly at her.

Guy Stone. And Adam Jaymes.

CHAPTER 60

Valerie stood aghast, trying to make sense of what she was seeing, what she was hearing. Why was Adam Jaymes there, and why did Stone seem so unsurprised? Her mind suddenly whirred through the events of the previous few weeks, trying to find some clue, some context, that would offer a logical explanation for Adam's presence in that moment, in that horrible house. But there was nothing. Not a single conversation, not a single word or inflection that could rationalise what was happening.

"You stink. Did you think I wouldn't smell your pretentious cologne?" The contempt in Stone's voice could not have been more pronounced and yet even as the words left his mouth, he stood absolutely still, staring at Valerie and not even glancing in Adam's direction. "Now, why don't you offer an explanation to Valerie, here. Why do you think I copied your pattern?"

"My pattern?" Adam replied, coldly.

"You know precisely what I'm talking about. Nine o'clock, every three days, a phone call just beforehand. Now, why don't you tell Valerie why I would have copied you."

Adam did not reply immediately, as though he was leaving a pause to prove he could not be told what to do. Not by Stone.

"Tell her!" Stone screamed, and he tilted his head slightly in Adam's direction, but still without actually looking at him.

After a moment, Adam spoke: "I doubt you were attempting to implicate me," he said. "From what I have just heard, you are keen to take full responsibility for all the people you've killed. Instead, I would suggest you were trying to make a point. To show me how a *real* man would avenge Pearl Martin's memory. That what I did four years ago wasn't good enough. That

335

the people who hurt Pearl were let off too easy. That only death could really punish them. It's something along those lines, I would imagine."

Stone nodded. "Of course, I didn't wish to implicate you, Jaymes," he said. "You think I'm some needy fame-seeker, desperate for people to see me hanging around with Adam Jaymes? Pathetic."

"And yet you did copy me," Adam replied, sharply. "Strange. You hold me in such contempt and yet you still feel the need to imitate me."

Valerie could not understand why Adam was baiting Stone so obviously, particularly as he did not appear to be armed. He was wearing a tightly fitted jumper and jeans that left no suggestion of a weapon. Stone, on the other hand, still held his knife and both she and Adam knew he was very happy to use it.

"What *you* did was pathetic," Stone said. "So, you exposed a few embarrassing secrets. So what? In the long run, you actually made things even worse."

Adam did not reply. He knew little had really changed since the days of 'Project Ear' and, indeed, many would argue the conduct of some parts of the media had spiralled out of control in the years which followed. Stone was right. Project Ear had failed.

"You claimed you were giving the people at the *Daily Ear* a taste of their own medicine, payback for what they did to Pearl," Stone continued. "You also claimed a higher purpose, to show those working in tabloid journalism the error of their ways. But all you actually did was feed the machine, remind the public how much they crave that sort of sensational journalism, how much they love to see lives being destroyed, publicly destroyed. And as long as there is a market for it, there are reporters willing to do it. You didn't avenge Pearl. You didn't set things right. The *Daily Ear* is worse than ever and what happened to Pearl is already happening again."

Valerie felt some comfort that Stone's attention was elsewhere, his gaze drifting across the darkness around them, his words aimed at Adam and not her. But as he spoke, with such calm anger, she could feel his words echoing inside her head, feeding her own remorse at what had happened all those years ago to a young actress struggling with her mental health. She knew that Stone's words held an uncomfortable truth.

"So, you murder a few reporters and think that will change anything?" Adam said, his voice strong and clear, demanding an attention that Stone still would not give him.

"That is where you and I differ," Stone replied. "I'm not pretending to seek a greater good. This was vengeance, pure and simple. My gift to Pearl. Someone finally delivering true retribution in her name, by killing those who hurt her. I put them in the ground because no one loved Pearl as much as me. That is *my* story. The man who loved Pearl Martin enough to kill for her. And everyone will know I loved her the most."

Adam's demeanour changed slightly. He turned sideways on, to look at Stone directly, and he put his hands on his hips, as though growing tired of the conversation. "Valerie was right," he said. "Pearl despised you. She hated everything about you. And I promise you, Stone, she would be horrified at what you have done in her name. You disgust me. And you disgusted Pearl, too."

"Liar!" Stone shouted, and for the first time he turned to stare Adam in the face, waving his knife in Adam's direction, the weapon suddenly very much a threat once more. "You kept her from me. All those years. Whispering in her ear, taking advantage of her, of how vulnerable she was. I know what you did, Jaymes. You and all the others. Keeping her from me. Keeping her for yourself."

Adam shook his head. "No, Stone. None of that is true. She utterly, utterly despised you. Right until the end. And if she were here right now, she would say exactly that. Pearl Martin hated you!"

In a flash, Stone lunged forward, plunging the knife towards Adam's chest, and screaming at the top of his voice. But Adam was ready for him. With both feet firmly on the ground, he slapped the knife to one side and then used Stone's own momentum to throw him forward, out of control, through the hole in the wall into the darkness beyond. He turned to Valerie, his face ashen and stern. "Run!" he said.

Stone was back, too quickly for Adam to react, and flew at him. The two crashed to the floor, amid the dust and rubble, with the brittle floorboards cracking and breaking beneath their weight. Adam threw punches where he could, but they landed unevenly, and Stone was on top, still with the knife in his hand. Adam held his arms up and grabbed Stone by his wrists. But Stone was in a frenzy, powered by years of hatred and jealousy, and he quickly freed his arms and held the knife aloft, over Adam's chest.

But then, suddenly, he fell sideways, blood spraying from his head, and he crashed to the floor, a dead weight. Adam looked up to see Valerie stood above them, a thick piece of wood in her hand, part of the broken wall.

"You… you looked like you needed some help," she said.

Adam gasped for breath, untangled himself from Stone's limp body, and quickly stood up. "Thank you," he said. "That was very well-timed."

"We need to get out of here," Valerie said. "And Ray – Ray's downstairs. Stone stabbed him. But he might be OK. We have to get him out, too."

Adam nodded and they both turned to leave. But within a single step, Adam tumbled down to the floor, and Valerie turned to find Stone with a hard grip on Adam's ankle.

"I'll kill you both," Stone hissed, and started to move across the floor towards Adam, stabbing the knife into the rotted floorboards to pull himself along. But Adam was ready for him this time. He twisted his body, sharply, instantly snapping himself free of Stone's grip, and then kicked him in the face. Quickly, both men were on their feet, fighting once more.

Although Valerie had every chance to flee, to run downstairs and escape, she found herself unable to move, unable to leave Adam in that dark house, the young man who had so selflessly risked himself to save her life. She watched, pressed against the wall, as the fight grew more brutal and savage. Adam was younger and faster. He moved with speed and precision, and Valerie could see how years of training for various fight scenes had stayed with him. But Stone was strong, in a frenzy, and he had the knife. And despite his terrible injuries, he was moving quickly, too. Each time Adam evaded his attack, Stone moved in closer, his anger building, his knife ready for another victim.

But she could tell from Adam's movements, the way he seemed to be drawing Stone away from her, that he had a plan. Suddenly he dropped to the floor and spun around on his hand, kicking Stone's feet from under him. It was a dance move, and one that took Stone completely by surprise. He screamed furiously as he fell to the ground once more, but this time Adam did not jump up, or run. The knife had fallen from Stone's hand, and Adam grabbed it from the floor. In a flash, Adam was on top of his assailant, holding the knife in the air, ready to end Stone's wretched life once and for all.

"Don't!" Valerie screamed. And for a moment, everything in the room stopped. "Adam. Don't."

Adam held Stone in place. He pushed his knees forcefully onto Stone's arms, keeping him pinned to the floor, and with his free hand he kept a tight grip on Stone's throat. For the moment, Stone was helpless with Adam on top of him, the knife held aloft.

"Give me one good reason I shouldn't end this monster right now," Adam said, choking on the words, as though about to cry. "One good reason, Valerie. After everything he put Pearl through. All the people he has killed."

Valerie stepped forward, just enough to bring herself into Adam's line of vision. She did not want to distract him, because she knew Stone would take advantage of any moment of weakness. But she knew she had to stop him.

"Because you are a good man, Adam," she said. "And I can understand why Pearl Martin loved you so much."

Stone wriggled with annoyance at Valerie's words, but Adam held him in place and lowered the knife to Stone's throat, allowing the point to press into his flesh but not enough to draw blood.

"I promise you, Adam," Valerie said, her tone soft and kind, "you will never be able to live with what you have done. To know that you are responsible, even partly responsible, for someone's death. I give you my word, it is something that will haunt you for ever. And I know Pearl would not want that for you."

The seconds that followed Valerie's words were silent as Adam's mind furiously raced through the options he had. From the moment he had realised Beth's identity had been compromised, that some lunatic knew who she was, Adam had felt himself hurtling towards this moment. The only way to keep Beth safe was to end the life of the man threatening to expose her. But then, he wondered, how would Beth ever look him in the face again, knowing he had killed a man in cold blood? Even a man as terrible as Guy Stone.

Adam tossed the knife to one side, and it landed on the floor by Valerie's feet. "Please take it," he said.

Valerie picked it up. In the distance, quietly at first, she could hear the noise of sirens screeching towards the scene. "The police are here," she said. But then she noticed something out of the corner of her eye, a brightness in the corner of the room that had not been there before. As she glanced over, she realised one of the candelabras had tipped backwards against the wall and the exposed frame of the building, dry rotted wood, had caught fire.

The flames spread quickly, covering the wall and creeping steadily across the floor and ceiling towards them. "Oh my God, we have to get out," she yelled. "Adam!"

Adam was distracted for the briefest of moments, but it was all the time Stone required. He twisted and turned, threw Adam aside and quickly jumped on top of him. He began punching Adam repeatedly in the face. His blows fell hard, blood sprayed into the air and Adam's head moved limply as he lost consciousness.

And then, Stone's attention quickly shifted elsewhere. He climbed to his feet and rushed at Valerie. Instinctively, she raised the knife to keep him away, but Stone was lost in rage, and the threat of a knife meant nothing to him. He smacked the weapon from Valerie's hand and shoved her against the wall, his hands quickly fixed around her throat, squeezing hard.

"You got my call, Valerie," he hissed, breathlessly. "I always follow up on my calls."

Valerie could see the flames enveloping the room behind Stone. She felt the pressure behind her eyes building as the breath was squeezed out of her. And in that moment, a moment she thought would be her last, an image flashed before her eyes.

Valerie and Alice are sitting in the lounge in Valerie's house, an array of objects spread across the floor between them.

"I want you to be safe, Mum," Alice says. "So, I made a few calls. Don't show anyone, though. They're not all legal in this country."

Alice picks one of them up, a small square device with buttons on the side. "This is The Paralyzer, it's a high-voltage personal stun gun," she says. "It's half the size of most, but it delivers the same charge and can disable an attacker instantly. Keep it on you at all times, Mum. It could save your life."

Valerie plunged her hand into her bag and grabbed at what she hoped was the Paralyzer. She then pushed it into Stone's ribcage and activated it. Instantly, he lost his grip on her and stumbled backwards, his limbs rigid as his muscles seized up. His eyes were wide, bulging, staring at Valerie, as he realised what she had done. And then he fell backwards, his body stiff and straight. He landed hard and crashed onto the rotting floorboards that were now alight and burning. The floor could no longer hold together, and a hole opened beneath the weight of his falling body. The floorboards collapsed under him and Stone disappeared.

Valerie dropped the Paralyzer onto the floor and rushed to help Adam to his feet. "Are you OK?" she asked.

He looked dazed and muddled, his face bloodied and bruised. But he quickly appeared to get a measure of what was happening and gripped Valerie by her wrist. "I'm so sorry. Where is he? Did he hurt you?" he asked, blood dribbling down his face from a large gash on his forehead.

Valerie shook her head. "He's gone," she said, "and I'm sure I'll be fine," she said, "but we need to get out. And Ray's downstairs. We can't leave him."

The fire was spreading, quickly, eating its way through the room. A layer of thick black smoke was beginning to drift down from the ceiling. Adam pulled Valerie towards the hole in the wall, and they hurried from the room and back to the staircase. As they rushed down the crumbling steps, Adam suddenly froze, and stopped them both dead in their tracks as he stared at something below them. "Oh, dear God," he said. "Valerie, don't look."

But Valerie wanted to get back to Ray, a great hope burning inside of her that he might still be alive. And even if he weren't, she would never leave him there, alone. And so, she stepped forward, past Adam, and looked to the hallway below. And there was Guy Stone, dead, impaled on the enormous broken chandelier, the large spike protruding through his chest.

Valerie recoiled, and turned away, to face the wall. She could feel her stomach muscles clenching, as though ready to force bile into her mouth. For a moment, she was unable to move, not wanting to turn and see that horrifying image again. But then she felt Adam gently squeeze her arm.

"We don't have much time," he said, gently. "You need to show me where Ray is."

And the mention of her beloved friend was all it took. Instantly, Valerie focussed her mind and turned to face Adam once more. "Down here," she said, and directed him into the room where Ray had been attacked. They found him on the floor, exactly where he had fallen, a large puddle of blood around him. Without saying a word, Adam lifted Ray's heavy body and hoisted him over his shoulder. Carefully, they made their way from the room and around the chandelier to the front door.

Burning embers rained through the hole in the ceiling onto Guy Stone's dead body, but Valerie was focussed on the way out, on getting Ray to hospital. In that moment, for Valerie, Guy Stone ceased to exist.

As they stepped back into the outside world, armed police surrounded them, shouting and yelling orders, shining torches at them. But after the horrendous experience inside the house, Valerie was in no mood to be told what to do. "A doctor!" she screamed. "We need a fucking doctor, you morons!"

CHAPTER 61

Crowds quickly gathered in the small, exclusive corner of north London as it was suddenly filled by the emergency services. Police, paramedics and fire fighters were working to control the fire, tend to the injured and keep the growing number of onlookers at a safe distance. They had swiftly created a line of vehicles around the entrance to Grosvenor House and cordoned the site off.

The police had been able to locate the main gates, lost beneath years of ivy and vines, and had forced them open so that two fire engines could manoeuvre up the drive for better access to the burning house. The towering flames, billowing smoke and flashing lights created an exciting visual for reporters, and many TV news services had quickly dispatched aerial camera teams to capture the spectacle and feed it live to their audiences. Amidst the chaos, word had quickly spread that at least one person was dead and that a major celebrity was involved and still at the scene.

Within the safety ring created by the emergency services, Valerie was sitting on the back seat of a police car, the door open and her feet on the pavement. She was wrapped in an emergency blanket and was drinking from a water bottle given to her by a fire fighter. She watched, silently, as a few metres away a paramedic, a proficient and reassuring woman called Amy, tended Adam Jaymes' injured head as the actor sat on the back step of the ambulance. Amy had cleaned, stitched and bandaged the wound, and Adam had sat calmly without saying a word or wincing, even once.

Around him, an entire world of people was busily going about their duties, and yet many were clearly distracted by him, looking at him, watching him, perhaps wondering if they could speak to him or even snag a selfie with him. But for Valerie, it was as though a veil had dropped. Adam was a huge, internationally famous, untouchable superstar, but suddenly he looked so small, so ordinary and vulnerable. Adam Jaymes could have died that night, and she knew he would have died trying to save her.

Valerie could hear Amy telling him she wanted him to go to hospital so they could review his head injury, but Adam declined. "It's… it's fine," he said. "Thank you, though. But I have my own doctor, and he's going to meet me at my apartment."

Amy then walked over to Valerie. "And how are you getting on, Mrs Pierce?" she asked.

Valerie waved the bottle of water at her and smiled. "I'd rather this was a gin and tonic, to be honest" she replied. "A triple."

Amy chuckled. "The NHS doesn't stretch to gin, I'm afraid," she said.

"What did you do with Ray?" Valerie asked, and Amy's friendly expression changed to one of concern.

"He's already gone," she said.

"I wanted to travel with him," Valerie replied, fighting the need to cry.

Amy nodded. "I can find out where they've taken him," she said. "Would that help?"

"Yes," Valerie replied. "I know it sounds silly, but I… I just don't want him to be on his own." Her voice cracked at the thought of Ray, lying in the back of the ambulance, with no one to hold his hand.

"That doesn't sound silly at all, Mrs Pierce. I'll come and get you when we're heading off. I'll make a call now and let you know."

As Amy left, Adam walked over to Valerie and leaned against the outside of the car. "We'll have a lot of questions to answer," he said.

Valerie huffed. "Believe me, Adam, by the time I've finished with them, it's the police who are going to have a lot of questions to answer," she said. "All of this could have been avoided. All of it. If they had just listened to me."

Adam made a noise in his throat, as though in agreement, and then said: "I meant to ask. Why were you here this evening? You and Ray?"

Valerie shrugged. "I wanted to get some photographs, for my next book, of where Stone grew up," she replied. "A contact gave me the address, but he told me the police had the property on their radar and if I wanted to get inside, I needed to do it tonight, or the police would probably beat me to it and close the whole site down. It didn't occur to me that Stone would actually be here, using it as his base." She sighed as the truth of the situation suddenly dawned on her, and she added: "That wasn't an email from my contact, was it?"

Adam shook his head. "Nope," he replied. "That was Stone. Reeling you in."

"So, this *was* my phone call night," she said. "It was all planned. And the only thing he hadn't allowed for was you. He hadn't anticipated you being here tonight. So, same question, Adam. Why were *you* here? Did your team of experts realise this was his base?"

Adam shook his head. "No, not at all," he replied. "Stone had created a whole network of false data trails. It looked like he could have been operating from any one of more than a dozen different locations: Edinburgh Castle, a whiskey distillery in Midleton, near Cork, Ljubljana, Tallin. Even Ricky's Cabaret Bar on Gran Canaria," he said. "But I'm not really one for sitting still and waiting for other people to give me the answers. Once I knew Stone was still alive, I looked for places he had lived." Adam gestured towards the burning building in front of them. "This seemed a good place to start. To check out, for some clues. And when I arrived, I could hear voices from upstairs and realised someone was already here. And that's when I found you both."

Valerie began to rifle through her bag. "You know, he had a whole wall of photographs and press cuttings. All the people he had killed. Articles they had written, about Pearl. Some were by me. But there was one picture I removed. I didn't think you would want it on the wall, for the police to find. It would lead to all sorts of questions."

She handed Adam the photograph of Beth. "Here," she said. "She's still safe. No one will ever know."

Adam looked at the photograph, and Valerie was sure she could see a change in his expression. He frowned, slightly, as though suddenly worried. And then he took the picture, folded it up, and slipped it into his trouser pocket. "Thank you," he said. "So, tell me, this book. Have you a title for it?"

Valerie nodded. "Guy Stone, the life and death of a serial killer."

Adam took a deep breath. "The life, death and second *death* of a serial killer," he replied.

A police officer approached them and addressed Valerie with an extremely apologetic manner. "Mrs Pierce, is your vehicle the dark blue Audi, parked at the corner?"

Valerie nodded. "Yes, that's me. Is it in the way?"

The police officer smiled. "Yes, I'm sorry, I do need to move it. But if you would like to give me the keys, I can have it moved for you."

Valerie unwrapped herself from the blanket and put the bottle of water onto the ground. "No, no. It's fine," she said, and stood up. "I need to get something from the glove compartment anyway," she said, feeling a strong urge for a cigarette. She turned and looked to Adam. "We'll need to catch up, Adam, at some point."

He nodded. "Take care," he said. "I'll see you again."

Valerie walked away, carefully navigating the bustling crowd of fire fighters and police officers. And just as she reached the police cordon, she glanced back and could see Adam on his phone, very animated. His voice, loud and excited, carried through the air and she could just hear him say: "Where have you been? We've all been worried sick!" And she wondered who he was speaking to.

The police officer she had seen earlier helped her through the barriers, and she quietly made her way to her car, ignored, almost invisible, to the crowd of onlookers, all of whom had now heard, for certain, that Adam Jaymes was somewhere in the middle of all the excitement. And they all had their phones out, ready to record the moment he came into view.

Valerie used her key fob to unlock her car, and then wearily climbed into the driver's seat and closed the door behind her. And as the quietness fell around her, she was overwhelmed by the emptiness left by Ray, and she leaned forward onto the steering wheel and began to sob.

There was a noise from behind her. It didn't register immediately, but she suddenly felt her private moment had been interrupted. That someone had climbed into the back seat of her car. She lifted her head from the steering wheel and went to turn around, but suddenly felt something hard, possibly metal, pushed against the back of her head. And then she heard someone speak, a woman she thought, but the words were deep and quiet, as though someone was trying to disguise their voice.

"Do as you are told," the voice said.

"What?" Valerie replied. "Listen, I have had the worst day of my life, and I am in no mood…"

"Do as you are told, or I will shoot you in the head, Valerie. Is that clear?"

The object, a gun, was pushed more firmly into the back of Valerie's head. She realised she was trapped once more. Guy Stone was dead, but now it seemed someone else was going to finish the job. "Who are you? What do you want?" Valerie asked.

"You'll find out," the voice replied. "Now drive. When you get to the entrance to the road, you turn left. Get going."

For a moment, a very brief moment, Valerie thought about running, or trying to open the door and screaming for help. But she could feel the gun, and she could hear the anger in the voice of the person sat in her back seat, and she knew she wouldn't last a second if she did not do as she was told.

And so, instead, she started the car and began to drive, and wondered where she was driving to.

CHAPTER 62

"As you can see, the building is completely ablaze, and the fire service is trying to bring it under control. This is one of the most exclusive areas in London and many of the houses date back as far as 1908. We understand this particular property has been empty for many years. As more information comes in, we can now confirm, via the police, there has been at least one fatality at the scene."

> *#BishopsSquareFire The road is filled with emergency services. Avoid the area. LOADS of diversions. People being asked to move their cars.*

"…believed to have died more than fourteen years ago, after attempting suicide by setting himself on fire at the funeral of the actress, Pearl Martin. It has been confirmed that a public statement issued by his family at that time, which had confirmed his death, was false. In truth, Stone has spent much of the past fourteen years in private medical facilities undergoing repeated treatments for his injuries…"

> *It's definitely Adam Jaymes. Just saw him. His face was a bit bruised but his body is SO hot. I would literally let him destroy me! #BishopsSquareFire*

"…images emerging which appear to be of the actor Adam Jaymes at the scene, his face badly bruised, and other reports that former Daily Ear columnist Valerie Pierce was also at the scene, speaking to police. Many will recall that Guy Stone received prison sentences for stalking the actress Pearl Martin, a close friend of Adam Jaymes…"

"...now confirm that a further two deaths have been linked to Guy Stone, and that others are being reviewed. Stone, who has already been labelled 'the Daily Ear killer' in the tabloid press, was born..."

#GuyStone One of the country's richest families hid its dirty secret and now people are dead. They need to be investigated.

"...confirmed they have now expanded the scope of the investigation and are reviewing the recent deaths of more people, all connected with the Daily Ear newspaper. They have declined to confirm if this includes the apparent drowning accident that claimed the life of controversial columnist, Lucy Strickland."

@ValeriePierce53 *PR firms, here's a little hint for your next launch event. Four words you should never see together on a press invitation: 'vegan sushi' and 'Valerie Pierce'.*

CHAPTER 63

Valerie could hear the sea. She could feel a cold breeze blowing across her face and there was a hardness beneath her body that did not feel like the comfortable mattress of her bed at home. Her senses gradually returned as she awoke, and she had a terrible feeling in the pit of her stomach; a great fear but, at first, she could not remember why.

As moments passed, she managed to force open her eyes and could see a beautiful morning sunrise in front of her; a cloudless, red and golden sky above an endless sea. She realised she had no idea where she was. At first, she wondered if perhaps she had had a particularly heavy night, overdone the Rioja and somehow ended up sleeping on the beach. But as she pushed herself up from the mound of grass damp with the cold morning dew, she realised she was high up, perched on the top of a cliff. She glanced cautiously over the edge and could see a lighthouse hundreds of feet beneath her, painted in large stripes of red and white.

She stood, her legs trembling and unsure. "This is Beachy Head," she whispered to herself. "How the hell did I get here?"

Her mind began to slowly offer some memories, flashes of the night before; the house, and Ray, and Guy Stone, and Adam Jaymes, and the fire. That terrible fire. And then she recalled the woman with a gun, in the back seat of her car. Telling her to drive, but only a short distance, just for a few miles. And then... and then...

"Pull over, here, in this layby."

"What? Why?" Valerie asked, but her question received no answer. She decided it was best to do as she was told. She slowed her car, pulled into a bus stop and put the gears into neutral. Around her was an empty, dark, London street. There

were no houses, just high walls surrounding large Victorian factories that were closed for the night. And Valerie knew, this time, no one was coming to help her. "Now, will you please tell me what the hell is going on?" she said, attempting to sound confident and irritated.

A bottle of water suddenly dropped onto the passenger seat next to her.

"No thank you, I'm fine," Valerie said.

But she felt the gun pressed hard against her head; she wasn't being given the option to say no. And she was tired, too tired to argue, or to come up with a plan, or to try to distract her assailant. She sensed that if she did not do as she was told, her life would end right there, a bullet in the back of her head.

She lifted the bottle, removed the cap, and noticed there was no 'click' as she unscrewed it. The bottle had already been opened. "What's in this?" she asked.

But, again, there was no answer. Valerie could feel a tear trickling down her cheek as she wondered if she would ever see Alice or her granddaughters again. Shakily, she lifted the bottle to her lips and began to drink.

As she stood gazing over the cliff edge Valerie could sense that she was not alone, that someone was stood just a few metres behind her. And so, she drew a deep breath, and turned. And then she screamed. "That's not possible," she spluttered, "for God's sake, what the hell? How are you here?"

The woman's pale complexion, bright blue eyes and shoulder-length black hair were instantly recognisable. She stood with a small black revolver in her left hand, pointed at Valerie. Her face was blank, expressionless, as though a ghost from Valerie's past was visiting, just for a moment, just long enough to take revenge for Valerie's many misdeeds against her.

"Pearl?" Valerie asked.

The woman frowned. "Don't call me Pearl," she said. "*He* did that. I hated it."

There was something familiar about the woman's tone, a hardness, a severity. And even though Valerie was unsteady and shaking either through cold, or fear, or the after-effects of whatever had been used to drug her, her mind was slowly beginning to make sense of what was happening. And she was able to recognise that the woman in front of her was not Pearl Martin, but her sister, Patricia.

"You look different," Valerie said. "That last time, in your office, the hair, glasses. It was like you were going out of your way to look like anyone apart from Pearl."

Patricia did not respond. She stood, gun in hand, staring at Valerie, as though trying to decide what to do next.

"Patricia, this is madness," Valerie said. "I do not believe for one second that you would willingly work with a man like Guy Stone. After everything he put your sister through. He must have coerced you, threatened you?"

There was a part of Valerie, her more cynical part, which believed it would not have taken much prompting for Pearl Martin's angry sister to be pressed into working with Stone. But when Patricia did not speak, Valerie suddenly felt differently. She no longer saw Patricia as hard and determined but tired and weary, as though the world had defeated her and beaten every last ounce of kindness from her. "But he's dead now," Valerie said. "You don't have to cover up for him anymore. Guy Stone is dead." She gestured with her hand towards Patricia. "Is that why you've dressed like this, like Pearl?" she asked, slightly appalled. "To please him? Feed into some fantasy that she was still alive?"

"No," Patricia replied, abruptly. "I needed his guard down, so I could get close enough to…" Her voice trailed off, and suddenly she stood straight, her grip on the revolver tightening.

"Close enough to – to do what?" Valerie asked. And then, after a moment of silence, Valerie's curious mind began to unpick some of the baffling events of the previous night. She began to unravel what had happened after Stone's death; Patricia's unexplained presence at the scene, at that moment, dressed like Pearl Martin, with a gun and a bottle of water laced with enough tranquilizer to render someone unconscious.

"You weren't at the house last night to kidnap me, were you?" she asked. "You were there for Stone. That's why you're dressed like that, to distract him. And the bottle of water. You were hoping to drug him, to kill Stone while he was unconscious."

Still Patricia did not respond.

"But when you got there, the whole house was on fire," Valerie continued, "the road cordoned off. And you realised we'd done the job for you. Stone was already dead."

"And then I saw you," Patricia replied, her lip curled with disgust. "Swanning around like some sort of hero. When you should have been dead. Stone's final victim." She gestured towards the cliff edge with the gun. "Now, move!" She issued the instruction coldly, and stepped forward, making Valerie instinctively step backwards, precariously close to the edge.

Valerie's heart was racing, the weapon in Patricia's hand now more than just a prop or a threat. Suddenly it was very real. And the drop behind her, hundreds of feet straight down on to rocks. It was the same place Pearl Martin had ended her life all those years earlier. Patricia had not chosen this place by accident. "Why here?" Valerie asked. "Why Beachy Head?"

"Because in your last miserable moments on this earth, you will experience exactly what my sister did," Patricia replied. "And your family will grieve in the same way we did, believing you had taken your own life. And they will spend the rest of *their* lives thinking they had failed you."

Valerie shook her head, trying to hold back tears that she could feel forming in her eyes. "But they won't believe it. Pearl had a long history of mental illness, depression. When she died, she had it all planned. She left notes, updated her will. She had arranged her own funeral. Her suicide wasn't spur of the moment, Patricia. You know this. She spent weeks planning for that day. And no one is going to believe for a second that I just suddenly decided I wanted to kill myself."

Valerie tried to be brave. Tried to behave as though she were taking everything in, calmly and logically. But her mind was beginning to race as she attempted to navigate a way through the insane conversation to find a safe path away from the cliff edge.

Patricia reached into her jacket pocket and retrieved an object that Valerie immediately recognised. "That's my phone," Valerie said. "What are you doing with my phone?"

Patricia pressed a button on the screen and Valerie's voice filled the air. But although it was indisputably Valerie's voice, the words were not hers. It was as though someone had written a script for her, created an entirely new narrative for the final moments of her life: *"I'm sorry for what I did, and I know some things cannot be undone. Some things can never be made right. But I have to take responsibility for my actions; the part I played in what happened to Pearl Martin; the lies I created that destroyed her life. Nothing can ever make it right. But I hope what I do next… I hope it makes a difference. And to Pearl's family, I hope my death brings you peace. And finally offers you closure."*

Valerie shook her head. "That's not me. I would never say that. Closure? Oh, for goodness sake."

"Really?" Patricia replied. "How ironic. Is tabloid gossip columnist Valerie Pierce claiming *she* has been misquoted, that what *she* said has been taken out of context?"

"You know that's not me," Valerie said. "Another of Guy Stone's clever tricks, I suppose." Valerie wondered why such a recording, even a fake recording, even existed. And then she remembered something Guy Stone had bragged about, the night before. The plans he had put in place for Valerie's 'phone call night'.

"A complex night of mishaps and misdirection that would have left you abandoned and alone, exposed, in the middle of nowhere. Without your ex-husband, or your daughter, or Adam Jaymes to hide behind. Easy pickings for me."

Valerie gestured to the cliff edge. "This wasn't you, was it?" she said. "You didn't just happen to see me wandering to my car and suddenly devise this whole plan. This was Stone, wasn't it? This is what he had planned for me, before he swapped my 'phone call night' for Lucy Strickland. He was going to trick me to travelling to Beachy Head, chuck me off the cliff and leave my phone behind, with that message on it."

Patricia placed the phone back into her pocket, and then looked at Valerie. "Yes," she replied, a cold matter-of-fact tone to her voice.

"My God, Patricia. Then you were working with him? After everything he did to your sister, you worked with that monster."

"I did not work with him," Patricia responded, angrily. "Don't you dare say that. I had no part in what he did."

"But you knew, didn't you?" Valerie said. "All along, you knew what he was doing, who he was targeting. And you said nothing."

Patricia nodded. "He told me everything," she replied. "Each time he killed someone he would contact me. Brag about what he had done, as though I was supposed to be impressed. Or grateful."

"You could have gone to the police," Valerie said. "You could have stopped it all."

"You don't know," Patricia responded, shaking her head. "You have no idea what he was like. How clever he really was. There was no way I could go to the police. He knew everything I did. Every phone call. Every text. Who I met with, what I had for lunch. It was suffocating. And if he thought, for a moment, I was betraying him, or if we tried to run away, to hide, he told me he would kill my son, that he would kill Ben. And I knew that he would, and that he could."

"And now?" Valerie asked, quietly, and pointed at the gun in Patricia's hand. "Be honest, Patricia. As much as you claim you kept silent under duress, you secretly enjoyed it didn't you? All those people you hated so much, and their gruesome deaths. You enjoyed it. And now, what, you are here, finishing the job for Stone?"

Patricia shook her head. "No," she replied, sadly. "For Pearl. I can finally finish this for Pearl." She then lifted the revolver level with Valerie's eyes, and her face distorted, just for a moment, as she tried to stop herself from crying.

A cold breeze blew across the cliff edge and a flock of seagulls began to circle overhead, screeching, filling the air with noise and distraction. Valerie noticed Patricia was leaning her head slightly to one side, as though trying to hear something, a sound carried on the wind. Then Valerie heard it too, a voice, distant at first but getting closer, calling out to Patricia.

"Auntie Pat… Auntie Pat… stop… what the hell are you doing?"

In unison, Valerie and Patricia both turned to the grassy hill that led down to the cliff edge and saw Beth rushing towards them, with Adam following behind her, his head still bandaged.

"No!" Patricia yelled. "You cannot be here, Beth. This does not concern you."

"Auntie Pat, that's enough," Beth said, sternly. She came to a standstill just a few metres from Patricia, with Adam gently holding her arm, keeping her from entering the line of fire. "You aren't thinking straight," Beth said. "What happened to Ben wasn't Valerie's fault. And you cannot do this. I won't let you. Not in my mother's name."

Valerie glanced over to Adam. "Please tell me what's going on?" she said. "How did you know we were here?"

"It was your phone," Adam said. "I found out Beth was in London, so I went to collect her, and then I checked in with the police. They told me you had gone to move your car and had vanished. I tried ringing you but there was no reply. Luckily, I had Alice's business card and I called her. She hadn't heard from you either. So, she checked the friend finder app on her phone, and she told me where you were. And I guessed you were in trouble."

"And I knew you would be here, Auntie Pat," Beth said. She then turned to Valerie, her pretty young face suddenly so familiar, as though an old friend had arrived to say hello. "Ben was beaten," she said. "Really badly. A few nights ago."

"What? By Guy Stone?" Valerie asked, and turned to stare Patricia in the face. "Why would he attack your son? You were doing everything he told you."

Patricia did not respond. She was staring at Beth, her eyes pleading for the young woman to leave, to turn around and pretend she hadn't seen a thing. But she kept the gun aimed at Valerie. "You can't be here, Beth," she said, her voice suddenly frail and sad.

"Ben's been emailing me for weeks," Beth said. "He knew something was up. All those people dying. He was certain they were all connected. He kept telling me he didn't think any of them were accidents."

"Oh, God," Patricia gasped. "He wasn't supposed to know anything," she said. "He shouldn't have been involved at all."

"I called him up for a chat, a few days ago," Beth continued, "and he accidentally put me on video. I saw his face. What someone had done to his face. I asked why he wasn't in hospital. And that's when he broke down. He told me he had been beaten, really badly beaten, but that you kept him at home. You told him he wasn't allowed to tell anyone he had been attacked. That he was never to tell anyone he had been at that marina."

Amidst her shocking story, there was a word Beth had used, a single word that rang most loudly in Valerie's head. *Marina.* And Valerie remembered something else Stone had said the previous night when he had been bragging about Lucy Strickland's murder.

"It turned out to be a tricky one, though, because I hadn't anticipated that she would bring…"

"Ben was with Lucy Strickland," she said, half as a statement and half as a question, as she tried to process all the disjointed bits of information she had in her mind and form them into a clear narrative. "The night she died. Stone was expecting Lucy to arrive alone. And all his murders were planned meticulously. No room for variation. But then Ben turned up. And Stone had to get him out of the way quickly, before he could carry out his plan for Lucy." Valerie looked at Patricia, and then glanced at Beth and Adam, hoping for an answer. "But how did Ben know Lucy?"

"Perhaps you should ask your friend, Adam Jaymes," Patricia said, a spiteful edge to her words.

"That's enough, Patricia," Adam replied, sternly.

Valerie turned to Adam and shrugged. "Well?"

Adam sighed and Valerie saw something in him that she had never seen before; Adam Jaymes looked ashamed. "He's been working at the *Daily Ear*," he said. "He was one of my corporate spies during Project Ear. He fed me information to use against the paper, its reporters, and managers. Against you."

"What?" Valerie asked, her face slightly screwed up. "But all that Project Ear nonsense. That was years ago. Why was he still there?"

"He enjoyed the job," Beth replied, "and he had aspirations. He thought if he could get promoted, become a manager or a director, he might be able to change things. From the inside."

"He's a good boy, Valerie," Adam said. "I promise you. Everything he did, he meant well. I think that's why he was with Lucy, that night. The night Stone killed her. I think he was worried for her and wanted to keep an eye on her."

"You know him, Valerie," Beth said.

"I promise you, Beth, I have never met your cousin," Valerie replied, exasperated.

"Yes, you have. It's Lewis," Beth said. "Lewis Greene. That's the name he used. He works in communications at the *Daily Ear*. You've worked with him. You saw him last week, at your club. You had dinner with him."

Briefly, everything Valerie thought about Lewis was turned upside-down. His bright smile, his kind and reliable nature, his impeccable manners. All of it vanished and was replaced with a grinding sense of disloyalty. But then she imagined him being beaten by Stone in the same way she had witnessed Adam so viciously beaten and any feelings of betrayal were quickly replaced by anguish. "Oh, my goodness," she said. "That poor boy. Oh, dear lord! He must have been terrified."

"He's going to be fine," Adam said, his words directed at Patricia. "I've got people with him now, private medical staff. People who know how to be discreet. They're checking him over. But you should never have kept him out of hospital, Patricia. Not with head injuries like that."

Finally, a tear rolled down Patricia's cheek, and she nodded. "Guy Stone... he sent me a picture," she said. "Of what he did to my boy. He had beaten him unconscious and stuffed him into the boot of a car. He told me where to find him. And he told me if I went to the police, he would finish the job. So, I drove straight to the marina and found the car. Ben had already woken up. He'd been conscious for about an hour, trapped in that boot. He was terrified. He thought Stone was going back to kill him. And he was so badly injured, his beautiful face, all covered in blood. But I couldn't take him to the hospital. All the doctors, they'd ask too many questions. They would involve the police. So, I just took him home, washed his cuts and tried to keep him safe."

Valerie looked at Patricia, the gun still in her hand, still pointing at her. "I'm so sorry," Valerie said. "I can understand how that must have driven you over the edge. But we can stop this now, Patricia."

Patricia shook her head. "No," she said. "I read that book of yours, Valerie. That sodding awful book. Hundreds of pages long, where you blamed everyone for what happened to my sister. Everyone but yourself. Not one single moment of reflection, not one single sentence where you offered an apology for everything *you* did to Pearl."

Beth went to step forward, to bring the situation to a conclusion. But Adam held her arm and gently pulled her back, shaking his head, knowing this was too volatile a moment to intervene. Instead, they waited for Valerie to respond, hoping she might offer some soft and kind words that might placate Patricia.

"I *know* what I did," Valerie said, her voice quiet. "And you are correct, it isn't in my book. But I have spent years reflecting on my time at the *Daily Ear*. Everything I said, everything I wrote. The impact I had on Pearl. And the truth is, I left it all out of my book because I was too ashamed to put it in.

"So, let me say it to you now, to all of you. If I could turn back time, I would change everything that happened. But I cannot, and all I have, now, is my words. And I am sorry for what I did, for the part I played in what happened to Pearl. For the loss of your sister. Adam's best friend. Beth's mother. I am truly, truly sorry."

But then, Valerie's demeanour shifted. She appeared annoyed, irritated, almost put out. She took a couple of steps forward, away from the edge of the cliff, and then stood with her hands on her hips and stared Patricia directly in the face, as though the gun was no longer a concern. "But what about you, Patricia?" she asked. "Where is *your* apology, to your sister? To Beth? Have you ever said sorry for what *you* did?"

"Don't you dare!" Patricia replied, waving the gun precariously in Valerie's face. "Don't you dare turn this on me. You know that was different."

"That's enough," Beth interrupted, cross and impatient. She brushed Adam's hand aside, marched forward and then stood next to Valerie. "What did you do?" she asked Patricia.

Patricia shook her head. "Nothing," she said. "Just… grown-up stuff."

"Funny, because the last time I checked I was a grown-up," Beth replied, indignantly. "Now what did Valerie mean?"

When Patricia failed to answer, Beth turned to Adam. "Uncle Adam? What's this about?"

He shrugged. "Honestly, sweetheart, I… I haven't a clue."

Exasperated, Beth turned to Valerie. "Tell me," she said.

But Valerie shook her head. "I'm sorry, my dear, but I can't."

"Why not?"

Valerie paused, her expression apologetic, as though she were being forced to share information she would rather keep secret. And then she replied, "Because a good journalist never reveals her sources."

Valerie's words, although trite, carried through the air with a terrible force. Slowly, Beth turned to her aunt once more, but Patricia could not look at her. She stared at the ground, tears streaming down her cheeks. Finally, the gun was lowered and then it fell from Patricia's hand, onto the damp grass below.

"I'm so sorry, Beth," Patricia gasped. "It's not what it sounds like."

Softly but sternly, Beth spoke. "You were the leak?" she asked. "You were the one feeding stories to the *Daily Ear*? From *inside* the family?"

Patricia covered her face with her hands, and then nodded. "Beth, you don't understand what it was like for me back then," she said, and then she dropped her arms to her sides and looked up. "Your mum had so much," she said, the words conveyed with a mixture of sorrow and anger, "she had this big house, and this career, and these rich friends. She had this amazing talent, so much success. I had nothing. I had a useless boyfriend, and I couldn't even hold down a job as a receptionist. I didn't want to lose her to this new life. I just wanted to keep up."

"Mum would have helped you," Beth said, "you know she would have helped. All you needed to do was ask."

Patricia shook her head. "I couldn't," she said. "Pearl knew Ben's dad was useless. She told me over and over that I deserved better. If I'd asked her for money, she wouldn't have seen it as helping me, but helping him."

"She still would have said yes," Beth said, a frustration building in her voice. "Whatever she thought of your stupid boyfriend, she still would have helped her own sister. You know that."

Patricia looked at the floor. "I couldn't ask," she replied, quietly, and with those words she exposed the true reason for her betrayal: she had been too proud to ask her sister for money.

"So how did it start?" Beth asked. "When was the first time?"

Patricia took a deep breath and looked Beth in the face. "When she got that first job, on the soap, it was only a six-month contract," she said. "And she was so worried it wasn't going to be renewed. The writers seemed to give all the best scenes to other actors. Pearl just felt invisible; she was certain she was going to be written out. All the other cast members seemed to be in the papers all the time. And I thought that's what your mum needed, to be in in the papers, too. One night she had a date with one of the other actors, and I thought I could help, do a bit of promotion for her. So, I called the *Daily Ear* to let them know where they'd be, in a restaurant, eating dinner together. And I suggested that perhaps someone from the paper might like to take a picture."

"Did Mum know?" Beth asked. "Did she ask you to do it?"

Patricia shook her head. "I was just trying to help," she said. "I was put through to the entertainment desk, and the reporter seemed really helpful and interested. He told me I was doing the right thing, that I was helping Pearl's career, that all celebrities and their agents were doing the same."

"But you asked for money?" Adam said, his words as much an accusation as a question. "You got paid for the tip-off."

"He offered to pay me," Patricia replied, bluntly, and didn't say any more.

"How much?" Beth asked. "How much money did you make?"

Patricia shrugged. "It wasn't about the money," she said. "I can't remember."

Beth scowled at her, and in that angry moment knew she did not believe Patricia's version of events. She did not see her aunt as a helpless victim, enticed into a shady system of tip-offs and pay-offs. She saw her as a liar, who had happily betrayed Beth's mother to make some quick money for herself. And as Patricia refused to elaborate, Beth sought an answer from elsewhere, and turned to face Valerie. "How much?" she asked.

Nonchalantly, Valerie frowned, as though casually doing a sum in her head. "A tip off, like that, back then… perhaps five hundred pounds. But I think Patricia will admit that as she continued to work with us, and her sister grew more famous, her fees increased considerably."

Beth turned back, to look at her aunt. "I guess this explains how someone with no job managed to pay for that house and all of those expensive holidays."

Patricia replied softly, hoping it was not too late to reconnect with her niece, "I didn't just do it for me," she said. "I helped your mum. It worked, that first time. Your mum was all over the *Daily Ear*, and then the rest of the press. And all the stories were positive. Really positive. And so, I did it again, a few times. And your mum started getting noticed by the producers. They gave her better scripts, bigger storylines. Her contract was renewed with a huge pay rise. Suddenly, she was being treated like she was the star of show."

"That wasn't you, Patricia," Adam replied, tersely. "Pearl's career took off because she was talented, and hard-working, and respectful. She did not seek cheap publicity or push other people out of the spotlight to get herself noticed. She waited quietly, in the wings, for her moment. And when that moment arrived, when the writers gave her an opportunity to show what she could do, Pearl shone so brightly that everyone realised she was the star of the show. And that had nothing to do with you or your tawdry tip-offs to the press."

There was a moment of quiet as Adam's loud angry words echoed around them all. And then Beth spoke: "But then it all went wrong, didn't it?" she said. "The stories started to get nasty. Everything Mum did was twisted into something negative. But you kept feeding that machine, taking their money. All those horrible articles, they all came from you."

After a pause, Patricia nodded and replied. "It was like someone at the *Daily Ear* made a decision that there shouldn't be any good news stories about Pearl, only bad ones," she said. "Everything I did, every story I gave them, was supposed to be positive, to help Pearl, help her career. But it all got distorted, every time, into something bad. I was trying to help, but I just kept making everything worse. And, Beth, every time they contacted me, I was terrified they would tell your mother if I didn't give them something. And I knew she would think I had betrayed her. I felt so trapped. I couldn't stop it."

"But they always paid you, didn't they Patricia?" Adam said. "Even when *they* were contacting *you*, cajoling you into revealing what was going on in Pearl's private life. Even when you could no longer pretend to yourself that you were acting in Pearl's best interests, you still took the money."

Patricia looked at Adam, anger etched across her face. "It so easy for you to look down on me, isn't it Adam? With your billionaire husband," she said, spitting as she spoke. "I was on my own. I had a son. I was just trying to make ends meet."

She then looked at her niece, hoping to find some kindness, or understanding in her expression. But Beth stood silently, staring at Patricia as though she were a stranger, someone she was seeing for the first time. "I was just trying to keep up with Pearl," Patricia said. "I didn't want her to leave me behind."

Ever so slightly, Beth shook her head and then looked down to the ground. There was so much she wanted to say, so much more she wanted to ask. But she needed time away from Patricia, time to think. She needed to be calmer, less fraught. She lowered herself, crouched down just far enough to pick up the gun. And then, without looking at her aunt again, she turned and walked away. As she passed her Uncle Adam, she reached out and handed him the revolver. And then she continued walking.

"Beth. Beth!" Patricia screamed. "Beth, wait. I didn't mean anything by it. Beth, please. Come back. I was only trying to help." But her words were lost, unheard. Beth was gone. Patricia dropped to her knees, sobbing, overwhelmed with anguish and shame, her painful cries echoing throughout the cliffs, carried on the cold morning breeze.

Valerie looked to Adam. Despite his obvious anger, she had expected him to move to Patricia, to console her. But instead, she was met with a cold expression, a stern glare; the famous actor unable to conceal his own feelings of betrayal at what Patricia had revealed. And Valerie knew why he would find Patricia's story so unforgiveable; Adam had seen first-hand the impact of all those leaked stories, not only on Pearl Martin's career or public profile, but the impact on her mental health.

Adam knew the constant paranoia Pearl had lived with, always wondering who was speaking to the press, and when, and why. He knew Pearl had cut people from her life, friends and even some family members, after accusing them, wrongly, of being the leak. And throughout all those years, there had been only two people Pearl had never suspected, two people she believed she could always trust, whose love and dedication were beyond reproach. Adam was one, her dearest friend. The other had been her devoted sister, Patricia.

And as Valerie gazed at the glorious sunrise, shining over the place where Pearl Martin had ended her life, she realised Beachy Head had now played a part in another awful chapter of Pearl's family; it was the place where a terrible betrayal had been exposed, one that left her family torn apart.

CHAPTER 64

Valerie sat in her car smoking one final cigarette to ease her nerves before she went inside the hospital. She was dressed entirely in black apart from a deep purple scarf around her neck, a necessary addition until her bruises had faded. She had collected a huge bouquet of flowers from a local florist, which was lying on the passenger seat next to her. She knew the day ahead was going to be filled with difficult conversations, and she was going to have to say a final goodbye to someone she had loved deeply.

But in the days that had passed since the terrible events at Grosvenor House, and the devastating conversation at Beachy Head, she had been able to reassess many different aspects of her life, and knew it was time to move on.

She stubbed out her cigarette in the little ashtray under the dashboard, checked herself in the rear-view mirror, picked up the flowers and walked to the entrance. She had checked in advance with the hospital's communications team and been told the media presence was now gone, and so she was able to quietly make her way through the busy lobby to the lift and stood alone as it carried her to the second floor.

As the heavy metal doors clunked and rattled open, she found Alice waiting for her, also dressed in black. Valerie stepped forward and Alice kissed her on the cheek. "How is he?" she asked.

Alice took her mother's arm and began to walk her along the short corridor to the entrance of the Chalkwell Ward. "He's in a lot of pain, but he won't admit it," she said. "And the police were with him all morning, taking another statement. I'm sure that's the third time they've seen him now."

Valerie huffed. "Nice to see them finally doing their job properly," she said. "You know that night at the house, that horrible night when Stone… when Stone stabbed him. There was a look on Ray's face I can't ever forget.

He genuinely thought he was about to die, that those were his last seconds on this earth. And yet all he could do, all he could think to do, was to tell me to run."

They stopped as they reached the door to the ward, and Valerie turned to look Alice in the face. "He could have screamed for help, but he didn't. His last action... what he thought was his going to be his last action... was to try and save me."

"He was very brave," Alice said.

"Yes, and that's my point," Valerie replied. "I don't think I ever appreciated how brave he is, how brave he has always been. To live his life as he did."

"What do you mean?" Alice asked.

Valerie was not used to being so candid with her daughter. But she had decided, after that frightening morning at Beachy Head, that secrets were usually better out in the open, exposed. And that included being more open about her feelings. "Our marriage lasted less than a year," she said. "When he left me for Pete, another man, I was devastated. Heartbroken. Humiliated. But everyone gathered around me, supported me and reassured me that I had done nothing wrong. Not a single person showed any compassion or understanding for what Ray had been through.

"All our friends turned their backs on him, and his family, his own parents, disowned him. He had to move away and start again, from scratch. I don't think I had ever really appreciated how much courage that took. Ray has had to be brave his entire life."

Alice took Valerie's hand and gave it a little squeeze. Over the previous few days, she had found an uncharacteristic, but overwhelming need, to be tactile with her mother and had taken almost every opportunity to hold her hand or embrace her. All her anger at Valerie had, for the time being, faded and Alice knew this was probably the last chance they would have to properly reset their relationship. For once in her life, that was something Alice genuinely wished for; a proper relationship with her mother. "And what about you?" she asked. "Are you sure you want to do this, today? You know it will change everything."

Valerie took a deep breath and then sighed. "Yes," she said. "Because after all these silly, stupid years, I have to accept that even though Ray is still undoubtedly the love of my life, I am not his. And it is time he and I both moved on."

She noticed that Alice's expression changed, as though her daughter was surprised by her unexpected words. "You don't mind, do you?" Valerie asked. "Alice, I loved your father very much. We had a wonderful life together. But we were great pals, more than anything else."

"Mum, it's fine," Alice replied. "I have a good understanding of your marriage with Dad. And, you know, Ray… he would have been a tough act to follow."

Valerie paused, her demeanour suggesting the conversation was not over, that she had something else she wanted to say. "I have a good understanding of what sort of parents we were to you, Alice. And I have had to come to the conclusion that I was a terrible mother."

Alice was so surprised by her mother's statement that she took a step back and, for a moment, was at a loss for words. She had always wanted Valerie to make some admission that her daughter's childhood had been far from perfect, yet it somehow felt like an overstatement for Valerie to claim to have been a 'terrible mother'. After a horrible night where Alice honestly thought Valerie may have fallen victim to Guy Stone, she no longer felt the need to label her in such an extreme way.

"Mum, you were not *terrible*," she said.

But Valerie shook her head. "Alice, I know how much I got wrong with you," she said. "Your father and I got so much wrong, and I know how much we damaged our relationship with you. At the time it all seemed so straightforward, so necessary. We had a family, we were in the public eye, and so dragging our daughter into the spotlight with us, it seemed the right thing to do. But I can see, now, how we used you, our own daughter, to publicise ourselves, to help our own careers. And that was a terrible thing for us to do."

Valerie reached forward and gently stroked the side of Alice's face. "Your father is long gone," she said. "But I'm not. I am very much still here. And I have the chance to make things better. And I want to make the most of this chance. So, how about it, kiddo? You and me, starting again. Properly. Cards on the table. Everything out in the open. I want to be your mother, Alice. And a grandmother to your daughters. So, how about it?"

Alice moved and, for a moment, Valerie thought her daughter was going to push her hand away from her cheek. But instead, to Valerie's surprise and relief, Alice cupped her hand in her own, and leaned against it. Tears began to form in her eyes, and then she said, "The girls are coming home."

"Oh goodness," Valerie replied, a huge smile on her face. "What happened? I thought they were loving it out there."

"No," Alice replied, and a tear rolled down her cheek. "They had a huge row with their dad," she said and then, half crying and half laughing, and with a hint of glee in her voice, she added, "They called his wife a stupid cow and pushed her into the pool."

Valerie smiled. "Oh, how wonderful," she said, with delight. "The girls are coming home!" Instinctively she held the bouquet of flowers to one side and hugged Alice. And for the first time in too many years, she could feel her daughter hugging her back.

"He's got them on an earlier flight, so I'll go and pick them up at the airport in a couple of days. I'm just waiting for them to confirm the arrival time," Alice said. She stepped backwards and wiped the tears from her eyes. "Perhaps you could come with me? Meet them at the airport, too?"

"Yes of course," Valerie replied, pleased to have been invited. "And... if you'd all like to stay at the house for a while...? You know. You are more than welcome. I'd love to have you all there."

Alice nodded. "I'll... I'll think about it," she said. "It sounds nice, though. I think the girls would enjoy it." She looked at the door to the ward, and then gestured back to the lift with her thumb. "I was actually on my way downstairs to get a coffee and a book from the little shop," she said. "So, why don't you go in and I'll be along later."

Valerie nodded. "Yes, I'd like a moment alone with him," she said. "Don't be long, though."

Before Alice left, she leaned forward and kissed Valerie on the cheek. And as she walked away, she called back: "And tell him to stop complaining about the food. The NHS is wonderful."

Valerie pressed the entrance bell and then entered the ward.

"Hello, Mrs Pierce," one of the nurses said to her, cheerfully. "He's having a bit of a moan today, so can you remind him, again, we don't do cocktails?"

Valerie chuckled. "Yes of course," she replied. "But if you did, fewer people would feel the need to go private." She noticed the nurse's good-humoured smile suddenly disappear. Valerie entered a small, single room just off the ward's main corridor and found Ray, lying slightly on his side, trying to operate the remote control for the television attached to the wall.

"You know, they don't have Netflix," he said. "That's just cruel."

Valerie surveyed the room and quickly located a glass vase, half filled with water. She dropped her handbag onto the end of the bed and set about arranging her bouquet. "This is a hospital, not a gay spa, darling," she said. "Now stop moaning and just be grateful you're not dead."

As Valerie busied herself with the flowers, she realised that as grateful as she was for Ray's recovery, she was also puzzled by it. Guy Stone had proven himself to be, if nothing else, a particularly efficient killer. And yet two of his victims, Ray and Ben, had both been left alive. She knew that, for Ben at least, that had not been an oversight. She did not believe for a second that Guy Stone would kill Pearl Martin's nephew, no matter what threats he had made to Patricia. But his decision – and she did consider it a decision – to leave Ray injured, but alive, baffled her.

She knew some killers operated within a code; personal rules that helped guide their actions. And she wondered if Ray's survival was a part of Stone's code, that he only killed people he directly blamed for what happened to Pearl Martin. Perhaps accidental bystanders like Ray and Ben were left immobilised, but alive, because they had not fitted within Stone's code?

Ray tossed the remote control onto the bedside table and tried to arrange himself, under the covers, more comfortably. But his stitches and injuries were still fresh, and he found himself in pain once more.

"Are you OK?" Valerie asked, pausing the moment she heard Ray groan under his breath.

"Yup, yup," he replied. "Just a bit achy still," he said. He managed to turn flat onto his back and then lay, happily, with his hands on his lap, smiling at Valerie. "And for the record, I am very grateful I'm not dead. And I'm very grateful you are not dead."

Valerie smiled and then quickly concluded her busyness with the bouquet. "There!" she said. The vase was now adorned with a blooming rainbow of colour, and she held it aloft, as though presenting it to him. "You officially have flowers." She carried the vase to the foot of Ray's bed and gave it pride of place on the little table used for his medical notes.

Ray reached for the remote control once more but only so he could turn off the television. He then tapped the top of the chair next to his bed. "Take a seat," he said, and Valerie obliged, kissing him on the forehead as she sat down.

"We're all over the news, still," he said. "I got a little bit addicted to it last night. I started watching one of the rolling news channels at 8pm and was still up at 3am. The night nurse came in and gave me a real telling off. I was like 'OK, calm down Hattie Jacques'."

Valerie stroked Ray's arm, reassuringly. "It will all blow over in a few days," she said. "They'll soon find something else to talk about."

Ray shrugged. "Oh, I don't know about that, Val," he said. "I've been thinking about the next few months. The police investigation. The investigation into the police investigation. The inquest. And I don't think it will finish there. You and I are now forever linked to a man who, without a shadow of a doubt, will become known as one of the most notorious serial killers in history. I think we're in this for the long haul."

Valerie chuckled. "Well, as I recall, you were quite keen to be famous," she said. "Saves you doing that silly documentary you asked me about."

Ray rolled his eyes and smiled. "I know," he said. "I guess this just isn't the sort of 'famous' I was hoping for."

Valerie took his hand and smiled at him. "You were only involved in all this because of me," she said. "That night, at Balans, when I asked you to come and stay with me for a while, you could have been killed. And it would have been entirely down to me."

Ray chuckled. "Well, if a gay man can't die for his ex-wife, who can he die for?"

Valerie squeezed his hand. "Stop cracking jokes, Ray," she said, a little crossly.

He nodded. "Sorry. It's a coping mechanism," he replied, a little glumly. "I don't think it's really hit me yet. What happened. My desperate attempts to find humour in all of this... it seems to be the only thing keeping everything else at bay." He reached up, and gently used his finger to lift the scarf around Valerie's neck, just a little, enough to see the bruises underneath. "It frightens me, you know. To think what would have happened if Adam Jaymes hadn't turned up when he did."

"Yes, but look how that turned out," Valerie replied. "He was almost killed as well. I think all three of us were just... very lucky, in the end."

Ray rested his hand back onto the bed and smiled. "When I get released, Adam and his husband are putting me up at their private villa in Mijas," he said, his voice hinting at a little pride. "They won't be there, but it's fully staffed, and they are going to hire some additional medical help, to keep an eye on me. Adam said I can have it for as long as it takes for me to have a full recovery. You can come, too, if you like?"

Valerie smiled, and knew that just a few short weeks earlier, she would have jumped at the chance of spending time with her ex-husband in some sunny, exclusive retreat. But, now, she had accepted that was not her place. Someone else should be there with Ray. And so, she quietly declined his offer. "I've got too much to do," she replied. "Although it does sound lovely. But you go. Live the life of a billionaire."

Valerie heard a noise from her handbag, a quiet buzz, and retrieved her phone, wondering if it was the text she had been expecting. Her eyes were met by a short, abrupt message on the screen: 'I'm outside.' She had conflicting feelings about what she had arranged, but after seeing Ray almost killed, right in front of her, she wanted to give him every chance to rediscover some happiness in his life. Even if that meant drawing their rekindled friendship to a conclusion.

"Sorry, darling, but I have to take a call, in private" she said, and kissed him on the forehead. She stood and walked to the door, but then glanced towards him, and smiled.

"What?" he asked, smiling back at her.

"All these years later, and you know what? You are still the most handsome man I have ever seen," she said. And then she blew him a kiss and left the room.

Valerie walked back to the entrance to the ward where there was a small collection of chairs just inside the door, and found her guest sat waiting for her; Ray's ex-husband, Pete. He had lost a lot of weight since Valerie had last seen him and appeared to have had some treatment for his male pattern baldness. Although his head was very closely shaved, he appeared to have a full covering of hair.

As Pete stood, he could see Valerie quizzically staring at his hairline. "It's scalp micropigmentation," he said, his voice filled with disdain. "It's like a big tattoo."

Valerie nodded and smiled. "It's very effective, Pete," she said, and then looked at the rest of him. "And you've lost so much weight too. I hate to admit it, but it's taken years off you. You're like a new man."

Pete paused, waiting for Valerie to follow the flattering comment with some catty put down. But instead, she just smiled and appeared to offer the compliment unconditionally. "Erm… thank you?" he said, almost as a question. "How is he?"

Valerie sighed. "Very, very lucky to be alive," she said. "The knife missed every major artery and organ. So, he's very achy but he's going to be fine. Physically, anyway. I think at some point what happened is going to impact on him mentally, emotionally. And he's going to need help. From someone who truly loves him."

Pete stared at Valerie and felt very perplexed by her actions and her words. He had never truly liked or trusted her but, on that day, she appeared to be saying and doing all the right things. And it felt the right time to be, if nothing else, gracious in return.

"Val," he said, "I know I'm the last person you would ever want to call. But I cannot thank you enough. To be honest, I never thought I would ever leave Ray. But circumstances were just… well, everything was awful. And I ended up blaming him. Wrongly, of course. But I had to get away, from everything, and that included Ray. And I've lived to regret that decision so much. So, the moment I got your call, I just packed straight away and was on the first plane home."

Valerie was able to maintain the veneer of civility but realised that, all those years later, she still hated Pete. She could not help but hold him solely responsible for the breakdown of her marriage to Ray. Her head told her that was nonsense, that Ray had been a young gay man pressured into marrying her by his God-fearing parents. But her heart had simply never made room for forgiveness when it came to Pete, the person she knew Ray had always truly loved.

However, this was her gift to Ray, the man who nearly died for her, who told her to run and save herself when he believed he had been mortally wounded. This was all Valerie could do to thank him, to offer him a happiness he had lost.

"He's in that room there," she said, pointing across the corridor. "He's

371

not expecting you, so it might be a bit of a surprise. But I know he's going to be thrilled."

Pete nodded, stepped past Valerie and began to walk towards Ray's room. But he stopped a few metres from Valerie and turned to her. "Val, you look amazing by the way," he said.

Valerie smiled. "Oh, well, thank you," she replied, surprised by the compliment.

"I mean, you know, for someone who was almost murdered," Pete added. And then he smiled at her.

Despite hating every inch of him, Valerie couldn't help but smile, and a wide grin appeared on her face. She watched as he disappeared into Ray's room. And amid all her feelings of loss and jealousy, she just about managed to find a small inner voice that wished them both well.

The main door to the ward opened next to her, and Alice reappeared carrying two hot drinks in plastic cups, both with lids. "I thought you might want a coffee," she said. "They didn't sell wine."

Valerie placed her arm around her daughter's shoulders and gently navigated her back into the corridor outside. "Time for us to go," she said.

"Oh, OK," Alice replied, a concerned tone to her voice. "You didn't have a row, did you?" she asked.

"No, no, absolutely not," Valerie replied. "But he's got another visitor and I think they need some time to talk."

As they began to walk towards the lift, Alice handed her mother one of the plastic cups. "Do you fancy a takeaway and a movie tonight?" she asked. "I just want to take your mind off everything, as much as is possible."

Valerie smiled. "Oh, I'm out tonight, darling," she said. "I have a hot date. But I'd love to do that another night. Honestly. Tomorrow?"

They reached the lift and Alice pressed the call button. "Oh, a hot date. That's sounds exciting. Anyone I know? And I hope he's taking you somewhere nice."

Valerie smiled. "Well… he's taking me somewhere… interesting."

EPILOGUE

It was a strange feeling; being out at night in London, alone, but feeling safe and happy, no longer scared. Valerie was enjoying a ridiculously heady sensation of freedom at a cabaret bar, sat in a private booth in the VIP area, and accompanied by a bottle of merlot and a small bowl of olives. Her seat, in a dark corner of the venue, was cordoned off and none of the other audience members could see her.

She was dressed simply, in black trousers and a mauve roll neck sweater that covered her neck, and she really didn't think for a moment anyone would notice her. But she had been advised to enter the bar through a special side entrance so staff could escort her to her seat without her being seen by anyone else; a precaution reserved for the famous. And Valerie was beginning to feel she was being treated like a celebrity.

The bustle within the club was exhilarating; voices, clinking glasses, clapping and laughter. It was something Valerie had not experienced in far too long. She had a clear view of the raised stage, glamorously decorated with swish red curtains and glistening sequins. And she could hear the audience, at least one hundred people, laughing and clapping as a pretty, young drag queen lip-synced to a blue version of 'Toxic', dressed like a beautiful, bejewelled germ.

And for a moment, a brief moment, she wished Ray were there with her, to explain some of the ruder lyrics. But she was trying her best not to think about him, or at least not to think about him as often. With Pete back in his life, she knew there could be no room for her. Her delightful reunion with Ray was now over, so she simply raised her glass, and silently toasted his health and happiness.

The audience applauded enthusiastically as the drag queen finished her performance and left the stage. As a brief intermission began, Valerie could hear movement across the club as some of the other customers headed to the bar to order drinks, chatting and laughing as they did, none of them with a care in the world. And Valerie realised how lovely it was to be part of that happy-go-lucky world once more.

And then, suddenly, she saw someone sitting near to her, in the booth, a dark figure in a hood, and her heart almost stopped. She caught her breath, and stared at him in horror, prepared to scream at the top of her voice. But then he pulled back the hood, and revealed his handsome face, smiling at her. Adam Jaymes.

"Sorry I'm late," he said, a little breathless, and unzipped the hoodie to reveal a smart shirt and tie underneath.

"Oh my God, you nearly frightened the life out of me, you bloody idiot, appearing out of the blue like that," Valerie snapped, and briefly placed her hand on her chest, as though to check that her heart was still beating.

Adam stared at her, the corner of his lips hinting at a smile. "I do apologise," he said, "but I assume you are not going to throw your wine over me this evening?"

Valerie was still holding her glass, and she mischievously swirled the contents before sipping from it then placing it back on the table. "May I pour you one?" she asked.

"Yes please," Adam replied, and waited as Valerie poured him a drink and then handed it to him. They held their glasses aloft and, without speaking, clinked them together in a silent toast. "Did you take my advice, about the side entrance?" he asked.

Valerie nodded. "Yes, although I'm still not sure it was necessary."

Adam shook his head gently. "Oh, you'll soon see," he said. "Valerie, right now you are the most famous woman in the world. Everyone is obsessed with you. All the papers are filled with articles about how you tracked down and caught a serial killer. Your life is different now. It may not have sunk in yet, but you are now properly world famous. You have very much crossed the floor. All those famous people you wrote about in your column for all those years? Well, you are now one of those famous people. And there's a whole new generation of journalists who will be obsessively writing about you."

Valerie was a little unnerved by his words but also knew there was a lot of truth in what he had said. Alice had briefed her about the content of the newspapers that day. There were hundreds of pages dedicated to Valerie Pierce; news articles, comment pieces and interviews with former friends and colleagues. Even the media's fashion editors had joined in, reproducing images of Valerie's best and worst outfits from the past thirty-plus years.

Valerie knew Alice had also been holding dozens of interview requests at bay, from print and broadcast journalists around the world. For the time being at least, it seemed, everyone wanted a piece of Valerie Pierce.

As her eyes focused more clearly on Adam's face, in the dim light of the booth, she could see he was still badly bruised, the swelling on one side of his face making his usually perfect features look uneven.

"It's been quite a day," he said. "Five hours with the police. *Five hours.* You?"

"I had them yesterday," she said. "It was quite desperate, to be honest, watching them scurrying about, picking up the pieces, trying to retrospectively solve a crime that's already been solved. And I believe DI Sally Price has been moved to other duties for the time being. But I think she'll be fine. We had previously discussed a different career path for her." Valerie topped up her own glass and then raised it to Adam; he raised his in return. "So, how is Patricia?" Valerie asked.

Adam frowned, and moved his head from side to side, as though unable to fall firmly on either a positive or a negative response. "She's doing as well as can be expected," he said. "It's a fantastic place. Secure and supportive. Private. She's getting all the help she needs. And Ben's with her. Although, to be honest, I think at some point, he's going to need some help, too. He went through quite an ordeal, bless him. And then to find out his own mother knew about it, about Guy Stone, all along… it's going to be tough on him."

"And the police?"

Adam shrugged. "Stone covered his tracks," he said. "If it weren't for the recording of your emergency call from the house, of Stone's confession, I doubt they'd have anything. But certainly, there's nothing to link Stone to Patricia."

Valerie could feel her excited buzz quickly disappearing as she was reminded of all the pain and suffering that had been exposed at Beachy Head that terrible morning, just days earlier. "And Beth?" she asked.

This time, there was no ambiguity in Adam's response. Solemnly, he shook his head, and his expression was drained of all its warmth. "No," he replied.

"She packed her stuff and left. Her mum and dad know where she is, and they've assured me she is safe, but they promised Beth they wouldn't tell anyone where she has gone. Including me."

Valerie sighed. "Oh dear," she said. "I am sorry, Adam. I know how much she means to you. I'm sure she'll come around."

Adam sipped his wine and for a moment seemed a thousand miles away.

"I hope you know..." Valerie started, but then paused and waited for Adam to look at her, to show he was listening. And she noticed there was something about his demeanour that was different that night, perhaps even a little odd. It was as though his famously analytical brain wasn't firing on all cylinders, his attention wandering from one thing to another. And she wondered if the dreadful beating he had received from Guy Stone had left him with more than just a few cuts and bruises.

When he eventually focused on her once more, she continued: "I hope you know... what I said, at Beachy Head? When I told you what Patricia had done? I hope you know it was in no way said with malice or spite. I had a gun pointed in my face, Adam. I was panicking. Just trying to think of things to say."

Adam nodded. "Valerie, I know," he said, a reassuring calmness in his voice. "And, in a terrible way, it was a secret that needed to come out. I just hope Beth is willing to forgive Patricia, one day." He placed his glass of wine on the table and looked directly at Valerie. "You could have gone to the police," he said. "Patricia kidnapped you, threatened to kill you. She could have faced years in prison."

Valerie nodded, ever so slightly, just enough to show she had acknowledged the point. But then she said: "To be honest, Adam, after all the pain I caused that family, it doesn't feel disproportionate to keep this one secret. And I have your assurance that she's getting the help she needs?"

"Yes," he replied. "Categorically, yes. Patricia will be there for as long as it takes, whether that be months or years. But she will never be in a position to do anything so... dangerous again."

Valerie felt a genuine sense of relief, partly for Patricia but mostly for her own safety. Her decision not to report Patricia to the police had felt like a necessary act of kindness, a small gesture to Beth and her family. But it had left her feeling exposed and she was pleased Adam and his wealthy husband were taking the matter seriously.

"And I did want to say to you, Adam," she continued, "to be clear, again, that first night we saw each other. When I told you if you did not help me, I would expose Beth to the papers. That was a terrible, terrible bluff. No matter how desperate I was for your help, I would never…"

Adam lifted is hand and said: "Valerie, we're good. I promise you, we're good."

Their conversation was interrupted by a ripple of applause as a glamorous drag queen took to the stage, sparkling in a floor-length sequin dress of red, white and blue. "Well, hello, yes it's me, Rue Britannia, your hostess with the mostess tonight," she announced. "I hope you're all enjoying your drinks, and please remember to tip the bar staff," she said. "There's table service, if you want it, and we have a special tonight on our cocktail jugs. Although, looking at you lot, I'd hazard a guess that none of you has any interest in jugs."

It was not the sort of humour Valerie would usually find amusing, but there was something knowing about the drag queen, almost as if she were delivering the lines ironically, and that made Valerie smile.

"Well, I am a bit nervous, this evening," Rue continued, "Because we have a huge star about to take to the stage."

There was a chorus of excited 'whoops' from the audience, and Valerie glanced to Adam, and pointed at him. "You?" she mouthed, silently.

Adam grinned at her and shook his head, but he clearly seemed to know what was going on. He then gestured back towards the stage.

"She's been all over the press," the drag queen continued. "We all know her. And, oh God, the gob on this one."

The audience was cheering and laughing and, like Adam, appeared to know who was next on the line-up.

"She's opinionated. She says what she likes, and she likes what she says. So please put your hands together for the amazing! The indomitable! The ever purple! Valerie Fierce!"

There was a roar of cheers and applause, and Rue Britannia stepped into the audience. A spotlight was shone onto the back of the stage and there, in a deep purple fitted trouser suit – very similar to something Valerie would wear except that it was covered in sequins – was a drag queen. She sported a sharp black bob, exaggerated dark make-up around her eyes, and had a cigarette in her hand that she was swirling around in an extremely affected manner.

She turned, as if she had noticed the audience for the first time and looked at them as though a little bored and unimpressed. And then she scowled disapprovingly at them as she strode to the mic at the front of the stage.

"What the bloody hell…?" Valerie asked quietly to herself, and then looked at Adam who had buried his face in his hands because he was laughing so hard.

"Oh, look at the filth in here," Valerie Fierce said, gesturing to the audience with her cigarette hand. "God, the amount of benefits you lot must have scrounged to afford a night out." She then focused in on one member of the audience, near the front, who was laughing particularly loudly. "Are you OK, dear? I see you've had a meal with the show. Was it the Chicken Tikka Lasagne? You liked that? I'm not surprised. It was from Asda. Posh, for you."

Valerie was a little perplexed but, also, a little in awe. The drag queen certainly looked like her, and even had some of her physical mannerisms. But it was the voice that was most striking. She had absolutely perfected Valerie's sharp diction, her clear voice edged with a slight huskiness that came from too many years of smoking. And even though Valerie Fierce seemed to be doing little but hurl insults at the audience, every comment was met with rapturous laughter. And Valerie began to feel oddly flattered that a performer had put so much work into a drag homage of her.

"A lot of people have been asking me about… you know… recent events," the queen continued, miming air brackets as she said 'recent events'. "And a lot of people have asked me: Valerie, they've asked. Valerie, are you now best friends with Adam Jaymes?"

The audience cheered at the mention of Adam's name, and there was a ripple of applause.

But Valerie Fierce was not impressed. She pulled a face and glared at the audience. "Oh please," she said, disdainfully. "Do you think I would be friends with an actor whose idea of auditioning for a part is having his face jammed up against the wall of a public lavatory?"

The air was filled with a roar of gasps, surprise and laughter, and the audience cheered at the sheer rudeness of the comment.

Valerie glanced at Adam, who was staring at her with a broad smile on his face. "I think," he said, brightly, "that was a direct quote from your book."

And Valerie, slightly awkwardly, nodded. "Yes, it is," she replied, and then leaned forward to offer an apology but Adam quickly intervened.

"No, no, it's funny," he said. "Believe it or not, Valerie, I do have a sense of humour about myself."

Valerie smiled, raised her glass to him and then sipped her wine. And she had a sudden awful realisation that she was starting to like Adam Jaymes.

"You should go up," Adam said. "The audience would go bonkers."

Valerie shook her head. "God, no," she replied, horrified by the suggestion. The audience was clearly enjoying a drag queen parody of her, but she could not believe they would be equally enthusiastic if she took to the stage herself. Her years at the *Daily Ear* had not endeared her to members of the LGBTQ community. And although her freelance work in the years since had softened the public's opinion of her, this was not the sort of venue where she would expect a warm reception.

"Oh, go on, Valerie. Go on," Adam said, excitedly. And then he leaned forward, out of the booth, and gestured to someone. A waiter quickly appeared, and Adam quietly spoke into his ear, motioning towards Valerie as he did. The waiter looked at her and his expression changed as he suddenly seemed to realise who she was. The waiter smiled and nodded enthusiastically at Adam. He then held out his hand, an invitation for Valerie to go with him.

"No, no, honestly," Valerie replied, shaking her head.

But the waiter looked at her with such eagerness on his face, such joy, that she suddenly felt it might actually be quite good fun. And so she raised her hands, as though giving-in under pressure, and shifted along the seat. "I could just kill you, Adam Jaymes," she muttered to him as she took the waiter's hand.

Adam laughed. "Break a leg, Valerie," he replied.

The waiter did not take Valerie directly to the stage. Instead, he quietly steered her around the outside of the audience, through the darker areas of the club, to the backstage dressing area. There were three other drag queens preparing their hair and make-up for their next performance, and Valerie was surprised at how much was packed into such a small space. Three clothes rails were filled with a colourful assortment of dresses and costumes, feather boas and hats. There was an array of wigs on stands, and two dressing tables that all three were trying to use at the same time.

The waiter spoke to Rue Britannia, who had quickly changed her outfit and was now dressed in a glittering *Wonder Woman* costume. "Oh my God, yes," Rue said with delight, as she realised who it was that the waiter had brought backstage. She then pointed him back to the club and appeared to give him an instruction. As he left, Rue took Valerie's hands. "Hello, my darling," she whispered into Valerie's ear, and then kissed her on both cheeks. "I am so thrilled to meet you. Now come with me. This is going to be fun." She led Valerie into the wings and up the steps onto the stage, although still hidden behind the curtains.

Valerie Fierce was in full performance mode, the audience in a cycle of hysterical laughter. Rue gently pulled the curtain slightly to one side to peer to the back of the club and seemed to be scanning the venue for something. And then, after a moment, she whispered to Valerie: "There. It's on. I just wanted to make sure you had your own spotlight." She then gently manoeuvred Valerie into place. "Just go on and look annoyed," she said. "The *other* Valerie will take it from there. She's going to be thrilled."

Rue stepped back, and then gestured for Valerie to walk out onto the stage. "They're going to love you," she said, and smiled.

Valerie felt a little out of place and overwhelmed. She wondered how she had suddenly found herself in such a position, about to take part in a live drag show, and she worried about whether the audience would react positively or negatively.

But she remembered the great efforts she had made to reinvent herself after leaving the *Daily Ear*, and the more compassionate tone she had brought to her writing, and in particular anything she wrote about minority groups like the LGBTQ community. And she remembered the way so many gay men and women had reached out to show their gratitude and support. And then she thought of her granddaughters, and how doubtlessly cool they would find it, if they were to see images and videos on Twitter of their nan performing with drag queens.

And so, she took a deep breath, and walked out onto the stage, immediately striking the pose Rue had suggested: her hands on her hips and with a scowling, angry expression. At first the spotlight was shining directly in her face and she could hardly see anything. But she could hear the audience and noticed a sudden change in the atmosphere; the laughter subsided and was replaced with an awful silence, and then gasps. But after a couple of seconds of doubt, when

Valerie felt sure she had made a terrible error of judgement, there were cheers followed very quickly by loud applause. And as her eyes adjusted, she could see Valerie Fierce, several metres in front of her, looking out at the audience, perplexed by what they were doing: "What? What's going on?" she asked.

And then she turned, and her chin dropped as she realised the *real* Valerie Pierce was stood on the stage behind her, pretending to be deeply annoyed. "Oh my God, you are fucking kidding me," the drag queen squealed, and began to roar with laughter. "No way!"

The audience was standing, applauding, filming with their phones, cheering at the hilarity of a drag queen being confronted by the very person she was parodying. And after Valerie had surveyed the venue, maintaining her mock air of disapproval, she walked gracefully to the front of the stage to meet her drag queen double, who hugged her and then brought her forward to formally introduce her. "Oh, my goodness, ladies and gentlemen, I can't believe it. May I introduce you to the *real* Valerie Pierce."

And as Valerie looked around the club, peering through the darkness at all the happy, smiling faces, she glanced over to the back of the venue, to her booth, to see if Adam was enjoying the moment too. But she saw that his seat was empty, Adam was gone. She continued to smile and wave but tried to see where he was. Then she saw him, stood by the door, his hood back up, about to leave. Just before he disappeared, he offered her a friendly wave and a smile, before he turned and slowly faded into the darkness as he left.

Valerie had the strangest feeling she would never see him again. That their brief association would soon become just a story, something she would talk about, years in the future; the time she had worked with superstar actor, Adam Jaymes, to solve a series of murders. But she knew she would never be able to divulge the full story to anyone. *Never* the full story. Because there were secrets she had promised to keep, and she intended to keep them for ever.

And as she looked back to the audience, still cheering and applauding, so delighted to see her on the stage, Valerie suddenly knew without a shadow of a doubt that her life was now forever changed. She was no longer the journalist who so jealously wrote about the lives of the rich and famous. Because in that moment she realised Adam Jaymes had been right. Valerie Pierce was now a part of the celebrity world. Whether she liked it or not, Valerie Pierce was now a star.

Lightning Source UK Ltd.
Milton Keynes UK
UKHW020403161022
410526UK00014B/752